"Bruce P. Spang masterfully intertwines themes of secrets, cover-ups, identity, self-acceptance, love, relationships, change, transition, friendship, support, loss, grief, growth, societal expectations, conformity, and conflict into a compelling narrative. Some themes, such as Jason's fascination with Watergate, are interwoven more subtly. The 1960s setting is vividly portrayed, with Spang capturing the era's political and cultural shifts with authenticity. Through detailed descriptions of the region and its way of life, the novel invites readers to experience its complexities, highlighting the realities of poverty, tradition, and the strength found in community. River Crossed explores how education can be a tool for empowerment and how individuals can create meaningful change in their lives and the lives of others. Jason's gradual realization of his capacity to lead and advocate is a central theme, inspiring reflection on the power of self-discovery and perseverance. Spang has penned a beautiful story that captures so much of human nature and the 1960s, and it's a book that no one should miss. It's beautifully written and would make an excellent movie."
—*Reviewed by Carol Thompson for Readers' Favorite*

❖

"River Crossed is a beautiful story about a man's journey to accept himself and fall in love with who he is. Author Bruce P. Spang masterfully captures the complexities of love and identity in a time when societal norms weighed heavily on personal choices. The setting of the natural beauty of the river and the backdrop of 1970s America mirrors Jason's internal turmoil. The way the author explained Jason's relationships shows the emotional upheaval he went through, making his struggles relatable and impactful. It was a treat to watch Jason grow emotionally strong. The pace was fast, the narrative style was fantastic, and Jason's development was inspiring. The heart lies in its authentic characters and their journeys, which truly made the story for me. River Crossed is a moving tale about the courage to embrace one's truth, offering an important message of self-acceptance and learning to love." —*Reviewed by Rabia Tanveer for Readers' Favorite*

❖

"Author Bruce P. Spang captures the complexity of self-discovery with remarkable sensitivity and addresses a whole community about love and authenticity. Spang's warm writing style draws readers into Jason's world through vivid descriptions that bring the West Virginia landscape to life. I found myself thinking about it long after finishing the book, and indeed every time I saw a river afterward. The emotional depth of Jason's internal struggles feels authentic and deeply moving, thanks to close narration and some powerful dialogue scenes. Spang's ability to convey the tension between personal truth and societal expectations creates moments of profound insight that are sure to resonate with anyone who has ever struggled with acceptance and belonging. The development of the relationships between the characters reveals a deep understanding of human nature and the courage required to live authentically.

Spang's portrayal of the transformative power of acceptance and love shows how personal growth often requires us to challenge our deepest fears and societal constraints, but also how rewarding it is to open up to others. Overall, River Crossed offers readers a powerful and touching exploration of identity, love, and the courage to embrace one's true self, and I would not hesitate to recommend it." —*Reviewed by K.C. Finn for Readers' Favorite*

❖

"I am quite selective when reading LGBTQ novels, and this book exceeds my expectations. Jason's journey to escape and then confront his homosexuality reflects a deeply human and relatable struggle with identity. This will resonate with readers regardless of sexual orientation. The tension between loving a man or a woman adds depth and a nuanced look at the fluidity of relationships and the complexities of love beyond binary categorizations. Bruce P. Spang invites you to reflect on how larger societal forces shape individual choices and identities. He cleverly demonstrates this with Jason's ultimate decision being influenced by a U.S. president whom he despises. Ultimately, River Crossed is a story of courage and choosing authenticity over fear. It leaves you reflecting on your own life, the compromises you've made, and the passions you have yet to chase. Truly, a deeply moving and unforgettable read." —*Reviewed by Vincent Dublado for Readers' Favorite*

❖

"River Crossed by Bruce P. Spang offers a glimpse into how various issues, such as gay rights, have changed over time. It also shows how religion can be weaponized against certain demographics. Bruce made sure all the events and the emotions of the well-developed characters were vividly captured. I also loved the suspense, which kept me looking forward to the events of subsequent chapters. This thought-provoking work also gets one thinking about embracing who we are, our identity, and why tolerance is important in society. The narration was also on point, which added to the overall beauty of the work. This was a great read, and I believe such literature is a step in the right direction toward bringing out various biases in societies. I look forward to reading something else by this author." —*Reviewed by Frank Mutuma for Readers' Favorite*

❖

"In my view this is a book for those in the process of coming to terms with being Lesbian, Gay, Bisexual, or Trans. It's an honest book in an age when honesty is rare. If you are LGBT or curious about that, be assured, there is another out there. It's a universal book, really, because everyone at some time struggles to find themselves and to acknowledge the differences between themselves and their families, or friends, or lovers. It's also a universal book because ultimately self-acceptance soothes and liberates like a breath of fresh air after a storm. Sometimes a bone-rattling storm. The hero's journey. This book will take you through the author's storm, and breathe alongside him, the fresh air." —*Reviewed by BC for Readers' Favorite*

———— A NOVEL ————

River
*C*rossed

 BRUCE P. SPANG

River Crossed

Copyright © 2024 Bruce P. Spang

All rights reserved. No part of this publication may be reproduced, stored in any retrieval system, or transmitted in any form or by any means, mechanical, photocopying, recording, or otherwise, without permission in writing from the publisher, except by a reviewer, who may quote brief passages in a review.

This is a work of fiction. All of the characters, organizations, and events portrayed in this novel are either products of the author's imagination or are used fictitiously.

Cover and Interior design by Ted Ruybal
100% Human Made. No AI used.

Manufactured in the United States of America

Wisdom House Books
For more information, please contact:
www.wisdomhousebooks.com

Paperback ISBN: 979-8-9907744-0-7
E-book ISBN: 979-8-9907744-4-5
LCCN: 2024917583

FIC019000 | FICTION / Literary
FIC027190 | FICTION / Romance / LGBTQ+ / Gay
FIC084040 | FICTION / World Literature / American / 21st Century

2 3 4 5 6 7 8 9 10
First Edition 2025
Second Edition 2025

Dedication

To Myles Rightmire, my husband and soulmate, for his patience, insight, love, and generosity.

To Carole Goldizen, my dear friend whose spirit is infused in this book and my heart.

To Katie and Matt Dobres-Spang for the pleasure of being their father and the joy of seeing them grow into compassionate, competent adults.

To Amalie, Marcie, and Sally Dobres for the love and the way they shaped and influenced my life.

To Head Start for what it does to change and improve lives.

This novel would not be possible without the help of writers and craftspeople who dug deeply into what needed to be said and let the story come to life.

My indebtedness and thanks to Reverend Richard Schmidt for his spirit, support, and the right word. And to his wife Pam for her humor and delight in the perplexities of this world.

Nancy McDaniel, my friend and wordsmith for her diligence in perfecting the text and for staying with me throughout its many manifestations.

River Crossed

John Michael Albert for his persistence in reining in the book and advice about how to do it.

Tessa Fontaine for cutting and reshaping the manuscript and giving it form.

Katie Edkins Milligan for honing and polishing the prose.

Table of Contents

Chapter 1 .1

Chapter 2 11

Chapter 3 17

Chapter 4 25

Chapter 5 31

Chapter 6 35

Chapter 7 47

Chapter 8 53

Chapter 9 59

Chapter 10. 63

Chapter 11. 67

Chapter 12. 75

Chapter 13. 83

Chapter 14. 91

Chapter 15. 103

Chapter 16. 113

Chapter 17. 123

Chapter 18. 127

Chapter 19. 133

Chapter 20. 151

River Crossed

Chapter 21. 165
Chapter 22. 175
Chapter 23. 187
Chapter 24. 211
Chapter 25. 225
Chapter 26. 235
Chapter 27. 253
Chapter 28. 255
Chapter 29. 269
Chapter 30. 277
Chapter 31. 285
Chapter 32. 287
Chapter 33. 295
Chapter 34. 305
Chapter 35. 317
Chapter 36. 329
Chapter 37. 337
Chapter 38. 345
Chapter 39. 353
Chapter 40. 365
Chapter 41. 381
About the Author 389

Chapter One

Every summer growing up, my mother drove me east to visit her parents on Long Island. We spent days at Jones Beach, walked the boardwalk and spread a blanket by the water as waves lumbered up the sand. She swam out past the breakers so far, I thought she would keep on swimming, stroke after stroke, until she slipped over the horizon; it was as if she wanted to swim away from herself, and nothing was left but the sea and her body.

In the evenings, we strolled down the streets of her hometown. She pointed to houses where Dr. Fenton lived—his daughter, her closest friend, a swell girl. Maples and elms shrouded the street. A few cars passed by. We walked for miles, past the Methodist Church where she was married, by the links where she found lost balls and sold them to the golfers. I found myself entering her life almost as if it were my life. Each time she returned here, I could feel her yearning to leave the life she was currently living and recapture what had been. She let her hair down and laughed with her brother's family, the music of voices rising, and she seemed more herself than I'd ever seen her at our home in Glen Brook, a western suburb of Chicago. Her exacting life there was one of a business executive's wife. Everything had to be just so. Appearances were everything. Not a napkin out of place.

I loved seeing her being herself. I wished I could help her stay that way, but I was the part of her new life she couldn't forsake.

That's why I felt an affinity for the east coast.

Growing up in the western suburbs of Chicago, heritage, if there was any, consisted of who owned the grandest house in the newest development. And no one stayed long enough to pass a house to another generation. Once the kids left, parents moved south to condos by the beach.

I yearned for deep roots. At least in the East, some of my favorite authors—Thoreau, Emerson, and Whitman—had laid claim to deeply American and disturbingly unconventional ideas. When I had a chance to go East to the original colonies, 50 miles west of the nation's capital, it was not so much to reclaim my mother's life but to find my own.

How was I to do that? To go where no one knew me. To slough off my status as one of the Follett boys. That would resolve part of the problem, but not all of it.

Another reason for getting far from home, one I kept to myself, was to erase what had haunted me for years. To escape the attraction I had for men, and to shake off the stigma I read about in the Statistical Manual of Mental Disorders.

I had spent two years at Vanderbilt Divinity School—there to avoid the draft and the Vietnam War—plenty of time to investigate a cause for my attraction. According to the DSM manual, I had a "sociopathic personality disorder." It sounded horrible. And it felt that way, too, like a muscle spasm that wouldn't go away. I was a sexual deviant. Saying the word "homosexual" terrified me. I'd read newspapers accounts of men losing jobs, of being sentenced to prison, even being killed for being homosexual. I didn't want to be sociopathic, nor did I want to be killed.

Chapter One

I thought of myself as a straight guy. Normal. That word suited me just fine. My goal was to look in a mirror and see that the face I thought should be there was my face, and not someone else's. But that other face kept reappearing despite my efforts to erase it.

My plan, put simply, was to put my life in order. If I went home, my father could have pulled a few strings, gotten me a job. (He was Vice-President of Motorola.) But if I could get away from my past and, instead, go to a rural town, spend time alone, and decide what I really wanted in life, I could sort out my ambivalences about who I was and what that meant about the way I wanted to be. I could avoid being like my mother, living one life on the coast and another in the Midwest. I could find a new life and keep it.

My friend, Ken McDonald, from Vanderbilt told me that the local Community Action Agency was hiring a Head Start Director. *Head Start* was a new program, part of President Johnson's "Great Society." Ken said I should apply. He had once aspired to be an Episcopal minister but, as a Black man, found even a liberal church was racist. A career in public services was the better option, so he moved back to his home in the West Virginia panhandle.

His suggestion appealed to me.

I thought that Head Start was a program for teenagers who needed a head start in high school. I filled out the application, citing my being a Director of a Folk School in Egan, Tennessee, and a youth minister in Nashville. I drove northeast to Pearsall Flats. The main street in town, Route 50, bisected the northern panhandle, running from its eastern end to its western border and straight on to California. Pearsall Flats, nestled in the Potomac River valley, rested between two ridges that followed the South Branch of the Potomac River.

River Crossed

◉

I learned in the interview that *Head Start* was for preschool kids. I deflected, speaking about my grant-writing experience and my administrative skills. Ken, as the Director of the Regional Community Action program, sat in on the interview as an observer, and afterward, he said, "It was pretty good."

"Pretty good?"

"They're interested in someone organized. Don't worry about your experience with kids." He patted me on the back. "It may work out."

"I have no idea what a preschool kid needs."

"Neither do they," he said.

Turns out he was right. I got the job: Director of Hampton County H*ead Start*. (That would impress my dad.)

I had no experience setting up a preschool program. I had a month to hire staff, find six sites to house the Centers, purchase equipment and food, and enroll students. I felt like a fraud, but it wasn't a new feeling. When I was in seminary, most people mistakenly assumed a theological seminary prepares one for the clergy. That's not always true. You can study Old or New Testament, sociology of religion, ethics, eastern religions, or systematic theology—which is what I did—and never enter a church. I did intern once with a Black Methodist church. I enjoyed the work, but I felt it would be a deception for me to be a clergyman. I wasn't sure of God. Established religion was not my strong suit. I was curious about how many different religions there were. Religions grounded in reverence for the earth appealed to me. Old Testament stories about men with inadequacies, and a god who blundered along with mortals to find their way, made sense

Chapter One

to me. I wanted to find out which one of the religions fit me best, if at all. I wanted to discover the feeling of reverence that James Agee wrote about in his book about Alabama tenant farmers, *Let Us Now Praise Famous Men*. That's what appealed to me: something outside the church.

Money wasn't a lure either. The job paid $8,000. Father would say to me, "Did we tell you about your cousin John? He earns $25,000 a year, And your brother. We're so proud of him. He makes $20,000 and is a manager for the lingerie department at Sears."

I'd squirm and nod my head. Wanting to please, to not offend him, I'd say, "That's great." But I didn't think it was great. I didn't want to wake up each morning, put on a suit and tie, polish my shoes, and head into an office.

At the time, my Vanderbilt advisor told me something surprising that changed my life's direction. He said I shouldn't worry about what the job was because, "You have an artist's sensibility. You're a poet. Face it, that's your calling. The work is secondary. It pays the bills. Jobs will come and go. Just don't let them get in the way of you as an artist."

So here I was taking a job as a Director of Head Start. Six hundred miles away from home. I knew I had to sort out the sexual confusion inside of me. I was pretty sure I could do that. I was less sure about feeding my soul and becoming a poet.

Wanting to get me settled, Ken showed me a newspaper advertisement for an apartment by the South Branch of the Potomac. It was in Springfield, not far from Pearsall Flats, just eight miles north, past Hanging Cliffs.

"Let's take a look," he said.

We drove on a road that looped over several small hills and then straightened out alongside the river. The Hanging Cliffs loomed over the water, separating the north and south sides. During the Civil War, Ken informed me, Confederate Army soldiers made their way into Pearsall Flats along this ridge. Under the command of Stonewall Jackson, they set up camp.

"He's pretty much a hero among the white folks. The Blacks—well, we have an entirely different view of him," he said, sweeping his hand toward the valley Jackson marched one cold wintry night. A roadside sign commemorated a house that was Stonewall's headquarters even though he only stayed there for 14 days.

Ken pointed to the river. "It snakes back and forth through the valley here. Mighty pretty."

We talked about the clergy path—getting ordained. "Did you ever give it serious consideration?" he asked.

"For several weeks there when I had no prospects, I thought I could give it a try. But I knew I would have been faking it. Being dishonest to those who are true believers."

"Dishonest," he said. "That's the right term."

After the bridge, we took a bumpy, dusty road beside corn fields. Hundreds of feet farther below that, the river basin leveled off beside small summer camps set off the road. Cottonwoods, 15 – 25 yards from the river edge, lined the bank. The road rose gently after that to a densely wooded area, then dropped precipitously to a narrow ravine.

From there, a quarter of a mile down the road, an expansive, renovated two-story lodge sat at the end of a steep driveway. An unfinished apartment was framed in on the right side of the building. I called out.

Chapter One

"Is anybody here?" I heard hammering and called out again.

A man greeted us with a falsetto yelp. He stepped out of a side room and waved us forward. "Ahaa! Hello there! Come on in."

A pencil was stuck over his ear. He wore a carpenter's belt with a hammer set like a gun in its holster. He looked as if God had assembled him in haste without reading the directions of what part belonged where. His shorts, ripped at the groin, exposed his white briefs. His torn T-shirt revealed the skin of his right shoulder, splattered with freckles. His broad shoulders contrasted with a scrawny, concave chest and thin, bony legs. His head, wide at the crown, had long, unruly, sandy gray hair that flopped over his eyebrows. Particularly odd was his mouth, large and wide, like a frog's. When he spoke, it would smack shut. He seemed entirely unaware of or unconcerned about his appearance. He gave us both immodest hugs of someone who liked full body contact, as if we were long lost members of his tribe.

He spoke quickly. "You must be the fellow interested in the apartment." He escorted us over stacks of two-by-fours and around packages of floor tiles. "So nice to have you here. Come out here—watch your step—we can sit on the porch. I fixed lemonade."

The main lodge was perched on a high ridge, wedged at the V of a valley where two sloped hillsides touched. A small backyard, completely enclosed by stone walls, was no larger than a putting green. Twenty feet long, eleven feet wide. Beyond and below it (not entirely visible from the porch) was a valley where the South Branch of the Potomac meandered.

Two cottages and one mobile home crested the opposite bank, shaded by large willow trees.

He introduced himself. "I'm Doug Waterman, but just call me Doug."

I told him I had taken a job as Head Start Director and needed a place to stay. I explained I didn't need much: I was single, a writer (a role I was surprised to hear myself say) and wanted solitude.

He explained that he and his wife, Angel, needed someone to watch over the place most winter days, since they both lived and worked in Wheaton, a town outside Washington, DC, and didn't make it down too often. He was a minister and a high school English teacher, and his wife was a bank teller. Because I would be taking care of the house for them, making sure no one broke in and calling them with any problems, he offered me a monthly $75 dollar rental.

"That sounds good to me," I said. It was too good to be true. There had to be a hitch.

"We have an agreement," he said, standing, reaching his arm around my shoulder, pulling me to him and patting my back.

I tried to slip away.

He said, "Perfect, perfect, perfect," squeezing my shoulder, and continuing to talk.

He took us into the main lodge. The ground floor's spacious living room extended the length of the building, a dining table on one half, and a stone fireplace with couches and chairs on the other. Upstairs, a long hallway. A dorm room with bunkbeds, and three small rooms. At the head of the stairs, a large master with a four-poster queen-sized bed and a window overlooking the river.

"Nice bed," I said.

"Lay back on it, you can see the river." Doug sat next to me, patting me on the thigh. The vein of water, glistening in the sun, danced over rocks.

I asked, "Can you swim in it?"

Chapter One

"Of course. We have a dock and a canoe. The water is wonderful. Let me show you."

From the back porch, Ken and I followed him down. Steep cement stairs descended to the river and a cement dock, nestled into a slate cliff. A canoe sat on the slate embankment. I dipped my hand in the water. Cool but clear. A fish darted back and forth.

Before we left, Doug pulled me aside. He stepped ahead of Ken and whispered. "I need to talk with you later about an arrangement." He winked, putting a finger to his mouth. "Not now. Wait 'til you move in. We'll talk later."

As I had thought, a hitch. Whatever it was, I would deal with it. I had a place to stay.

Chapter Two

Later in the week, Doug called to tell me he was ready for me. He said I wouldn't be in the apartment while he added exterior walls, insulation, sheetrock, and a tile floor to the apartment. It was far from finished. He'd put me in the main building. A river-facing bedroom. He said we'd discuss 'the arrangement' privately at the lodge that night. "Oh, my boy, so good to see you! Do you have your things? Let's get you moved upstairs. A river view." He gestured toward the apartment. "I still have only the new bedroom to do—and the plumbing in the bath and kitchen. Let me show you around anyway."

My apartment had good outdoor light. It had a small kitchen with a stove, a refrigerator and a small half-circle table under the window that faced the driveway. He showed me my study. He'd made a desk out of two short filing cabinets with an oak slab over them. Based on my suggestions, he'd put in wall-to-wall bookcases on either side of a small fireplace. There was a couch covered with a red mottled blanket.

"It's a fold-out bed in case you have visitors." Doug winked at me. A doorway with no door led to the unfinished bedroom. It looked more like a long closet. The interior plywood hadn't been nailed to the studs, so you could still see through the walls to the outside.

"Perfect," I said, because there was plenty of space for my books. A view of the river. Privacy. Solitude. All I wanted.

River Crossed

Doug told me he had to get back to Maryland.

"Before I head off, though, "he said, "I wanted to go over the arrangement we have with people who use our place." He gazed off at the river. "You know Angel and I have another home in Wheaton. I work two jobs so we can afford this lovely retreat for our family—our boys love it—and, of course, our church groups. And yet—and I think you'll understand."

I didn't understand as yet how Doug beat around the bush in a conversation. Still, I later learned that's how he eased his way into a conversation by repeating himself, telling things he'd already said, shifting to a new topic, and finally coming out with what he wanted to say like someone pushing the choke and fidgeting with the air filters, before pulling the cord to start the mower.

He turned his chair toward me and reached across the table for my hand. Before I could pull it away, he took it and fixed his eyes on me.

"Now, as Christians, Angel, my dear wife, and I wrestle with this. But we feel that sometimes you must look the other way, sort of turn the other cheek. Christ taught us to do that, didn't he? You know what I mean?"

He offered a closed lip smile, nodded his head, and continued to explain. "We have this arrangement with a very nice gynecologist—he's Jewish—and a car salesman—he sells Mercedes Benzes in Cumberland. It provides us with supplemental income, so we can bring our church groups here for retreats. You understand?"

"I don't," I said.

"Of course, you don't. What we have arranged is that they can come here during the week anytime that they want; a little private get-away. They have keys. And what they do is their business. You

Chapter Two

see what I'm driving at?"

"They have parties down here?"

"Oh, my dear boy, not quite," Doug let go of my fingers. He stood up and pushed his hands in his pockets and paced back and forth.

"You seem to have an open mind. Let me be frank: They're married men. But—let me try to say this diplomatically—they have women friends, if you know what I mean. They come here for some privacy, to get out of town where no one will be the wiser. It's out of the way, if you catch what I'm saying."

"Do they come together as a foursome?"

He laughed. "Oh, no, no, my boy. They are careful about that. Very discreet. One at a time. They come only on certain days. It's private. It's just a get-away for them and their girlfriends."

"So, they fuck and go?"

He seemed rather startled by my frankness. "That's a way of putting it," He turned away, and then he turned back.

"Do you have a problem with it?"

I said, "Do they like sharing the goods?" Doug's face reddened.

"Just kidding," I said.

He laughed. "Very funny, indeed."

"I guess I don't mind," I said. "What do you want me to do? Keep to myself?"

"Exactly."

"I can do that. I'll just read and write," I said, more amused by the arrangement than worried, as I had been when he first sat me down. "There you are. That's it!" He clapped his hands and took a seat again.

"What if I'm here when they come?" "Keep to your room."

"If I come back from work and they're here?"

"All I ask is if they're here, you're discreet. Give them privacy. Wait until they're ready to go, and just let them be. Can you do that?" Doug leaned over, putting his hands on my knee.

"I can sit on the porch or just head down the road if need be."

"Exactly," he replied.

He patted my knee and squeezed it slightly, "I knew we could count on you. This little arrangement Angel and I have made is delicate. We don't let our boys know, or anyone. Is that clear?"

"Who would I tell anyway?"

"Yes, yes, yes. You're right! And if you want to bring a little friend here, well," he winked, "that's your business. Boy. Girl. We're very open-minded. But we would prefer you wait until we have your apartment done, if you know what I mean." He shrugged and smiled at me. "You never can tell, can you? You might come across someone up to no good. We all have our needs," he said, chuckling to himself, taking a brief glance at my crotch. "Don't we?"

"I guess." I looked down, wondering if I'd left my zipper open. "Then we have an agreement?"

I stood up to shake his hand. He lifted my hand up to his chest, pulled me close and, lightly, kissed me on the cheek.

"Oh, my boy, you'll love it here, I can just tell!"

I put my books on some shelves in my temporary room, hung my clothes on the wooden closet rod, went downstairs, and stepped onto the porch. The river was murmuring to itself. The air was cool and fresh. For the first time in my life, I had a place of my own, not

Chapter Two

in my parents' house, not in a campus dorm. I had a place away from people, no TV, no phone. Off the grid. I slipped off my pants and walked down the fifty cement steps—counting each one—and dangled my feet in the water. The steady current massaged my feet and tugged at my legs. Across the river, the trailers were vacant. No one there. For an hour, I sat there, cooling off, not thinking of anything, just listening to the water, taking in the surroundings of my new home. To my left, a ridge rose precipitously to a ledge where several stunted, scraggly hemlocks jutted out, their branches leaning over the river below.

Home, I thought. It was a word I had to get used to, a word I liked. No longer a vagabond, I was safe in the folds of these foothills, by the bank of the South Branch of the Potomac. If you looked at a map, this water drifted northward where it joined the North Branch and became the Potomac River which, in turn, flowed southward, headed into Maryland and then to D.C. where President Nixon, if he looked out of the White House, could see the same water that flowed by my room.

Chapter Three

My first task as a Hampton County Director was to attend a series of Head Start Director workshops. I had spent time boning up. It was a comprehensive program designed to engage the entire family. Education for preschool students. Health care. Nutritional education. They encouraged parental involvement in the local centers. In Hampton County, there would be five centers, each situated in different regions, each staffed by a lead teacher, a teacher's aide, and a cook. Fifteen to eighteen students could apply. A bus would pick them up at the same time as regular students and leave them off in the afternoon. I drove out to visit each area, meeting ministers, inspecting churches or other municipal centers, that might want a children's program.

At the orientation workshop, a motley group gathered at the Hilltop restaurant—some with elementary school backgrounds, some former administrators of social service programs, most with degrees in early childhood education. I felt like an outsider. My ignorance of childhood development, particularly early childhood education, kids under five years old, was a major deficit. When the trainers spoke about developmental benchmarks and sensory-motor level functioning, I had no idea what they meant. Even less of a clue how developmental levels translated into purchasing equipment for the centers and hiring skilled, competent, disciplinary classroom staff. I slunk down in my chair, made notes, and pretended I knew what was going on.

During a break, I browsed through books and materials on a table. I picked up a thick Jean Piaget volume on activities for preschoolers, showing how to set up blocks, puzzles, and word recognition games.

Another new director, responsible for setting up programs in two adjacent counties, saw me and walked over.

"Do you understand that?" she asked.

I held the book at arm's length, staring at it. "Why do you ask?"

"I just want to know. Do you?"

She had a kind face with a large gap between her front teeth. Her glasses had slipped down her wide nose, so she had to look over the rims. I wasn't sure what to say. I'd never heard of Jean Piaget.

"You want an honest answer," I said, stalling.

"That would be good," she said, offering a half-smile that seemed playful and put me at my ease.

I looked around to see if any other director was nearby. I whispered, "I don't know shit." She laughed uproariously. Her whole body shook. She covered her mouth out of embarrassment yet kept on laughing. Her laugh was contagious, so I laughed, too. Her blue eyes danced with delight. When she regained her composure, she said, "I'm sorry. You seemed so studious. I thought you were an expert. It really struck me as funny."

"Clearly."

"I might as well be honest with you, too." She was whispering. "I don't know shit either."

I laughed.

Chapter Three

She poked me in the arm. "Quit it. You're embarrassing me. Let's take a walk."

She had three children, one of whom was in elementary school, one in junior high, and one in high school. She'd been a fourth-grade teacher, which seems like relevant experience to me. She told me she was disconcerted by the thought of sitting in training for three more days. She held up a manual they'd passed out that explained, step by step, center set-up expectations. We had to get a program up and running within four weeks, including one week dedicated to training staff.

"My Lord," she said, "if we sit here and have them go page by page over this manual, I'm afraid I'll either fall asleep again or be so confused I wouldn't know how to start anything, including my brain." She tapped her finger at her head and widened her eyes. "The clock is ticking by golly. We better get hopping or else we'll be out of a job."

"What'll we do?" I asked.

"Get the heck out of here and set to work. We got the manual." She patted it. "I say, let's start the doing now! I don't know about you, but I don't even know where my sites are. Let's blow this joint and get a decent lunch. You and I can figure out what we're doing. You read this stuff by Piaget. You seem the studious type. I'll read the ones on activities. We'll make this work."

We passed by a table with displays of children's toys and educational materials, and she picked up an armful. "You take these. I'll take those. That'll get us started at least." As we were walking to the table to pay for the books, she asked, "Am I right, you're the new director for Hampton County?"

"I guess so," I responded. My uncertainty must have been rather transparent because she laughed again, a full body laugh that got me laughing too. The little space between her two front teeth was charming. Her eyes filled with a playfulness that put me entirely at ease.

"I guess so," she repeated. "That pretty much sums it up. Oh, my dear, I'm sorry," she looked me in the eyes, "but I'm quite sure that you're probably even greener at this than I am. That makes me feel good. My name is Carole Goldsmith."

Carole knew of local merchants in Hampton County willing to supply us, including a Ben Franklin 5 & 10 Store in Pearsall Flats and several smaller food stores up Route 50. She put together a shopping list, based on perusing our manuals, the books we bought for research on what the grants allowed for supplies in each center. Like a hired hand, I followed her lead and hoped she didn't see the little boy doing his best to keep up with her.

Over the next four weeks, nonstop, we started each day at 6 AM and ended the day past 10 PM. We planned to hire her staff, and then, mine. I stayed overnight at her house whenever I could and met her kids—high school boy, junior highschooler, and daughter in elementary. The junior highschooler, Steve, loved playing football. His being around gave me an excuse to take a break from work. We would toss the ball, him racing across the yard, snatching my throws. I felt competent playing ball. I also liked that he became attached to me. He sat right next to me at dinner. Every time I stayed over, he was there waiting for me, tossing the ball in the air.

Chapter Three

His father, as a farmer and preacher, kept him busy with chores and never played with him. I became his second Pa, as Carole told me. It felt good. I liked feeling as if I were a dad, feeling what it might be like to be one.

Once we got the word out, ministers clamored at our doors. Every center came with new refrigerators and freezers, stoves, and early childhood supplies that the Sunday School teachers could use. Churches in the outlying areas of Hampton County, after some initial skepticism, were more interested and willing to house a Head Start Center than any of the conservative, established churches in Pearsall Flats. Carole suspected it was racism.

Pearsall Flats had a large Black community right in the middle of town, a six-block ghetto that might as well have had walls surrounding it. No white people ever went there.

I visited several homes in the Black area where I knew there were preschool kids and let them know about the program. They seemed to be appreciative. One mother told me. "Mister, you ain't going to find no church in this town that will have any one of us. No, sir. Not a chance."

I was discouraged. If the Black children attended Head Start in their white churches, it would erase their invisibility, but it would also highlight years of discrimination.

I wondered what magic could open the doors of a church. Carole invited me to dinner to discuss my options. Forty miles away, down a road that snaked along the river, I drove, thinking about my successes and my failures. I felt over my head. When I arrived at Carole's house, she had sliced Velveeta cheese, mounded Ritz crackers on a plate, poured a Diet Coke in a glass, her favorite. She had us sit on the couch, and asked, "You don't look good. How was your day?"

I suspected that was what she asked her husband when he came home. As a Pentecostal farmer who got up early to do chores and a minister who made house calls in the evening, he was often late. I felt honored to be his substitute.

"Fine," I said. "Made some contacts."

"Good ones?" she asked.

"About as friendly as rattle snakes." She sensed something was amiss.

"Are you alright?" she asked. By her tone of voice, I knew that she really wanted to know. I didn't grow up with people like her. Her easy charm made me feel like anything I could say, no matter how offhanded, would be heard, and taken seriously.

She leaned forward. "Something's wrong. Tell me."

"I can't seem to get anyone to buy into having a Center in Pearsall Flats."

"Uphill battle?" "More like a wall."

"There's something else?" She touched my hand.

"I feel like a fraud."

"Fraud?"

"It may sound crazy, but I'm no director. Inside of me, right here"—I tapped my chest—"there's this little boy. Jung called him a homunculus. That's the real me. He's gripping these strings. He's manipulating this adult puppet, desperately trying to prop me up. He wants me to maintain this image of an adult. But he's overwhelmed, worn-out, exasperated."

"I get that," she said. "I do. It's not the same. Yet when I think

Chapter Three

that I'm now the wife of a minister. Can you imagine? Lord knows I didn't go to church years before I met Jack. A college student, I was a free thinker. A bit wild. Now, I even think some wanted me to be a virgin. Thank God I have our neighbor. She's a Presbyterian. She sees me as who I am. Just Carole. No expectations. Otherwise, I don't know what I'd do. I mean, if I'm not what others think I should be, who am I?"

"Exactly," I said. "I'm supposed to be some expert here. Reality check: I don't know the difference between, as Piaget calls them, the development stages. Besides, I'm supposed to sell them our program. I hate being a salesman. It seems crazy. I don't know if I can do it."

"Oh, Jason, I . . ."

I put my hands to my face and cried.

She put her hand on my shoulder. "I think you need to give that boy some slack," she said. "Here, give him another cracker. Tell him he's doing a good job and needs to relax. Your little boy may be a minor, but I think he needs a beer, too."

I laughed.

"Come here," she said and put her arms around me.

The front door opened, and Jack stepped in. A sly man, skinny but broad-shouldered. "What's this?"

"Oh, honey," Carole said. She didn't skip a beat. "It's Jason. He's had a bad day."

"Tell me about it," Jack said, tossing his coat on a chair. "You should hear the complaints I got today. We need new cushions. The roof is leaking. My sermons are too long."

"I've told you that a hundred times," Carole said. She stood up, gave Jack a hug, went to the refrigerator to get us all a beer. He left us alone to do some paperwork.

In my bedroom, I took out my journal—I hadn't written in it for several days—and pulled out a pen.

First week at the job feeling very much as if I'm auditioning for a role in a play where I have no script and don't even know who the character is I am acting. I wonder if everyone when they take on a new job, especially one with authority, feels similar. What else could one feel?

When I met with one minister, he showed me around his church and asked me what I had to offer. When I told him about how we'd pay for upgrading the kitchen, buy toys that they could use, and hire staff, he pinched his glasses back on his nose, cocked his head, and seemed impressed. Here I was with the keys to the money kingdom. When he asked if we offered a good Christian education, I had to tell him it was a government program, and we had to honor the separation of church and state. "A Yankee program is it?" he said.

"A government program." I said again.

"Same difference. You a Yankee?" he asked. I told him I came from Nashville. Figured a little lie wasn't too bad. Don't know if he'll bite on the offer or not. I sometimes think the south is really another country and I am an outsider. In any case, I fake it until I make it.

After that evening, whenever Carole greeted me, she asked, "How homunculus doing?"

I was never sure how the little man was doing until she asked. But I found that he felt better just knowing someone knew he was there, was looking after him, and offering him a beer as if he were an adult.

Chapter Four

Pearsall Flats, the center of the county, had the greatest number of children who would qualify for Head Start. I had to get a center there. The need was as real as the racism. As I met with ministers—first one church, then another—they were polite, congenial with an air of southern gentility. They never mentioned the issue of race, but they knew what I meant: the Blacks would be with the whites, and that, no sir, wasn't going to happen in their church. I met with four boards, gave them the pitch, talked about service to the poor, the call to reach out to "the least of us," but no dice.

"Sound like a good program. Very noble," one minister said. "Let me tell you, son. Not likely to sell anyone in this town about the president's Great Society. No one appreciates Yankees' programs. We don't want anything to do with that turncoat president. He sold us out with that Voting Rights bill. He's not popular here. I'll tell you something you don't understand about us. We're steeped in the blood of the Confederacy."

I nodded. "Any advice?"

"Not sure I can help. Keep trying, I guess. You got a long road ahead of you, son." He stood and ushered me to the door. "But it was a pleasure to meet you."

I had a coworker, Anne, at my office who told me folks thought I was a communist. Anne seemed to know everything about everybody. I made note in my journal:

Anne's whole life revolves around the people in Pearsall Flats. The same way Kafka was fascinated about people, their actions and desires, their exterior manners and inward angst. Anne is like a novelist, except her gossip never stays too long in her head since she is always publishing it to her public, gossip about me included.

Before the week was over, Ken introduced me to his friend, Maddy Bloom, a white local businesswoman. She was a Southern widow with a surprisingly liberal bent. Although petite with soft grey hair, she carried herself like Eleanor Roosevelt. Both gracious and fierce, she met with the minister and church elders of the First Presbyterian Church and told them to find out what I had to offer, not to bury their head in the sand. When they complained, she told them, "It's your Christian duty." As one of the church's founding families—she had a family pew set aside and had financial clout behind her—she got me a meeting with them.

Beforehand, I worked on a clearer theological justification for having a Center, building on Maddy's Christian-duty theme. After I typed up my presentation, I showed it to Carole.

"You make a good argument. I don't know that theologian Bonhoeffer and that other fellow Bultmann, but they seem to be deep thinkers. Let's see how it goes."

She had made more progress in setting up her centers than me. She'd already booked her sites and had planned on the next weekend, for us to purchase equipment, having checked out the best buys in the region.

I had Centers in all the outlying areas: a historic site at Capon Bridge, and three churches that were further away. That was a big accomplishment.

Chapter Four

But Ken told me I had to nail down Pearsall Flats Center. "I hate to tell you this," he said. "Hear me. The program is dead in the water if we can't get a Center in the county capital. You know what that means? You'll be out of a job." He slung his arm around my shoulder. "Make it work. I don't want to lose you. I'm looking forward to our spending more time together."

While the Pearsall Presbyterian Church was a block from the Black neighborhood, it had never had any Black members. Most, if they attended church, worshipped at a small Black Baptist church on the other side of town. I planned to cite New Testament scripture, explain how Head Start was consistent with Jesus's altruistic message of reaching out to the least of us. This time, Carole offered to come and support me. Time was running out, and I knew it. We met in the church board room at a large mahogany table. The minister, a young, gaunt man with thinning black hair, sat in the head chair. He opened with a prayer. He introduced the elders, all men who looked sour-faced and bored. He told me to get on with it.

Speaking from my notes, I stood up and launched into what amounted to one of my best sermons, quoting testament passages and some recent South American liberation theologians.

Across the table, the seven men folded their arms, stared at the desk, wholly uninterested in my presentation. Two of them doodled on scratch paper. I kept on too long. Carole screwed her mouth to one side, ran her hand under her throat, signaling me to stop. I asked if they had any questions. No one spoke. The minister interceded, asked how many children would be in the program. I told him. A suit-dressed elder asked how we selected them. I went over the selection process. He asked if I knew if they were Presbyterian or Baptists. I said it didn't matter; they were children of God. What I wanted to say was that it was more Christian than anything they had in their church.

No one made eye contact with me. I felt invisible. They probably knew I was a fake.

The minister called for a vote. While they discussed if they would or wouldn't accept a Center, Carole and I waited in the hallway. The minister came out to meet us after ten minutes and shook his head.

I asked, "Why?"

He stared at me. "We don't need to share our deliberations."

I slammed my fist against a chair. "Can't you persuade them? You know it's the right thing to do."

He stepped back and said, "They make these decisions, not me."

I asked if we could talk with them again. They couldn't do this to the kids. Carole put her hand on my fist and said surprisingly, in a quiet voice, "Please let me say a word to them."

We went back inside. She smiled at them. She had no notes. Instead, she looked across the table and said, "I noticed, when we arrived, that you have an incredibly old refrigerator and stove in the kitchen. It's even older than the ones in my kitchen." She laughed. "As a housewife, I'd say, from the looks of them, pretty soon, you'll be needing new ones. I know that's what me and my husband ask pretty near every year at our church. He's a farmer and a minister, too. You need a good kitchen to have a robust church. You need good cooking for a strong congregation. The womenfolk expect that, don't they? The way to the heart goes right through the belly."

Several elders chuckled at that comment.

Chapter Four

"Well," she continued, "I know you may not like the Great Society, I have my own doubts, too, with federal programs. But there's some self-interest here to consider. Here's the deal: we can take care of that kitchen. As part of our program, we'll buy you a new refrigerator and stove, and, in addition, a freezer. If the program leaves, you keep them all. Free and usable the day we start. You can even store your food in the freezer. Take that out of your budget considerations. We'll do it for you."

Smiles transformed their sour faces. Everyone perked up, leaned forward, listened to her as if to the word of God. She wasn't done. She told them how our pre-school equipment—outdoor play areas, toys, and educational material—could be used by the church for their Sunday school.

"The building blocks, I noticed, in one room were chipped and worn. We can get you new ones," she said. "And, in addition, we'd fix up the rooms, putting on a spanking new coat of paint and install new blackboards." The elders asked where the merchandise would be purchased from. She dropped name brands, the highest quality: Whirlpool, General Electric, and Westinghouse.

We waited in the hall again afterwards. She assured me that I had made a good, thought-out plea, but she chuckled and said, "You know they couldn't give two hoots about gospel and all that theology. They're businessmen. Dollars and cents. That's what makes sense to them."

Within five minutes, the minister called us back to the room and told us we could have three rooms for our program, full use of the kitchen and the playground outside the school. We smiled. Thanked them. Carole called them each by name and shook their hands. She nudged me to stand up and follow her. I had no idea what their names were, so I picked up on what she called them. I was faking it again. But we'd made a deal. Carole had done it. I crumpled my notes and tossed them in the wastepaper basket.

The minister offered a prayer before we left.

On the way out, he asked us to stay a moment. "I'm glad it turned out the way it did. I'm new here and must apologize since I have no leverage right now," he explained. "But mark my words, I will soon. I'll support you 100 percent. We need to open these doors to all of the community. I suspect you will still face some blowback with the race thing: that's still a thorn for some of them. But I will stand by you, I guarantee you that."

After that meeting, when selling our program to anyone, I mentioned the children but focused on the list of what we could give them, item by item. At the end of those sales pitches, I had made deals. I learned that, for businessmen, God had a price tag.

The afternoon of the Presbyterian meeting, I made some notes to myself when I got back to the lodge.

Carole won the day. Funny, in all the classes at the divinity school, we talked about sociology, religion, ethics, but no one ever talked about capitalism and religion. Soon as we mentioned a new stove, they jumped at it like fish to a fresh worm.

The real American religion is capitalism. We worship products, profits, and prestige. My dad said he couldn't believe in what he could not see (or own), but he could believe in what was before his eyes. Appearances are reality. I think that is the way most people think. If I ever became a minister, the first thing I would do is call that out. I would give a lesson on capitalism and how so many of God's children have been disenfranchised. I wouldn't be a mousy, frightened man afraid of the church board.

Chapter Five

Through Ken, we advertised in the local papers for new staff. With five centers in Hampton County, and less than two weeks to start-up, and with each site needing a teacher, teacher's aides, drivers, a cook, and assistant cook, we had thirty positions to fill just in my county alone. Since we also had to do Carole's hiring, we crammed interviews into one day-long set, from 7:00 in the morning to 8:30 at night.

Federal guidelines required us to have a parent involved in our interviews. Over the phone, I met a woman, Edith, who lived up the road from me. Her three-room, ramshackle house was right off the road to the lodge, swallowed by the long grass, nestled under a large willow. She had three children, all eligible for Head Start, so I invited her to sit in.

I arrived at their house early on the interview morning. I knocked. A voice called out, "Come in." In the living room, I found a man sitting in an armchair, staring, aiming a shotgun at me.

I backed up. "No, no. You got me wrong."

"What you mean getting my woman up so early without asking me?" The barrel of the gun had two dark eyes.

Instinctively, I raised my hands. But he laughed.

"Scared you, huh?"

Peering behind my hands, I saw him bent over laughing.

"You should have seen your face," he roared. He howled, tears streaming down his cheeks.

Edith came in the room and screamed, "Bill! What are you doing?" She came up to me, grabbed my arm. "Come in, Jason. Bill, that's not funny. You nearly scared the piss out of him." "Sorry," he said.

I shook his hand.

Edith wore high heels and a stylish, red polka dot dress. She was well made up with eyeliner, lipstick, and rouge.

"When's it over?" he asked.

"Not sure," I said. "We got a slew of people to interview. It could go as late as 9:00 or later." Bill seemed worried then, for real, so I added, "I'll take care of your wife."

At 7:00 PM, our 48th candidate came in, a middle-aged woman wearing a permanent scowl. Carole, Edith, and I were exhausted. The woman sat down and immediately launched into several minutes about her employment history, the name of her boss, the type of skills she had, pretty much answering all our questions before we even spoke. Edith then asked from our preset questions about her experience with children; another oration followed. The Senate could have hired her to filibuster.

I started to ask my question and realized she'd already answered it. I stuttered. I asked the next question on the list. Carole, misunderstanding, told me to go back. I told her I had asked it, and she said she hadn't heard it, and both of us, catching each other's eyes, realized how absurd it was, how neither of us could remember what had been said. Carole started to giggle, covering her mouth. I tried to

Chapter Five

hold back but burst out laughing.

The lady glared at us.

"Excuse me, I should go." Carole headed out the door. I followed.

Edith pulled her chair up and said to the lady, "Hon, we've had a long day. A really long day."

We scurried out the door into the hallway. It took us several minutes to calm down. Every time we looked at one another, we laughed again. And again. And again.

"This looks bad," she said. "We can't be doing this. It's a government program."

"Yes, yes, it is. Let's get it together."

She leaned against the wall. "You first."

We took deep breaths. Avoided eye contact. As dignified as we could, we walked back toward the office door. Every time we reached for the doorknob, we collapsed again into a fit of laughter. Finally, we agreed that only one of us should carry on since if we both went in, one of us would lose it. Carole went in and I hustled down the steps and paced up and down Main Street. I walked to the town hall to gaze at the Confederate soldier on the pedestal, slowly regaining my composure. Here I was having to prove a Yankee program could save lives, and I couldn't stop laughing.

When I pulled up to the lodge, exhausted as I was, I discovered the night was far from over. Someone—the gynecologist or car salesman—had brought his lover over for the first time since I moved in. His black Mercedes Benz was parked under the back light.

A dealer's plate. The car salesman.

I was supposed to give them privacy and not go into the main house. As fatigued as I was, I wasn't going to sit in my car. It was cold. I tiptoed into the living room, and sprawled out on the couch, hoping to get some rest. The grandfather clock's pendulum swung back and forth, and upstairs, I could hear the brass bed creaking in time to it. Rapidly at first but, as the minutes passed, slower, at last faintly until it ceased.

When the man came down the stairs in his Italian leather shoes, he noticed me. He told the young woman, who eyed me with a half-smile, to wait a moment. He double stepped up the stairs and returned with a bottle of champagne, still cold, unopened, dropped it in my lap and patted me on the head.

He introduced himself as Harold Berlin. "Enjoy," he said.

While he waltzed his beauty to the car, I opened the bottle, poured it in a wine glass, toasted to a full staff that we had just hired and the start of a new career.

For the next few weeks, I picked up appliances, wrote proposals, typed staff contracts, dialed-up agencies, bought food, carted in toys, and greeted the new families along with their children. My hands were in everything. At the end of every day, I'd sit at my desk, my fingers cramped from typing, thinking my hands needed a day off, something else to do. I was becoming, much to my chagrin, a businessman just like my dad—a human doer. Only in the deep night when I journaled and pondered what had become of me did I feel the artist come alive. Lonely, the artist had only himself to talk to. But he still existed.

Chapter Six

By late October, I had settled into a routine. Working late. Having dinner with Carole and her family. Coming home to the river.

The Vietnam War continued unabated. That worried me. If it went on, there was still a chance I could get drafted. Nixon said the end was in sight. Congress had stipulated that we needed to withdraw our troops by the end of the year. Peace negotiations were ongoing in Paris. I didn't trust Nixon, yet congressional action made the end more certain. That was a relief.

I visited the Centers nearly every day. Sitting with the kids on the floor, playing with blocks, reading them stories, having them in my lap. In those moments, I felt like a kid again myself. They called me, disconcertingly, by my father's name, "Mr. Follett." And the director role forced me to think of myself as an authority. Every day, simultaneously, I felt more like an adult than the day before and still more and more like a child who was acting a part that, even if I didn't want to admit, enjoyed it.

Ken thought I'd gotten into a rut, talking about Head Start and nothing else. Once a week, late in the afternoon, we stopped by the Cozy Kitchen for coffee. He liked to talk about theology, pestering me with questions, checking to see if I'd read any more of the liberation theologians. If I hadn't, he'd slip a book to me. "Read this." He had given it some thought, he said, one afternoon, how the ministry was more secure than a government job. How it has much less paperwork and guidelines.

"You know, if you had a small church, you could freelance. You could write poetry. You'd have more time to yourself," he said. "Wouldn't that appeal to you? I bet you'd have time to write a novel." I told him that I would only do that out of desperation. He suggested that I expand my social horizons and meet people who were both intellectually interesting and involved with the arts. For him, it was the only way he stayed sane.

He invited me to meet the Bentleys—Tess, a patron of the arts, and her husband, Jerome, an Episcopal priest very active in the Community Action Program. They were rich. Jerome had inherited millions from his father who owned a petroleum company. Tess had her own money, from a coffee plantation in Brazil. They lived in Dresden, over the mountain from Pearsall Flats. Ken had met Jerome at a regional meeting of the Community Action Program, and they hit it off.

We rode in silence to the Bentley's house. I looked at the tree-lined roads, the soft light of the moon cresting over the hills. It was a cool evening, the first hint of fall in the air. By the time we reached Dresden, light snow had begun to fall.

Tess, dressed in a stylish red silken fabric, welcomed us at the front door, cautioning us to watch our steps. I stepped into the foyer and gazed around. A dark oak coat rack. A small, framed British landscape oil painting. A metal umbrella stand.

She extended her hand to greet me, smiling. Her dark eyebrows lifted. She looked charming, inquisitive, staring at me as if appraising my worth.

Chapter Six

"Jason. I've heard so much about you from Ken."

Ken shrugged his shoulders and grinned, helping me out of my coat. "I hope he didn't disclose too much about my shady past," I offered. "Oh, he's said quite a bit." She took my overcoat, brushing off the lint, creasing it carefully, and hung it from a rack hook. "Is there something I should know?"

I was embarrassed and shook my head. I stepped into a living room. The finest furnishings—armchairs upholstered in bright colors, deep plush couches, chandeliers with glass pendants—surprisingly sophisticated for a parsonage in a small rural West Virginia town.

I heard Tess whisper to Ken, "You didn't tell me that he was so good looking."

I brushed my hand through my hair, pulling it off my forehead. Ken shot back, "Do you think so?"

"Silly boy. Appearance makes the man."

She directed us to a room down the hall. We stopped at the threshold. The room was swank, old-world elegant and filled with a few other guests. I hadn't known it would be more than the four of us. No one seemed to notice us, though. They remained seated and engaged in conversation. Several men fleetingly gazed at us yet continued talking. They acted as if Ken and I had come to the wrong room.

I felt awkward. I took several breaths. Ken patted my arm.

"It will be fine, just go with the flow." The hands of a grandfather clock seemed arrested at 7:13.

Tess strode behind us, took note of us standing there, and sang out, "Come along, my dears." Almost as an afterthought, she thrust her arm in mine and escorted us into the room. Once in the room, she played leading lady, making sure we were introduced to the rest of the players. She turned to her husband, who had been so engrossed in conversation with a handsome young man that he hadn't noticed the new arrivals.

"Jerome," she intoned, "Do the introductions, dear."

Jerome stood and greeted us. "So sorry. Enrique was telling one of his fascinating stories about the military academy. So good to see you, Ken, and who is this?"

He shook my hand. "Did I catch your name?"

"Jason."

"Oh, yes, of course."

He took my arm, pointed to Enrique. But he skipped over a man who said nothing but nursed his drink. Intentionally or unintentionally, I wasn't sure. The man wasted no time in making note of the slight. "Jerome, my dear, is there something wrong?" he asked, tilting his head to the side. "You forgot me, dear."

Jerome ushered me over to the man. "This is David Bridewell. One of Tess's finds. Quite an interesting chap." David met Tess at the Kennedy Center in Washington. A pair of opera buffs, the two of them drove together and stayed nights in a DC hotel.

At first, his handshake was firm, and then it went flaccid like a fish squirming out of a fisherman's grasp.

He raised his eyebrows and said, "Simply charmed." He patted the chair next to him. "Put yourself here so I can get a better look at you." Remnants of adolescent acne, deep pot marks, scarred David's cheeks. Quick to tell me he was a confirmed bachelor, he pointed at and informed me exactly which artist painted which paintings in the room, giving the exact date, place, and style. He bragged that

Chapter Six

he could tell me when any piece of classical music was composed by what composer and premiered by what orchestra. His passion, however, was Wagner and the Ring Cycle from Tristan to Isolde. At the party, before I had a chance to tell him anything about myself, he asked me to come to his place. "I have the very best Deutsche Grammophon records. The very best. And the latest. You will love them as much as I do," he said.

Sitting across from us was Enrique, the 16 year-old son of a South American general who had been talking with Jerome when we came in. Swarthy, lean, and virile, he flirted with everyone, including me.

Jerome offered us a drink. As the night wore on, any time my glass was half-full, he grabbed it, and said, "Here, let me refresh it," before I could say no. For him, it seemed that a good dinner party meant inebriation. In the case of this party, he was right.

With a string quartet playing in the background, we sipped wine and talked of the arts, of Nixon's failed presidency and his run-ins with the press. There was an air of something splendid, other worldly, about the occasion, almost as if we slipped through a time-warp and were dropped in a 19th century soiree.

Ken, sitting on the other side of me, warned me about David. "He likes boys."

I recoiled and straightened up. "What did you say?"

Ken laughed. "Don't be shocked. It takes all kinds, these days. It's not my style, I assure you. But what can I say?"

I wondered if there was some underworld, some hidden society that had been right in front of me. I spent my adolescence living in the suburbs, my twenties in seminary. Maybe this was the real world. I looked over at David immersed in conversation with Tess.

He seemed to be a nice enough fellow. I figured if he made a pass at me, I could handle it. I tried to follow Ken's cavalier attitude: no obvious judgements. Just accept people for who they are.

As the host, Jerome seemed lost, never quite sure of what he was doing. He downed one drink after another. His thick, brown hair was slicked back from his forehead. He wore a dressed-white Episcopal collar and kept up a commentary about his trials as a local priest. Anytime he paused, David jumped in.

"I can't compete with the Jerome, never even tried, but I should have my say, don't you think?" He spoke of Wagner's Ring Cycle recordings—"how luscious they were"—his hands flapping as if he were directing the wind, then he said, turning to Jerome, "Oh, poor Jerome forgets to introduce me since I'm having an affair with his wife."

Jerome, not to be outdone, retorted, "That's nothing. Everyone has an affair with her. That's her role as a clergyman's wife!"

David whispered to me, "Look at him. He's like a lord on his throne." Jerome did, indeed, seem artfully poised at the edge of the chair, back straight, knees together, looking horribly uncomfortable, entirely out of place and yet regal, like someone expecting others to attend to him.

I got up to fix another drink and David joined me. I asked him where he lived. It proved to be the wrong question. He complained about his aunt who owned a huge mansion, right in the middle of town, a historic landmark, and had relegated one room to him. "Just one room, mind you. It's in the back. I enter by the back door like a house servant. Sometimes I'd like to strangle her. It wouldn't take much. She's such a fuss budget. She even has me on the Community

Chapter Six

Action board in our county. She disdains my friends. She hates my music. But I give her credit: she pays the way. It's the best I can do until she dies. Then I plan to live like king David."

We finally migrated to the dining room: platters of vegetables, delicately brocaded cuts of beef, and a bountiful bowl of salad. The clink of silver on plates, and ice in crystal. Tess described each dish. Each had a name. More wine, different for each course.

Time unwound itself.

Enrique mostly listened. He snuggled next to Tess, kissed her on the cheek and told her how lovely she looked. He was aware of those who paid close attention to him. If he caught a glance, he'd soon be by your side, fawning over you. Man. Woman. It didn't seem to matter. It seemed he was gay too. Or bisexual. He stayed with Jerome and Tess on his holidays, but David told me he'd stayed over several nights with him. "It was magnificent," he told me. "Pure delight" as if Enrique was a lavish food.

I was uncomfortable. Tess sat next to me. Earlier, David had told me that she liked younger men, single and available. The muscular fit of their shirts, the quickness of their stop, and their love of art. I noticed the way her eyes took me in—Enrique too. I felt like a stray on display in a pet store. My skin tingled. I couldn't figure out who wanted who. Everybody wanted everyone. If David was looking at me, I turned my head and focused on Tess.

Glasses clinked. Liqueur filled lowball tumblers. The conversation, like a musical score, swelled and dissipated with lapses into silence rescued by another story, a quick exchange, a lively retort, until Tess suggested that coffee might be in order.

The kettle screamed as steam spurted out of its spout. Tess

pulled me over, walked me through the steps of making coffee the "right way."

"Now hurry. The water is ready. This is what you must do: scoop out ten scoops. No. First, level them off. Yes. Good. Now pour them in the filter. Make sure the coffee is level. That's it. Now pour the water gently into the filter." Her face flushed.

"Good Lord, what are you doing? Stop pouring. Stop!"

Flustered, I spilled water on the counter. She laughed at my mishap, shaking her head, a smile radiating from her lips. She mollified me, taking the kettle.

"My! You have so much to learn, young man. Let me show you. If you keep pouring, the acids from the coffee stir up and spoil the taste. But if you wait, let the water settle, then the acids will not come to the top." She poured the water as one would run one's hand over a pet. Gently. Lovingly.

She said quietly, "It is an art form like your writing Ken told me about. You must do it as carefully as you choose words for your poems. Yes?" She took my hand again and then passed the kettle back, "Let it catch the aroma. Now you finish."

I did.

That moment with Tess in the kitchen seemed portentous. The touch of her hand on mine. I sat back at the table, feeling it like an afterimage on my hand throughout the night. I felt young. Innocent. Loss and regret had not been woven in my heart. I felt saved, happy to have her blessing, happy to be there and full of expectation.

Every time, after that when I've made coffee, I followed her instructions and thought of her. Her tenderness and patience like she was teaching me to make love for the first time.

Chapter Six

Enrique excused himself, saying it had been a long trip from the academy, and went upstairs to bed. Soon after, David left. The chill of night slipped in the room when he opened the door. Jerome offered us another coffee and took more for himself, put his feet up, quiet. I sat in a large high back chair across from him. Ken sat on the floor, his legs folded under him, by Tess's chair. Tess played the "Four Last Songs" of Richard Strauss and told us about the songs and the woman who sang them. She loved classical music—her German heritage. She explained these were Strauss's swan songs, published after he died.

"Three of the four are from Hermann Hesse's poems," she said. "Oh, I know him," I exclaimed. He is one of my favorites." She was delighted.

She read the last poem "Beim Schlafengehen" in German, then in English. The German sounded foreboding, deeply mournful. The English seemed less dramatic.

> Now that I am wearied of the day,
> my ardent desire shall happily receive
> the starry night
> like a sleepy child.
> Hands, stop all your work.
> Brow, forget all your thoughts.
> Now all my senses
> yearn to sink into slumber.
> And my unfettered soul
> wishes to soar freely
> into night's magic sphere
> to live there deeply and thousand-fold.

I was struck by one line: "Hands, stop all your work." I looked at my hands holding the coffee cup. They were in that moment complacent. Self-absorbed. Unhurried. The evening had let them rest. The music swept over me. I could feel Strauss's every emotion. I was carried off and didn't want to come back to the room and conversation. I looked out the window at the snow falling and thought of the guests, the intensity of their voices reaching out for something intangible. With the music and the voice of soprano, Elisabeth Schwarzkopf, it seemed like a fine crystal was cracking, crumbling back to sand, and rising like a phoenix into the night sky. I had seen the others leave, and the voices that were left were speaking in lower tones as an old Victrola winding down, and finally saying nothing. Silence. Our eyes all taking stock—Tess of me; me of her; Jerome like a Buddha, pondering mysteries of Ken and me, of all of us.

Ken rose and said, "Wonderful evening." I too rose and, as a gesture befitting the evening, kissed Tess's hand, and said, "Simply delightful." We left with her standing in the doorway, waving graciously as we trudged to the car.

I knew I had chanced upon something both frightening and wonderful, dangerous yet magical, something like a lure with a sharp hook that had gotten under my skin.

The next night, after coming back from work outside on the deck of my lodge, I gazed at the moon, yellow-robed, and above it, the myriad stars and the constellation Orion—the belt of stars. I felt a whole lifetime had passed through and by me the previous night.

Chapter Six

I held in my hands a cup of coffee and a strange sadness. As I'd poured the water in the makeshift napkin filter, I knew my hands had been taught to do it right. I stood alone with the cool air in my lungs, wondering what would become of them, those hands that were learning what it meant to be an adult with a life of their own.

Chapter Seven

Coming back to the lodge one evening after work, I saw Doug's van parked in the driveway. He was putting the final touches on the new apartment. The lights glimmered out of the apartment kitchen window. I knocked, and he told to me come in.

"My boy, it's nearly done! I've gotten the tile floor in the bedroom done. Look," he said, pointing, obviously pleased with how the tiles fitted together.

"Nice color." It was an understated blue interwoven with white.

"I've gotten you a bed, a mirror, and a dresser," he said. He pulled out several dresser drawers. "Lots of space. But be careful of this one, the knob is loose. Use the one on the right. I think it will hold up if you don't yank on it."

He showed me a phone he'd installed on the wall by the door in the kitchen, which was good, because I'd been getting complaints that some people couldn't reach me. He said he was exhausted and asked if I'd like a drink.

We sat in the living area by the fireplace, drank several glasses of wine, and nibbled on mixed nuts and cheese and crackers he'd set out. The circles under his eyes had darkened and gotten puffier since I last saw him. He seemed worn-out.

I asked how he was doing. Maybe because no one ever asked him, or maybe because what he carried inside of him had never been released, but for whatever reason, he opened up. He told me that his relationship with Angel, his wife, had never been easy. He started at the beginning, told me how after they were married, the first night of their honeymoon, he began to undress, and she attempted to disrobe. He sat on the bed and touched her, and she recoiled. He cuddled next to her and tried to make love with her, and she burst into tears, slapping at him, cursing at him, screaming how she knew he would violate her. He held her in his arms. She told him that her mother, a righteous Christian widow, had told her how awful sex would be, how painful it was and that it wasn't right, never had been, the pain was the result of Eve's unfaithfulness tempted by the snake, but how it was a wife's duty, something she had to endure to perform her marital duty. Doug tried to console her, but it was no use. No matter what he said or how he acted, no matter how he tried to teach her the pleasures of the body, she dreaded it, found it disgusting and would always shower after, wiping away the stain and insisting he do the same.

I asked him how he managed to go on.

The side of his lip turned up in a weak smile. His face barely changed, his cheeks and jowls drooping. "Oh, my boy, how I've wrestled with that. I've prayed to God to help me. I don't want to be unfaithful to her. We have two delightful boys, really," he said and, gesturing toward the wine, asked, "Can you, please?"

I poured him another glass, and he continued. "It's ugly. It's not something I'm proud of, not under the sight of God. But I had to do something. I had to do it; don't you see. Or I'd go mad. The wanting and what? Disgust. It was too much. I felt trapped. I had needs. And she, bless her, she couldn't. She wouldn't. So, I just stopped trying.

Chapter Seven

Angel was happier. Much so. She loves the boys and church and the bank and her piano lessons. It keeps her quite busy."

He stopped and rubbed his face, pushing at the skin, shoving at it as if he were trying to rub something off.

I leaned forward. "It's alright. You don't need to say anymore."

"Oh, don't say that!" He nearly spilled his wine, pointing the glass at me like it was a weapon.

"Don't tell me to stop. I've never, please, let me finish."

"Go on, then."

"I feel I can tell you. I just do. That you'll understand. And anyway, you should know. Yes, you must know. I can't have that between us, a secret." He pursed his lips and stared at me. "Alright, if you must know, I have made peace with it. It's what I had to do. Angel, she knows. She doesn't like it. But we never speak of it. Never. Can you understand?"

I nodded although, as much as I tried to fit the puzzle together, to know what this "it" was, I could only guess he'd made an arrangement like the one those from Cumberland had made.

"You see, I don't find sex to be disgusting. Not at all. I love it. Don't you?" "Sure."

"Good then. As you should. You're a handsome boy. I'm sure you've enjoyed it. As you should. And I do, too. I'm a very sexual person. I have great needs, don't you see? Now, he leaned forward. His expression was gentle. "Let me be frank. I just find it disgusting with women. Don't you see? It was all too much. An effort. A trauma. It nearly drove me mad. Nearly so. And then I met an opera singer—he was a member of our church—who loved the outdoors, and I brought him here, and one thing led to another, and I discovered that love can happen, just happen, and I was, after years, years of torment, happy."

I swilled the wine in my glass, staring at it. My jaw tensed. I didn't want to reject him. Not now. Not after he told me what he did. Yet I felt a certain revulsion. I came to rural West Virginia to put as much distance between me and homosexual temptation, figuring the men of a small town would pose no threat and now here it was again, twice in a matter of days. I'd sensed, even as I tried to deny it, that he was attracted to me. His hands always found an excuse to touch me, to pat me on the back, to tap me on the leg.

He looked at me, his eyes pleading for sympathy. "So, you're gay?" I said.

"Oh, no! I wouldn't call it that. I just prefer men." He laughed. "Can we leave it at that?"

I said we could.

I thanked him for trusting me with his story and rose to go upstairs.

"Wait, my boy," he said. "I must tell you sometimes I'll be bringing some friends too—you know—I have to trust your discretion. You understand? Angel must not know." He bit his lip, and his face flushed, his cheeks, his ears, even his neck. "Discretion, please."

"Not a word."

He stretched out his arms to hug me, and I accepted them. His hands roamed my back. I wanted to pull them away. But I stood as still as I could. He kissed me on the cheek, stepped back, gazing at me before I went up the stairs to my room.

Chapter Seven

Upstairs, I took out the journal.

I came here to live off the grid. I thought that maybe, to shed my dystonic feelings and quell the rumblings of desire, a faraway place would give me a reprieve. But now Doug tells me this. He has sex with men. Yet he claims that he's not gay. Nor is he straight. Probably best to call it curved. What it is for him I don't know any more than he does, but for me getting away from my fears has turned out to be the opposite of what I intended. I find myself immersed in gay life. That fellow David, he's on the make, avid for any young piece of meat. Maybe this is some kind of test. I must face it and confront my demons to get to the other side. Funny though, I listened to Doug's story with such equanimity. I feel almost comforted knowing what he is going through is a quiet agony that, I suspect, many men experience. I won't end up like him. I sure hope not. Eventually I'll find a woman who will love me.

I need to be careful she's not like Angel. That would be horrid.

Chapter Eight

A week later, Ken asked me a favor: to act as an adviser to a youth group who wanted to plan an archeological dig in Capon Bridge, not far from where I had a Head Start center. There was a federal science grant that might fund the venture. Since I'd written grants, he thought I could help them write one. He introduced me to the student leader, Terry Hatch, a 16-year-old with a winning smile. An athletic boy who proudly put his body on display with tight jeans and a tight T-shirt. He gave me a strong handshake when we met.

Terry engaged comfortably in conversations with us, suggesting one of his high school science teachers who might like to be involved. He seemed very mature. After Ken left, Terry stayed in my office, asking me questions, clearly interested in me. He seemed to like it that I didn't fit the conventional administrator mold. Before he left, I promised to meet with him and the youth group Friday evening.

The group met in the Town Hall basement. Terry introduced me to everyone—black and white students, some girls and some guys. (This was the first time I'd seen black and white in a mixed group.) I was impressed. Terry comported himself with the self-assurance of an adult. The other kids listened to him. He presented the idea for the summer program. A famous archeologist, a Dr. Hammersmith (now retired), would work with them as they excavated an area near Capon Bridge where an important Civil War battle, or more likely, a skirmish had occurred. Most students, looking for work, had jumped at the chance which promised a stipend, and free room and board. The grant needed to be submitted by December to be considered for the following summer. I told the group I'd do anything I could to help them.

It was a sweltering day, and the basement was stiflingly hot. During a break, I went up the stairs to stand under a large oak to get some fresh air. A light breeze wafted over me. Terry followed and we began to talk. The vaguest hint of a chill in the air nipped at us.

Terry shuffled his feet, catching my eyes; he didn't seem interested in talking about the grant. He looked troubled, his jaw working back and forth. I asked him if he was alright.

He said, "Fine. I'm fine." He leaned against the oak.

I asked him about the social life in Pearsall Flats, if there was anything to do.

He said, "Nothing." He clammed up, a stark contrast from his easy-going conversationalist meeting persona.

I asked about school. We exchanged some words about his classes. He stuttered as he spoke.

Thinking the conversation was over, I said, "Well, buddy, it's been nice talking to you." He lurched back, offended.

"Don't call me buddy," he blurted out. "Just call me Terry."

Maybe 'buddy' had negative connotations in the South.

"I might . . ." he said, hesitating mid-sentence. His voice pitched louder. "I might as well tell you. You'll find out anyway. You probably know them. We were over at Orlando's last weekend. You know who he is?"

"No," I said.

Chapter Eight

"He's a cleaning lady. He cleans all the offices around here."

The mix of he and lady confused me. "Is he a she?" I asked.

"He's kinda both. He dresses like a girl, but he's a guy. I go there with Jimmy, you know, the black guy in the group."

I nodded, still not sure what he was getting at.

"There were these two guys from Cumberland there. They have a yellow Comet. You might have seen it on the streets. They pick up other guys."

"Really?" I said, surprised at the turn of the conversation. "They come down here all the time."

I nodded again. Terry rocked back and forth as he talked, but he seemed comfortable telling me what happened.

"Orlando's place is nice. Beautifully decorated. Paneling and all.

Lots of paintings. Originals. About seven rooms." "Is Orlando a decorator, too?" I asked.

"No, no, she just cleans." He looked at me.

I said, "Go ahead," not sure where he was headed, nor what I could say or do to help once he got there. I decided listening was the best thing to do.

"Well, one of those guys was, you know, gayish, a fem, and had blonde hair to here, longer than yours." He touched his shoulder. "He was gyrating like a top and got sweaty and took off his shirt. He had no body hair. None."

"Was he bald?"

"No, he had long hair. He had no body hair on his chest and legs. When he came back in the main room—he left for a while with his friend—when he came back where we all were, he was dressed in skimpy shorts. You know the kind you can see through with sort of fish netting."

I ran my fingers through my hair, brushing it aside. I put my hands in my pockets. *Good God*, I thought, *what is going on? I come to a bucolic town tucked in the hills and discover its crawling with gays. What did he just say? Something about fish netting.*

"Shorts you can see through," I said, picking up where he'd left off. I wondered why he would tell me this. But he kept talking, so I listened.

"He was dancing crazy. All jumpy. He couldn't dance really. I can dance better. Jimmy—you know." He pointed back to the room. "He and I were doing the horse. You know how it goes? Yes, you do. Like this." He did few leaping steps, back and forth, for a second.

"Oh, I see."

The conversation had both disgusted and excited me. I didn't move. I was afraid. I wondered if I should change the topic again, but I was afraid to give him the message I didn't care what had happened to trouble him. Maybe he was reaching out to me, a stranger, to help him, to keep him away from Orlando's. Regardless, whether he meant it or not, he'd gotten me aroused, and that is not what I wanted to be, not with a new job. Not with a kid.

"His buddy, the blonde, was alright. He was...." He hesitated again. "Well, he was natural, you know. Not gay like. Anything can happen at Orlando's."

"Shall we go back into the meeting?" I tried.

"No, wait," he said. His head slumped forward. He had rolled a piece of manila paper in a tube and was playing with it, sticking it in his mouth and rubbing it back and forth. I wondered if he did it intentionally, or out of nervousness, or excitement from telling the story, or if he was coming on to me. Had I somehow given him the wrong idea?

"When Jimmy and I were putting on our shoes, getting ready to

Chapter Eight

leave," he said, "this guy came who was our age and started, right there, before we had time to leave, to give another guy, a little older, a blow job."

"What! Didn't you leave?" I asked.

"No, we stayed. It happens all the time. Orlando just laughs. He, I mean she, isn't like other adults. She doesn't force you at all. She's nice, you know. She offered us a gin and tonic, but I knew it was vodka and coke. He treated us like adults."

I was desperately trying to act like an adult. I felt dizzy and staggered a few steps backward.

He was mixing his pronouns, blending them together. He didn't even seem uncomfortable, but I was dying. Here I was listening to a teenager describing what I'd never experienced, never knew existed, never had even imagined.

"Jimmy and I, we went back to the side room after a few, and that blonde, he came in with us and we had a pretty good time."

"I imagine you did."

"Yeah," he laughed. He put the paper tube in his mouth again. He looked at me. I was quiet and stared at him. I was frightened and awed and dumbfounded by his story. It seemed unreal. I felt worried for him, a kid exposed to all of it. What must he be thinking? What was he thinking about me? Or about himself?

I sensed I was being drawn into a dark underworld, a web of temptations that left my body shivering because of the intensity of my mixed feelings.

I ended the conversation there. I shifted to talk about the proposal again, that we needed to write a draft and that he needed to get the names, addresses, and telephone numbers of the kids who were interested in being involved.

He quickly straightened up, as if putting on a mask.

On the way back in, I said that what he'd told me was confidential, although I wasn't sure it should be. I told him that we'd meet next Friday, and we could invite several people who might fund the project.

At the end of the night, I walked slowly toward the car. My plan had been to put distance between myself and sex, to spend time on the river, to figure out what was going on with me. But here I was in Peyton Place on speed. Odd. Very odd. First, David. Then, Doug. And now Terry, a minor, and God knows how many other kids. They were all gravitating toward me like flies to sticky paper. What was it about me that let them feel so comfortable spilling their stories as if I were some convenient depository for their gay angst?

It was like I had moved into homo-central. Compounding my dread of having to face my fears, I was now faced with another dilemma. If I told authorities what was happening, I would violate Terry's confidence. If word got out just as I was setting up my program, I risked alienating the community. I'd be ruined.

There wasn't any right thing to do, at least not one I could think of. I was determined to blot it out of my mind and to focus on, thank God, my seven-days-a-week job. I had to evaluate the staff I'd hired, meet with Carole about reports that were due at the regional office, and attend an upcoming intensive training session in Annapolis for new directors. It wouldn't be hard to keep busy.

Back at my place, I wrote word for word—sometimes not even sure I wanted to believe it—what Terry had said. But I put it on the page as if, by doing so, I could set it aside, close the cover of the journal, and pretend that it never happened.

Chapter Nine

Carole and I attended the Annapolis new directors training session. November tourists had gone, and the red, green, and blue Christmas lights already hung from door fronts and the pier to lure, later in December, the holiday crowd. The weather had shifted. A cold front had slid down from the north, making it almost like a holiday. The trainer, a professor of early childhood education, taught us the rudimentary principles of teaching preschool children. The sessions ran into the early evening, so Carole and I took any break we could to walk down the Annapolis streets. The marine docks had slips for boats of different dimensions—little cutters, medium-sized sloops, and large schooners—tied to bollards. Across from the harbor, the lights from a restaurant, set on a hillside, glimmered on the water.

Annapolis was refreshing. By the second day, I felt as if I'd escaped the dreadful revelations of the past few weeks. Carole and I sat at the end of a pier, our feet dangling over, the waves pummeling the pilings. The sounds of the incoming slush and outgoing slurp were hypnotic. Bundled in our winter jackets, we talked about our lives. Carole told me about John, her husband, how he was kind, yet distant, and I told her about my parents how they were rich and proper. I explain that, although I had attended Divinity School, I wasn't a believer.

Given what her husband did, she was a believer of sorts. But she was a skeptic, too. Over the years, while raising three kids and teaching, she'd skirted death several times. Several major surgeries, one where she died but was brought back to life. She knew what to take seriously and what to take with a grain of salt. As she said, "I'm still here."

The waves whooshed beneath us. Time with all its surging momentum slowed down. We weren't rushing to meet with staff, to purchase items, to collect weekly sheets, or to intervene in squabbles among staff. We were wanderers, off by ourselves. Carole was as close as a devoted friend could be. For me, love had many guises, some as strange and exotic as the allure of Tess and her coffee. But our love seemed to be one that didn't demand commitment. She'd put her arm in mine, and we'd walk, stop in a shop to look around, make comments about couples that we saw—married couples that looked miserable, young couples that had passion in their eyes. With her, I felt that, if I could find someone like her, I could be a good husband. I could live the life I wanted to live. I wrote a poem trying to capture the feelings I had. She liked it, read it aloud back to me. It was the first time anyone had read a poem of mine aloud:

Propositions on Chesapeake Bay

> Bay water humped the wharf.
> Red lights stitched the harbor.
> The tide thwacked the pylons.
> A woman had her arm in mine.

Chapter Nine

"We'll remember this always," she said,
pulling me close, "as a place within,
held and known—a place of our own."
She was not mine. Nor was I hers.

Yet the harbor contained us.
We had nothing to lose but sound.
Replicable, it would never gain
a deeper voice than ours, nor remain

as she clutched her hand in mine
like the white masts scoring the night,
like the water reddened around us
while the waves that came to shore

were there and were no more.
It was more than the waves
that came to shore; it was more
that they are and we would be

no more. The lights, faint
on brackish water, bent
and broke like lives torn in
and out with tidal stains
that never let us go.

After she read it, she said, "I never said that!" I told her, no she hadn't but I needed a protagonist to make it work.

"You poets," she said. "I do know what you're saying, and I feel that way, too. I don't need it to be in words. I just want to hold onto it as if it were a feathery thing inside my heart." She kissed me on the cheek. Whatever happened those four days in the misty romance of that town sealed an unspeakable covenant of our friendship.

Although we didn't want to admit it, we were falling in love. But it wasn't a romantic love, not heated, passionate. It was a tender love, one borne from our common struggle to find ourselves and to strive to do some good in this world. By the end of the session, we felt like a couple. We were married in the best sense of the word, married to a mutual understanding of life's joys and sorrows, of what each of us strove to do with our lives. Leaving there felt like a severing of a sacred artery. I wished I had the courage to tell her more about me. But I wasn't sure if that would push her away or draw her closer.

Chapter Ten

I could hear the water from the doorway off in the distance like a whispering breath, a silver ribbon slipping over rocks in the sweep of the valley by the lodge. In the room the light puddled beneath the lamp on my desk and into my open journal. Doug had finished the apartment, and I'd moved right in. The phone was hooked up, and I was officially now back on the grid. But getting comfortable was harder than I expected.

Less than a year earlier, the Vanderbilt graduate dorm life had provided an unsolicited intimacy. Not necessarily what a reasonable person would want, but some level of intimacy all the same. The groans of a guy across the hall jerking off and about to cum; the fellow quite ineptly trying to get his date to give him a blow job, bemoaning her resistance, whining like a little boy until she agrees, and the room goes silent; the Red Sox/Yankees conversation getting heated, statistics screamed out as if it were the end of the world; and the midnight footfalls in the tile hallway—they all offered a connection to life. There was, as Ken said when we talked about the years at Vanderbilt, a sense of community. There were people around me at any hour of the day or night.

I could knock on the door of Bryan, the med student, and chat. I could ask Jack, the law student, to toss the football. I could slump in a couch in the lounge and catch an episode of *The Untouchables* on

TV, knowing certain guys would be there. "Great show—thirty-eight gunned down. A slow night but we're only halfway through."

At the lodge, when I came home, after I fixed some mashed potatoes and pan-fried chicken, after I sat on the couch to read, after I slipped off my clothes at night, the only sounds I heard were the creak of the door from my hand pressing it open, the rustle of bed sheets from my legs kicking at them, the scratch of the pen on the page from my hand, and the water, outside. The isolation made me attentive to my own actions.

For the most part, that was alright. I liked listening to the modulations of the river: its playful morning patter when I sat on the deck; its buoyant exuberance at midday when, earlier in the fall, I swam; its listlessness in late afternoon after I came home from work and sat on the dock; its deeper groans at night. As I lay down to sleep, often, I was startled by an acorn thumping on the roof, charmed by the swish of branches against one another, and mystified by the howls and hoots of night creatures.

Yet there were times I wanted to talk with someone. In those moments, often in the silence of the night, I would put Beethoven's Emperor Concerto on the record player, set the needle lightly on the rim, and turn up the volume. I'd stand in the middle of the room and let the music swallow me—caress my body with sound. For 30 minutes I could feel as deeply as the music felt, feel the pulse of dum-dee-dee-dum-dum. I'd extend my arms and, by knowing the score as well as I did, anticipate when the violins would slide over the top of the piano, where the bass would charge ahead and where the piano would fly up and down across the keys, and dance around the room, moving as the music moved. It was exhilarating.

Chapter Ten

And then, after the needle lifted and the machine clicked off, the silence was changed. It vibrated with the negative space of the distinct reverberations of the music—as if the music had chased away the loneliness and reconnected me with humanity. I reentered a communal, physical space not so much alone. Transported by the music to a heightened sense of experience and then slipped back into the everyday world, with a better sense of it. And, too, the post-music silence gave me time to think, to plan, to make sure I didn't make any missteps. It gave me opportunity to deepen my resolve that I'd keep clear boundaries between Terry and myself. Heeding Ken's warnings, to keep firm boundaries with David, too. And, taking my own counsel, I'd keep distance from Doug.

Chapter Eleven

Carole insisted I hire a secretary. "Your handwriting," she said. "It's hopeless, like chicken's scratching. And your spelling is not much better. Your typing, well, the erasures and smudges won't do. Not for official documents. This is a government program. You need someone who can decipher your scrawl and make it look official."

Hiring a secretary felt like admitting I really was a grown-up. I interviewed five candidates, asking each, at the end, to type up a handwritten memo. The last two could whip out a memo in seconds. One of them was a middle-aged woman and former high school secretary who'd shake her head and emit a low growl anytime she came across a misspelling. (Ones I intentionally put in.) While she was the most professionally qualified, she was too interpersonally cool and judgmental. The other came in wearing mud-caked boots and bib overalls. Long stringy hair, parted in the middle, and no makeup. She apologized for her appearance. She had to cross the river. The skiff stuck in the muddy bank, and she had to pull it up on shore. She asked if she could use the bathroom to spruce up.

She laughed while typing the memo, catching the errors. She'd figured out they were intentional. After the interview was over, she asked if I was going north out of town. She had to row back to the opposite shore where she and her husband, Larry, were tenant farmers.

I hired her.

River Crossed

On the way back to the lodge, I left her off by the river. She walked to the bank, shoved the skiff in and rowed against the current, fighting it with fierce adjustment of the oars, to a willow tree on the opposite bank where she tied the boat. Her husband, a striking man even from a distance—skinny, blonde, and tall—waved to me.

Each morning, I'd stop at the river and pick her up. If I was going back in the afternoon, I let her off. If not, she would hitchhike. Due to her persistence that I see their place, I went to their farmhouse—ferried across in her skiff—for dinner. Her husband had gone to visit a friend. Afterwards, she and I sat on the porch, gazed at the stars, and let the silence be like the river: carried along, unhurried.

She lived a laid-back life and let each day come as the river came, high or low water. She and her husband planted, tended, harvested, and husbanded the crops from the land, two young and happy hippies.

The other Head Start staff thought she was grubby at first, not professional enough. But they came to like her for her forthrightness, her intelligence, and her ability to temper any complaints that came to her attention. If something came up that was troublesome, she would let me know right away, head it off with a calm comment, assuring those involved that I would be there to help.

My lead teacher at the Mountain Top Center, Deloris, a Black woman, complained about a driver named Hetzel. When she chewed him out for arriving late again with several kids, he called her a "bitch." She thought she heard, but wasn't sure, that he also called her a "nigger."

I needed Hetzel to drive kids who could not take a bus and

Chapter Eleven

lived off the beaten path. I even loaned Hetzel $300 to buy a new station wagon. I wanted to trust him, given he had a large family and needed work. But I wouldn't tolerate racism. There was enough of it already with the town's segregated neighborhoods.

As part of my regular routine, I visited his house a mile out of town, a five-room structure backed up against a used-car lot. If I could prevent him from sounding off at staff, I could make sure six kids who wouldn't get services because of where they lived got picked up and delivered to the Center. I had to make compromises.

Hetzel enjoyed my visits. We sat in his living room, which also served as a bedroom for his fifteen-year-old daughter, Bobbie. Hetzel told me about his alcoholism, which, right now, was under control. His wife, Betty, a woman twice his size with the arms of a stevedore, yelled, "You better be. I swear." I told him I depended on him and expected him to control his temper and his language. I also told him that I'd fire him if he made any racists comments. He needed to know that.

He said, "I've got it under control. This time no trouble. I've had enough trouble." He needed money. He was on the straight and narrow. He showed me a girly magazine that he hid under his chair. I glanced at it. "You can take it with you, if you want," he said, shoving it toward me like an apology.

"No thanks."

He picked up the magazine. "Pretty hot, aren't they?"

"Sure," I said, offering a wry grin.

Betty baked me a fresh loaf of bread. It was warm. I thanked her and she walked me to the door. "'preciate what you're doing for him. First regular job he's had in years. No one's round here likely to hire him. Know what I mean?"

"We need to keep him sober," I said. "He needs to keep his mouth shut."

"If he musses up, he'll get hell from me. I can tell you that."

"Get him up earlier. He's been late getting kids."

She grabbed my arm, held it tightly. "Just tell me what you need."

As I was leaving, I heard her scream at him. Her shrill voice shook the house. I never heard him talk back. She was General Patton, and he was a buck private in that house. For a long time after that, he toed the line. Deloris had no further complaints.

Without a TV, nothing between me and the night, it took weeks for it to dawn on me that my time, whatever it was, was mine to do with what I wanted.

One night, to take advantage of a full moon, I walked up the road, to see what it was like to be in the dark. No flashlight. Just the refracted light of the moon, to guide the way. Looking back, I may have been yearning to fill a void that I had felt since coming back from Annapolis. I had been feeling empty. Lost. Confused.

I trudged halfway up the road. The large pines and oaks loomed overhead, and moonlight slipped like threads through their branches. To the right side of the road, close to the top of the ridge, a path, one I'd never seen during the day, veered though a copse of hemlock. I followed it up a steep embankment. Needles were spongy and soft under my feet. The hemlocks' presence—their trunks—made me feel small, diminutive. I may be nearly six feet tall, but they were 60 to 80 feet tall. The wind creaked and rustled

Chapter Eleven

their branches. A cloud blotted out the moon.

An enormous oak, 12 feet in circumference, blocked the path. Dark as it was, I could barely see my hand. As I gazed up through its branches, I remembered looking up in the nave of a cathedral, the faint light seeping through the lancet windows, in France. The sense of being enclosed by the enormity of that chapel made me appreciate how generations of worshippers had come there, knelt, and appealed to God to hear their prayers, hear their tiny voices in the vastness of the space. That's how I felt in the presence of the oak. It felt old, even fatherly. As I waited for the moon to reappear, I squatted on the ground. It was cold. There was no need to close my eyes since only a flicker of light came through the hemlocks. The wind pulsed the upper limbs. Leaves tittered. Time held its breath.

Growing up, if I was outside at night, suburban traffic frequented the road. Lights from the Benson's house across the street illuminated the yard. There was always a sense of other people—someone walking a dog, someone grilling a steak—pervading the neighborhood. There was no sense of wildness. Everything was tamed. The roads, each of them, led to other roads. Alongside the roads, evenly spaced, were houses. The landscape, if that is what you called it, was peopled, filled with others. It was orderly, secure, confined.

Not so where I was standing. No one was here. On the hillside, my eyes adjusted to the dark. I leaned back, listening to my breath, the rise and fall of air as my ribs expanded and contracted. The ground around me, the trees above me, I felt that whatever worries I had—the responsibility for the new program, the worries about Terry and the underground life, the confusion about my own sexual feelings—seemed unimportant. It was as if this darkness and these trees had absorbed them all and made them incidental in the great scheme of things. Black Elk, the Lakota visionary, believed in the power of plants and trees to heal any ailments. The sacred hoop of the native people had at its center a sacred tree. The tree brought together the four powers of the earth. I wondered how long would I have to sit in that spot, listening to the tree breathe, for me to know of its power, how it could shape my own destiny?

As if someone had thrown a light switch, a cloud shifted and the moonlight flicked on, illuminating the pathway around the oak. I walked under the oak and felt its spell pressing down on me. It felt as if I had touched, however briefly, a sacred space. I was under it, under this large, aged oak. *Understood*, I thought. Yes, that was it.

While I was busy trying to be someone, to find myself, this oak continued as it had for a hundred years, to be setting out its roots, shedding its leaves. What came to me right then was the idea of how insignificant I was, and I didn't feel bad about it. Being as small as I was had seemed the right size to be.

Out beyond the oak, there was an open space. A shale hillside led to a ledge that extended over the river. I inched toward it on my hands and knees. Down to the right were the lights of Doug's lodge. Directly below me, the river, its currents painted in moonlight, snaked under the cliff. Up to my left, I could make out the crest of a farther ridge and from that precipice, off in the distant valley, the dim light of a farmhouse shimmering like a fallen star. It was the only light in the wide sweep of lowland. It seemed as if one star, unmoored from the heavenly constellations, had settled there. I held onto the scrub hemlock, grasping so that I did not fall. A strange dizziness came over me

Chapter Eleven

from being exposed to everything above and around me.

After that night, I often walked up the road on moonlit evenings to that place above the river. It helped me feel placed when I was feeling displaced, sure when I felt unsure, grounded when I struggled to sort out who I was. The crickets sawed their songs. Even late in the fall, frogs sniggered in the grasses on the riverbank. The road, pale and milky under the black trunks of trees, led up to the path and to the forest looming over me. I learned what Martin Heidegger, the German phenomenologist, meant by the word, *Dasein*, the in-dwelling in a place. Underneath the limbs whose shadows fell across the road, I was dwelling within and beneath a world larger than my own. I worried about copperheads warming themselves on the radiant heat from the road, where I could not see as well as I would have liked to see. But on cooler nights, I imagined they would be hibernating. I came to trust that visibility was tactile and auditory. My footfalls on the road. The brush of branches on my arm.

The word "night" was not out there, some distant thing; it surrounded me, pressed in on me. In the recesses of the night, forest creatures could hear and see far better than I could and yet I was among them.

After time on the ledge, I would go down the road to the porch light, dim yet distinct, spread lightly across the hillside beside the lodge. I called it home. It was separate from the darkness that had also become another home to me, one that I could be in and find myself, find where I was when the daily duties pressed against me and made me feel alone.

Chapter Twelve

After Tess's dinner party, David invited me several times to hear a new recording of Wagner's Ring Cycle. I was leery, but my mother always told me that her father loved the Ring Cycle. My grandfather, grandmother, mom, and her brother went to hear it at the Metropolitan Opera in New York. David's kind of offer was one I could only refuse so many times.

The minute I arrived at his house—one room with access to a kitchen and bathroom—David readied the space for the opera. Strutting about on the balls of his feet, he arranged what was for him a music hall, whistled melodies from what I came to know as Das Rheingold, the first of the four operas, and told me that he had to make everything just right.

Shelves lined two walls of his room. Books, records—and his clothes—all neatly folded and arranged by color. He puttered with objects, dusted off a bust of a Wagner, catalogued several books that he'd left on a chair, insisting that for the Ring Cycle everything had to be in order. I asked if he needed help and he waved me off, "Oh, no. Enjoy the books, my boy. Take time to relax. Put up your feet—here use the stool—and let me wait on you. It is such a delight having you here. Such fun!"

David had Quadraphonic sound—music coming from four corners of the room—so he placed two chairs in the room's middle.

Sound surrounded us. He had me sit in the right chair, lining it up with the speakers, making sure the angle was just right.

"I'm so sorry this is all I have to offer you," he said. "I don't even have a bathroom of my own. My aunt, the witch of Mooresville, has relegated me to this cell. I must say, I've made it into quite a lovely space. Don't you think?"

"It's fine. It's quite lovely."

"I agree. As for her, if I could, I'd plan one of these nights to club her in the head. That would do, a good whack. It wouldn't take much. If I were Dorothy, I'd simply toss water on her. She's such a trifle," he said, lifting a bottle. "Something to drink?"

"Sure."

Before we listened to Wagner, he lectured me about the selection, how in one part we would hear the first hints of jazz, how Wagner played off a chord, did riffs on it, modulated it, refined it.

It takes nearly 15 hours to hear the entire Ring Cycle. It is an enormous task. Even when the music soared, even when conflict between characters rose, I was often baffled about what was going on. David would pick up the stylus, careful not to scratch the record, and describe the action. He explained the ill-fated love of Siegfried and Sieglinde, and the magic ring, fashioned from Rheingold, that empowered anyone who had it to rule the world.

The excerpts that he loved the most, he played repeatedly. We sipped whiskey. He stood and twirled around, his face filled with bliss, humming to the violins that soared to a fever pitch. The drunker we got, the more the music felt like being intoxicated by God.

After an hour or two of listening, we took a break to read passages from his stories as well as those of his favorite writers. One

Chapter Twelve

passage that he rendered twenty times—fidgeting with an adjective, a verb, changing it each time he recited it—was a scene in which a man (presumably him) awakens in the middle of the night, aware that his lover (a young woman) he wants desperately to see, is asleep beside him. He lights a match and, cupping it in his hand, lifts it to see her angelic face.

"Isn't that perfect?" he asked, holding the pages out to me.

"Oh, yes, quite wonderful," I agreed, although I felt that the prose was overblown, idealized, and dishonest.

He must have sensed my ambivalence because he offered to read from Hemingway whom he worshiped as much as Wagner. He picked a book off the shelf, sitting me down, "Listen to this. It's from one of his short stories." He read it slowly, taking care to pronounce each word as it had a life of its own. When he finished, he looked up at me, took two fingers to his mouth, blew a kiss, laughed his deep throaty laugh, and said, "Ahhh. Better than sex!"

After several more drinks, he became unmoored, paced around the room talking about his time in Florence, his dear friends, telling stories about Enrique who would come to stay with him. His father was a member of a military junta.

David's idea of a conversation was to leap from one topic to another as if sticking his finger in a cake's frosting, tasting it, and then abandoning it while he shifted his attention to piece of pie on another counter.

"Now where were we, dear boy?" He loved to gossip. He even dished Tess, his supposed confidant and best friend. "The ghastly woman. Ahh, Madame B, how could she have married Jerome? Despicable prig. Did you know his father owns Metro Petroleum

Company? Filthy rich. He shows it, doesn't he? Full of himself. Full of money. Did you know I kissed him once? Oh, yes, at a dinner party. All the guests had left. Madame B had gone off to polish her silver and I sat on the floor by his knee."

He eyed my glass of Jack Daniels. "Would you like more?"

"Yes." I let him fill it. "Go on." I was unsure what to make of his scathing comments. I liked Tess. I had no reason to denigrate Jerome for his wealth. But I sat back and listened.

"I sat on the floor and looked at him. 'Jerome,' I said, 'kiss me.' And, you know, he did. Not one of those pecks but a real kiss on the lips like he meant it. I was delighted. There's a homo in everyone, hiding, just waiting to be released. When Madame Tess came back, I told her that I had kissed her husband and now I wanted to kiss her. It was all quite fun."

"Did you kiss her?" I was lightheaded.

"Of course, my dear boy, of course!"

He laughed and flipped his hand out. "It turned out badly. Jerome was infuriated and walked off, not to return for the night. He didn't want anyone insinuating he was a faggot. Can you imagine? One kiss! But he was, don't you see? He was. He just couldn't accept it." He raised his eyebrows, "Aren't we all?"

I shook my head. "I'm not sure I'd make that generalization." I wasn't about to let him find out about me. I was feeling both abhorrent about his cavalier way of speaking about all of his supposed friends and, much to my surprise, amused with his sexual playfulness. After Terry's experience with Orlando and hearing Doug talk about his extramarital affairs, I'd already had enough innuendos to last a year.

He must have sensed my discomfort.

Chapter Twelve

"Of course, of course. It's all fun. Just my joking!" He stood up. "Come with me." He pointed to a doorway on the far side of the room. "You should see this. Now that you know about Jerome. It only seems fair."

He showed me a portrait that Tess had given him to store, one Jerome despised as too explicit, too erotic to be hung in a minister's home. It exuded sensuality. The dress, red with black velvet, shimmered. The low-cut neckline, exposing the long neck, thrust down to her breasts, the fullness of them under the light. Her head tilted delicately back with an allure in her eyes, her lips parted slightly. There was something enchanting about it, even stuck as it was in the dim corner of David's closet. Something of another life and of a yearning.

Later, he told me the painter insisted she wear that dress, the luxurious sheen of it, for days on end. She admitted that she'd fallen in love with the artist. They'd had a brief affair. It was then she realized the mistake of marrying Jerome. He was the wrong man for her. She craved an artist. That was why I was so appealing to her. But back then, what could she do? The die was cast, her fate sealed. Jerome must have thought, if the painting could be stored away, her desire for other men could be hidden away, too. But that yearning carried on throughout their lives, enriching for her and a curse for him.

After closing the closet door, David asked if I was hungry. I was. He ordered take-out. Later, when he opened the door for the delivery man, he gasped, "It's you!" A young man stood on the porch, and David gave him a kiss, ushered him in.

"This is Tom Samuels," David announced as if presenting royalty. "He owns the White Horse Restaurant and is a dear, dear friend. Aren't you, my dear?"

Tom handed David the bag and the bill. David scurried to his desk, rummaging through it for money, not finding any. I took out my wallet and said, "David, I've got it."

I gave a ten to Tom. He eyed me carefully, pulled out a wad of bills, and gave me change.

"Sit, sit down," David insisted.

I moved to the bed so Tom could sit in the rattan chair. His blonde hair fell loosely across one eye. He had the insouciant air of one not easily impressed. Skinny and gaunt, he moved gracefully even when crossing his legs. His effrontery enchanted me. He was an incisive and yet impertinent asker of questions—who I was; where I was from; how much money I made; where I went to school; if I had any long-term relationships; why, with a master's degree, I choose to work in a God-forsaken place. When asked about his history, he was bitter but not brief. He'd been discharged from the military—an ugly affair he didn't care to discuss—and had returned to Mooresville to run the restaurant after his alcoholic father died. His life was drudgery. His mother, who passed away when he was eight, was a hypochondriac. When diagnosed with cancer, she settled into dying, a quick exit from a horrid marriage.

Tom looked at David, and asked, "Where'd you get him?"

David giggled. "He was for sale. I got him at a discount!"

"Figures," Tom. He turned and, taking my hand in both of his, said, "If you have time, come down to the White Horse. I'll give you special service."

I laughed. "I'm sure you will." He winked at me. He was attractive. His eyes, dark and heavy lidded, cast a spell. I was equally put off by his aggressive lines of inquiry put me off and desirous of

Chapter Twelve

spending time with him—alone and without David.

Tom kissed David on the cheek and, glancing back at me, stuck out his hand. This time, his handshake was tender.

As soon as he left, I inquired how David knew him.

David chirped, "Oh, birds of a feather fly together." Their families knew each other, since they were boys.

"He's quite interesting," I said. "What, does he work for the FBI?"

"No, my dear, the questions are his defense, I'm sure," David said. "Behind it, there's gold."

I looked at my watch.

"My dear boy, it is much too late for you to be driving off. Too much whiskey. Stay here. I have an extra toothbrush."

"I couldn't."

"You can. I insist. I wouldn't want you driving. It would rankle my conscience," he said. He took out a set of pajamas and tossed them to me. "Bathroom's down the hall."

When I came back to the room, he'd gotten into his pajamas, flicked off all the lights but one by the bed, and pulled back the covers.

"Do you mind sleeping on the right side. I prefer the left. It's a king-size bed. There is plenty of room" he said.

My heart was pounding. "That's fine."

Once the light was off, I could see out the back window at a light above the garage. It illuminated the yard with a dull yellow light. I tossed and turned, still dizzy from too much to drink. Midway in the night, I felt his hand resting on my stomach. I pushed it aside.

"Oh, sorry," he said.

Hours later, the same hand had slipped inside my pajamas. It caressed my cock. I meant to shove it away, but it felt good. His mouth followed his hand. And he was good. He knew what he was doing. I let him have his way and tried to imagine I was with someone else, but no one came to mind, so I let my mind empty, be like the lamplight in the yard—pooled and receptive. When he finished and wiped off my belly with a cloth. He turned over and went back to sleep.

What had gotten into me? Hadn't I given that up?

By morning, I was irritated, even slightly angry, with him and even more so with myself. I declined his offer for breakfast, drove away and vowed never to visit him again.

Chapter Thirteen

I met Suzie in mid-November at a regional Head Start conference in Winchester, some 50 miles east of Pearsall Flats. From the start, I took to her. Or better way to say it, she took to me: she waylaid me, invited me into her motel room, told me, flat-out, that she liked to have sex. She was voluptuous with pouty lips that lured me to her with every word she spoke. I should have seen what it would be like from the first night with her.

After an official from Washington discussed the future of Head Start and Carole told me she had to go to bed early—one of her migraines.

I had nothing to do. I went back to the hotel. Wandered down the corridor toward my room and glanced into a room where a party was in progress. Standing in the doorway was a young woman—it was Suzie—with her radiant smile.

"Where are you going, handsome? What does the big boy like to drink?"

We sat drinking on her bed because all the chairs and most of the floor space was taken. Everyone knew Suzie. She never failed them. She threw the biggest bash at the conference.

With a master's degree in early childhood education, she consulted with Head Start programs in the region. She attached herself to me. After most people had left—she had a roommate who had stripped and discreetly slipped into bed with a nice-looking guy who taught kindergarten—she closed the door and came over to me, saying, "Honey, I believe in free love."

I must have looked startled.

"Oh, you never heard of free love? No strings attached. How's that for a deal?"

I said, "Not bad, I guess."

She unbuttoned her blouse. Stunned, I pointed to the other bed where the long-haired guy was cuddling with her thin blonde roommate. The guy was propped up on a pillow staring at us, waiting to be entertained or aroused by our striptease.

"Oh, don't mind that," she said, dismissing them with a flip of her wrist. "They do their thing and we'll do ours."

Taking her by the arm, I walked to the door. "I prefer not to have an audience."

She scribbled her number on a card.

"You'll call?" she asked.

"Yes," I said and did. It wasn't that I wanted to settle down. I didn't. But I needed something.

A week after Winchester, I drove to Dresden and knocked on Suzie's apartment door. In the half-light of the doorway, she stood in a light blue negligee, a white ribbon tied right at her neckline as if all I had to do was pull on it and she'd be unwrapped like a birthday present, ready.

She fixed dinner, a simple meal, pasta with a cream sauce, mixed vegetables, and a salad. A candle flickered on the table. She rolled the noodles on her fork and licked them with her tongue. She

Chapter Thirteen

sucked them, drawing one into her mouth as if she were taking me into her. I don't remember if we spoke or, if we did, what we said. I remember being aroused, captivated by her eyes suffused with the yellow candlelight. As soon as we finished our plates, we left them in the sink and made love. I pulled on the white ribbon and her whole negligee collapsed to the floor. She had no shame. She liked men, no doubt about it.

We made love and I came too quickly and wanted to go again to prove myself. Her phone rang and she picked it up.

"Hi, Alex," she said.

I could hear Alex's voice, a muted baritone. He asked if he could come over.

She laughed a throaty laugh. "I'm what you might call indisposed." She laughed again. "I'm not sure he swings that way, if he's like that." She looked at me. "No, I'm sure he's not." She leaned over and kissed me on the lips and tapped me on the forehead with her finger.

She hung up. She twisted in the bed and put her hand on my penis, rubbing it gently, cupping it and lifting it up, holding it, almost by way of apology, although it wasn't an apology as much as a "Hello, I'm back."

"Don't be jealous," she said. "He's a lovely guy. You'd like him. A painter. Very handsome, like you."

Her hand brought me back to arousal, her nibbling lips on my chest, teasing my nipples. She took my cock in her mouth. I swooned as I imagined Alex, this other man, here with us. I quickly came again. She sat up, brushed my hair back, looking at me as if trying to break some hidden code.

"Would you ever do it with a guy?" she asked.

I hesitated. Here I was again! I shook my head, but I was intrigued. I wondered what he looked like. As quickly as those thoughts came to my mind, I tried to erase them.

She massaged my stomach and legs, tuning me up like a mechanic. But I felt a mixture of desire for her body, for her delight with sex, and disgust at her being as free as she was, her delight in men, Alex, and whomever else she had as a lover. I think, in truth I envied her notion of free love, how it opened doors, ones I wanted to open—joining her and Alex—yet could not, would not, dare to open for myself.

I yawned, pressed my hand down my leg. There it was, my sex, wet still and now soft. I laughed to myself, thinking how Alex would be there, lying in the same bed, that next night. His cock, the cock of another man, would be relaxed, sated, under her hand. Love, if there were such a thing, would have surrendered itself to him. Some night thereafter, she would be onto the next guy—a Craig, an Andrew, a Dan. I wondered if it would be the same for them as it was for me? If they would find whatever it was, whatever they needed, and call it whatever they did—free love, free sex, a good lay, a quickie, some nookie—and leave her as I would the next morning when the neon light down the street was blotted out by daylight. I laughed again to myself, shuffled to the side of the bed, and picked up my underwear. I looked out the window. The neon sign Benny's Laundry, flickered. The red and blue splashed across Suzie's ceiling: scribblings of night life, blinking on and off. My breathing slowed. Suzie crawled to my side, cradled her arms around my neck, tapped the back of my head, "Hey, you in there?"

Chapter Thirteen

I turned to smile at her.

"Sure, that was nice."

"Something wrong?" she asked. She rubbed one finger down my chest to the gooey remnants of my desire.

"Come on. I'm no dummy. Something really excited you, right?"

I put her hand down, squeezed it hard.

"The call from Alex?" she asked.

"Maybe."

"Hey, calm down. Look, he's a nice guy. He's even willing to meet you, you know if you're into it."

"You told me."

"You interested?"

When one part of yourself is reaching out and the other is holding back, it's hard to know what to say. There was a cavern between *yes* and *no*, some deep ravine that, if I dared to step into, I feared would swallow me whole.

"I'll think about it."

She squeezed my arm and scooted to the side of the bed. "I'll fix us some popcorn. Let's watch a movie."

"I gotta take a leak first."

"Be my guest."

She slipped off the bed, pulled on a robe and left the room. The red and blue lights danced on the wall and ceiling as if they were alive, as if they were trying to tell me something that, as yet, I could not decipher.

I continued to see her, driving to Dresden regularly to have dinner at her place. I had to hand it to her—she made each night memorable. She greeted me in different colored nightgowns. Before dinner, as we sipped wine, we'd waste no time. She'd slip off my clothes and fondle me. I'd kiss her breasts, licking lazy circles. We'd pause to eat creamy linguine, beans with almonds, and a garden salad, sometimes with avocado, sometimes with tomato, and then, after dinner, she'd drip a chocolate sauce on my erection. We lounged around naked on her couch and eventually headed to her bedroom to make love.

What more could a guy ask for?

Close to midnight one night, the phone rang. She held her hand over the receiver and whispered, "It's Alex," then winked and added, 'You'd like him. Remember?'" I laid back as she discussed her plans for the week. Yes, Monday would do, and she'd meet him in Cumberland. Yes, I was good, very good.

I once asked her about monogamy. She laughed. "You must be kidding. And miss out on all the opportunities?"

After that night, we met two or three times a week. She started coming to me half the time. When we went out in public, when I had her down to my house with Doug and his wife for dinner, when she held my arm and leaned her head against my shoulder, I felt proud. Angel, Doug's wife, told me, as we were standing on the porch, that we made a lovely couple. She liked to see me happy. I liked the feeling of approval. I enjoyed knowing I was a normal guy. No one could doubt me.

Gratifying as it was, I knew I wasn't special to her. It bothered me, but not enough to break up with her. I wanted to believe that I was special since she called me twice a week. I realized that deep inside I was more conventional than I thought. I wanted a monogamous relationship.

Chapter Thirteen

◉

One night, I turned in the bed and looked into her eyes. In the milky light from a streetlamp outside her apartment, they were a muted gray.

"Are you in love with me?" I asked.

"Love?" she asked.

"Yes, love."

She laughed and ran her fingers against my cheek, drawing them down to my lips. "Oh, my sweet one."

I let go of her. A flicker of hurt and resentment sparked in me. I felt that I couldn't breathe, as if my lungs had stopped working.

She reached out and grabbed my shoulders. "Don't be like that."

She propped herself on one elbow and poked my nose. "You know what I mean. You're acting like a hurt little boy. Come on, let mama love you."

I recoiled, got out of bed, and stood. The floor was cold. I grabbed my underwear from the wicker chair. My mind was racing.

She'd told me how she believed in free love; she gave it unstintingly, inviting me over twice a week, coming, if I asked, to my place, staying the night, never denying me her body, knowing how to arouse me, willingly and eagerly at my disposal.

My reaction didn't seem right. How easy it would be to strip, turn, and fall into her arms. She sat upright on the bed, her breasts, beautiful and perfect, inviting me to come back, nestle close to them, hold them, and forget any slight. Tempted as I was, aware of my arousal, I was equally aware of a more powerful yearning for something more permanent, something she was not able to offer, something I'd have to find elsewhere.

My shoe laced, I perched on the bedside. "I'm sorry. I need time. It has been great, quite wonderful."

"You talk as if it's in the past," she said, her hand on my shoulder.

She was puzzled by me. And she wasn't the only one. I was puzzled, too. We had had a lovely evening.

"I don't know. You know I'm a writer. I spend so much of my time writing about what happened to me. Last week. Last year. The year before. My childhood. And even yesterday. It seems like I live in the past, you know, writing about what happened before, mulling it over, trying to figure out what I felt, and find myself going there before I've left the present. I often feel as if I'm already thinking about and writing about the present before it happens. It's like I'm outside of myself looking in, wondering how it would look on a page."

"Silly boy," she said, her voice muted. "Silly boy."

I leaned over to kiss her.

"Remember, darling, when you come back, I'm here, always in the present," she said. She ran her silky hand over my thigh.

I walked to my car. I sat for a while, the engine running, watching her behind the shade—she had gotten up—her figure moving from the bedroom. A light went on in the living room and another in the kitchen. It looked as if there was no darkness left in her house.

Chapter Fourteen

On the weekend, a sunny, surprisingly balmy December day, while I was sitting on the veranda, I heard a car come down the driveway. Not expecting anyone, I got up. I watched Carole hop out of a blue Ford beside my green Volvo.

"I thought I'd find you here," she said. "I was feeling housebound."

"I'm delighted," I said. I reached out to take her hand.

"You've seemed down of late," she said.

"Come in," I said, opening the door. "Coffee?"

"Tea," she said. She wandered into the book room, ran her finger over the bookcase. "You need a woman. The dust is thick. Do you have a cloth?" She wiped the shelves. "I hope you don't mind. I love to dust. It makes me feel I've accomplished something."

"Help yourself,"

We sat on the wicker chairs on the veranda. She turned toward me, inspecting my face. "You look unhappy. You haven't even called."

I stood up and walked to the edge of veranda.

"You know I'm dating a girl up in Dresden, right?"

"I have a nose for trouble. What is it?"

"It's kinda embarrassing."

"I just don't get enough embarrassing things these days," she said.

I told her about Suzie, free love, my being one of many. She leaned forward in her chair, resting her elbows on her knees. Then she stood up and took a step toward me at the edge of the veranda. She lifted her cup. "Does anyone live in those trailers?"

"They came once, a month ago, spent the weekend, and left. I think it's a getaway. They're an older couple."

Carole turned toward me. "Listen, Jason, you're a sensitive guy. I know you. Fooling around, I suspect, is what a single guy like you must do. But you deserve more."

"You think?"

She put her arm around my waist. "It's cold. But let's walk down to the river. I love sitting by it, watching it go by."

The river was low. Carole scooted next to me on the steps and put her hand on my knee. "Listen to me," she said. "I don't have much experience. John is only the second guy I've been with. Yet I see you, how you look at us and how you inquire about our lives, and know you want what we have. Is that right?"

I nodded.

"You shouldn't have to settle for being second, or third, in line."

"I wonder sometimes if I ever will," I said. I tossed a rock into the river. It splashed. The ripples spread out and were swept downriver.

"You will."

She had a way of getting to the point. I thought about telling her about my aberrant feelings. She was the one person whom I could trust. I wanted to tell her other things about myself, tell her of my ambivalence, but she stood up.

"Come on," she said. "Lunch. You look like you could use a good meal. We can drive up to Cumberland. There's a really fine German restaurant. I have a craving for bratwurst."

Chapter Fourteen

We strolled arm in arm along the downtown streets. Christmas displays were resplendent We went in a store selling stone Buddhas and tie-dyed T-shirts, chatted with the clerk, acting as if we were a couple.

We laughed watching two kids who looked as if they'd just had a fight, the girl with a long ponytail striding ahead and the boy, five feet behind her, head down, following her like a miserable duckling.

Carole whispered, "He looks like you looked when I first saw you this morning."

In all the time I'd been with Suzie, we'd gone out once or twice to dinner, once with Doug and Angel, but we never spent the day outdoors, never strolled down a street.

By the time, we got back to my place, it was late afternoon. "I have to scoot," Carole said. "John will be thinking I'm having an affair."

"No free love for you?" I asked.

She laughed. She leaned over to kiss me on the cheek. "Unless it's with you." She pinched me on the side.

"Ouch."

"Don't get too sassy with me," she said. "There's a side of me you don't know about. I can be quite fierce if need be."

"I bet."

She drove off. I went back to my room, sat for a while staring at all the books—the theological texts, the collections of poetry, the novels—and wondered if any of them had ever been as helpful to me as one day with Carole.

Another weekend. Nowhere to go. A long time alone. Just the room, the river, the sun steaming in the window, and me. The windows were as open as my heart felt. I sprawled on the couch reading *Look Homeward Angel*, remembering Erling Duus, my mentor, the man who introduced me to American literature, had taken me on one of his pilgrimages to the "Old Kentucky Home," Thomas Wolfe's childhood home, which was still standing alongside other turn-of-the-century homes in Asheville, North Carolina.

It had been mid-summer. Heat poured off the pavement. The air felt reined in, immobilized. Nothing moved. A hefty white-haired lady sat on the porch, greeted us and asked if we'd like a tour. She showed us the room where young Tom had lived, the parlor where the boarders met, and the dining room. To be in Wolfe's home, to smell its musty odors, to touch the window curtains, to see the large sprawling handwriting of his manuscript, was to be in a place with two lives. One was imbued with his words, alive in his imaginative portrayal. The other was the relics of an old, rickety building—far less interesting, and, had Wolfe not lived there, a place that would have been long ago demolished.

In the last months, I'd had that dualistic feeling about my life. Wanting to be Suzie's lover yet cherishing being alone. Alone with my journal yet having to endure the daily drudgery with my job—buying groceries, filling out forms, cashing checks, planning training, writing grants. Alone while climbing the hillside at night above the river. Alone with Beethoven's symphonies. Yet having to put on the administrator's face.

I traced my finger over Wolfe's elaborate sentences that seemed to pick up momentum, swerve and grab more details, and then, with an easy grace, unwind and scroll down the page.

The story of Wolfe's Eugene, searching for his place in the

Chapter Fourteen

world, striving to make sense of his alcoholic father, his quirky, overbearing mother, seemed more real than anything I was doing.

I pulled out my journal.

When you feel small and become frightened, you reach for something larger than you. So it is with me now as I feel both inadequate about my life, yet unsure about my job. I reach for other people, more experienced, older, and wiser with the sense that they must know more than I do. Especially Carole. If anything, as T.S. Eliot said "Do not let me hear / Of the wisdom of old men, but rather of their folly, / Their fear of fear and frenzy, their fear of possession, / Of belonging to another, to others, or to God." He might as well be speaking about me—all my fears, and, it seems, the fears of many others.

How is it that we get stuck in the rut of our lives? We move in the same circles as the needle in the groove of a record, playing and replaying the same song, the same phrases, the same cliches that we said last year, and the year before, and never, not even when we are bored, bother to lift the needle.

Immersed as I was in my thoughts, it took a moment for me to hear the cries. Someone was wailing outside. Rousing gradually to the noise, I sat up, listened. Sure enough, out the kitchen door I could hear a sharp clear cry of a baby.

It was frightful.

Out where I lived, down a dirt road, four miles off the grid. No houses nearby. To either side of the driveway were miles of forest, long, low slopes of pine and hardwood that rose and peaked at ridges alongside the river. I scrambled to my feet and raced out the door. I ran, following the sound.

The cries were coming from the bend in the road, some five hundred yards—it seemed—beyond the driveway.

I dashed up the road, glancing at the eight-foot gulch on either side. I felt awakened. I cocked my ear. The wind fussed the treetops. The wail came again, this time back down the road but also up the slope in the woods. Had I miscalculated? I sprinted, slid down the gulch and, trampled into the underbrush, pushed aside branches and saplings, getting swiped in the face, heading as close as I could to figure out the spot where I heard the mournful cry.

Nervous, sweat dripped off my forehead. I heard a skittering sound; leaves of a low bush rustled. I kneeled and peered under the underbrush.

Nothing.

I went back to the road, stood at the top of the driveway for 15 minutes, walked back up the road, stood quietly for another ten minutes. Maybe I was deluded.

Had I really heard it?

I ambled to my apartment, deciding whoever it was, whatever it was, I was not going to rescue it, not the way it eluded me.

I tried to read Wolfe with little luck. The cries came again. They went on for five minutes and then subsided. Then again. I felt awful. Whatever it was, no matter what I did, rescuing it proved useless. Good, I thought, let it be. If it wanted help, it would have responded to my voice, making some sound, letting me know where to find it. I walked down the steps to the river. I watched my breath. The currents swiveled around the boulders, sending up a slight mist that was carried toward me, caressing my face.

I returned to my apartment, read another chapter, poured some

Chapter Fourteen

wine in a glass, turned on the phonograph, turned up the volume of Beethoven's Emperor Concerto to block out the cries. Something was wrong. Yet, whatever it was, it didn't make sense.

I stepped out of the kitchen door.

That's when I met him, crouched by the door, a palm-sized puff ball of black and white fur—a kitten.

He gazed up at me and made a raspy mew, more like a cat this time than a child. I looked down at him. This was not good. I hated cats.

But this was not a cat. It was a kitten—a small one at that. I bent down and picked it up. It purred and nestled into my hand. I was not about to let it into the apartment. I put some milk in a bowl. It lapped it up. I gave it more. It lapped it up. Hungry little one. I wanted it to be safe, at least, until I could find an owner, so I found an empty box in my closet, put a towel in it and put it by the door. The kitten purred when I tucked it in. I patted it goodnight and shut the door.

But it cried, just as it had done when I first heard it—one throaty ululation after another. I opened the door, picked it up, told it to be quiet. It purred in my hand, nestling its nose against my wrist. I admired its persistence. I figured one night wouldn't hurt and brought it inside to a pillow on my bed.

As it turned out, the kitten, who I named Toby, knew me better than I knew myself. He put his little paw to my face that night, scrunched into a ball by my neck, his warm body against mine. When I woke in the morning, he licked my face with his raspy tongue.

I fed him milk and bought him some canned food in town. I asked at work if anyone wanted a kitten, but no one seemed interested. I couldn't let him starve.

By the end of the week, with his new name, he purred when I

played Beethoven. He sat on my desk when I wrote and would slap at my pen if my sentence was getting too long. He followed me wherever I went—down to the river, out on the porch, and even in the shower (until I turned on the water). Right by my side, like a miniature bodyguard.

After a day at work, he greeted me, mewing that he'd had a good day, caught a few mice, which he left for me at the doorstep, and sunned himself in the wicker chair on the porch. I was learning I didn't know anything about cats, but Toby was giving a crash course day by day, teaching me the mysterious ways of cats.

Lou, my secretary, had wanted me to meet her husband, come visit, have dinner, and stay the night. I didn't want to impose on them, given their limited resources, but one night, after work, the week before Christmas break, we drove to the boat ramp. I stepped into the skiff, held onto the low gunwales, taking care not to rock it. Lou rowed us across the river, angling the stern upriver since, as we caught the current, the boat would be drawn downriver. On either side of the river, small trees, darkening the water, made it difficult to see where the boat was headed.

She called out, "Grab the branch," and I saw it—a long limb sticking four feet out from the shore over the water—and latched onto it.

"Good," she said. "Pull us ashore."

The boat swung around, dragged by the current, almost throwing me out. We dragged it up the bank and tied it to a tree.

She led me to their farmhouse about a hundred yards up on a knoll. It had a wide, covered porch and a bank of windows facing the river.

Chapter Fourteen

The clapboards were gray, some festered with yellow-green mildew. Larry, her husband, stood on the porch, waving at us. Golden-haired, long-waisted, swarthy, dressed in bib-overalls with no shirt, not even in the cold weather, he looked like a working man's Phoebus/Apollo. He extended his hand to me as I stepped up. He grabbed me by the shoulders and hugged me as if I was a long-lost uncle.

"Really glad you came over. Lou keeps telling me all about you. It's been a while."

Larry and I hit it off right away. He offered me a joint, homegrown marijuana, and we smoked it, and several more, and sat around, listening to the river.

We had dinner. Corn from their crop, lamb chops from their lambs, winter kale from their garden, and, later, ice cream from the fresh cream they churned. The meal took hours and our conversation meandered from laments about Nixon and the War, to their farm. How they managed, as tenant farmers. Selling crops at market, marijuana on the sly, and cows to local butchers.

Larry was the most naturally affectionate man I'd ever met. I envied him. He felt comfortable with his body. A man of touch, he slung an arm around my shoulder, pulling me close to him. and chatted with me as if it was the most normal thing in the world. After dinner, he offered me another joint and took a seat between Lou and me on the couch, the only piece of furniture in their living room.

"You know," he said, sticking his hand on my knee and pressing his large muscular fingers onto me. "I'm jealous of you. You get to see Lou way more than I do. If she wasn't so in love with you—you know, man, like maybe not love, but admiration—I'd feel bad. But you're one cool dude, you know. I see how she could get into you."

He kept his hand on my knee as if it were a stick shift on a tractor. He smelled of hay, musty yet sweet, and earthy manure. He bent his head toward me, his hair against my cheek.

"You're one cool dude, man," he said again.

We smoked another joint, passing it between us.

I got a hard-on. He said, "This weed, it makes your body electric." His hand grabbed ahold of my erection. "You can't help it, can you? That's what's so nice." He smiled at me. "Look at me," he said, and nodded at the bulge in his pants. "It makes you remember we're just bodies. Sensual bodies and that's what is so cool. That makes us who we are." He lifted his hand and leaned over to kiss Lou. "She's just like us except it doesn't show. That's why women are so mysterious."

I thought of Suzie, her seemingly unquenchable need for love, for touch, for intimacy. Maybe I had the same free need for abiding love, something tender and durable. I felt so comfortable with Larry. It was gentle. Even playful.

When it was time for bed, Larry pulled out the couch, Lou threw a sheet over it, several blankets, a thick comforter, a pillow. She whispered to me and hugged me. "I'm glad you came over. You should do it more often. He doesn't have many guys to talk to. He likes you." When they had gone up to their bedroom, I pulled the couch to the window where I could hear the river. No sooner had I dozed off than I was awakened by the creaking of a clarinet of bedsprings above. Larry and Lou's moaning. I couldn't help hearing them. I gave up trying to sleep. I walked to the porch, wrapped in the comforter, and listened to the lovely chorus of their love and the river below me. I made a vow to come back here as often as I could. Crossing the river, I'd felt like myself with no disguises. I slept soundly like one who'd been enveloped in love.

Chapter Fourteen

◉

A few days later I wrote.

We must discover gender through experience. Larry grabbed ahold of my erection the other night, touching me as if that were a normal thing. For him, gender means nothing. Male. Female. What is the difference?

We have whole clandestine worlds, as with Terry and Orlando where gender is fluid, not as polite society were to cast it, not as psychiatrists label it. Yet what is gender anyway? What is the gender of a blanket? Or the lamp on my desk? Or the beetles swatting the screen? Toby's tail is twitching. He's asleep, yet his senses are alert. Does he know that he is a he? Does he care? The sun could be a girl as well as a boy. The moon could be masculine. What difference would it make?

We can be turned on by anyone. I wonder.

Chapter Fifteen

Late December, some oaks, more modest than other trees, were still clothed in leaves. For a while longer than usual, the weather had remained balmy, some days reminiscent of summer. But we had a huge snowstorm, aimed at us from Chicago, heading our way.

It was Christmas time. My mother had invited me back home, but I was looking for an excuse not to go. Tess had already invited me to their holiday dinner, so I stayed in West Virginia.

Jerome greeted me at the door. The stentorian voices of other, well-oiled guests ricocheted off walls. Beside Jerome and Tess, it was their two children, as well as Ken, David, and Enrique. I was surprised to see Enrique, until I considered how far he had to travel from South America, but then realized, of course, he had driven over from his academy outside Washington.

Tess handed me a Jack Daniels on ice and kissed me on the cheek. I sat on the arm of a couch next to Enrique. He told me his semester at the military academy had gone well. He liked his teachers and got mostly A's. When he went for a drink, David came over. He asked if I had read *Islands in The Stream* yet, a Hemingway book he had given me.

"It's compelling," I told him, still uneasy since our night together. "Particularly the end when he is lost in the mangroves. But I worry his main character isn't well rendered. Seems too cut and dried, an echo of his previous male characters."

He pulled me aside, pointing his finger at Enrique.

"He stayed with me last night," he divulged, smiling, pleased with himself.

"How nice," I responded.

"He slept over. He is quite something. I must say."

I tried to steer the conversation in a different direction. But he nestled close to me and went on.

"Latin men make such good lovers. You know I always believed that if you want something, go for it. Take action. Do it. And it pays. It always pays, right?"

I was calculating what to say when Enrique walked over to us and saved me from having to respond. He asked if we wanted another drink. I took a quick slug of mine. David had already drained his. We gave him our glasses, and he traipsed off to the kitchen.

"Quite a number, hey?" David nudged me.

"Yes, he certainly is."

When Enrique came back, David suggested that Enrique come over to his place when I was there. We could all listen to music together. Enrique blushed and looked at a cigarette in David's hand, the ash dangling, about to fall. He was just a boy. I shook my head.

"No, David," I said. "You must be crazy." I stood up, disgusted with David, with myself, and strode across the room to talk with Ken.

"Something wrong?" Ken asked.

"You know what you told me about David. It's true. He's even having affairs with someone who's underage. And I don't like it."

Ken took me by the arm, ushering me from the room. "Keep your voice down," he said. "I know what you're saying. I don't like it either. But not here, not now. It wouldn't make a bit of difference. Think it through. Don't make a scene. Talk with him later." He added several ice cubes to my glass. "Okay. Let it go. He's on our board."

Chapter Fifteen

I stayed after David and Enrique left to help tidy up. Enrique drove back to Maryland to stay with a friend. David, who hated to drive in the dark was anxious to avoid the storm. The children had been sent to bed. Flurries had begun to fall.

Jerome seemed delighted that I remained and plied me with different aperitifs: first, an amaretto, then a drambuie. Finally, an exotic cognac to tease my taste buds as I wiped off plates. Cleaning took us more than an hour. After Tess had hung each pan from its hook and returned silver serving dishes to their cupboards, we relaxed to a Mozart symphony. Dark had drawn down its curtain. I had just gathered my overcoat to leave when the phone rang.

Jerome's tone was uncharacteristically urgent. "It's David again."

Tess held up a finger to me, miming for me to wait. She joined Jerome on the phone and her expression fell too. She began scribbling on a notepad and repeating words in an odd cadence. "Yes, of course. We would be happy to. Yes. Right away. Of course. Yes. I understand. It must be awful. I will. Expect us."

She placed the receiver down gingerly and clasped her hands across her chest.

I looked at her, "Well?"

"His aunt has had a cerebral hemorrhage. Sounds as if she's still alive."

I watched Jerome place a hand on her shoulder. A flash of tenderness crossed her face. Her eyes welled up. But still, she brushed him aside.

"We have no time for that. We must get to him. Now."

She moved so quickly from grief to full-blown command mode that we were swept up in the velocity of her decision making. She snapped out orders, "Jerome, stay with the children. Stay by the phone in case we need to call. Check with any regional hospitals to see if they have specialists for such things."

She turned to me and pointed to the door. "Jason, let's go."

On one severe curve in the road, Tess asked out of the blue, "Do you think he killed her?"

What could I say? I said nothing.

"He hates her guts," she said.

"I know."

"He told you, too."

"He had told me he'd like to strangle or bludgeon her. But who says that in seriousness? I do remember," I said, "that he said if he'd be left out of the will, she would regret it."

"The poor soul." She pressed on the accelerator. "He's liable to do anything when he's drunk too much."

Gusts of powdery flakes battered the windshield. She negotiated each twist and turn like she had trained at Le Mans. I resigned myself to the vertigo. I gripped onto the ceiling handle, braced against the dashboard. Headlights of passing cars burrowed through the snow and flashed past us. Tess intently turned at a steep curve and lit a cigarette.

The hospital, set on a knoll, seemed to float like a solitary brick building against an angry sky. The saplings planted in front of it shook and shivered in the winds. "He said that he'd meet us here," she said, pulling into a parking lot.

"What do we do?" I asked.

"He said," she raised her voice over the wind whipping at the car,

Chapter Fifteen

"he'd let us know if they needed to transport her to another hospital."

Just then, out of nowhere, David tapped on my window. Both Tess and I jumped, and she rolled down the window.

"How is she?" Tess asked.

He murmured, "Dead."

With the wind howling, she didn't hear him.

"What?"

"Dead!" he screamed.

She gasped, reaching her hand out toward him. "What can we do?" she yelled.

"I'm going back to her house, to my place. Tom is driving me. The police are there. They have some questions." He pointed to a car that had pulled in front of us. "Come over there. I may need your help."

He blinked and gazed up at the hospital. "Dead on arrival. Nothing we could do."

We watched him walk away. Tess rolled up her window and puffed on her cigarette. It had a minty smell.

"Let's hope he didn't do it," she said.

"What if he has?"

"Dear God, let's not think of that."

"But I'm not going to lie if the police ask."

"We'll have to see. There's no telling. This is horrid," she said. She placed her hand on my leg, squeezed it. "Be circumspect."

When we arrived at his house, a police car was parked outside. David stood in the doorway waving us in. Two officers on either side.

Tess held onto her hat from the blast of the wind, and I scrunched down, covering my face as we trudged to the doorway.

"High pressure, that's what causing the storm," David said ushering us in. We took turns giving him a hug.

We introduced ourselves to the officers. One was skinny, tall, and young, his hair long and curly. He had a notepad. The other was stout with a ruddy complexion, crow's feet etched deep into his cheeks. That one said, "We have some questions of Mr. Bridewell, but you can join us."

David guided us through the front parlor and stood at the edge of the dining room. "There," he said, gesturing at the Oriental rug.

It was a deep burgundy pattern, elaborate with strands of blue and faded reds and gold. At first, I wasn't sure what he wanted us to see. I cocked my head, as did the officers. He must have seen our quizzical look, so, more emphatically, he said, "There," aiming his finger at a large spot to the right of the dining room table's clawfoot paw.

The spot had no clear configuration. It spread out in extending splotches, some nearly a foot wide, some two feet wide, some thin and narrow, pooling out from a central stain that the rug pattern had camouflaged. Blood. Lots of it. Inches thick.

Tess looked at me, I looked at her, we both looked at the carpet. I was thinking of a game of Clue, imagining the lead pipe. Neither of us looked at David.

"Mr. Bridewell, can you tell us what happened?" the older officer asked.

"I found her," David said.

"Where were you when it happened?"

"I wasn't here, clearly. I found her afterwards."

"Where, may I ask, were you?"

David pointed to us. "I was at Tess's Christmas dinner."

"Is that right, ma'am?"

Chapter Fifteen

"Yes."

"When did he leave your party?"

"Oh, I'm not sure," Tess said. "When was it, Jason?"

She dragged me in. "A little after ten."

The younger officer made a note.

"What time did you arrive here, Mr. Bridewell?"

"Probably about eleven or so," David said. He was chewing his fingernails. Tess made a face. He stopped and shoved his hands in his pockets.

"So, you got here about eleven. What happened next?"

David blurted out a great moan. Choking back sobs, he apologized, then, containing himself, told what happened: "I came home and put on some music. I didn't know something had happened to her. How could I? But something felt odd. I couldn't tell what it was. Maybe it was that I usually could tell if she was up because I could hear her walking upstairs. It was eerily quiet. I decided to go to the kitchen. I usually do, to get some milk. I like to have it before I go to bed. Helps me sleep. Something still felt odd. Something was not right. Do you know how that is? The cat was nowhere in sight. And I smelled something. Horrid smell. That's when I looked in and saw her shoes—dress shoes. She must have come from a party. I called out to her. And then I stepped in it. The blood. So much blood. I called Tom. He called emergency. But there was nothing to do. Was there? I found her there. Blood coming out of her from all over. Her mouth. Ears. She must have realized what was happening since she had cupped some of the blood in her hands—they were caked—and her blouse was soaked and she had tried to reach the phone—see it there on the side table?—and, as you can see from the blood stains, she almost made it. Not that it would have made a difference. The doctor figured it took seconds."

At first, none of us spoke. Finally, the officers asked if they could talk to David alone, so Tess and I retreated to his room.

"Do you think he did it?" I asked, sitting lightly on the bed.

"I sure hope not," Tess said. "Sounds as if he did find her. I know David. He can lie, but he couldn't lie about something this serious. He would fall apart."

"We'll see."

David returned to his room after an hour. When he did, his eyes red and swollen, he was visibly shaken. "They act as if I did it. I can't believe it," he said, his arms flailing around him. "They asked question after question. I think they wanted me to slip up. How could I? I saw what I saw. I loved her. You know that. This is so absurd. I need a drink."

He grabbed a bottle from the shelf and offered us a glass too. Whiskey. We accepted. He all clinked our glasses.

"My thanks for coming. I don't think I could have managed without you."

Tess said, "Oh, David, we had to. We just had to be here, didn't we, Jason?"

I concurred, looking at him. His face was blanched. Tess smiled gently. She looked at me and raised a brow. David seemed unsure how to proceed. He stared at us like we knew what to say.

I leaned forward, "This is good whiskey."

"My aunt, she gave it to me last Christmas. Very good brand. Her favorite—George T. Stagg Kentucky Straight Bourbon Whis-

Chapter Fifteen

key," he said. "She spoiled me."

"I'm not sure what to say except, well, except we're sorry," Tess offered, sipping on her whiskey. I could tell she didn't like it.

David looked at the floor and picked up a piece of lint, held it in his hand and blew on it.

The lint fluttered upward, balanced mid-air, then drifted in the air.

"Just like that, here and gone," he said, taking a deep breath. "I suppose you don't want to go back to see the scene of the crime?" he said, breaking the suspense—we'd been following it—of the lint rising up, suspended.

"The crime?" asked Tess.

David turned to her. "Oh, that's what they seem to think it is."

"No, David, we saw it."

He said, "I just don't believe it." He folded into her arms and sobbed, gripping her, repeating, "There was nothing to do. There was nothing to do."

When David stepped back unsteadily, Tess picked up his hand and cupped it in hers. "Of course not," she said. "She went quickly. That's best."

As the police weren't about to arrest him, we stayed with him for several hours, well into the morning, consoling him. We learned later that, based on the blood tests, the massiveness of the internal hemorrhage, and the condition of his aunt's body, she had, indeed, died earlier in the day when David was with us at Tess's dinner. The police called off the investigation. Although moody and distracted, not able to carry on a rational conversation and acting like someone fleeing the scene of a crime, David made plans for what he would do after her house was sold: escape.

Chapter Sixteen

One Tuesday in January, after a long day with Carole in Peters-borough, I came back to my apartment to find a car parked outside. It wasn't one of the men from Cumberland. An old Impala, powder blue, the engine still running.

The teenager I'd met months earlier, Terry, stepped out of his car, smiling. "I found out where you live," he said.

I stopped in my tracks. "How'd you do that?"

"Talked to some people and I know this area. We camp, my dad and me, up the road from here." He pointed up past the lodge.

"Well, to what do I owe this surprise visit?" I asked as coldly as I could. "Do your parents know you're here?"

"Of course," he said.

I didn't believe him. I was tempted to tell him to call them.

I felt uneasy with him, a minor, there at my place. After our conversation, I'd made a point of only seeing him in the weekly planning meetings and keeping a professional distance. I didn't want to be embroiled in some scandal. I feared how his story aroused me. I distrusted his sexual openness and was angry he'd shared it with me.

"I think you should get back home. We can meet at my office later this week," I said.

"I'll just stay for a minute. I got some stuff I want to show you." He reached out to me, set his hand on my arm. I looked at his hand, at his doleful eyes and solicitous expression and felt myself softening.

In the apartment, he looked around. "Nice digs," he said. He strutted, moving quickly from one side of the room to the other, brushing back his hair, jerking his neck back and forth.

I told him to sit down, relax. What was it he wanted to show me? We could talk.

From his bag he pulled what appeared to be a magazine-like booklet, the size of a small novel. "Look," he said, flipping through the pages of gay pornography.

"Where did you get that?" I asked, stepping back.

"Mitchell got it. His uncle. He knows about Mitchell."

"You shouldn't have stuff like that," I said. "That could get you in serious trouble."

"It's neat," he said. "Look, this one looks like Jeff, you know, the tall kid, a basketball player. We joked with him that it looks exactly like him. Don't you think?"

"You show this to other kids?" I asked.

He said, "Here's one that turned everyone on." He held open a page with two guys sucking each other's cocks, a close-up shot that showed their eyes, bright and wide, gazing at the camera. More stunned than I'd been the night he told me about Orlando, I stood by him, letting him talk about how one kid in the booklet reminded him of someone he knew, someone I'd met at the town hall, as if in a hallucination.

"You want to keep it?" he asked. "I've got to hide it at home."

I couldn't bring myself to say no.

He put it down on the couch. Still standing, he took a paper bag and a bottle from his back pocket.

Chapter Sixteen

"Ever try to sniff this?" he asked.

"What is it?"

"Glue," he said. "You put some in the bag and sniff it."

I had heard it wasted your brain. Before I could stop him, he unscrewed the lid on the bottle, poured it in the bag and inhaled. He made a few spastic steps forward and stumbled. His legs gave way, and I grabbed him, holding him up, my arms under his arms, and carried his limp body back to the couch. I propped him up. He didn't move.

I called, "Terry. Terry."

I lifted his eyelids.

He came to, smiling and stared at me vacantly as if someone had erased his frontal lobe.

He said, "What happened?'

"You collapsed. Are you alright?"

I shook my head. "That stuff will fry your brain. Throw it away." I brushed his hair back from his eyes. He seemed like a little boy.

"You idiot," I said. I felt like a big brother. Here was this powerful young man who, in public, displayed all the confidence in the world, now stretched out on my couch, passive, letting me take care of him.

He reminded me of Suzie when she wanted to have sex. Instead of talking and being busy fixing dinner for us, she'd lie back on the couch in her apartment, her legs opened, looking languidly up at me. The first night I went to her place and wasn't sure how to initiate sex, I did the same thing. I lay back and she caressed my chest and stomach, and we made love.

But this was very different. Here was a kid out of control. A minor. He was passive. I felt flushed. Anxious. I went to the bedroom dresser for a washcloth, something I could wet to put on his face to revive him. When I pulled on my dresser drawer, the knob came off, the screw holding having lost its thread. Doug had warned me to be gentle with it. I flung it on my bed. A quiet rage stirred in me.

"Get up," I yelled. He laid back, staring at the porn, his legs parted, and I saw distinctly that he too was aroused. No time to waste, I picked him up, hoping to walk him out of his stupor and to his car, to be done with him.

He flung his arms around me, pulled me close, his chest on mine, and kissed me. For a moment I melted, feeling his lips on mine. His body against me, he reached down and grabbed my erection and tried to pull me back to the couch. His tongue wormed its way into my mouth. He knew what he was doing. He knew that he could seduce me. Everything in my body wanted to let go, to reach down and touch him, to admit that he had won. I was his. I took several steps toward the couch when the telephone rang.

It was Mitchell, his friend. He wanted to know if Terry was there. Immediately, I slammed the phone down.

"You gave your friends this number?"

"That was Mitchell?"

"Who else did you tell?"

"If Mitchell called, my mom's looking for me."

I clenched my fist. "You didn't tell her you were coming here?"

He hung his head.

"Call her now," I said and shoved the receiver in his hand. "And I want to talk to her, too!"

He called his mom and explained to her how he came to work on the grant. I got on and apologized and told her, yes, we did work on the grant and, yes, he would be right home, and, most of all, I was very upset he'd not informed her of his whereabouts. Before he left, I typed

Chapter Sixteen

up several pages of notes that he could use to show his mom our progress and told him that I didn't want him coming here unannounced.

I asked him why he gave Mitchell my number. He didn't want to say. I told him I needed to know. He said, "He thinks you're gay. He gets that vibe. He says that you have that look in your eyes."

"I see," I said. "Mitchell isn't prescient, you know."

"What's that??"

"It means he can't read minds."

"Oh." He stuffed his hands in his pockets. "But are you?"

"No," I said. "I'm sorry."

"But—"

"I got caught off guard, that's all."

He asked for a hug—I gave him one—and he left. I went out on the veranda and took in the cool air. My body was shivering. From the cold or from the excitement or from the fear, I couldn't tell. A knot twisted in my belly. I hated the way he made me feel. How my body betrayed me. When he grabbed ahold of me, his body next to mine, there was a part of me that wanted to be as free as I was with Larry on his couch. Yet I also wanted to deny it, to bury those feelings, to quit the project, to tell him to find someone else to write the grant. It was as if he had torn me open and was ripping me apart, exposing the inner side of me that I had to hide. I had to get rid of feelings that didn't want to be rid of me. This was another test. I almost failed it. But I had drawn a line. Just barely.

I boiled hot water to brew a cup of coffee just as Tess taught me, using a paper napkin for a filter, which, strange as it sounds, comforted me, just following a routine I had learned from an expert.

I called Ken the next day and asked to meet with him.

◉

Before I could say a word, Ken asked, "What's the problem?" He must have sensed my distress.

"I don't want to write that grant," I said. "I can't. It's too much."

"Did something happen?" he asked. "Sit down. You're upset."

I told him that Terry had showed up at my place.

"But that's not a big deal," he said. "Why didn't you tell him to go home?"

"I don't know. What I do know is that I don't like some kid showing up at my front door. It's not right. I wouldn't stand for it," I said.

My voice must have given me away. "Okay," he said. "What really happened?"

I looked at my hands. They were shaking. I could barely speak. "He . . . he. What can I say? He . . ."

"Did he try to do something to you?" Ken asked, scooting closer to me.

"I don't want him to get in trouble. I just want out, that's all," I said. "I shouldn't have let him come into my place."

We had a long talk. I gave Ken a brief version of what happened. Ken convinced me to finish the grant and that would be all. I didn't have to do anything else. He would take care of monitoring the summer program. Relieved, I told him I would do my best. As I was leaving, he said, "Can I give you a hug?"

I nodded. As he held me, he said, "It wasn't your fault, Jason. The kid is messed up. That's all. Let it go."

"I wish I could," I said.

Chapter Sixteen

◉

I went to the Pearsall Flats Ace Hardware store to find a new knob for my dresser.

As I searched the aisles a young, man, slight with light blonde hair, probably dyed, asked, "May I help?"

I showed him the knob. "The thread is stripped," I said.

He took it from me, held it up to his liquid brown eyes. "So, it is." He brushed back his slack hair. He touched the knob as if he was touching me—my legs, my chest, my face—to determine if I, too, was stripped. He had that same look that Terry had the night before.

What was it about this town? Was every kid gay? Did Orlando have them all under his spell?

The corner of his mouth turned up, his lips opened, his eyes dropped. It was as if we were transfixed, stalled in time, caught in each other's invisible web, unable to move yet aware of each slight movement, every breath we took.

Why couldn't I control myself?

I stuffed my hands in my pockets.

He put one hand in his pocket and looked at me, his head nodding very slightly to confirm what we both knew was true. Then he looked at the knob, his thumb rubbing it.

I said, "We . . ."

"Yes," he said, "Follow me," he said, leading me to an aisle across from us.

He pulled out drawers, fidgeting with knobs of different sizes, holding them up, comparing mine to them until he found a match and a nut to match the screw.

"Do you need to paint it?" he asked.

"Yeah, a green."

"Flat or gloss?"

It felt like something had finally snapped inside me, some internal coil that had been tightly strung, and my inhibitions had sprung loose. What was happening to me? Why couldn't I get control of myself?

He found a small can, added a brush, and escorted me to the check out. I kept my hand deep in my pocket. When he brought the items to the cashier, writing the cost on a slip, he eyed me once more, noting where my hand was. "Is that all I can get for you?"

I said, "Yes, that will do. Thank you," although I felt as if I could have taken him in my arms, stripped him of his white Ace shirt and buried my face in his chest, making love to him right there on the tile floor. It was as if my id was on overdrive. I may have passed the test the night before but here I was failing it.

I never went back to the store, at least not physically. I did, however, swim in a fantasy of his dreamy brown eyes that were like a far field filled with late fall grasses.

When I wrote in my journal that evening, my thoughts kept veering into the darkest part of me.

My attitude toward myself is destructive. I hate this thing I call "a self." My body repulses me. I want to flail it, tear my loins out, strip naked, rip out sinew by sinew, until I am lean and healthy, not a dilapidated essence, overweight, out of shape. I hate my sex. I am extreme in what I imagine. It's not right. Dare I say what it is? Can I admit it to myself? My little pornographic film flickering in the back of my mind. Fellatio extreme. Semen of an adolescent as he slips the pump out of a gas tank and notices drops drip out onto the cold

Chapter Sixteen

cement, but it's not gas; it's him. He's got a match in his hand. Vivid images, vital essences wasted in an over flux of extremes. I think I'm destroying myself. What I am is hate. I hate my thoughts. I hate myself. I hate my sex. Why do I exist? How did I get caught in this trap of desire? Why am I as I am? Can I ever be free from all of this? These perverted imaginings?

I put my pen down. I looked at it as if it had the answer to those questions. But it didn't move. It sat there. I flicked it across the room where it slammed against the paneling and landed on the couch, nestled there, unmoving.

Chapter Seventeen

Every month the West Virginia Head Start Directors were convened at a state park to get national updates, go over the latest guidelines, hear from speakers, and generally let off steam about the inevitable local problems boiling up on their own. I was just glad to get out of town. At Blackwater Falls State Park, some fifty miles south of Pearsall Flats, I met with Carole. From the lodge, you could see hundreds of feet down a canyon into the Blackwater River.

After spending the day in classroom management training, Carole and I walked along the canyon wall. It was a surprisingly warm day in January, almost springlike, but much too early. Dusk had settled. The sunlight held tenuously above the tree line; its slanted rays diffused by the trees.

"Well, now I know," Carole said.

"What?"

"This will be a perfect place to come and leap," she said, eyeing the drop-off.

"I will join you," I said, taking her arm in mine. "The void does have an appeal to me right now." She gave me a look.

"You alright?"

"I'd rather not talk about it," I said. "Some kid who I work with on a grant pushed some of my buttons."

"How so?"

"Just asked more of me than I could give."

"Sorry."

I tugged her arm. "It's good to be here. I needed the break."

We kept walking.

In two of her Centers and one of mine, we had serious problems. Either a teacher was too slack a disciplinarian, kids literally bouncing off the walls or the teacher was too strict, the kids defeated, cowering in corners, waiting for the teacher's tirade to end. Still, a morning panel discussing the merits of trained and untrained staff had been so boring my eyes had felt as if they were falling out of my sockets. Carole had to nudge me to keep me awake. The facilitator, Mary Ann Bivins was famous—or infamous—for droning on. Words dribbled from her like water from a leaky faucet.

"That Mary Ann," Carole said. "She can talk a cow to death."

"What is it with her?"

"Some people have this gene that just won't let them shut up." She giggled and pulled me by the arm. "Let's go down to the falls that everyone talks about."

"It's some distance, you know."

We kept on walking.

"I had to drive her up here, did I tell you that?" Carole said. "She doesn't drive. A two-hour drive, mind you, and she opened her trap soon as she opened the door, not a moment wasted, started to talk about her program, about how lovely the scenery was, about her poodle. She speaks as if there is no punctuation—just one long run-on sentence."

We followed a path along the canyon that, at a quarter of a mile, dipped down among the trees, following the ravine toward the

Chapter Seventeen

river. Muted by the pines, we could hear the rush of water to our left side. When we arrived at the falls, there was a bridge. We leaned over the railing. Mist, thrust up six stories, moistened our faces. The roar made it hard to hear.

"Shall we?" Carole yelled.

"You first," I replied, bowing to her.

Careful not to fall on the slick surface, we sidestepped our way, holding hands, holding onto the railing. The water jack hammered into the basin in a frothy black and white stew. I could feel the earth shaking under my feet. Much to our surprise, a small pathway led behind the falls. We followed it. Inside a hollowed-out cavern behind the waterfall, the roar was even more deafening. We yelled but couldn't hear one another. We stood, arm in arm, and watched sheet upon sheet of water pour over, crash into the rocks, again and again, holding as still as we could. For fifteen minutes—maybe more—time stopped. The power of the crashing waves felt like just our secret. *Portentous*, I thought. I felt humbled, small, incidental against the majestic power.

Once we emerged from behind the falls, we were thoroughly drenched. We climbed back up the path. The night was on us now, only a faint glimmer of reddish-yellow light over the distant trees. When Carole spoke, she spoke in a hushed tone as one does in cathedrals, in the presence of the sacred.

"Could you believe it?" she said.

"Hardly. It seemed like we were in the presence of gods."

We'd only worked together for six months and, although we trusted one another, nearly loved each other, we hadn't spoken much about our personal ambitions.

She asked, "I know you like your work here, but what do you *really* want to do? You live by yourself, spend a lot of time talking about men I've never heard of—Agee, Stevens, and Eliot, all writers—and I sense much of your life is wrapped up in them. What is it you want to do?"

Amazed that she could sense something in the heart of me, I froze on the path and looked at her. She tilted her head. "Well?"

"I'm not sure I want to say."

"Why?"

"Well, it seems too outrageous."

"Come on," she said, taking back one of my hands. "It can't be all that bad."

I told her that I didn't just want to write, which is what I'd told her in Annapolis, but I wanted to be a writer, to make that my livelihood. If I could write anything as well as any of those men she mentioned, could make their art, I would be happy.

"An artist, huh?"

"I guess," I said. "Although I don't know my way there."

She tapped on my chest. "It's there." She kissed me on the cheek and took my arm, tugging me. "We should get back. You know how they are. They'll all be talking about how we're having an affair. Ahh, it's such an obligation."

"What?"

"To provide them with gossip, silly," she laughed. "I think we do a good job, don't you?"

Sure enough, the next morning, over breakfast, the director from an adjacent county, a close friend of Carole's, noticed how drenched we were, and asked her how well we liked each other. As we walked to our next meeting, Carole took my arm and whispered, "We must not disappoint them." We strode into the plenary session like two birds in love. In our way, we were.

Chapter Eighteen

After work with the rain pouring down, Lou invited me back for dinner. Larry had been asking about me, and I hadn't been there for weeks. When I was at their house, I could erase any pretense of being a director, of having to be an authority. But much as I tried to blot out what happened with Terry, I still wanted those feelings that Larry let me feel to be as natural as taking a breath. What convinced me to go back to their house was also memories of my father's executive friends, who wielded their authority like a sword over everyone. I worried I was falling into the same trap. I didn't want to act like a monarch with sole authority. I wanted to let loose and be some version of myself other than being a boss.

Larry offered me a toke when I arrived at their house. I sat back in a chair and said, "Well, that was good. I just got rid of the director," which was how it felt.

After dinner and after getting stoned, we played hide and seek, which Larry called the ultimate game. We scampered to cubbyholes, under beds, behind doorways, under porches like kids. Nothing more happened that night. But Larry never ceased to amaze me with his uninhibited affection.

A week later, when I went over again, he offered me some hashish. "It's good stuff, dude. You must try it."

We sat on the couch, scrunched next to one another. After

inhaling some, I felt every nerve in my body amplified: the feel of fabric on my leg, the elastic of my watch band on my wrist, my lips against one another—my body like a radio tower with all the signals feeding into it.

"Good stuff, man," he said and put his hand on my thigh. The heat of his hand, even the pulse of his heart, the sound of his voice—everything excited me. He kept rubbing my leg. "Amazing, isn't it?"

"Phew!" I said. "It's almost too much."

Lou said, "You should feel what it's like to make love on this stuff."

"Hey, man," Larry said. "It's normal, the way the body is. It's beautiful. Look." He grabbed my hand and put it on his erection. "See, man, you can't help it. Neither can I. That's the beauty of it. Your whole body goes wham." I was feeling strangely comfortable, unjudged. My body like a sparkler after a match touched its tip. "Good, huh?"

"Yeah," was all I could say.

Lou laughed. "You guys are lucky. When you're aroused, it's all out there. I guess that's penis envy, right?"

Larry said, "Oh, but your body is so much more mysterious."

We let the sensations, waves of them, flow through and around us. He patted my face. "Time for us to head up to bed. You okay?"

"Sure, fine."

I was amazed that he'd touched me and didn't want to make love with me. That wasn't it. He only wanted to celebrate our bodies, how we were wired, and how it pleased him to see that I was like him, and he was like me. He and Lou went up to their room and I listened, once again, to their symphony of love. It was as if they were tutors telling me to let it be, to forget about deviant or non-deviant

Chapter Eighteen

behavior, some aberration in a psychological manual called mental illness. I didn't trust my body and what it really wanted although, lord knows, I wanted to trust it. I would owe it to them if I did finally trust it, I knew, because it would be being like Larry.

The next time I visited, while Lou was fixing dinner, Larry, dressed in jeans and a blue work shirt, rolled two joints, and kneeled in front of me and offered me one.

"Nice," he said. "Now, I'm going to fill your lungs with the next hit and . . . can you do something?"

"What?"

"Just go with me. Let yourself go. Don't think. Don't analyze. You're in your head way too much. Let go of it. Just go with your experience. Okay?"

I nodded. He lit another joint. This time he shimmied between my legs, pressing himself against me. After he took a hit, he put his lips to mine, breathing the smoke into my lungs. I just inhaled, letting it fill me. When he removed his lips from mine, he kept close to me, staring into my eyes like a lover.

That was the thing about Larry. He could be intimate yet at the same time keep his distance. I wondered if he only wanted to let me experience what he experienced or if he wanted more. He never exactly kissed me. He seemed to be bent on teaching me sensuality, letting my body feel what it felt, but made no move to touch me erotically. He held me like a brother. He told me that he liked the way I smelled and wrapped his arms around my waist. I looked into his eyes, seeing in them, a reflection of me. I listened to his breath and noticed the minute movement of his cheeks, his lips, his forehead as he gazed at me. We held onto one another, not saying a word.

He stood. "Good stuff, no?"

"Real good," I replied. "I appreciate you; you know."

He touched my nose with his finger. He stepped back, and shook his head at me, smiling. "The trouble with you, Jason, is you need everything to make sense, to be rational. You lose something special."

"I don't understand. 'Something special'—what's that?"

"Madness, that's what it is. That's the thing most people miss."

"But I don't know if I even want that," I said. "What are you driving at?"

"You seem to pretend to live like a rebel living by yourself. I get that. I like it. The monk by the river. The artist in the cave. Yet you crave being legitimate. You're not free. You're chasing after success."

"Hey," I said. "My friends are not conventional. Ken is a liberal, a Democrat in a Republican town. He may go to church, but he is willing to—"

"But don't you see that if you still want to be accepted by people, any people, if that is what drives you—and this is what is important and what I'm telling you—you are lost. I'm not saying," he said, "you're a homo. I don't think you are any more than I am. But there is a part of you, admit it, that is deviant. This is my one clear thought, the one thing I have wanted to tell you since I met you: if you accept what everyone else thinks, if you strive to be accepted, to be normal, you give up what is special about you. Instead of that, why not go for the wildness? Embrace being mad, being deviant, not fitting in. Go for the wildness in you. Even if you might not always be happy, you'll be pleased with being who you are."

Chapter Eighteen

I fell back on the couch, stunned. What he had said hit me like a punch to my jaw.

He tapped my chest. "Let it sink in. I've been thinking about this for a long time, ever since Lou first met you and told me what you were like."

I put my hands on my thighs. I was shaking. He put his hands on my shoulders. "Hey, it's alright. You don't have to listen to me. I just sensed there is something in you holding you back. That's all. I didn't mean to upset you."

He let go of my shoulders, kissed me on the cheek, stood, and putting out his hand, reached out to me. "Come on. Let's eat."

Throughout dinner, I could still feel his hands on my shoulders and his lips on my lips as if his body had left an afterimage. I ran my fingers across my mouth. He had made love to me without making love; he had entered me, and it seemed I had entered him. He had sensed something in me that I myself couldn't put into words anymore, something I was sure (wasn't I?), that I could dispel.

Larry was right. I was not a wild man. I was a man with a job. I was an administrator. For Larry, sex was sacred and celebratory. I wanted it to be like that for me. What could I do to break out of my need to be legitimate? I wasn't sure, even if I could, if I wanted to break free. What was wrong with being normal? Having a marriage, a son, a respectable life was not so bad. Why did I have to honor the rebel in me? For days, I kept pushing his thoughts away, yet they kept coming back. Not only can love flip a life around, but it can happen in a few hours—or even within a few minutes—with the right person, and can burrow into you, take possession of you, and transform your life.

Chapter Nineteen

The Community Action social worker, Anne Snyder, greeted me at my office. A rumor was swirling about a boy molested at the Petersborough Center by one of the teachers.

Good God, I thought.

I told her that they were rumors, nothing more, and I couldn't comment on them.

She persisted, "We heard the teacher keeps a journal."

I pointed my finger at her. "Anne, this is one issue that you need to drop. The teacher is fine. I met with him. He's doing a good job. Let it go."

"But—"

"Let it go."

She left with a great show of disgust. I was prepared for her questions. But I should have been more prepared. Ken warned me about Anne.

"She's a wonderful lady. She'd give anyone the shirt off her back. Her clients love her. She knows everything about everyone, which can be to your advantage. Work with her closely. She's in your office. But be cautious. Draw a line if she gets too close to anything bad. It will be all over town in the time it takes to strike a match."

She was like the local Associated Press. She regaled me with Pearsall Flats Civil War stories, how the town changed hands more than any other town—at least eight times; how Stonewall Jackson encamped one January in a two-story house on the edge of town; how the Yankees could never keep hold of it. What she must relish telling others about me, I always thought: twenty-eight, still single, living off the grid, having long hair, being alone without a phone for over a month. I feared if she ever got wind of Terry having come to my place, she'd make that my ruin.

My office fronted Main Street (Route 50), across from a Confederate soldier statue. It was the first brick building in town, an ideal place to view the incoming or outgoing traffic and any oncoming storm.

Mid-afternoon, a call came in about a Head Start family. The Heavener house caught fire. A mother and her two children. The mother, severely burned, escaped, but one child had died. The other was in critical condition.

I asked the caller which child survived; she couldn't say.

Jay Heavener had made an indelible impression on me earlier in the year. The one thing I enjoyed most about visiting each center was getting on my knees and playing with the children. Sometimes I acted like the big bad wolf and chased them. Sometimes I played with their blocks, helping them build a tower. I sometimes wondered, on those days, what it might be like to have kids of my own.

On one visit, a boy called me over as soon as I walked into the room, before I could even get down on the floor to play.

"Mr. Follett, come over here, please."

I looked at him: blonde hair, alone with a stuffed bunny rabbit.

"Come over here," he said again.

Chapter Nineteen

The teacher whispered, "That's just like Jay. He likes attention."

I whispered back to her, "I better be going then. I do need to run to a meeting." I called out to him, "Next time, Jay."

"No. Come over here, I want to give you something."

The teacher shrugged her shoulders, and I walked over to him.

"Come down here," he said.

I scrunched down. It was just him and the bunny. What could he have to give me?

He kissed the bunny's nose, and then he touched the bunny's nose to mine. Before I stood up, he also leaned and kissed me on the cheek. Several of the girls seated near him giggled.

"What was that for?" I asked.

He smiled and said, "I love you."

All that day, I kept putting my hand to my cheek and smiling to myself. Here was a kid who, if he loved you, made no bones about it.

Because of Jay, Pearsall Flats Center became my favorite one to visit, to play with the kids, to read them stories, to stay and to eat lunch. Jay was always by my side or in my lap. The teacher cautioned against giving him exclusive attention, but wherever I went, Jay followed. He asked if he could call me by my first name and I told him that he could, (to which the teacher took umbrage). Over many meetings, I built a true bond with him. His unbridled affection seemed to reach out to everyone, even the teacher who pretended indifference, even the cook who fixed him special snacks. He was a special kid.

I snatched up my car keys and told Anne to call the staff of the Pearsall Flats Head Start Center and tell them what happened. As I sped over to the hospital, I prayed that Jay was still alive. As the prayer ran through my mind, I felt guilty. Either way, a child had died. And who was I to ask for it to have been one and not the other? But I couldn't help it.

The hospital was cold. The wind howled though the sliding doors.

The emergency nurse told me the mother and the surviving child were now in the ambulance, waiting to be transported to another facility. I looked at an opened triage doorway where pieces of a charred shirt and a smudged blue blanket lay on the floor. It was Jay's shirt, one he always wore, a bright yellow with red, cross-stitched stripes.

"Where is Jay?" The word caught in my throat.

The nurse looked surprised. "If you're a reporter," she said.

"I'm not a reporter. I'm the Head Start Director. Jay is a student in one of my centers."

"You will need to talk with the doctor."

A gray-haired physician confirmed it: Jay was the child who survived. Jay and his mother had very severe burns, third degree, and were going to be driven to a better facility that could treat them. He said that the other physician on the case was consulting with two regional hospitals, to determine which would be better.

A month before, at the Christmas pageant, Jay had gamboled over the stage, playing one of the goats in a play. His long shaggy blonde hair and impish face gleamed as he hopped on all fours and bleated. The audience roared with laughter.

Another physician, in his thirties, came in and informed the older doctor they were going to Winchester Hospital, but they

Chapter Nineteen

needed to get some paperwork done first.

I said, "Look here, I know the boy and his mother. Can I go out to the ambulance and let them know what is happening? They know me."

The two physicians looked at one another, wincing, "Young man, it's pretty bad. I don't know if you want to do that."

When I insisted, they handed me a surgical mask. The EMT stepped out of the ambulance and also pulled me to the side.

"Listen," she whispered, "It's awful. I don't know if he will make it. Are you sure you want to do this?"

I bit my lip, fighting back what I knew would be tears if I didn't act, "Believe me, ma'am, I do."

I slid into the front seat. I could see the back of Jay's head. His hair, a tawny blonde, short and scraggly as if it had been cut with dull scissors, was nearly burned off. It looked as if it took him an enormous effort to hold up his head. But he lifted his head when he heard me call his name.

His skin was blackened. It had cracked open. The skin beneath was oozing what looked like thick tomato-sauce. His lips were swollen, moist and blackened. Large boils potted his arms, shoulders, and back. He recognized me. His eyes widened ever so slightly.

I wasn't sure what to say. "Your hair was cut."

"No," he whispered, "It burnt off."

As if he were gazing at another world, wanting to find his way back to this world, he looked at me intently. A faint smile. He stared at me, and all I could do was focus on his eyes.

Although his face was charred, his features would come back—there had been progress in the treatment of burns. His expression seemed to plead for me to tell him that he was fine, that they would save him.

This fire would be the test of character that shaped him, formed him, that he would prevail. But I didn't know that. I didn't even know if he could be saved. I blotted those negative thoughts from my mind. I had to think positive things to keep me in the ambulance, to make me believe something I really didn't believe.

He asked, "Jason, where did the lady go?"

"She'll be back. Just left for a moment. They're going to drive you and your mom to a hospital that can really help you."

He dropped his head down again. I looked at his mother, Alice, who was on the stretcher beside him. She was quiet; a dark distance seemed to surround her. She could barely look at Jay, only giving him fleeting glances. Her leg was strapped in a splint; her hands and arms were bandaged. She said, "I sure hope they hurry. I hope they can get my son to the hospital."

The ambulance door swung open. The EMT needed to get back in, scooting by me as I stepped out. She held a needle. She needed to give him another shot. Jay's head sagged. He screamed, a low faint wail of someone who can barely open his mouth, someone gagging on something too large for him to swallow.

How much pain, I wondered, *can he endure?*

The ambulance sped off, sirens blaring. Through the window, I could see the EMT, who had moved into my seat, holding his head up.

I walked off to the side of the hospital. The wind lashed at the pines; the snow, still thick and steep in the ravine, made the landscape looked incongruously white in contrast to Jay's charred skin.

Chapter Nineteen

I went back to the office. I couldn't be alone. Anne fixed me a coffee. After I sat in my chair, she asked, "Are you alright?"

"Sure."

"You want to hear what happened?"

I leaned back in my chair, told her what I'd seen. How Jay looked. Wiping tears from her eyes, Anne, in turn, told me the story.

The Heavener home was a tinderbox down a muddy, rutted road set beside trailers and other shabby houses. A three-story, unpainted structure, it had dried out so badly the clapboard had pulled away from the frame, curled, and left gaps that were stuffed with paper and cardboard.

"Unkempt," Anne said. "Run-down and old."

I didn't tell Anne I'd been to the house once. That wasn't how I would describe it. I made a point of visiting as many homes as I could. Yes, the house was nestled along the far side of the river outside of town. Yes, I could feel the wind through the windows. But, the rooms, jammed with furniture, old cloth chairs and couches, had a homey, lived-in feel. Alice had pasted different red-and-green Christmas wrapping paper on some walls.

Anne told me to drink some of the coffee and pulled Danish out of a brown bag. "Here, have some of this. It will make you feel better." She pulled her chair beside my desk and explained how the fire started.

Jay was playing with his younger sister, Lynn, while Alice got supper started. Lynn was dressed up as a princess in one of Alice's old skirts. Jay found a box of matches and lit one and Lynn must have gotten too close. Her skirt caught fire. Jay tried to pat it out, but Lynn broke away from him, screaming for her mommy, swatting at the flames herself. She ran desperately around the room, igniting curtains, upholstery, and wallpaper.

Once the furniture caught fire, the wind, gusting through the house, caused the fire to build and to leap from room to room.

Jay chased Lynn through the front hall, its narrow corridor, and into the kids' playroom. His mother followed, screaming for her daughter to stop. By the time she could grab Lynn, it was like taking hold of a torch. Alice threw an Afghan over her, but her daughter, hysterical, twisted free. It all happened in a matter of seconds.

I asked Anne how she knew all this. She told me Alice, distraught, had told a neighbor about it as they were waiting for an ambulance. Why couldn't she save her? Why?

With the downstairs engulfed in flames, the heat and smoke pressing against them, Alice and Jay watched Lynn thrash once more, fall to her knees and collapse.

By then, Jay's shirt and hair had caught fire. His mother grabbed him and flung a blue blanket around him, smothering the fire and screamed, "Stop it. Please, God. Stop it."

Jay called out, "Mommy, mommy are we gonna die?"

His question saved them. It gave Alice the strength to get them out. The flames rattled the house. The front hallway was consumed in flames. Alice grabbed Jay in her arms and bolted with him up the stairwell to her bedroom and slammed the door. Wood crackled and snarled like rifle shots. The bedroom door shuddered. The smoke unbearable, seeping snakelike through the slats. Jay was coughing and calling out "Mommy, Mommy," pressing his body against her. She picked up a lamp from the bed stand and smashed the window. There was a momentary hush, then she felt the cool air and a shift in air pressure. Like a vortex, a blast of air swept in, then out the window, almost knocking her over. She heard a roar. Flames shot through the door.

Chapter Nineteen

There was a snowbank from snow cascading off the roof. Alice scooped Jay up, leaned and dropped him out the window. He smacked into the snowbank and tumbled into the yard. Then she leapt herself. Her ankle snapped on impact, but she picked up her son and hobbled to the roadside.

Several neighbors gathered and covered them with blankets. Someone called 911. Before the sirens arrived, the house exploded into flames, the windows blasted out, the roof imploded. Alice called out, there was another child inside. There was nothing they could do. The firemen arrived and hosed it. But it was ashes—like a matchbox that had consumed itself.

The ambulance sped them to the hospital. Jay's father who worked at the State Highway Department was out in a truck. A neighbor called his office. He drove to the house, thinking he could salvage something.

He wandered about wreckage, dumbfounded, repeating, "I can't do nothing. I can't do nothing."

I couldn't listen anymore.

Anne sipped her coffee and mused, "You know this will make the news. I bet they cover it."

I sighed. "Yeah, I'm sure it will."

I thought about Jay who was now in the ambulance, sirens blaring, blisters on his back, his charred face, in shock with pain.

One unanswerable question came to me: Why him?

I wanted to hope that he would miraculously recover—that God had made a dreadful mistake. That it was wrong. I felt as if a vortex of feelings had swept me and dragged me in a dizzy swirl.

"My God," Anne said. "You're crying. Look at you. Just look at you."

"Oh, shut up," I laughed. "What of it?" I needed time to think. I stood up, grabbed my coat, walked out the door, and went down the street, past stores with post-Christmas sales. The winds, and now sleet, lashed down the street. It wouldn't give up. It was like the night, years before, when I'd heard Reverend Martin Luther King Jr. had been shot and all I could do was repeat was one word, No, No, No. All I could do was wait, hoping that what happened had not happened, could never happen, but it did.

When I came back, Anne told me the regional hospital in Winchester couldn't treat them. Too severe. They were on their way to a burn center, clear across the state, in Morgantown. Would Jay survive another ninety miles? Why did the local hospital send him to a hospital that couldn't treat him? Did it come down to his being poor with no insurance?

I seethed. Anne offered to take me out, to buy me dinner. It was her way of being thoughtful, but I told her, "Maybe tomorrow."

I had the number of the burn center. I told her I'd wait and see if they made it there. She told me to call her once I found out.

I stayed at my desk well over two hours. Called the hospital several times. Wind rattled the windows.

The cleaning lady came in, asked, "May I clean up?" and I looked at her—a large woman, nearly six-feet tall with broad shoulders, large hands, pink nail polish, and a gentle, husky voice. She looked very stylish like someone going out on the town, not someone working late at night.

She said, "Honey, you look like you could use a good hug. Come here."

She wrapped her arms around me and patted me gently. She wore

Chapter Nineteen

a lavender-smelling perfume. I didn't cry, although I wanted to.

In the arms of a stranger, I did feel comforted. She made no fuss. She told me, "It will work out alright, honey. Trust me, Orlando knows. I just know it will be alright." Then she emptied the trash bin, vacuumed the rug, and dusted the desks, all the time gazing sympathetically at me, repeating, "It's okay, honey. It's real sad. It is."

Through the fog of my grief, understanding dawned. This large cleaning woman was the Orlando in Terry's story, the one who had the parties of the underworld that haunted my imagination. I didn't feel repelled by her. She was genuine. Her comfort was a welcome consolation.

Three days later during a violent snowstorm, I arrived with Jay's father—Junior—and his grown son from another marriage—Roger—at the West Virginia University Burn Center. At the last minute, I changed my work schedule and offered to drive them. I wanted to see Jay who was stable but still in critical condition.

A physician greeted us. He gave us masks, white gowns, and sterile gloves. He cautioned us to be upbeat, encouraging, and to keep our emotions in check. Jay needed us to be positive.

Junior went first. I watched him, through the window in the door, stand at the end of Jay's bed. Jay's face looked blubbery yet slack. Junior stayed ten minutes, talked with a nurse, leaned over his son, whispered something, and left.

I followed him back out to the waiting area. He stared at the floor and said to me, "I couldn't take it. I didn't realize . . ." He told me that Jay asked him to kiss him. "Like how he always asks for a kiss when I leave off to work in the morning." His body jerked as he sobbed and talked. Roger put his hand on his father's neck and rubbed his back tenderly.

Junior told me, "Go see him. He wants to see you. I've got to see my wife, let her know he will be okay." He stopped himself, then bit his lip, "He will be okay, won't he?"

I nodded.

Father and son went to the elevator and pushed the button.

I slipped the mask over my face.

When I entered Room 217, Jay was propped up in bed. His face glistened with white cream. His mouth was turned upward, twisted oddly. His eyes and face were disguised in wrinkled skin. He gasped briefly as if catching his breath, then wailed—a high-pitched ululation like a cat—then became quiet. The white sheets had blotches of red on them.

He nodded when he saw me. I started talking immediately. He said nothing. I showed him a Beatrix Potter book I had bought him and put it on the table by the bed. I felt awkward. My hands were shaking. I was not a member of the family. The doctor has said only family members were allowed to visit. I moved my chair to the side of the bed and read him the story, showing him the pictures.

When I finished, he managed to ask me one question, through the cream and the gauze. "What happened?" I could have cried. I understood, then, that he didn't remember. I told him about the fire, and how I had seen him at the hospital. I pointed to the bottles of liquid, the stint in his forearm, explaining how the liquid was helping to make him better and the shots that the nurses gave him would fight infections. He listened, blinked his eyes and muttered

Chapter Nineteen

something. He lifted one hand and pointed. He wanted to watch TV. I turned it on.

A nurse came in the room, conferred with the attendant who had admitted me and briskly marched over to me.

"May I ask who you are?" she asked.

I had to think fast, or the visit was over.

"Well?"

Jay spoke up, "He's my buddy."

I smiled and repeated, "Yes, I'm his buddy."

She leaned into me, tapping me on the shoulder, "Look, I don't know who you are, sir, but I haven't seen him act this enthusiastic since he arrived, so stay awhile." She winked and left.

Sitting beside him while he watched, I noticed thick, dark nodules of bluish-red skin on his neck. Then I realized they were his blood vessels throbbing. His blood was working hard to flush out the toxins.

Did he remember the last moments with his sister? Had anyone told him what happened to her? Had anyone hugged him? Could you hug him? What was he thinking? Questions chased around in my head.

I had to do something for him. But what?

When the show ended, he pointed to the book again. It was about a bunny that sneaked under the fence and grabbed a carrot. I read it once more. I talked with him about Pearsall Flats, the kids in the Center. I pulled from my jacket pocket a big card that other kids had signed and showed it to him, then propped it on the nightstand. He asked for water. His hands, bandaged like a mummy's, lay beside him as if they didn't belong to him. There was a water bottle on the stand with a plastic straw and I put the straw to his mouth. He took a long sip. He asked me to read about the bunny rabbit the third time. He began to cough, deep raspy coughs, and I grabbed some tissues on a stand nearby and caught the gooey, black globs in it.

The nurse came. "Go ahead. You are doing fine. Let him drink. Let him cough it up."

I gave him water, and he coughed. He hacked violently, his whole body shaking. The phlegm was putrid, sooty, a viscous liquid the color of ash.

Several more nurses gathered in the doorway. I felt uncomfortable, thinking I must be doing something wrong. I began to perspire, partly from the mask, partly from anxiety.

Which of them knew I was not family? I smiled weakly at them, but they couldn't see my face.

I stood and offered, "If you need me to go, that's alright."

The head nurse came forward and pulled me aside.

"Listen," she said, "Whatever you are doing is a miracle. He has been unwilling to drink anything. His lungs are congested. The antibiotics have kept him alive, but he must have the will to live. He needs to drink. Stay as long as you like. You're bringing him back to life."

She cupped her hands over my hand and squeezed it. There were tears in her eyes.

I stayed for several hours, watched the nurses change the dressings, explaining to Jay, as best I knew, what they were doing and how it would help him. He continued to drink, and I read the story more times than I could remember. When I decided I must go—hearing on the TV news the storm had let up slightly—I told him I would be back. One nurse stayed in the room.

"Give me a kiss before you go," Jay asked.

I looked apprehensively at the nurse. She nodded and turned away.

Chapter Nineteen

I lifted my mask, kissed him on the forehead very lightly.

Jay asked, "Please kiss me again."

I said, "I can't, Jay. I might infect you. We must be careful."

I looked at the nurse. She said, "You can with your mask on."

I asked Jay if that was alright.

He said, "Okay." He seemed content and settled back on the pillow.

On the drive back, I thought about how he had reached out to me that first day at the center, told me before I even knew him, that he loved me, and now, at his worst, came back to life with me beside him. I felt for him as a father might for his child. It was a love that had a tenderness to it and yet had a depth, too. The words of the Potter book played on a loop in my mind, and I let them take me away.

I drove back to the office. It was a weekday, and walking in, I realized I hadn't given anyone a heads up that I would be gone all morning and, as it turned out, most of the day. As soon as I walked in, Lou informed me that Ken wanted to meet with me. It was urgent.

Ken, normally soft-spoken and circumspect, a man who prided himself on his composure, was irate. He said that staff members were mad that I had missed two morning meetings when others were working, to visit a boy from another Center. "Even in extenuating circumstances," he said. "it's the worst time of the year to disappear."

I listened to him. I explained that I was helping a Head Start parent who didn't have transportation and that it was a medical emergency that I thought fit into my responsibility as the director.

He patted me on the knee, "Jason, this world is full of nuts. You know it; I know it. The fact is it's well beyond your job description, although, I agree, it was a good thing to do. Don't get me wrong. It's just that there were some emergencies here too, and at other Centers. We have so many kids here. No one knew where you were."

"I don't feel like giving in to their petty concerns," I countered.

He scrunched his mouth to one side, and leaned forward. "I think I can be straight with you as a friend and as your boss. In the larger scheme of things, yes, you're right. If, say, you were a minister—"

I jumped in. "Don't start with that."

"Hey, let me finish. It would be noble. But, right now, you are a director of a program with multiple centers. What you still don't get is that you are still new, an outsider. They play up to you—you're the new Head Start Director, the guy with his hands on the money—but they're waiting for you to screw up. And, I'll be frank, you did. You need to hear me: you didn't inform anyone. You should have called me or Carole. You didn't even tell your secretary. What were you thinking? You don't have a leg to stand on."

"An outsider," I said. "I don't think about that."

"This is a southern town."

He had me pegged. Most of my life I had scoffed at the authorities. Now I WAS The Authority. Now I was the one who people expected to act like a director. I was accountable. I needed to tell people where I was and what I was doing.

I shook Ken's hand and agreed to take the day as a personal day; it wasn't worth the fight.

"Thanks for being straight with me," I said.

"One more thing," he said. "You know our friend David Bridewell, pretty well, don't you?"

Chapter Nineteen

I must have startled because Ken laughed and put up one hand. "No, no, not anything to worry you. You hang around with him, though?"

"At the parties," I said. "I go to his place on occasion. We listen to his Wagner collection. Why do you ask?"

"He's well known in Mooresville. Him and his aunt, the one who died, have been active in Community Action—supporters. Advocates."

"I think I knew that. That's good."

"It is and it isn't."

"Why is that?"

"He likes to tell stories. True, untrue, doesn't matter."

"I know," I said, "only too well."

He patted me on the back. "Good." He laughed, "There are a lot of strange people out there. Be careful with him." He put his finger to his lips. "Better safe than sorry. We're always learning. Just watch your step as a word of caution."

I drove home wondering if David had talked to Ken about me. Most likely he did, or Ken would not have warned me. It had been a very, very long day, and I was tired.

Chapter Twenty

On Friday, later that week, having learned that Jay was breathing better, I sent him several children's books and a long letter. I returned to the lodge after work, hoping to enjoy time alone to do some reading and writing. When I pulled into the driveway, however, I found four cars parked and had to squeeze mine into a space near my apartment. Music was playing from the lodge building. Lights illuminated the windows on the second floor. A note was taped to my door. I pulled it off, went in, sat on my couch, and read it, written in a long-looping scroll.

Dear Mr. Follett,
You are invited for dinner. Doug asked us to give you this
Special invitation. It's at 6.
See you then!

—The Boys

It was 5:30. I stretched out on the couch, Toby up on my chest, and closed my eyes. A strong bass beat throbbed through the walls.

I kept thinking about Jay, his skin peeling off, his hands, curled, shrunken as if he'd stuck them in acid.

Someone called, "Hello, you there?"

It was Doug. He was standing at the doorway, tapping on the window. I got up and unlocked the porch door.

"My boy, so good to see you!" he said.

"Yeah, thanks," I said.

"Something wrong?"

"Long week."

"Oh, so sorry," he said. He patted me on the back and changed the topic. "I need a favor. A big one."

I sat back on the couch, and he joined me. "I have a bit of a problem. You see I've invited some friends—we did talk about this, remember?—and I thought it would be a perfect weekend, you know, having my friends here, being free to . . . . Well, you know. Angel is visiting her relatives. I decided to have a little party while she is away. You know, friends. Everyone is here. You'll love them. Artists. An opera singer. Dears, really. I so looked forward to having them here, some me-time, if you know what I mean and—"

"Get to the point, Doug," I said, knowing how he could babble on without any thread of coherence. "I'm tired, Doug. It has been a long week. So please just let me know what you want."

"Yes, yes. Thank you," he said and turned stone-faced. "It's a slight problem. My son, you've met him, Jan, the one who's at Georgetown, called to let me know he's coming down. A surprise. I didn't have the heart."

"Here, tonight?"

"Afraid so."

"Does he know?" I asked scooting back from him.

"Well, not really. That's where you come in. I don't think it would be wise to have him stay in the main lodge. I figure he could stay here, sleep on your couch. I imagine he'll be heading back tomorrow sometime. If not, maybe he could."

"Jeez, that's."

Chapter Twenty

"I didn't have the heart to tell him not to come. He loves it down here. He wanted to surprise me. Angel probably told him I'd be lonely here. And so, I told him, sure and . . ." patting the couch, ". . . he could sleep right here. I have sheets, a pillow, and blanket. He'll be fine. He's in college. He surely has met, you know, some . . ."

"You think so?"

"In Georgetown? He's a big boy now. I imagine he's met a few. Could you put him up for the night?"

"No, no way," I said. "It has been a rough week. I just . . ."

"Please," he said.

"Doug, I . . ."

"Please, I really need your help."

His cheeks had fallen, the distress crept into his eyes.

"Shit. Alright. But you owe me. When is he coming?"

Doug looked at his watch. "Anytime now. I told the boys—that's what they call themselves—'Doug's Boys,' to tone it down. You know. And just act as they would at work. Keep it straight. They know how to do that. They have to. They'll be good. It should be fine, really."

Half an hour later, Jan arrived. Only nineteen, full of himself, a strapping young man with dusty reddish hair, I watched him drive in. As planned, I intercepted him and told him that his dad had some unexpected guests, friends, and wanted me to let him know he could stay in the apartment.

Jan cocked his head to the side. "Is there something you're trying to tell me?"

I must have hesitated because he quickly added. "Okay, what's up?" A pre-law student, he already had a lawyer's savvy. Even carried the leather briefcase of a lawyer.

"It's just that some of them are artists. A little on the fringe."

As Jan greeted everyone with smiles, I hovered by his side, and along with him, shaking hands, acting as a chaperone. He seemed comfortable—initially. His being at ease surprised me. He went around to each of the guests, shook their hands, and told them who he was as if trying to impress a jury. As he observed the men who, I realized, were strangers to him, he became more self-conscious.

In a few minutes, Jan lighted next to me and stayed there. I was his protector. He engaged me in conversation about college, his girlfriend, and summer plans. The two of us were sequestered on the couch in a bubble of our own while the other men chatted in groups of two or three. I could see that "Doug's Boys" had a keen interest in Jan's wide-eyed, freckled boyishness, but were, as Doug had asked them, being good. Some would come by and chat with us. We are acting in a play entitled "We Are Straight" and everyone knew their lines.

As the night wore on, I learned that Doug's Boys consisted of two couples and two unattached strays. One couple, Dominique, a powerfully built Black man, a decorator, and Alan, a scrawny white man, dressed conventionally, and unstylishly in slacks, a button-down shirt. Another couple had flamboyant outfits—stultifying colors like an advertisement for stereotypical gay men: pink jeans, open collar, frilly shirts with necklaces, rings galore, and bracelets. Another guest, an opera singer with a booming voice, wore a subdued black outfit that hid his enormous bulk.

One man arrived late. A sleek professional dancer in cut offs

Chapter Twenty

that exposed most of his legs. He pranced into the room and introduced himself as Stephon. His femininity had no bounds. His hands fluttered like wings of a bird. Since he hadn't been warned to play it straight, he flung himself at me and at Jan, pawing us, saying how gorgeous we were. Were we brothers? Where were we from?

He would have kept on, but Doug hustled him to the kitchen where he was told to toe the line.

The rest of Doug's Boys acted their best as if nothing was going on. They acted as if someone had shackled them in straightjackets, joining in our conversation, hovering around, eyeing each other, rolling their eyes when one of them stepped out of line.

Jan never left my side—an imprinted puppy.

During dinner, as the wine made its way around the table, the casual talk about Nixon and the useless war drifted into show business and, since several of the boys were professional actors, the conversation veered into bawdy stories about one or another affair of a Rock Hudson and other closeted gay actors. Having had a few glasses of wine, Doug made no attempt to steer the talk back to more conventional topics. In fact, as he drank, he let down his guard. His hands flipped wildly about in ways I'd never seen before, and he spoke with a distinct lisp. It was almost as if, by being with other gay men, their gayness had freed David to be like one of them, uninhibited.

At first Jan seemed bemused, not making eye contact with his dad, attempting to ignore the other men, listening while shoving his peas into his potatoes.

Doug offered Jan wine, "Come on, son, give it a try. You're old enough."

"He sure is!" piped in the opera singer.

"Oh, honey, he's one ripe tomato!" rejoined Stephon, ruffling his hand in Jan's hair.

Jan blushed.

Stephon said, "It's alright hon', I just love red hair."

"I remember that age," Alan said. "How old are you honey?"

Jan muttered, "19."

"My God, I got my cherry burst on my nineteenth birthday," cried out Stephon. "He was the starting fullback and, I can tell you, it was first-and-ten-do-it-again until we both reached the goal line. He knew how to use it. Yes, he did!"

A burst of laughter rippled across the table.

"First and ten, to his burst cherry!"

Doug went to get another bottle of wine, stopping as he went to kiss Stephon on his neck. He acted as if it was natural as his kissing his wife.

Jan's fork scraped the plate. His ears had turned a beet red. Several of the men glanced over at him. Dominique, the black man from the mixed couple, looked at me oddly.

Stephon stood up, came behind Jan, placed his hand on his back, "Have we offended you, honey?"

Jan stiffened. His fork fell to the plate. He looked up at everyone. All eyes were on him.

Stephon, not sure what to say next, tried to lighten the moment, "Listen, honey, if you want to, you can bust my cherry anytime!"

Everyone laughed, including Doug who said, "Oh, you must be better behaved. Just stop that."

But before Stephon could respond, Jan's chair shot back, nearly

Chapter Twenty

knocking Stephon over, and Jan bolted from the room.

Doug cried out, "What did I say?"

Dominique, his face grim, signaled with his eyes for me to follow Jan. I pushed myself back from the table, "Excuse me."

Doug grabbed me by the arm, his eyes teary. "I'm afraid I made a mess of things," he said. "Can you talk with him?"

I pressed my hands on his shoulder. "Have you told him?"

The room was quiet. I saw the others, some holding their napkins, most bowing their heads, not sure what to say or to do.

"No," Doug said. "I figured he was old enough to figure it out."

I followed. Jan stood on the far side of the porch, leaned against one of the pillars and stared at the empty sky.

"You can come to my room if you want," I offered.

He turned around, tears in his eyes. Much to my surprise, he grabbed ahold of me and sobbed. I gingerly put my arms around him, patting his back. I held onto him for several minutes while he cried. When he calmed down, I steered him into my room. I sat him on the couch and drew him a glass of water. I sat next to him. He sipped.

"I didn't know," he said.

"He's gay."

"Yeah."

He rubbed his forehead and shook his head, his hand pausing on the side of his face, the shock setting in.

"It's a lot to take in," I offered. "I'm sure this isn't how he wanted you to find out. I'm sure he wanted to explain it sooner or later, but, right now, well, I suspect he's as confused as you are about what to do, since, you know, he has his friends and he's—"

He looked at me desperately. "But why did he invite me here with them?"

Not sure what to say because I didn't know any better than he did, except that Doug was a guy who didn't like to say no to anyone, even if it cost him heavily, I told him, "Maybe he just thought you would be alright, that you're old enough to know."

We talked for an hour. He asked questions; I offered answers. He wanted to know how his dad knew them, and I explained that gay men, particularly men in the arts, had ways of finding one another. As I talked with him, I thought about how difficult it would be for anyone to come out, how others might act, how it could destroy a relationship, stain it forever. The more I thought about coming out, the more abhorrent it felt to me.

After an hour, Doug came to the door and stood there, looking in the windowpane. He couldn't look directly at his son, so he looked at me, his eyes plaintive, beseeching, seeming to want my assurance.

I gave him a weak smile and said, "Come in, Doug, have a seat." I stood to go out, leaving them alone for what I figured would be an intense father-son talk, but Jan grabbed my hand and pulled me back down into my chair.

We sat for several minutes looking at each other, the floor, our hands, feet, or the books on the shelves. Finally, Jan spoke up. "Dad, why didn't you tell me?"

With a fearful look in his eyes, Doug said, "Son, it's hard to explain because . . ." he trailed off, ". . . because, well, it is hard for me to admit to myself. I was afraid I might lose you."

Jan began to sob again. Doug sat immobilized in his chair. I put my arm over Jan's shoulder. Eventually, Doug scooted over and put

Chapter Twenty

his hands on his son's leg.

"I don't want to be this way," Doug said. "I wanted to spare you."

"But we're family," Jan blurted out.

Doug started to cry. His face tightened up. His eye wrinkles deepened. His mouth sagged. He looked old and ashen, as if life had been drawn out of him.

"I know," he said. "I've let you down."

Jan hugged his knees and rocked back and forth. Doug rocked, too, head down, reaching to rub his son's arm reassuringly.

"What Jan wants to know, I think," I interceded, "is if you still love his mom and you will still be family. Or is this . . ."

"Yes, yes, of course. I love your mother dearly, and she knows—yes, yes, she knows, has known a long time—and none of it matters to her or to me because, son, you are what matters to us."

I stepped into the kitchen to let them talk by themselves. I thought about my father, what he might say if I ever admitted I was gay. I winced, felt a knot in my stomach. I hoped it would never come to that. I could keep to the straight and narrow. I could stay being an artist. That was enough. Yes: I could both defy my father's expectations of me and remain in that bored, seemingly endless, pool of men called normal while living, as Wallace Stevens, another life entirely.

At the end of their conversation, they hugged. Jan left, admitting he couldn't stay overnight, not now, not with them. That was the word he used, "them," as if it signified something disgusting. I walked him to his car, hugged him, and watched him drive off.

River Crossed

After Jan left, with all the other men drinking in another room, Doug curled up on the couch. He wanted my assurance it would be alright to tell Jan about his frustrating sexual life with his mother. I assured him it was not. He should keep that to himself. He wanted assurance that he had listened to his son's concerns, and I assured him that he had done his best.

"Angel's going to kill me," he said. "Once she finds out about this, she will be livid. I dread the day. I wish I could erase it. My, my, I screwed this up, didn't I?"

"Yes, you did," I said.

"No sympathy from you."

"You hurt him, Doug."

"I know."

I carried him to the glass sliding doors of the main lodge. Stephon came out, took him from me, put his shoulder under Doug's arm, and lugged him up to his bedroom.

The men asked me to join them for a drink. They regretted making a scene and apologized. Dominique, the decorator, whose partner had gone to bed, sat by me and handed me a glass of wine. He asked what happened.

I felt strangely exhilarated to be, for the first time in my life, among people who were gay. There was no supposing. They were gay.

"How are you?" Dominique said. "I mean it must have been difficult with his son and all."

I told him that I felt conflicted, sympathetic but irritated to be the intermediary, put on the spot, not sure what I could do to help the kid, after all, and sure that I couldn't absolve Doug from what happened.

These men didn't fit the stereotype of what I thought an evening

Chapter Twenty

of gay men would be like. They had such a range of personalities from shy to laid-back to downright outrageous. I enjoyed being with them because I didn't wonder, as I did with straight men—or men who acted straight—that, if I glanced too long at their bodies—as I now found myself looking at Dominique's—if they'd suspect I was queer. They were queer. They did eye me, checking me out. It felt good knowing that they were interested in me not as a competitor but as an attractive man.

For a moment, I wasn't fighting with myself, but that didn't last long.

I found myself saying inside my head that I was not one of them. A rising tide of feelings—I should; no, I shouldn't; I'm not, I am—pressed on me, receding and extending farther and farther inside of me, only to pull back, drain out of me, and leave me stranded in between, neither here nor there, feeling good at one moment, confused another, then frightened, terrified, and, as I drank more, indifferent and strangely relaxed. It was all still as new to me as it had been for Jan.

When the conversation wound down, when I got up to head back to my apartment, they each offered me a hug. Dominique followed me outside. He asked if I wanted company. I turned to face him. His hand was on his hip. My arms were at my side like a soldier at attention, afraid of letting down my guard. We were the same height, same weight; we matched. His face was angelic, round, kind, expressive. His lips, moist and tender, touched mine. He didn't press, didn't force, didn't impose himself. Flesh met flesh as if testing the waters. I closed my eyes. His flank pressed into mine, very still, letting me respond as I would. I gave way to his entreaties in a mutual arousal.

How had he known?

How had I signaled him?

The way my eyes lingered longer than they should? Having drunk more than I should, did I entreat him to follow me?

The moon loomed large over the willows across the river. We flowed like the river, now faintly audible down the embankment, under the moonlight, melting into desire. This stranger whom I'd barely spoken to knew I was attracted to him enough to follow me to the porch. My heart hammered in my chest. It felt as if it might explode. I could feel myself wanting him, and not wanting him, smelling the wine, his musk, feeling his body, the whole of it against mine. Letting go of his arms, I pushed him away and told him, "Not now" although my body was screaming, "now, now, now."

"You sure?" He turned his hand upward toward me, the pink underside sweet and desirable.

"Yes."

"Wait," he said.

I stopped, my hand already on the doorknob.

"Don't run away from yourself, Jason."

"I'm . . ." I wanted to tell him I wasn't, but I was confused. He didn't say, "Run away from me." He said, 'from yourself.'

What did he mean? Did he say it wrong?

I felt like weeping and stood silently looking at him. Willowy, his legs set apart, his eyes with a quietness like that of water in an eddy, clear and welcoming, pleaded with me. I felt his body had become magnetic pulling me toward him, while my body pleaded,

Chapter Twenty

"Please let me go."

His hands turned down and fell to his sides.

I closed the door and locked it. I stared at the lock, thought about how, if I wanted, I could just flip it back open. I couldn't fathom how I'd fallen in love with him in the stretch between the main lodge and my room. I felt more exposed than ever before.

Did I have to accept, as I did when I was with them, that they were not unlike me? Could I, as when I was with Larry, let the part of me I could control out to play and still put it back after that? Was there, as Larry said, a wildness inside me that wanted to be out? Or was I just deceiving myself? For much of my life, I'd managed to keep up appearances, to dress like my dad, to be an athlete, to act normal, to date girls, to be straight. But now, far from Illinois, not bound by my parents' expectations, in a completely different world where I had to make my own way, where the old props were no longer there, I felt vulnerable, exposed, out-of-control, not myself, not the way I should be. What was dangerous was that—I saw now—something larger, more encompassing was forcing me to rethink who I was. It was a potential for new love. If I let that in, if I unlatched the door, I worried I would never come back to being normal.

A memory of my mother came to me. Her out beyond the white caps at Jones Beach, swimming back and forth, suspended there against the horizon, her arms lifting and her head dipping and turning, and how it seemed, when she was a solitary figure in the blue, she'd never come back and would keep swimming as if it were her destiny, and she would be lost to us forever.

Chapter Twenty-One

Jay graduated from intensive care and started rehabilitation. His mother, Alice, moved with him, to a room next to his. They were doing well. But without insurance, the state wouldn't cover rehab long-term. The best they would offer: a visiting nurse to home care to train them in a few sessions to do physical therapy with Jay. Alice was recovering well from her burns, and she could walk without crutches. So, mother and son returned home at the same time to a small trailer Junior had purchased on the outskirts of town.

When they came back, I arranged to see them one day after work. It was selfish of me, though. At least when I was with Jay, I could put aside what happened with Dominique.

Alice welcomed me inside. Jay ran, limping, into my arms. He wanted me to play with him, so I sat on the floor. Alice sat on the couch and told me the nurse wanted her to stretch Jay's fingers. They were laced with scar tissue that prohibited movement. They needed to be stretched. Jay picked up a truck. I studied his hand, like a claw, raw pink skin marbled with white scar tissue. He could pick up the truck, but his stick-like fingers moved like chopsticks.

"We can't do it," Alice admitted. "I know myself"—she showed me her hand—"it's mighty hurtful to do anything, and the poor boy cries and fusses so. I just can't bear to see him in more pain. The lady who comes does some of it, but Jay runs from her. She wants us to do it twice a day."

Jay's blue eyes fixed on me. I opened my mouth and then thought better of it. Alice had lost one child, saw her burn to death. To watch Jay suffer was too much, too much to ask.

I tried to cajole him into doing the exercises, to squeeze the ball, pretending it was a magical stone, and he tried, attempting to please me, but soon, wailed, and cried, "I can't no more!" He stomped out of the room, his arms folded across his chest.

Alice said pointedly, "See? He's willful."

A week later, an official complaint arrived at Head Start from the Department of Human Services. Jay's parents were being charged with neglect. I had to attend a hearing and give testimony. I consulted with Ken who hired an agency lawyer to give us advice.

I told the lawyer that yes, technically, Jay wasn't getting proper treatment and, yes, the family hadn't complied but for good reason. The lawyer was attentive. I told him that I couldn't afford to lose the trust of the family. Clearly, I felt compromised.

The lawyer laughed at me, "Couldn't afford?" he said. "Young man, whom do you think is being compromised? That kid has no future—and you know it—if he doesn't get the proper help. His parents need to pick up the ball and run with it. What good is he without the use of two good hands?"

Too much was happening too quickly. Much of it I wanted to avoid. I steeled myself for the hearing, scheduled for later in the month. I tried, not successfully, to blot out Dominique's words, "Don't run away from yourself."

Chapter Twenty-One

I visited Carole's office, stayed late, had dinner with her, enjoyed being a part of her family. Even as a Pentecostal with a mind of her own, she enjoyed an evening at a bar, where we went after work, getting a booth at the far end to avoid being seen. She joked, "Lead me unto temptation," and clicked her mug against my glass. I felt frenetic, but she told me that, whatever happened, I'd done my best.

One night, on the way back to my place, I stopped in to see David's place. We went to a bar in Mooresville and listened to his plans to move to Italy where he could, as it called it, "play the field." In a few weeks, I was drinking too much, even by myself. Nothing seemed to be right. All my balanced, orderly life felt wobbly. I couldn't reconcile what I wanted to be with what I was.

I found myself unleashing on David. All my stored-up disgust with how he had used Enrique. I told him it wasn't right what he was doing to him.

"Not right?" David said.

"Don't you get it?" I asked. "He's only eighteen. He is practically a minor."

"Get off your high horse, Jason," he said and smiled. "Hey, we all have our different takes. Wait until you're my age. I bet you'll be thinking differently."

I wondered, after I left, if I'd been trying to convince myself to quit feeling as I was feeling. I couldn't change David. The best I could do was to change myself. I had an urge to run away, really run away, quit the job, get out of Pearsall Flats, and escape.

When Tess called and invited me to come to Washington, D.C., I jumped at the opportunity.

Tess, who had come to my place several times in recent weeks, bringing records I should hear and staying long enough to hear them after dinner, had invited me to see "Giselle," a ballet about a nobleman who falls in love with a peasant. I had never seen a ballet.

"This is opening night, so wear your Sunday best," she told me. I packed my best suit and tie, shined my shoes, and drove to D.C.

We met at her suite, overlooking the National Mall.

She was svelte in a purple and black dress that made her appear taller, thinner, and younger than she was. We rode in a limo. She loved the good life, the arts, wanted to enjoy them with someone—Jerome hated ballet—and I seemed the right man to appreciate the night life of Washington.

In the lobby of the Kennedy Center for the Performing Arts, I felt like a peasant boy in the company of the noble class: women in lush dresses, beautiful, graceful, picking up their skirts as they ascended the plush, red-carpeted stairs, women who were used to being seen and knew they were worth seeing. And men in tuxedos and waistcoats who carried champagne glasses in their hands, never spilling a drop, who knew how to act elegantly and believed everyone admired them.

Tess introduced me to several couples who asked me what I did. When I told them, they were gracious, telling me how nice it was that I helped the poor. Lord knows they need it.

With seats in the fourth row, I could see the dancers up close. I watched as the male dancers leapt like a buck, suspended over the stage, their legs in their tight leggings, their arms extended. I imagined

Chapter Twenty-One

one of them reaching out to me, pulling me into his arms, and carrying me off as he did one of the maidens. When they landed, their footfalls were barely audible. Lighter than air.

After the first act, we strolled around the grand foyer with its chandeliers, and I noticed a terrace outside the three-story windows, and beyond it, the lights of the Capitol and the Potomac. I asked if we could go outside and she laughed, "Why of course, silly boy. But first let's enjoy some champagne."

A waiter gave us two long-stemmed glasses. We stepped out into the nippy air, both shivering. She clutched close to me. We walked to the white-marbled railing and looked at the Potomac. The streetlamps reflected from the water, oval orange smudges whirling and struggling in the icy current.

Tess put her hand on my cheek. "Why, you're freezing. Is something wrong?"

"Nothing," I said, stepping back from her.

"No, there is something wrong. What it is? Tell me. I can feel it hanging around you like a noose."

I told her Jay's story.

She listened sympathetically. When I finished, she said, "I'm so sorry. Really, I am. He sounds like a terrific kid. I will see what Jerome and I can do. We donate to that hospital. There must be ways to get him more support. Let's get more champagne. The second act will be starting soon."

She took my arm, cupped her hand over mine, and said, "There is always the second act. I know it well."

In Giselle's second act, the deceitful nobleman Albrecht who must atone for his ill treatment of Giselle dances to his death, leaping again and again as if hunted down, bounding across the stage, his arms outstretched, his body of air more than on the stage. I drank in his beauty and athleticism, his grace and power, and his death. For days, his image kept coming back to me. I'd extend my arms, straightened up and extend my legs, pretending I was him, dancing out of my body, floating in the air above everything like a fantastic otherworldly being.

On Monday, the serpentine Route 50 rose and dipped like a twisted cord that pulled me back to my work-a-day life.

Staying in Washington for two nights, going to the National Gallery of Art, having lunch and dinner in fine restaurants, all had helped me forget about Jay. Being with Tess was enchanting. She had money to spend, and she spent it on the arts. It confirmed for her that she had a life outside her marriage, a life where she was free to be who she wanted to be. I felt like a man, someone admired by a sophisticated woman. I acted more carefree than I had for months and sensed that my identity—that elusive sense that I was, or needed to be, someone—seemed entirely dependent on whom I was with. If Tess wanted me to be her young paramour—or, at least, act like one—for her society friends, I was only too willing to be that for her. If Suzie wanted me to be her lover, her handsome boy-friend, I had been willing—and might still be willing—to do that, too. If David wanted me to be his princely fantasy to indulge, I was even willing to do that. If Dominique, whom I had just met, wanted to flirt with me, entice me, lead me on, fall in love with him, I was almost willing to play along. If Jay needed me to be his buddy,

Chapter Twenty-One

to reach out to him, and comfort him. If his parents wanted me to accept their limitations, and if the Community Action Program lawyer wanted me to be honest and testify against the Heaveners, I was willing to do that too. A well trained child of a business executive, I was taught be a chameleon in any social situation, to adjust how I acted to please whomever I was talking to, to put on the right face, to act the role, to stand when a woman came to our table at dinner, to open doors for elders, to nod my head and listen attentively even if what they were saying was entirely boring—and I was only then realizing how I was like a hateful windup toy that, once correctly set in motion, would do just what as it was designed to do.

And for what? Who was I? What did I want?

What confounded me was how easily I could move from one self to another.

I was also aware that David, however he managed to know any information he learned about my relationships, had probably heard I'd gone to Washington with Tess. Maybe he even knew about Doug's gatherings at the lodge. I wondered if Ken's warning about David was something I needed to heed or if it would amount to nothing. I tried to convince myself, more and more, that I was OK, that I needn't worry about being gay. Tess liked me, after all. Maybe that kind of weekend love could be enough to change me into whatever, at the moment, I wanted to be.

Every time I visited Jay, Alice would complain to me about the nurse, her demands. I felt like I was walking barefoot on a razor edge. His forthrightness, his affection, and his tenacity had endued, even as his hands still looked more like animal claws than human hands. Any false move, and I felt as if I would slice open, caught between loyalties to Jay's family and my professional duties.

I waited and waited but the call about the exact day and time of Jay's hearing never came. I hoped that Glunk, the nurse, had put it off. I busied my days driving to different Centers, checking in on staff, roughhousing with the kids. I kept busy, distracted my mind from the testimony, and visited Jay less frequently. But I'd taken a photograph of Jay and kept it on my desk, and every time I went back to the office, his captivating smile broke my heart.

One evening, I went to my office and there was a note: the hearing would be on March 8th. I put it in my calendar and circled it and tried to breathe.

When I next visited Jay, Alice didn't mention the hearing. At the end of my visit, she came to the door with me and thanked me for coming. "It means a lot to him and to me. Jay, he misses you when you are not here."

"I miss him, too."

"I know," she said and shook my hand and held it a long time as I left, something she had never done.

A week before the hearing, Anne charged into my office exclaiming, "They've left town. The Heaveners have up and gone!"

"What do you mean gone?" I asked, baffled.

"They moved out. No forwarding address. They're gone."

I drove directly to their trailer. The door was locked. I pulled on it and peeked in the slotted window. Everything was gone, the furniture,

Chapter Twenty-One

toys—cleared out. I must have stood there for five minutes. Then, I hunted around out in back. I have no idea what I was looking for, but a small vegetable garden, newly planted, had been dug out of a bramble of weeds. Each row had a string and at the end of it, a seed envelope staked to a Popsicle stick: lettuce, radish, and carrot. It brought a smile to my face. I knew who had planted them.

About a week later, I got a postcard from Alice that said, "Doing well. Jay misses you," and scrawled in the lower left-hand corner, was a picture of a bunny, smiling and holding onto a carrot and in block letters, "Love, Jay." I held onto the card, closed my office door, and cried.

Chapter Twenty-Two

I felt obligated, once I heard that David was flying to Italy, to go to his farewell party. When he appeared at the door of his room, I was aghast. He'd gone on a starvation diet and looked like a Dachau survivor: gaunt, eyes hollowed out; facial skin sagged and sallow. Rather than looking younger—his goal, I knew—he'd aged ten years. His voice was scratchy, too. When he asked how he looked, turning around in a circle, raising one hand like a matador, obviously pleased with his new physique, I said, "You look swell."

He seemed to have forgotten my chastising him, smiling, delighted to see me.

I loved how his deep throaty laugh reverberated and changed pitches. He circled the room, walking on the balls of his feet like a dancer. Excited about his "grand egress" as he called it—we were to have dinner with someone I'd met earlier—he had me drive to the restaurant for his special occasion.

At the White Stallion restaurant, he searched for Tom, the owner, the man I'd met who brought pizza that first night I stayed with David. Tom had planned the night's festivities. He was my age, and, as I remembered, still had shaggy blonde hair that fell over his forehead. He dressed casually in jeans and a tight T-shirt that revealed a well-toned, sleek, glabrous chest.

In a side room, we ate steaks, huddled around candlelight—it reminded David of Florence—and talked. David had Tom sit next to me; he regaled me with stories of local restaurant ownership.

"There is no privacy here," he whispered, looking across the table. "Everyone knows everyone and, if they don't, they soon will. It's the price of living in a small southern town."

David, loquacious as usual, did much of the talking, telling of his grand plans. He was certain that he could pick up some nice Italian men and make a life for himself. He bragged how slim and trim—"svelte" was the word he used—he was. After a few drinks of wine, a fine Italian variety, his pallor reddened. He looked better drunk.

"It's OK to be off the wagon," he raised his glass in a toast—"for one night and one night only." He reminisced how one night in Florence, years ago, he picked up the son of J. Paul Getty. He nuzzled close to me and said, "Let's go back to my room. One last time, hey, for old time's sake." I wasn't attracted to him—had I ever been?—but he'd been good to me over the year, and I felt an obligation.

I told David to go home. Said I'd meet him there. The bartender offered to give him a ride. He hugged me and kissed me on the cheek and said, "My evil wayward boy" and left, waving to the others in the restaurant like an old politician on his last campaign. After several more drinks, Tom suggested that we should go back to David's place. He came with me, sitting in the car, while I went to wish David a bon voyage.

David was seated on the bed, paging through a magazine. He handed me an album of Copland's music.

"My dear boy, this is for you," he said.

Chapter Twenty-Two

"His music reminds me of you. It is sweet and elegiac, filled with a lovely yearning and sadness. Here give me a kiss," he said, tilting his head to me.

He tilted his head to me, and I kissed him.

"Can you stay?" he asked.

"Actually, Tom is in the car. He's waiting. I've got an early meeting, bright and early. Sorry, I wish I could. You understand?"

"Yes, I do. I do. Tom, he's cute, isn't he?" David glancing out the window. "I have often consorted with him in my imagination."

I laughed. "Well, that's where I have most of my affairs!"

He laughed and then he patted the chair next to him. "Take one second. Come on. Have a look at these."

I looked down at his magazine—photographs of naked young men. One held his erection with the half-dazed look in his face of one about to ejaculate. I fell into a trance. He turned the page. Another man holding another guy's erection, large, bigger than his hand and cum was spurting out, eyes closed in rapt pleasure. My eyes fixated on the image. He turned another page. A young man sucking on a cock. I shoved at my pants, and David reached out to caress me.

"Just this once, let me, again."

I consented, thinking it would be my little gift to him, "Okay, okay." I unzipped my pants and pulled myself out. David was thrilled. I looked at myself. All I wanted was release. The urge, pent up for weeks, boiled in me. David took me in his hand and sucked me just as he had once before. It was heaven. Something about being with David made everything feel like it mattered so much less.

In a few seconds, Tom burst into the room. I turned around, my pants half-off. He didn't look at me. He nodded to David and said,

"David, what the hell are you doing?"

He came over and sat down in an empty chair across from us as if oblivious to my being exposed. I wanted him to join me, to join us.

The two of them stared at one another.

I stood in between them like a badminton birdie, waiting for one to take a swat at me.

"Come on," I stumbled over to Tom, pulling at his belt, "Come on!"

I tried to undo his pants, but he resisted with a cute smile, "No, Jason. Not now. Stop it, Jason. Not here."

He pushed me away, "Zip up, Jason. You're drunk. You're a sight to behold. Look around you. It's—don't you think—a bit unsightly? Any passerby"—he pointed to the open windows. "—can see in here."

I didn't listen, I kept at his pants, drunk as I was, which forced him to stand and nudge me away forcefully. I stumbled with my pants down and fell on the floor.

"Leave me alone. Not here."

He quietly spoke to David, "The boy is clearly drunk. He needs some coffee to sober up. Do you not agree?"

David agreed, "Yes, sad case. Never seen him like this. There is something evil in him. Too bad." He waved his hand at me, dismissing me, as if I were of no more use to him. "Be gone with him. Get him out of here."

His rejection startled me. I looked at the mirror hanging by David's desk and became aware of what a fool I was. I pulled up my pants and stated with resolve, "I'm going home. I don't know what came over me. I've got to get out of here. I'm done with both of you."

I lunged to the door, shoved it open, grabbed the railing, and staggered down the steps, lost my balance and toppled to one knee,

Chapter Twenty-Two

stood up and aimed my feet toward my car. I needed to erase the whole episode. I needed to get home, get some sleep, get back to myself.

Both of them followed me.

David rushed toward me, holding something in his hand. It was the phonograph album of Copeland's work. I had forgotten his gift.

"Here." He placed it in my hands. "Do take care of yourself." He leaned in and kissed me on the cheek and added, plaintively, "Dear boy, my dear evil boy, I shall miss you."

I flung myself into the car. I hated him and hated to leave him. This would be our last time together and I knew that I had messed it up horribly. "Evil" was the right word. What was I doing? He had been good to me, had taught me an immense amount about opera, and had cared for me in ways I never could have cared for him. I started to pull away when Tom banged on the roof of the car. I stopped. He hopped in the front seat, "May I come along? You need to drop me off at the restaurant, remember?"

I drove the car, careful to stay in the right lane, to the restaurant. There were four or five cars still in the parking lot. A blue-green light illuminated the red front door, and a streetlight showed overhead.

"Can we talk a second?" he asked.

"I need to get home. I need to get back."

"Can you at least turn off the car?"

"I need to go home. I need to get up early. I need to get out of here."

"Please?"

I groaned. I looked at him with as much disgust as I could muster.

He leaned forward, patting my knee, said, "Oh, honey, you're so drunk." And with his other hand, he grabbed my keys from the ignition.

"Give those back to me!" I raised my fist, surprised by the rage erupting inside of me.

"Calm down, just calm down, honey," he tried to soothe me, speaking soft and low.

"Don't honey me!"

He held the keys over his head. "Now, now. You're in no state."

"Give them back you mother fucker."

"You need coffee, Jason. It's dangerous for you and for anyone else on the road at this hour. Come on in. A cup of coffee, that's all. One cup? Come on." He pulled on the door handle and pointed to the front door.

"No."

"Please."

"It's on me. And I will play David's record. You'll have a chance to hear it."

"On your word: one cup."

Inside, Tom placed the record on the turntable. Appalachian Spring played on the speakers. The bartender built like a football player, eyed me carefully, and leaned over the counter.

After we drank two cups of coffee, Tom insisted we sit in the side room in a booth.

"It's more comfortable."

I could hear the latch of the front door turn.

Tom and I sat side by side in a booth by a window. I told him that I wanted to be a poet. He listened. With the room empty, we sipped our coffee. He looked at me, his hand lightly caressing my cheek, and I reached over and touched his leg. He massaged mine.

I thought, "What am I doing?"

Chapter Twenty-Two

My hand strayed to his crotch. He was aroused. He pulled on my belt and zipper.

"Wait," he said. "Wait right here. I'll not be a minute."

He went to the back room and emerged with a blanket, a comforter, two pillows and said, "Come over here. Make yourself comfortable." I walked over to the make-shift bed. He undid my pants and let them down. I looked down at myself, aroused again. He stood, slipped off his clothes, and we sat, naked, holding each other.

The light from a narrow window stabbed my eyes. I propped myself up on an elbow. I was hung over, no clothes, one large comforter covering me. Tom was curled next to me. I put my hand out and touched the chilly floor.

My head throbbed. I could barely remember what we did. Slipping out from under the comforter, I hunted for my clothing. My pants and shirt were on a table, my socks and shoes on the floor, my underwear on a chair. Hurriedly, I pulled them on and tiptoed to the door, wanting to get out before he awoke. The door was locked.

I went to the plywood door in the back and jerked on it. Locked. On the far side was another set of windows. Locked.

I returned to jerk on the door, hard. I shoved against it. I lunged against it again, hoping I could crack it, break the lock, pull it off its hinges.

The sun was higher, cresting on the bar, glistening.

I was trapped. I had to get out, yet I didn't want to talk with him. I wanted to disappear, pretend it never happened. I pulled out my keys and realized they weren't my car keys. They were keys to the lodge. Tom still had my keys.

I walked back to him. Strewn on his side, the comforter pulled around him, his naked feet protruded from the bottom like a little boy, he looked harmless. I thought about how he must have taken me, his long fingers caressing my body, how I must have gone along, how my body didn't deny him, even when it was painful, how I must have followed his lead, let him have me as he wanted.

Drunk, I thought. God I was drunk. That's what happens when you're drunk. That's what happened with Dominique. Drunk. Drunk! Drunk!

I slammed my fist into the wall. Still, infuriatingly so, while he slept. Sound asleep, his face cupped in the pillow, peaceful.

"Get up! I gotta go. Let me out of here!"

He startled and flung an arm up to protect himself. Once he realized it was me, he replied softly, "Calm down. It's okay." Groggily, he stared at me, leaned on one elbow, rubbed his face and brushed back his long blonde hair. He kicked back the comforter slightly.

"I want out, now," I shouted.

Sitting up, he said, "Coffee first?" He giggled. "You look like someone dragged you out of a closet. Excuse the pun." He gestured to the kitchen. "Are you sure I can fix you some breakfast?"

"No, I told you. I want out. Now. Let me out."

"You going to meet someone?"

"None of your fucking business," I was nearly crying. "Damn it, I'm a director of a program. Don't you get it? I have a meeting. I need to get to my office."

"You need your keys," he said, and reached into his shirt pocket. "Here." He went to the front door and slid a bolt, one I had not seen in the hazy light of the hallway, lower in the door, knee-level. I could

Chapter Twenty-Two

have opened it at any time if I had paid attention. I stepped outside.

He called out the door after me, "Can I call you?"

I turned to him and just stared.

With his comforter around him, he put his hand to his lips and blew a kiss to me.

I smiled and realized that he still had David's record.

"The record," I said. "I need the record."

He turned and went back inside, and I stayed standing in the parking lot in the bright morning light. He came back with the record, handed it over, and stood before me.

"It can be wonderful," he said quietly. "If you let it."

For a moment, I let him hold my hand.

In the rising light, I drove through the long, narrow valley by the broad banks of the South Branch of the Potomac, winding by pastures with cattle and sweeps of corn and hay fields—a fecund life. It swept by me as my feeling of desolation and foreboding swept over me. I had, once again, stepped outside my old limits, my own sense of who I was, except this time I had really crossed the line. I had made love with another man. I wanted to erase the memory of the night, of how foolishly I acted at David's house, of how I given in to Tom. Maybe David was right, maybe there was something evil in me that led me to act as I did

I was out of control, and I knew it. I felt ashamed. This wasn't the way I was. I kept saying that to myself. Not me. Not me. What a fool I was. I had gotten away from him, but not from myself. I was on the road again, yet where I was headed, what had become, and would become of me, was unclear. Something had gone terribly wrong. What my body was telling me ran contrary to who I was.

My body had its own intelligence that I didn't understand or want to understand. I needed to stop this back and forth.

Yet here I was in the same old place.

My trial wasn't done.

Evil. Maybe that's what was wrong with me.

Nothing was in the past. I needed those feelings to be in the past. But I couldn't seem to outrun them no matter how I tried. They kept catching up with me.

I had escaped from Tom. I gotten out of the restaurant. Yet I wasn't free.

Would I ever be free? I didn't want to know. I was afraid to find out that maybe I was hopeless.

Yet it wasn't over.

What was happening to me?

I kept repeating the same things in my head and repeating them more rapidly like a record at the wrong speed. The more I said them, the more the repetition bore into my brain with no sense I could gain any release from them and cast out the horrid feelings I had about myself.

My body had become my enemy.

I wanted what had been to disappear.

I had escaped. But I wasn't free.

Would I ever be free?

I didn't want to know.

The lines of a James Agee poem came to mind: "This mine to touch with deathlessness their clay, and I shall fail, and join those I betray."

At home that night, I took my journal, a bottle of aspirin, and a Budweiser, and sat on the couch and wrote.

Chapter Twenty-Two

If I could just kill the guilty one who can't contain himself, I can do that better than anyone: a short course in how to die. I'll just take more of these aspirin, as I took other drugs, and as any modern man, die. This is the best way. I could not shoot myself. I know little of guns, and I might miss and blow off my nose, or something silly. I just want to slow down, lean over neatly in my robe and be dead, and forget what I have done. I slink along doing my job, getting my petty assignments done like a robot, completely unoriginal, fat as everyone else except David who looks like death himself. I sleep too long. I become sated. What I am is another man like a clog in a machine. At twenty-eight, never having written anything significant, having no particular vision, what is the use of living?

My thoughts hurry.

I should feel something. This is taking a long time. Wait. I feel as if I'm slowing down. The night in the valley is dull, faint over the lodge. Oh, look, I can't think right. I'll take a few more, finish off the bottle. I feel dull, but not dull enough. It should be quicker. There, I noticed my skin burns. That must be a reaction. Something else should happen. I think I'll just wait at the desk. When death comes, I'll flop over to the side, near the fireplace like F. Scott Fitzgerald. My hair is combed, so I'll look neat. Who would want all these books? I hate to say it, but I do not love anyone. That may be the problem.

My parents are alright. But I have a difficult time believing they are my parents. For what I know of them, they have done a fine job of trying to make me into someone I am not. To my friends, I thank them for the pleasure and the pain. My stomach is knotted. That is a sign. I don't have much to say for myself. I'm an illusion to myself. I think sometimes that if I could have, I would have liked to meet myself, been formally introduced, and found out what I was all about. Unfortunately, I lost track of myself. I kept going along with what happened and hoped for the best. I'm fading. I can feel that. When I am dead, I will be like my high school classmate Keith Klee, voted Most Humorous, who went into his backyard on Mother's Day, poured gasoline over himself, and burned to death. Now he's known as the guy who burned himself on Mother's Day. A sick joke. A suicide.

I wish someone close to my age would die or have something horrible happen to them so I could watch my reaction, observe what I would do. I'm getting cold. Distant. That's how I feel much of the time. Look at all the books on my shelves. They make me look intelligent when I've read only half of them.

Toby has leapt on the desk. He knocked the pen from my hand. His purr is like a motor from a boat far from shore. I press him to my chest. I'm tired. I've written all this already. But I feel incredibly awake. The fellow who roomed next to me in college, the premed major, used to take aspirin, whole handfuls of them, when he pulled an all-nighter. I don't seem to be getting any closer to death than when I started this. I'll sit with Toby, read for a while, then go to bed. What was the Dylan Thomas line? And death shall have no dominion. He had it right. At least for now.

The next morning, the aspirin jar sat on my desk along with the journal open, and a half-empty bottle of beer.

I thought of David on his romantic fantasy trip, imagining that, when he returned to Florence, he'd be a young man again and other men, seeing him, would fall in love with him, as they had decades ago, and wouldn't see him as I did as a pathetic, old man, no longer handsome, worn out, gaunt, lonely, and alcoholic. I'd winced thinking of him, of myself, of Tom, and stepped on the back veranda to look at the river that was shimmering in the early light.

Chapter Twenty-Three

Long rows of single tenements, built in the 1920s, lined the street. Without any trouble—Suzie gave good directions—I drove to 126 Piedmont Road, found a parking spot, checked the street number once more and locked the car.

The building loomed against the ashen sky. It had a small vestibule hinting at a former elegance—a beveled-glass front door, and, inside, glimmering chandeliers and wainscoting. A large, hand-printed sign tacked on the wall said *Door Open, Come Up, Third Floor.*

People were jammed into the apartment. Suzie greeted me with a kiss. She had been hanging on the arm of a guy with long blonde hair—the guy, as it turned out, who owned the apartment. She inserted her arm in mine and introduced her friend.

"This is Alex. He owns the place. A close friend. Aren't you, Alex?" She leaned in to kiss him, an I've-known-you-a-long-time-and-known-you-well kiss.

I must have looked startled when she turned to face me.

"Gosh, Jason, you look envious. You remember Alex, don't you? I talked on the phone with him."

Alex leaned closer to me and said, "So you are Jason. It's nice to put a face with the—"

"Panting."

"You guessed it," he said, squeezing my arm.

Why I had come to see her, come to the party? I couldn't say. But here I was, and she said we could spend the night. Maybe I could get back to being myself.

Suzie escorted me through a gaggle of people, introducing me like a celebrity, tossing my name off easily, "Hey, guys, this is Jason."

There were a mix of young, long-haired hippies and college-aged, preppy types—each stylish in their own way, either the John Lennon or Eldridge Cleaver look. The women wore their hair like Suzie, long, straight, parted down the middle, unless it curled, in which case, they had Afros.

One couple sat on a tan couch. A guy in his twenties, thick-chested, heavy set, in Army fatigues. His arm was slung around a Karen Carpenter type woman with long brown hair and narrow, gaunt facial features.

We walked over to meet them.

"This is Stan," Suzie said, "just back from 'Nam. A war hero." I offered him my hand. He peered at it as if it were a foreign object. Suzie leaned over and kissed him on the cheek. He grabbed her by the face and welded his face into her, French kissing her. But she didn't seem to mind—free love, after all.

Stan's girlfriend surveyed the scene as if it were an old movie and extended her hand to me, offering me a few words as if to apologize. "He does that to all the chicks. I'm Chance."

As Suzie led us back to the main room, she whispered, "He's got some weird thing wrong with his head. A lot of 'Nam vets have it. Messes up their minds. It's like they're re-playing the war. He's just another fucked-up guy—stoned most of the time, which makes him tolerable, but he goes off the deep end now and then, so watch him."

Chapter Twenty-Three

"I'm sorry," I offered. "He just grabbed you."

"What do you expect from men?" she said. Then, catching me out of the corner of her eye, added, "That's why my way is better. Most of them aren't worth it."

"Explain this," I said.

"Explain what?"

"You believe in free love, but you seem to"—I hesitated, then said it—"hate men."

She laughed. "Oh, don't you know me enough by now? It's pleasure before politics!" She looked over her shoulder and waved at Alex, smiling. He was trying to get her attention, motioning toward the front of the apartment.

She escorted me into the kitchen. Cases of Jack Daniels, Jim Beam, Johnny Walker, along with three beer kegs, two tubs of ice. Three guys took turns downing straight shots and chugging beer. They belched. The room sounded like a cow barn.

Suzie shoved by them—"Excuse me gentlemen—or should I say, slobs,"—and they parted, waving her by. She barged by another cluster of guys, opened the refrigerator as if she owned the place, and gave me a Budweiser. Before I could take a few sips, she kissed me on the cheek and scooted off arm in arm with someone I didn't know.

I stood for a moment alone and awkward, and then saw Vince. I'd met him once at a dinner at Suzie's place.

Vince saw me too and came over. "Well, I can see the free-love queen is making the rounds." he said laconically. "The girls are having fun." He nodded off to our left where Alazia, his girlfriend, was dancing in the living room with another cute guy.

I surveyed the scene, nodded, then remarked as coolly as I could, "Suzie's checking out the merchandise for any items on sale."

He laughed and replied, "There are a number of the male items on the discount table," he said, pointing to several doors on the other side of the room. "I wouldn't advise going in there. Trouble, with a capital T."

He suggested we get out of the kitchen—he needed to talk. The wind whined outside like the high-pitched call of a coyote. A sliver of cold swept across my legs. Down the hallway a door swung open, then banged shut again.

A young man came through and pulled it shut. He strutted like a prince, thin, broad shoulders, shirt open at the neck. A girl trailed after him, adjusting her skirt.

When I turned back around, Vince had disappeared.

A guy across the room was staring at me. I looked him over—jeans, loose red shirt, shiny black European-style shoes. Attractive. Mixed Asian-American with a pale-chocolate complexion and almond-shaped eyes. He stood beside a screen where images flicked on and off from a slide projector. They were images I recognized of people in the room. They were taken in the summer, with people in beach attire by a lake, oiled and tanned, smiling, swimming, saluting the photographer with beer bottles.

My eyes swung from the slides back to the guy staring at me.

Occasionally the crowd watching the pictures burst out laughing or applauded a scene where couples were indiscreet—a hand up a blouse, down a bathing suit.

With his wan smile and deep-set eyes, the stranger intrigued me. He looked different from the rest of the crowd. He moved with the grace of Albrecht in the ballet as he strutted across the stage to his dear Giselle. I was conscious of his eyes. Somehow, I could feel them on my

Chapter Twenty-Three

body. They felt intimidating, arrogant, as if he had the right to look. He seemed to look at my unpolished shoes. I lifted one foot, then the other, rubbing them against my pant leg, hoping to shine them.

Guitars stained at the higher notes, and the drums throbbed so intensely I couldn't tell if it was them or my heart pounding in my chest. *Not now*, I thought, *I must put these thoughts aside. I have something to prove.* I had to find Suzie. She promised.

"What are you doing!?" a voice blared over my shoulder.

I turned. It was Vince. He pointed at my shoes.

He grabbed me by the arm and led me to a hallway. I vaguely remember him mentioning something to me earlier about his dad. "So, I called him again," he said. "Decided to call and tell him I cared. And my dad—you wouldn't believe this. You know what? You know what? He hung up on me."

Tears welled up in his eyes. He wiped them away, but they kept coming. I put my arm around his shoulder.

"That's awful." I patted his back, which didn't seem to do much good. I was never much good at consolation since, no matter what I said, the pain was there and would remain there.

"Here," I took his glass. "Let me get you another drink." I steered him to an empty chair and told him to stay put. I slid by a cluster of people, holding his glass over my head, staggering slightly.

Someone nudged me, and I bumped into a side table, losing my balance.

"Shit," I blurted out. Whoever it was, was gently propping me up with a hand on my waist. He kept moving. I glanced back at the man, his almond eyes, high cheekbones and heavy lips. As I pressed my way through the crowd, I tried to figure out what it was about him—his gaze, the way he stood, his contrapposto hips poised like Michelangelo's statue of David—that attracted me.

The first time I traveled to Florence, in my early twenties, I remembered the light in the rotunda highlighting David. I stopped and stood, strangely aroused as if I was seeing a god. The magnetism of the marble—smooth, flesh-like body, as if David could reach over and pick me up in his arm. The stone figure, chiseled by another man, who wanted me to see what he loved, what attracted him—and I did see it and felt that same attraction. The effect renamed my desire. I knew it even as I wanted to deny it. I wandered around the base of the statue, gazing up until my brother nudged me onward.

I glanced away from the stranger, thinking how self-absorbed I was. Everyone was on the make. I was no different.

I needed to keep away from that man.

The Rolling Stones blared in my ears. People in small groups chatted about nothing. I delivered Vince his beer. Then I noticed Suzie leaning on an inebriated fellow miming magic tricks. I walked up to hear what he was saying to her.

"I can change you, pretty-one, into a princess," he told her.

She tilted her head to the right and flipped back her long brown hair. "Why, don't you know . . . I already am one!"

He laughed, "And so you are! What does that make me?"

Without missing a beat, she said, "Why that makes you . . ." she pawed her hand lightly through his hair . . . "that makes you a toad."

Then she slapped him on the cheek, hard, and said, "Quit flirting with me, buster. I have no interest in you." She turned to me, grabbed my arm and boasted, "This is my kind of guy!"

She turned and whispered in my ear. "That's what I like about

Chapter Twenty-Three

you. I had to seduce you. You're such a shy one."

She clung to me for a minute, and we glided from group to group, arm in arm. Then, as soon as I found her, again, she left. "Later, honey, I need to spend some time with Alex." She grabbed a man by the waist from behind. He turned and gave her a kiss. They dispersed into the crowd.

I checked my watch. I'd planned, and she'd promised, that we'd spend the night together. It was early, just 11:00 P.M. I could wait.

I leaned against the wall. The stereo blasted. Beer drained out of one keg after another. Faces swept back and forth, reeking of scotch and bourbon and beer. Several guys vomited in the sink. A hand grabbed my beer, shoved another in my hand, "Try this. Have another drink, buddy."

I stared at the slide show. One picture after another, until one slide was left on the wall for a long time. Everyone hooted, "Eric! Eric! Take it all off."

It was an image of a man in a thin skin-tight blue Speedo, his hands on his hips, emerging from the water. Waves licked his calves. Water poured off his sleek swimmer's body. He had a lovely, shy smile on his face and looked more like Eros than Eric.

Two women, standing a few feet from me, looked at the slide and laughed. The blonde said, "I've heard he's a stud. Unbelievable in every way, if you know what I mean. She went out with him several times and, you know her, she likes them well-endowed."

Her friend, a red head, giggled, "I'd love to get my hands in that Speedo."

"That's what they say. Unbelievable."

The real Eric stood to the right of the projector. He didn't look like a stud at all. He bowed his head, obviously embarrassed by the fanfare. He waved at the projectionist to change the image. (A sea gull flying off. The underside of its wings pale orange in the sunset.) He looked up. I was stunned: He was the same Asian man who had given me the eye. He saw me standing across from him and smiled and began to walk toward me.

Panicked, I moved away.

I found Alazia, Vince's girlfriend. I was delighted to have a woman, any woman, by my side and pulled her close to me. I wanted to tell her about Vince, how upset he was, but she waved her hand at the dance floor. "Where have you been?" Inserting her arm in mine, she handed me another beer—how many was it, six?—and invited me to dance. We shuffled back and forth in a tight square, wiggling and flinging our arms out. Her eyes seemed dilated—probably stoned—as she shoved her hips at mine, grabbed me by the neck, and licked my lips. She shouted something at me above the music. Blitzed as she was, I could not make it out. She spilled her drink.

Vince, who appeared out of nowhere, scowled at me and grabbed her by the arm. They wandered away.

Another woman came up to me and called out, "Hey handsome, let's shake it," and we danced wildly, bobbing up and down, until she flung up her hands, "I'm beat," and went to get another drink. I stood in the center of the room. I knew no one.

Several fingers crept up my back. Suzie cuddled up to me, lacing her hands around my waist.

"Some hot dancing," she intoned, rubbing her breasts against my back.

Chapter Twenty-Three

I turned around, kissing her on the lips. "Where you been?"

It was nearly 12:30 A.M

"Oh, hanging around," she pursed her lips and put her finger to mine. "Why do you want to know?"

"Worry about you."

"Don't concern yourself. I can take care of myself."

I leaned close to her ear and asked, "Where's the bathroom?"

She pointed to the hallway.

I draped my arms around her neck. "Let's get out of here. Go back to your place."

"Sure, honey, we'll do that. You know we will." she said and gave me a long kiss.

Another guy bumped into us.

He latched onto her, slinging his arm around her shoulder, offered her a joint, which she took and inhaled, then held it up for me and gave me a hit. She patted me on the face.

"Relax, baby face," she said, pinching me on the cheek. "Just have a good time. That's why we're here. This is the Good Time Special. Hop on and ride."

I had to pee. I held my arms out as I walked down the hallway, keeping my balance, since the room seemed to sway. I stepped over a couple of guys slumped on the floor like bookends, smoking pot. Once over them, I bolted to the only doorway in the hallway. I pushed but it was jammed shut as if someone were leaning against it, forcing it closed. I shoved harder. The door cracked open. I heard muffled voices.

The Marine, Stan, appeared in the bathroom door's crack. "Bug off, buster." Behind him, gawking at me, reflected in the mirror, was his girlfriend, Chance. She was pressed against the wall. Her hands covered her face. She was sobbing.

She pleaded, "Let me out, Stan. Please let me out."

He closed the door.

I could hear her voice muttering something.

I pressed on the door, tried to get my foot or hand in it. I stuck my hand against the jamb, but he shoved it back.

"My hand. Let it out," I yelped.

I shoved at the door and knocked. I listened intently. Chance pleaded louder. Something was wrong. I leaned against the wall, trying to figure out how to get in without causing a scene. The two stoned guys gazed up at me. One asked, "Hey, what's going on?" I shrugged. There was thudding on the wall.

I shoved my shoulder into the door. I shouted, as evenly as I could, "Hey, man, come on. I gotta go."

I kept knocking. No use. *This is stupid*, I thought. From within, a belt unbuckled, and a zipper unzipped.

I knocked three more times. Clothing rustled. There was a moan.

One of the guys on the floor yelled, "Hey, quit knocking. You're disturbing the peace."

I couldn't think straight. Flustered, I stepped back and gazed into the kitchen. I thought, if no one was there, I could pee quickly in the sink, or a bottle. I wanted to help Chance, yet I hardly knew her, and Stan seemed like a guy who could turn on you in a minute.

I went outside through the back door and relieved myself over the balcony, the urine streaming out in a fine arc, falling down three stories between two parked cars. Standing exposed in the

Chapter Twenty-Three

cold sobered me up. Down the alley, streetlights swayed in the wind and glimmered, iridescent, with the heavily falling snow. I felt released from the world. I wanted to get out of there. I'd had enough. I needed to get home.

A muted shriek punctuated the air. The bathroom window was opened slightly. I crept over to it and stood on tiptoe to see in. But all I could see was a single bulb swaying back and forth. I heard voices, garbled at first, then heated, strained. I propped myself up higher to make out what they were saying.

Chance called out, "Stan, let me out. Please. No, I don't . . ."

He fumed, "Sit down there. Take it. I told you to sit down. Hurry up. Do it. I'm hot, baby."

"No. Stan let me out. Please. Stan."

There was quiet. A groan. Some movement.

"Sit down, bitch."

Back and forth. It seemed interminable. He insisted. She pleaded.

I had to do something. Yet I had never encountered something like this. I leaned against the clapboards, getting colder, stuffing my hands in my pockets. I wondered what someone would say if they came out, seeing me there by myself, perched on my tiptoes, peeking in the bathroom. Snow spit over the porch, heavier, thick flakes, shambling across the platform, gathering around my shoes.

"No, Stan. No," her voice strident.

His voice, gruff, "Sit down, cunt."

A whomp, dull and blunt.

I chugged the last swig of my beer, rolled the bottle over the railing, shook my head to clear it, and stepped back into the hallway. I had to do something. If nothing else, I could break down the door. Or get Suzie. She knew him. Maybe she could help.

Suzie and Vince and Alazia were outside the bathroom door.

"What's happening?" Suzie demanded. She banged on the door, hard.

"Bad things," I said." That guy, Stan, is pushing, you know, on his chick. She ain't buying it."

As I was about to say something else, the bathroom door swung open. Stan was screaming, "She needs some help."

We rushed in. Chance, her hand to her face, was bleeding profusely. Suzie grabbed her and took her to the kitchen, pressed a towel with ice cubes to her nose. Chance mumbled about him smashing her face on the sink, but kept apologizing for him, "He doesn't know what he's doing: He's a good man, he's just drunk."

Suzie held the ice pack to Chance's broken nose.

She barked at me, "Get more fuckin ice!"

I grabbed a towel and turned to the refrigerator, filling the towel with a pile of ice cubes.

"Men," Suzie muttered. "Men are so fucked up. I'm sick of them. Well, you are, aren't you? You never know what you want, and when you do, you mess it up. War, peace, sex. You men have no idea what you are doing. Men fuck it up. Force themselves on someone. Use her like a puppet. Like a fuckin' puppet. All you're interested in is taking care of yourselves—just like this goddamn war, this polluted city, just like everything you touch."

She held onto Chance and glared at me, "How can you stand to be a man?"

I backed up and bumped into the kitchen table.

"Watch yourself." She laughed. "You're all such fools."

Alazia set her arm gently around her shoulder. "Suzie, calm down,

Chapter Twenty-Three

will you? You're making a scene. Have another beer, come on. It's not a big deal."

"Oh, fuck off. Fuck you all. You're all fucked!!" Suzie screamed and pulled Chance close to her. "Just leave us alone. We don't need you."

Alazia, Vince, and I stood by, watching Chance with her ice pack and Suzie with her beer, silent, not sure what to do or say.

The party dispersed—many people put off by the screaming. Suzie convinced Chance to come home with her.

"I'm out of here," Suzie brushed my cheek with a kiss, patted my arm, hard enough to hurt, said, "Sorry it didn't work out, hotshot. Maybe it wasn't meant to be. Who knows? Maybe next time, right? Give me a call."

"Yeah," I said, "Next time."

I didn't look her in the eyes. I didn't want to. This world of free love, of get-what-you-can-when-you-want-it had lost its appeal. I was struck by the indifference, the way nothing seemed to matter, how anything could happen—violence especially—and the show carried on. I yearned for something, or someone, who really cared and was committed. Carole had told me that I deserved it. Yet how was I to find it?

Since I had no coat or hat, I milled around in the apartment, and finally left, cold, trudging in drifting snow to my car, feeling guilty for not breaking down the bathroom door and rescuing Chance, for letting Suzie go off without me.

Discovering the keys were locked in the car, I had to hurry back to the apartment, find a coat hanger, and trudge back once more. As I fidgeted with the hanger, inserting it along the door gasket, my hands numbed up. Alternately blowing on my hands, stuffing them in my pockets, and jimmying the lock, I was getting nowhere fast. The snow shifted to sleet and the sleet intensified. After ten minutes, I'd managed to hook the lock five times, but each time my hands floundered when jerking it up.

Behind me, lights flickered on a car, its windows steamed up. I hadn't noticed it, but figured a couple was making out.

A wiry young fellow leaned out the driver's side door, "You look like you need help."

By then, my hands felt like cast iron. I waved at him, "Damn right, I do."

He hopped out of the car and stepped through the low-lying drifts. "Carl's the name."

A second guy hopped out of Carl's passenger seat, ducking his head against a gust of wind.

Carl manipulated the coat hanger adeptly. "I do this all the time," he joked.

His friend, stomping off his boots, came over to me. I didn't recognize him until he stood next to me. It was Michelangelo Eric.

"You look cold," he called out.

"Freezing," I admitted.

"Here," he said, taking off his buckskin mittens. "Put these on and get in our car."

I recoiled at first, "No, I don't need them."

He laughed. "That's bullshit because, man, in these mittens, your fingers aren't all stuffed in little cages: You can wiggle your fingers around inside them, keep them moving, keep them warm."

He handed me the mittens. I did what he told me to do. I stepped in his boot prints and followed him back to their car. He opened

Chapter Twenty-Three

the front door and told me to get in, then got in next to me. I was shivering so badly he grabbed me by the shoulders and put his scarf around my neck.

He put his hands to the heater that blasted hot air. I took off the mittens and put my hands up to it, too. They stung. I flinched.

"Look at them," he said. "Give them over."

He took my hands and held them, rubbing lightly. A sensation like prickly knives shot through my fingers. I winced.

"It may take some time," he said. "When circulation comes back, it will hurt. Then, it will tingle."

I took a deep breath and leaned back, staring at the roof's interior.

He asked my name, where I was from, what I did—the usual. I inquired the same.

He lived outside of Cumberland. Was a therapist. A local boy, a former dancer, and still did theater. I asked another question, "Who's your friend?"

"Oh, Carl," He laughed. Through the foggy window, we could see Carl leaning against my car door, sawing back and forth with the hanger. "He's a buddy, an old roommate from college. We go way back. We haven't seen each other for a year. He lives in the Midwest—Illinois, University of Chicago, and is here visiting his parents, so we're catching up."

"I come from Chicago."

"Is that so?"

"He's very good at breaking into cars."

Eric laughed. "That got him in trouble when he was a kid."

I blurted out a question, "You live alone?"

His tone immediately softened. "I do. Why do you ask?"

I shrugged. Shoved my hands between my legs to keep them warm.

He asked if I was single. I told him, "Well, sort of. I used to date Suzie, you know, the one at the party."

He laughed. "Quite a woman I've heard—free love, if you're into that."

"What are you getting at?"

"I just prefer commitment. Everything has a cost." He shrugged. "To each his own."

We sat quietly, not looking at one another, just breathing, watching Carl's systematic manipulation of the coat hanger.

"Anything wrong?" Eric asked.

"No, just thinking."

He squeezed my hand, "You can talk if you want to."

"I sense that," I said. But I didn't want to talk.

Carl, through the window, was perched on his heels, craning his arm up as if suspended. In a moment he reached for the door handle, and then a gust of snow obliterated his image.

In the quiet, my thoughts wandered back to the party.

I said, "I heard that you're quite a stud."

"Who told you that?"

"Inside, when they showed the photo of you, two girls said you were really something."

He laughed so hard his head rolled back, and, after he recovered, said, "Well, it's nice to have a reputation. But I'm afraid those girls don't know me very well."

"You're not a stud?"

"Please. Not in the way they think I am."

"I don't get it."

He patted me on the leg and said, "Let's say I'm not much interested in girls."

Chapter Twenty-Three

I looked at him and he nodded his head.

Outside, Carl, back into view, leaped mid-air, "Yippee!" The front door of my car swung open.

Carl started back toward us, his fist raised, the hanger like a sword aimed at the sky.

"Guess you're saved," Eric sighed.

"Thanks for everything."

"You warm again?" he asked.

"Yes, definitely."

He looked me in the eyes as he had in the party and I looked back at him, not flinching this time. It was just for a moment. The door handle made a clicking sound.

I stepped back outside, and Eric followed. We crouched down to avoid another blast of sleet. I offered his mittens back to him and he shook his head. "You may need them."

"How will I get them to you?" I asked.

"No problem," he insisted. "They're yours."

"But I want to get them back to you. You've been so kind."

"Okay," he said, reaching into his pocket, and handed me a card, "Call me."

Behind us, Carl escorted me to my car, made sure it started, then said, "Glad we could help."

"You're amazing."

He said, "I think it was fate," and winked at me.

Although poorly plowed, with ridges like cross-country ski tracks, the roads were passable. The main road had larger clearer patches because of the traffic.

As I drove, the snow turned into a deepening slush. Snow, pummeling the windshield, buffeting the pavement. I drove cautiously, keeping to the center of the road unless there was an approaching car.

A mile from the house, I saw a particularly clear section of road—the last stretch, I thought—and accelerated.

The car quickly picked up speed, but it was not a natural acceleration. Something was wrong. It slid, first a quick jerk to the right; next, a swerve to the left. Black ice. I slammed on the brakes—a mistake. The car spun laterally down the road, out of control. I let the brake go and downshifted, momentarily stalling its momentum. At best, I could only control the direction I was headed, not the skid. I was going off the road one side or another.

I clenched onto the steering wheel, preparing for impact into the hillside effacement. After several lurches, the car pitched forward, jammed against something, caught, tilted sideways and slammed to a stop in a ditch, teetering precariously on the driver's side, the headlamps glowering at the glassy rock abutment. The passenger's side, lifted, its wheels off the pavement, was partially in the oncoming lane.

I swallowed, took a breath. My mouth was dry.

Past 2:00 A.M.

Stuck.

I'd have to crawl across the passenger's seat to get out. Anyone coming either way could hit the car.

I kept the engine running to keep warm.

I checked to see if I'd been injured, moving my neck, arms, and legs. I checked the car mirror. The dashboard gauges were normal.

Chapter Twenty-Three

Then I saw headlights.

A car was coming right at me. I scrambled for the door, but it was jammed. The car kept coming. At the last minute, it swerved too, veered into the other lane and then coasted to a stop behind my car. I grabbed my mittens, and with all my effort, shouldered the passenger door open.

The other driver climbed out as well and was standing on the wide side of the road. He appeared to be a businessman, dressed in an elegant blue jacket. He spread his arms out for balance and skated on the ice over to where I stood. He shrugged and said, "There is not much you can do. You are wedged in there, fella."

Together, we tried to push me out, shoving the car from the side while I rocked back and forth on the gas pedal. My tires splattered him with slush.

He offered to call the State Police in Cumberland, where he lived, then he drove off. I hunkered down, my arms hugging my side, my hands surprisingly warm inside Eric's mittens.

The next cars to pass were two trucks and several sedans. Each came by slowly. I waved at them, but they kept going.

Finally, a large yellow van crept up the road, pulled over and stopped. Two men, bulky, one holding a bottle in his hand, glided over, sliding on the ice.

"Whee," the larger of the two exclaimed. "This is something!"

The larger one had a red flannel jacket, rolled up at the sleeves and distinct tattoos—guns and roses—on his arms. The other had a baseball cap, pulled down, but I could see he hadn't shaved in several days. I was wary. These were the type of men who might just as soon lay waste to me as say hello.

I stepped back toward my car.

"This is a fuckin skating rink," the guy with a red baseball cap called out.

I took off one of my mittens and offered my hand, but they ignored it. I shoved my hands back under my arms, telling them my name, but they didn't seem to hear what I said. The car, angled in the ditch, fascinated them.

"Holy shit. Look at that sucker," the one in the cap laughed.

"Hey buster, looks like you are in deep shit."

"You want a drink?" the first one offered, passing me the bottle. I wanted to prove myself, to act as if I was one of them. It seemed the best ploy. I wiped off the end with my sleeve and took a sip, whiskey, Jim Beam, not very good—and it burned like a fire in my throat. Bigger than me, sure of themselves, masculine in the way of brawny men, I felt inadequate beside them, scared, and unsure what to say or do.

I took another swig and passed it back to him. I wanted to act like a real guy. Flannel jacket told me baseball cap was a mechanic. "We've been over at his chick's house," he said. "He works in Morgantown, and here he's head over heels for this girl halfway across the state. Out of his fuckin' mind in love. Don't you think that's crazy?"

The mechanic knelt by my front fender, got on his belly, and checked out the underside of the car.

"You are fucked, no doubt about it."

"It's in the ditch, both side tires. In there good." He nodded, then turned to me, "But otherwise car's fine. No damage I can see."

I held the bottle as they consulted about what to do.

"Too heavy for the three of us," the friend said, pulling up on the fender.

Chapter Twenty-Three

Lights appeared on the curve, a car coming fast.

"Get the fuck off the road. That guy is humping it!" He grabbed my arm and ran, pushing me toward the ditch. "Get off the road fella."

The car caught traction, braked, slowed, straightened itself out, and drove in the other lane. It was completely in control by the time it reached my car. It was a green Pontiac with studded tires, and passenger rolled down the window and called out to us, "Need some help?"

Two more men, obviously drunk, in their early twenties, and husky, hollered, "What's happening, guys—a street party?"

They paid as much attention to me as a road sign and surveyed my car as if they were going to buy it, bending down to check the fender and frame, kicking at the tires, conferring in hushed tones with the mechanic and his friend. They came back to me and the five of us drank from the Jim Beam bottle.

"Okay, let's do it," the mechanic said, handing me the bottle. He told me to get to the back of the car with him and the other three went to the front. Stooping down, he motioned to me with his head as he held onto the bumper.

"Should I get in the car?"

"Fuck no, man," he said, "What the hell you wanna do that for?"

"What are we going to do?"

"Well, buddy, we're going to lift this son-of-bitch outta here," the mechanic informed me.

"Put the bottle down and get your mitts on the bumper."

I did as I was told. I felt honored. I was one of them. I would do my part. It didn't matter that it was my car. What mattered was that I was included in their fraternity.

He counted one, two, three. The car rose, in one swoop, out of the ditch and smacked down on the road like it had been dropped from heaven.

The mechanic smiled at me, "Light as a fuckin feather."

We cheered and high-fived each other. I stood stupefied. I felt like I'd had three nights in one. All thoughts of Eric and what I felt for him seemed irrelevant. I was a guy.

We finished the bottle. The mechanic, as a salute, threw the bottle against the embankment, and it shattered.

"That takes care of that," he said and told me to get in the car to see if the fucker worked. I started the ignition and drove it a few feet.

I hopped back out of the car. I wanted to shake their hands, but it didn't seem right, so I took off one mitten and saluted them like a soldier.

"No problem," the mechanic said, laughing and turned away.

He stood for a second, and in a hushed tone asked, "You all set?"

"Yeah, I am."

The black ice had dissipated in the time we spent hauling the car out, but I drove cautiously the last half mile to my home. When I parked in the driveway, I realized I hadn't really thanked them, but then, maybe they didn't need it. They did what they did. And that was that. No need for thanks. It felt good. It felt right. It felt not so bad.

I bent over in the cold night air to check my car: only a slight scrape and little dent on the left side. Nothing serious, considering.

The globe lamp over the door spread a faint halo, a little oval-shaped blessing, on the snow. My hands felt warm in the mittens. I went inside the apartment put them on the counter by the phone with the card with Eric's name on it on the dresser next to my bed.

Chapter Twenty-Three

It struck me that two very different types of men had saved me. One was kind, gentle, and soothing. The others were strong, tough, and resolved. And for me, late as it was, I was wondering more than I ever had before which type of man I was and, finally, wanted to be.

Chapter Twenty-Four

Over a week had passed since I'd met Eric. His card was still on my nightstand, and I pretended not to look at it.

I went out with Suzie on a weekend fling with her friends Vince and Alazia, who had driven Suzie to rendezvous with me. We rented a room in a bed and breakfast in the northern part of the county. For dinner, we went to a combination grocery store/diner. A few tables were set to the side of a lunch counter, and we ordered the special, a turkey dinner with mashed potatoes and mixed vegetables. Classic Americana.

We watched a turkey shoot. Fifteen men, each with rifles, gathered inside by a window at the back of the store beside our table to watch as well. Dressed in bib overalls, they looked to be farmers.

Outside the window, at about forty yards was a bull's-eye on a tree. There were three rounds. First one man would shoot, then another, and another until the first round was finished. The winner announced, they toasted him, guzzled a beer, opened another, and chatted as the targets were set back up. By fourth round was reduced to a shoot off among three winners for previous rounds. The older man took a long time steadying his rifle, aiming it properly and peeled off three rapid shots; a younger man, scrawny and lanky with the makings of a beer belly, went to the window, pulled up his rifle, shouldered it and bam, bam, bam. It was over. A third stout fellow waddled to the window, having to lift each leg as if it were dead weight to get out of the way, sat on a stool, rubbed the rifle with a cloth and fidgeted with the trigger. Someone badgered him, "Hurry up. Sam, we don't have all night." He kept polishing his rifle, raised it, adjusted himself on the seat, and took aim. He fired once, then looked out, squinting his eyes to see the result. Then he fired again, checking once more. Last time he fired, he nodded his head. He won, all three bull's eyes. The store owner presented him with a twenty-pound turkey, still in feathers.

That night, we slept together in the same room, Suzie and I in a bed across from Vince and Alazia. It was cold. Suzie nuzzled next to me, kissed me on the neck. I found myself unresponsive, my arms by my side, my body unplugged, without sensation. Across the room, I could hear them making love, the soft whimpers and moans. Suzie wanted us to join in, fondling my penis, but I felt offended, her taking the lead. I shoved her hand away.

There was a voice inside me—was it the little boy?—that kept saying, No repeating it until I became dizzy. My thoughts kept going back to Eric, the way he held my hand and rubbed it, how gentle he was with me. I craved gentleness. wanted him back.

"Is something wrong?" Suzie asked.

"Give me some time," I said.

She put her hand on my cheek. "My poor, little boy."

"Don't call me that."

Even when, some months before Suzie had a girlfriend over with her boyfriend, and they'd made love in the living room while we were in the bedroom, nothing held me back. I enjoyed listening to them as I made love to her, but not now.

Chapter Twenty-Four

The image of the laundromat lights across the street from her place came back to me. What was I doing with her now? What was I trying to prove? I told her to wait, but she kept rubbing me again. My penis recoiled. I started to sweat. The room closed in on me. I could barely breathe.

Before she could finish, I shoved back the covers, pulled on my shirt and whispered, "I've got to go."

She sat up in bed and grabbed my T-shirt.

I jerked it away. I was drenched in sweat. All I could think about, all I could focus on, was getting out the door.

Vince called out, "What's going on?"

"I'm not feeling well. I need to go."

"Hey, don't do that. The fun is just beginning," he sat up, bare chested and swung his legs to the side of the bed.

Suzie grabbed me from behind. "Come on, hon."

"This will be a special night," Vince said, stepping toward me, naked, half erect.

I averted my eyes. "I know," I said, pulling away from Suzie. "But I feel sick. I need to get home."

Suzie crawled out of bed and came up to me. "Why you're drenched. You shouldn't be going out on a night like this."

"I'm OK. Just let me go," I insisted, kissing her on the head and pushing her away.

She called me every few days for several weeks, and, once, unannounced, she came to my apartment to talk. By then, we both knew that our relationship was off again, for good. We had a beer, and she told me that Alex had invited her to move in, and she was thinking about it. She asked if I had kept her pink negligee, and I told her it was hanging in my bedroom. She went to retrieve it and came out hold up Eric's card.

"Eric Kendrick?".

I blushed. "Eric. From Alex's party."

"How do you know him?"

"I met him that night. His friend helped me. I locked my keys in the car and his friend, he got them out. I borrowed his mittens, and I wanted to return them." Sweat beaded on my brow once more, and one droplet dribbling down my cheek.

She wrinkled her brow. "You know he's, well, he's—."

"Gay."

"Yes, he is."

My face flushed. My hands were cold.

"Well, you know, that's okay with me. He's a nice guy."

"Is that all there is?" She sighed and came over to me and wiped the sweat off my brow with her thumb. She knew. I could see it in her eyes. A half-grin came across her face. She nodded her head and looked into my eyes. "It's okay. It really is. You don't need to be afraid." She gave me a hug, pressing her cheek against my chest. "Hey, it was a good run, and I enjoyed it. Hope you did, huh?"

"I did."

"Take care, sweetie," she said, kissing me. "Take care."

I threw myself into work. Mercifully, there were always events that drained the day, minor crises in Centers—toilets stopped up, ovens not working, children with measles.

A regional Head Start Conference, slated for Washington, D.C.,

Chapter Twenty-Four

offered Carole and me three glorious days in the Capital, all expenses paid and for once, I was torn about going until Doug offered to take care of Toby since he had some work to do in the lodge.

The presenters offered new ideas for staff development, better approaches to engaging hard-to-reach parents, and innovative educational curricula. I couldn't manage to retain much of anything. At lunch Carole and I sampled every cuisine—Chinese, Thai, Indian, Italian, and French—within walking distance from the hotel. At night we went to nightclubs in Georgetown. In one, we saw Mary Travers perform, her voice not as pure as I'd hoped. During a break, she was on a balcony smoking, her golden hair draped over her shoulders, her cigarette held up so she looked like Lauren Bacall in Key Largo, deeply inhaling.

Before the last day, Carole had to return to Petersborough because her lead teacher had been hospitalized with pneumonia.

Left alone, after milling around in the hotel lobby, checking out several of the booths that offered early childhood materials—developmentally appropriate toys and games—I wandered out on K Street, not sure of the city layout, and followed the flow of pedestrians. Cars blared their horns, squealed their tires—the intoxicating sound of city life, quite a jarring contrast to my apartment by the river.

I came to an intersection, not sure which direction the streets went—toward the National Mall or south toward Georgetown—I turned to the right, glancing in shop windows, noticing across the street a store with blazing red lights with a bookstore sign Adult Only. Stunned, I loitered for a moment, wondering how that could be, how an adult bookstore could be located right in the middle of the commercial district, right down the street from the big department stores, not blocks from the White House. A steady stream of men came in and out of the door—some young men my age, some older in business suits—as casually as if they were going to get a cup of coffee.

I'd been in an adult bookstore in Nashville, but that was years ago. I'd vowed never to go into another one, the temptation too great. I walked toward this one as if under a spell. I stepped through the door.

On one wall, there was a magazine rack with several men browsing, paging through magazines. A heavy-set guy stepped by me, and I followed him skirting by a man who stood at the elevated register. I looked up at him. He glowered at me, his fat face with squinty eyes looking like the Cheshire Cat passing judgement on everyone who entered. His two meaty hands rested on the counter. I took several steps and picked up a magazine, going for inconspicuous.

I had done nothing wrong. I was, after all, an adult. Or at least, had the rights of one.

Other men moved from one side of the room, not making eye contact, slinking by one another. Some were absorbed in magazines, some were looking at videos, some disappeared into a side room you entered through two black curtains. It was like everyone agreed to pretend that no one else existed, complicit with each other's anonymity. The magazine that had been a prop to preoccupy me turned out to be a homosexual magazine with beautiful men, young men, naked, and erect, staring at me.

I leafed through one page after another. My chest felt as if someone had shocked me with AED pads.

The man at the counter gave several men quarters in exchange for dollar bills. The traffic in and out of the back room was as busy

Chapter Twenty-Four

as a subway station, when the black curtains parted, and someone exited, just as quickly, someone else entered. I ducked my head and joined the current.

I ventured through the curtains, pushing them aside.

There was a long narrow hallway, walls painted midnight blue, with open booths on either side. Men in the booths were looking at videos on small, twelve-inch screens. Many left the curtains opened so the films were plainly visible. Blue-gray light flickered in the darkened hallway. The bodies of men, their faces gray in the reflected light, floated by me.

A short, angular man with a congenial appearance, glanced back at me from one booth, his eyes swiftly appraising me from head to foot, as if he recognized me.

Maybe, I thought, he was at the conference?

He put a coin in a red slot and a video appeared on the monitor, a video of a barely legal boy sitting on a chair, completely naked. The man smiled at me and nodded his head, motioning for me to join him in the booth. He pointed to a space beside him as casually as someone offering a seat in a subway. His hand gripped his crotch. He looked down and back up at me. I wiped the sweat above my upper lip.

"Join me," he whispered. "It is alright. Come on." He held the curtain back with one hand. He had a lovely smile. Large white teeth. He motioned again. My legs felt hot inside my pants. The hair seemed to bristle against the fabric.

"Hey, my boy," he pleaded in a mellifluous voice. "Time's a-wasting."

My hand reached out to his, the tips of my fingers touching his. My feet turned me around. I bolted into the other room and out the front door, doing double-time down the street before I could take another breath. I charged around the block to the intersection and kept walking until I could make out a park—the National Mall—and the White House and, off in the distance, the Washington Monument, its giant girth framed against the blue sky.

I pressed by people, a seemingly endless gaggle of them—tourists with cameras dangling from their necks, businessmen or government bureaucrats in suits and ties, laid-back hippies in their sandals and jeans—toward a visible destination, the white marble monument. If I could get there, if I could walk up those stairs, I might find my old self, the innocence of that time as a senior in high school on a field trip to Washington I scaled the steps to the top.

I perched on one of the monument's exterior marble slabs and peered across the Reflecting Pool at Lincoln's dark visage, hidden inside. He came to this city reviled and scorned and managed to make the right decisions to hold himself and the nation together, yet assassins waited for him as they are waiting for us all, and they finally got to him. My assassin was not hidden, he was inside me, wanting to kill whatever hope I had of being normal. I walked all the way across The Mall and stood at Lincoln's enormous feet. I felt a cold dread seep inside of me. I stayed there over an hour, sheltered within its sanctuary, and his words immortalized on the walls:

> With malice toward none; with charity for all; with firmness in the right, as God gives us to see the right, let us strive on to finish the work we are in; to bind up the nation's wounds; to care for him who shall have borne the battle, and for his widow, and his orphan—to do all which may achieve and cherish a just and lasting peace, among ourselves, and with all nations.

Chapter Twenty-Four

My breath steadied. This war raging inside me, whatever its final resolution, had endured for years. I thought if I could only have charity for all of it, if I could bind up my own wounds, I could go on. I needed to make some choices. I needed either to give Eric a call or toss his card away. Getting into a booth with some stranger was not what I wanted. I didn't want to be like Suzie, going after whatever was there.

I headed back to the conference. But, throughout the afternoon, the smile of the man in the booth flashed in my mind, a quick flicker of temptation that soon dissipated only to recur, to be blotted out, and come again, which I realized, as it appeared, reminded me of Eric's face that night in the snowstorm, smiling, waving at me as I headed to my car. His smile kept returning like some reckoning that had to be faced, an appointment I had, sooner or later, to reconcile.

When I got back to the lodge, I let Toby into the kitchen, fed him, and played with him. I set him upside down on my lap, and boxed with him, his paws swatting at my hands like Muhammad Ali.

I took off for a walk to clear my head. Toby followed me. He sniffed, leaped at leaves, and kept pace.

The moon-lit road with its rocky surface had a chiaroscuro effect, black with white edges, like close-ups of the moon. An early spring flower stirred on the roadside, waving its faint white blossoms.

The more night walks I took, the more convinced I became that we—human beings—had never befriended the night. Black was to be scorned. It was always associated with how heroes stole fire from the gods. We were fire people.

Oh, I thought, maybe my task is to befriend the night and to defy the light.

At the side of the road was a slim opening through the trees, a path that led to a ledge. Walking up and down several slopes, my hands in front of me to avoid snaring saplings, I came to a white pine, six feet in diameter with branches obliterating the sky. I'd encountered it many times, but still, its sheer bulk intimidated me. Early people worshipped trees such as this. At night, the tree's physicality, its mass—dark and dense, looming, broken only by slivers of moonlight through its branches, reminded me of the massive exterior of an unlighted building in Washington, D.C. But it was a living being, not brick and mortar, not just something to be knocked down to make way for a new structure. It was far older than I was, more powerful, with roots set down before the Civil War, more rooted to a place than I had ever been. As I stood in front of it, it seemed to announce, "Behold. I'm the center of the earth."

I looked up at it, tried to take it all in, walked around it, touched its rough bark. I let it know I meant no harm, that I, indeed, knew it to be grander and more powerful than I.

From there, a slate slope with jagged slabs rose toward the cliff. Bent over, my hands in front of me, my feet stepping carefully, I inched up the slope, using the stars, now illimitable above me, as a guide. Toby, steady and sure on his feet, walked beside me as if to say, "Hey, this is no problem. What's the big worry?" At the slope's crest, I knelt on my hands; a few feet in front of me I could see a vast empty space, and, below, the river. I swung around to sit down, digging my heels into the slope. Toby moved into my lap. He licked one of his paws. I wondered if he had cut it. The slate, shattered like

Chapter Twenty-Four

broken pottery, would cut my hands if I weren't careful. I held onto a scrub red cedar, twisted and gnarled a few feet from the edge. I didn't want us to fall. The sapling was a lifeline. It had four large nails in it, twisted upward as if to hold something—maybe a rope for swinging into the river. Even in the dark, I could see splotches of a pale luminous yellowish-green moss on its north side.

This was my spot. I had been here before. The first time, with only the thin cedar to hold onto, with the rest of the ground falling away from me in all directions, I felt like a man in free fall. As I spent more time there, though, claiming it as my spot, my fear lessened, and I came to find solace in being set apart atop a ridge. Every few weeks, at nightfall, I climbed the slate hillside, slipping and sliding, grabbing at the roots of other shrubs until I got to the top. Toby came with me. He seemed to enjoy the evening jaunts. From there, I could look back through the underbrush and upper limbs at the house below, a pale flavescent patch of light from the lodge's back porch leaking out on the back patio. The light had a sturdy quality, etched, as it was, against the black.

The moon at its fullest, I could lean over the cliff and see its light languidly threading the water. The clear and sharp bark of a lone dog carried across the fields. Far in the distance, a farmhouse had one lighted window. It seemed I was not on the same planet as the people in the valley. In the summer, the farmhouse light seemed close, but later, in the winter, it seemed farther away, and beyond it, the road which curved by the farmhouse was striped by car beams against the white snow. When the river froze, the length of it was a long white unbroken line. I wondered if, when lights went out after dark, when candles burnt down, when oil was used up, people would see again gods configured in the galaxies. I could make out Orion, the great hunter with his belt, and his lover Artemis, goddess of the moon. He reminded me of Toby who, on some nights, would sneak off by himself, stealthily, each paw placed precisely when he sniffed some mouse or mole in the shrub. I liked to find Libra in the skies, my sign, the scales that I tried to keep in balance and, of late, kept tilting one way or another. There was always Ursa Major and Ursa Minor, the two bears chasing themselves across the southern sky. Occasionally, a shooting star flared and blinked out after a few seconds. How silent was the night, just like the Christmas carol, silent with only the hint of nocturnal insects, their susurrant sounds, restless, still active.

Without a television, only a record player, I came to rely on the overlook as my window into the larger world. Being there reminded me of Thoreau at Walden Pond wanting to confront the essential facts of reality, to live deliberately. He'd set aside a career, gone off to be by himself, and let the natural world be his teacher.

Certainly, I wasn't like him. But I could at least for an evening, let go of trying to be one way or another, and just let myself be with the entirety of it all. I could forget if I were gay or straight, if I should rip up Eric's card or call him up, if I should start dating someone else, if I should be as others wanted me to be, or if I should be myself. If, indeed, I knew what I was. Out of my confusion, the wildness of the natural world offered a reprieve. It took me in as one of the creatures, as an animal like Toby who, whenever we came to our perch above the river, seemed pleased I finally had come to appreciate the wildness he loved, and cherished being there.

Young Cherokee boys were brought to such places far from their village and told to wait without food and water until they

Chapter Twenty-Four

had a vision. Being a long time alone inside their head allowed them, if they listened intently, to discover their own voice in the night sounds. I imagined the inside of their bodies had as much darkness as the outside. They could feel themselves being filled up with the dark, being absorbed by it, pulled away. It became part of their being. In our culture, boys folded themselves in front of a TV, clicked on a remote control, and flipped through channels to find meaning, to become one with some sitcom. Outside their windows, the dark became less and less their own, wholly unfamiliar as if abandoned and forgotten. For me, it had become a friend. It enveloped me. I could sit with it for hours, and did.

I could have scuffled down the slope on my rear end, my hands reaching carefully for one limb after another, feeling quiet inside, serene. I could go back to reading or writing with my mind cleared, Toby in my lap, letting me rub his belly. That was the grace of living alone and being far from others. I trusted that, when the wind stirred, when the leaves shuddered, when a howl rose in the dark, I did not belong to the animal world as Toby did. But I was no longer a stranger to it. I listened to the owls, raccoons, ferrets and Toby hunting familiar ground and became, for a moment, a creature familiar with and part of the night, and then, went back to the light—my cave—to dwell in the confines of my books and my writing.

Chapter Twenty-Five

With Suzie no longer part of my life, Tess worried I'd feel lonely. "Let's spend more time together," she said one night when she called me on the phone.

Worried about Jerome getting jealous, I suggested we should meet in town, not at my place.

"My Jerome, he's such a worrier. But I must tell you, he's harmless. Most of the time I'm gone, he's quite happy. He can drink all he wants, and mama isn't there to hide his bottle or to scold him," she said, laughing. "In fact, most of the time when I come home, he doesn't even know I'm back until he smells the coffee brewing the next morning."

"But you said he came after David with a gun."

"Oh, yes. That was unseemly. He created quite a scene. But nothing happened—and nothing had been going on, not with David. No, no, no, not with him. I'm sure, Sir Dragon, you understand," she said, patting my leg.

She had come to call me "Sir Dragon" after one of her favorite children's stories because I lived, as she called it, in a cave.

"Oh," she said in her husky voice, "I like how you go here to your cave and hide out to write your poems. That's quite unusual. Most young men your age want to be in the middle of everything, out to a dance, out climbing the ladder. You're different."

From that night, she took me further under her wing. And just as I had with David, she and I listened to a lot of music together. She introduced me to more composers that I didn't know—Richard Strauss, Chopin, Bach, and Vivaldi.

When I didn't have a recording, she'd buy it for me on one of her DC excursions and play it for me.

From Beethoven's opera, Fidelio, one night she played the aria "Gott! Welch' Dunkel hier!" (God What Darkness Here). Florestan, imprisoned, starving to death, sings of his longing for his wife, Leonore. I fell in love with the music. The music dips and then swells, and he sees "ein engel im rosigen Duft." (An angel in the golden mist.) His voice rises to a fever pitch, and then, with the notes suspended in air, the aria is over. Done. The abrupt end sucked the air out of the room. Even when I did not know what it meant, I felt as if someone had snapped my heart in two.

"How was it?" she asked.

"My God," I said. "What can I say?"

Embarrassed that I was crying, I started to stand, but she leaned over and pulled me to her. Maybe it was the aria's desperation and longing, but I felt as if there was something imprisoned inside me. When Florestan sang of his longing, it was a longing that I had, too. Tess didn't fully understand why Florestan's voice had such an effect on me. I tried to explain that it was because it was a man's voice. I didn't tell her that the aria reminded me again of Eric, my yearning for him.

She rocked me in her arms and cooed, "My boy, my dear boy."

I felt the little boy in me melt. Felt that at least someone understood him or wanted to.

Later she explained that Florestan's longing for his wife Leonore was so intense because he was locked away in a dungeon and was

Chapter Twenty-Five

sure that it was the end of his life. He had no idea that his wife, determined to free him, had disguised herself as a man and snuck into the prison. I could have laughed because I, too, wanted some lover to set me free.

As I played Fidelio, again and again, as I played Richard Strauss's Four Last Songs—another piece she gave me—my longing for Eric and for someone to love was married with other artists with the same pangs, the same yearning as mine.

The music spoke to me of that loss, that sadness, but spoke in a way that made me feel better because it also spoke of beauty.

Tess told me that every one of these composers lived with some private torment.

"What do you mean?" I asked.

"Well, take Tchaikovsky," she said. "Such beautiful music. But can't you hear in his violin concerto the agony?"

"Yes, I love that. The sadness."

"Well, I probably shouldn't say this since I don't want to offend you, but since you seem to be so open, not inclined to judge someone for a failing, I will. Tchaikovsky was tormented by his homosexuality. Of course, he tried to deny it. But there it is, coming out, cast nonetheless in the spell of his music."

I said, "It makes his music even more meaningful. That's good to know."

In last song in Fidelio, when Leonore saves Florestan, an exuberant outburst interweaves the sad chords of earlier arias into an ode to joy. The violins soar through agony. The music taught me to express a range of emotions in my poems. I gathered the inspiration—sadness, joy, anger, and excitement—and dove deeper into depths I had not fathomed before.

River Crossed

After weeks of our quiet, short visits in my cave, to celebrate our time together, she brought two new records, two bottles of wine and a bag full of fixings for a meal—salad, pasta, a clam linguine sauce, shrimp, crab legs wrapped in white butcher paper, some haddock, and fresh beans. She had heard a symphony in Washington and was brimming with delight. She had me put on a record and told me to sit while she prepared dinner. Her treat. I put on Mahler's Symphony No. 5, careful to place the stylus on the record rim, not to scratch it. Joining her back in the kitchen, I started to uncork the wine, but she told me to open other surprises she'd brought.

One at a time, I opened them. There was a Melitta coffee set with the filter and paper filters. She said, "Now you can make coffee the right way. We will have some tonight." She pulled out a skillet. "The best, heats quickly," she said, holding it up, "just sponge to clean it off." There was a set of carving knives. My only knife was a short, dull blade that she held up by its black handle and unceremoniously dropped in the trash can. There was a set of six wine glasses. She took two of them, washed them, and set them to dry. There was a corkscrew, one of those you rest on the lip of the bottle, with two wings on either side of the cork that you press down and pop the cork up, never damaging the cork. I used it and poured two glasses full.

She clinked my glass to hers, "To Sir Dragon in his cave."

I held Toby in my arms, rocking him back and forth. He nestled into my armpit. He enjoyed being held, liked to scrunch up on my neck, curl around, and fall asleep. Tess thought he was a perfect companion.

Chapter Twenty-Five

"He's taken to you," she said. "He wants to protect Sir Dragon, too," Tess told me to turn up the music and aim one speaker at the kitchen. She swooped around. She threw a carton of shrimp into the refrigerator. Pulled out pans and skillets. Cut and snapped the beans, boiled the water, crushed the garlic, toasted almonds in butter. The aromas suffused the room. Her movements, so adept and practiced, seemed musical.

"Listen, listen to the music," she said. "The second movement is so powerful. I love it."

Trumpets blared, a stupendous fanfare intoxicating the room.

Then, it slowed. Soft melodic strains crept in. Cascading back and forth, first intensifying, the horns dominating, and then slackening, the strings stepping forward like tidal waters slinking forth across rocks in a river. The violins swept in to create a counterpoint to the horns, tugging back and forth for dominance.

"You like it?" she asked. "It reminds me of you. The initial flash and bravado and then, almost unexpected, the quiet and, well, sensitivity and passion."

"That must be a compliment."

"You should be more comfortable with those qualities. So few people in our lives see us as we are, as I sense I do with you. You must take them in because they will come few and far between. You can count on that!"

She laughed, her deep husky laugh, and tossed some garlic in the skillet. "I thought I should initiate your new skillet, so it feels at home."

I walked over to admire her work. Little chunks of garlic, golden brown, shimmered in the olive oil and gave off a woody scent. Shrimp rimmed a plate with a cup of cocktail sauce on the counter. She speared one with a toothpick, dipped it in the sauce, and fed it to me.

"Good, yes?"

"Very good."

"Fresh. Here, have another," she said, offering me another one. She took a sip of wine.

"Good food is the secret of a good life."

The music had grown rich with violins, a deep yearning sound that almost made me weep. She poured me more wine. We took our plates to the porch, sat in the wicker chairs at the wicker table and sipped the wine.

"Savor each bite, "she said.

We listened to the river. She put another record on the phonograph, a Beethoven piano sonata and we sat on the couch. She leaned against me and rubbed my thigh, wistful.

She was much older than I was, as old as any of my mother's friends. Her face had an elegance to it that showed, even with the years, an exuberance and vitality which made her attractive. She was aware of it, but, at the same time, I could tell she was frightened that her beauty was fading and would soon vanish. When she was young, as I had seen in a photograph, her auburn hair cascading off her shoulders, her youthful body wrapped in a blue bathing suit on a rock ledge overlooking the seashore, I imagined that she was a fiery young woman.

I was intrigued by her touch. I yearned for a woman's touch, and let it be.

When she turned to me, I do not remember if it was Beethoven or, by then, Mahler again, but it was as if the music had turned with

Chapter Twenty-Five

her. She delicately unzipped my pants and unbuttoned the buttons of my white shirt. She slipped it back off my shoulders as delicately as she had removed the butcher paper from the fish. Each piece of clothing was folded, as if it were precious and placed on the chair by my desk. She stood in front of me and asked me to hold her wine glass, while she undressed.

She pressed her finger against my lip. She nestled next to me and kissed me. We glided onto my bed. She enjoyed sex as much as she enjoyed music and fixing a meal. She took her time. I was surprised how comfortable I felt. None of the anxiety I had felt with Suzie came back.

On the record was Mahler's 5th Symphony. She held my erection and giggled like a little girl—"It is so hard and yet dignified. Yes. That is the word, dignified." We lay back down on the bed, me inside of her. She orchestrated our movements: for long stretches we listened to the violins ebbing under the horns, then the woodwinds where I started to move as she leaned back—"Good, good. Oh, that is nice,"—and, as the music softened, she pulled me close to her—"Shh. Quiet"—and I held my place, resting on her until I felt the trumpets and, below them, horns and trombones blaring. She let go of me and I moved again until at last, timed with the crescendo of the symphony, I came, and by then, she was with me saying, "Oh my, yes. That is good. Yes. Yes." We were quiet for an hour, and then, with arousal, she insisted on another record, and we made love again.

I did not feel any pressure to perform. She seemed like a connoisseur who was not about to let a moment slip by her without tasting it fully. While enjoying each other's bodies, we were ageless.

She held me close to her after the last time and hummed, rocking me back and forth.

"You are quite wonderful," she whispered. "Quite wonderful."

I'd had others comment on me as a lover. Suzie said I was good at it. Most of the times I felt as if I managed to do alright with women, but never with much assurance that what I was doing was, indeed, pleasurable to them.

With Tess, it was the two of us. I felt a strange sense of gratitude, as if I had been initiated into adulthood. I leaned back and gazed at her face in the milky moonlight. Her high cheekbones. Her mouth, quiet and calm. Her eyebrows fluttering.

"This is the best music appreciation class I have ever had," I told her. She gave a hearty laugh." Oh, Sir Dragon. Very nice."

Late one Sunday evening, I was already in a robe, ready to go to bed. Tess swooped in unexpected on her way to Washington. We spent several hours in bed, she gave me several record albums, one by Chopin and another by Strauss, both her favorites, inscribing them to Sir Dragon.

My head beside hers on the pillow, I said, "Shouldn't we call it off? I don't want trouble. My director told me to be careful. Rumors spread quickly here. I can't afford to lose my job. I must be careful. Don't you see?"

"Don't fret. Nobody knows. You have nothing to worry about."

She undid my robe, knelt between my legs, and took me in her mouth. For a moment, I let go of time. My double lives left me exhausted. For weeks, I had no interest in work—paperwork, budget

Chapter Twenty-Five

crunching, food deliveries, visits to Centers. All of it weighed on me. Deadlines for completing grant requests had passed. I had to get to work early in the morning and get back to a solid work routine. Yet here I was, letting her have her way and, despite my fears, my enjoying it. Whatever role I was playing—the paramour, the cheater, the daring lover—had an appeal. It was dangerous. That made it more exciting.

Tess stayed overnight. She told me to wake her early in the morning. She wanted to do some errands on the way to the city When I woke at 7:00, the rain had shifted to a light freezing drizzle that spit against the window.

I lifted her arm, and she stirred. She resisted at first. "Oh, please don't wake me. It feels so lovely, my dear man, to hold you." She touched my sex and seemed to want to do it again. But I reminded her of her errands and told her that she had insisted I get her on the road by 8:00. We showered separately.

She made breakfast. It was her way: she wanted to treat me as if she had been my lover for years. With a knife, she sliced oranges. "You cut them thus," she explained, cutting them against the grain. "Then you make slices and at the tip of each, you loosen the core." She wielded the knife dexterously with her long, thin fingers.

"Why do it that way?" I asked.

"Oh, my dear, so you can eat them!" She took one slice, pulled the skin back, leaving the juicy core for me to suck on and eat. She laughed her deep throaty laugh. "We eat them as such in Brazil." She looked into my eyes with a feverish intensity. Her one eyebrow lifted slightly. "Exactly."

We ate a breakfast of coffee, oranges, and herbed scrambled eggs. She smoked one of her Newport cigarettes with its nice, mentholated, air freshener smell. It was perfect, a nice end, the last time—although I didn't know it then—that she would come to my cave. Before she left, she sat at my desk, pulled a pen from her purse, and wrote the names of several books that I might like, one a biography of Beethoven. "Be well my darling," she said, kissing me. "How I love coming to your lair. You are my dragon. Only mine."

Then, she drove off to Washington where she intended to spend the weekend. I was back to myself. I was already planning my night, after work, I would spend it writing.

Chapter Twenty-Six

Doug called me to inform me he had invited friends to come for the weekend.

I was in no mood to welcome anyone. I had been looking forward to being alone, doing some writing, playing with Toby. Tess had called and asked if she could drop by. I told her that it wasn't a good idea. She asked if something was wrong. She was distressed because she wanted to tell me in person that Jerome had been assigned to a new parish in Charleston—it had all happened very quickly—and they had to move. She wanted to come over to say goodbye.

Could she just make a quick visit?

I told her no. It wouldn't work. Not now. But I told her how wonderful it had been.

"You mean it's over?" she asked.

"I'm afraid so. I need to straighten out some things in my life."

"Is there someone else?"

"I think so."

She hung up rather abruptly. But later wrote me, keeping me in touch with her art world and music.

Maybe it was for the best. I hated goodbyes. It was like an artery being closed off and knowing, afterward, if you were going to survive, that you had to open it up and let the blood flow and find a new pathway to the heart.

Later, after she moved, she wrote me, addressing each letter "Dear Sir Dragon," and keeping up her role as a mentor, told me about her life, the latest musical recordings, and poetry books I might love to read.

At 3:00, a car came down the driveway. It was a long-limbed black man—Dominique with his partner, a pale, gaunt-like Andy Warhol—who knocked on my door. I was coy. I told them I'd left the door open to the main lodge and that Doug kept the beer in a refrigerator in the mudroom. Later, I watched from my window across the yard as they came downstairs and stood on the main house veranda, admiring the view. I tried to ignore them, yet I felt a strange tug from Dominique's honeyed voice.

I could hear them tramp back up the stairs. I had a twinge of loneliness. I didn't know where Doug was. I put a record on, ate some rice and beans, and played with Toby who liked to chase a toy mouse I'd bought for him.

As if my feet had decided to act before I had, I found myself at the glass doorway to the main lodge. It was unseasonably cold outside. My breath made little white puffs in the air. The river burbled in the background. Shuffling, my arms around my chest, I knocked and slid the door open.

"Hello," I said.

They were sitting inside. Dominique's partner stood up. His thin hair, drawn severely back on his skull like a hospital patient, made him look sickly. He limped when he walked.

"Nice to see you again," I said.

Chapter Twenty-Six

Dominique's glance was riveting. He stared right at me, and, it seemed, right through me. I averted my eyes, embarrassed. He wore a tight, brown, one-piece outfit with no belt. He leaned toward me, extending his hand, speaking softly, said, "Nice to see you, too."

I asked, "Would you like to come over for wine?"

Wallace, the partner, turned to Dominique who nodded, "Sure, that would suit us fine."

"Come over any time. I've got some music and all."

We downed an Austrian bottle of wine and uncorked a French one. Toby was attracted to Dominique and nuzzled in his lap, tucking deep into the folds of his pants.

I held the bottle up. "We might as well finish it."

"Please," Dominique said, and I poured the remains in his glass, twisting the bottle just as my father taught me. Dominique said that Doug gave them permission to sleep in the master bedroom, in the luxurious four-poster bed.

"He treats you like royalty," I said. "I was never allowed to sleep in it while this apartment was being built."

"You must come and join us," Wallace said.

"How kind," I said.

"That is nice music," Wallace said. He was leaning on the mantel and holding the record jacket of Beethoven's Emperor Concerto. He dangled his wine glass by his thumb and forefinger.

"I like it," I said. "I can imagine Beethoven writing it. The power in it. Listen to how it builds. It seems to go almost out of control like some mad rush and then pulls back." I waved my arms and conducted the piece. Wallace stood, gazing at me, then at the record jackets, and finally at Dominique. I kept putting on new albums. I put on several

Frank Sinatra albums and Wallace's tapped his foot.

"You know," he said, "Doug told us you were straight and, might want to keep some distance . . ." He trailed off.

I said, "It gets pretty lonely here sometimes. It's nice to have you over."

Wallace gestured to Dominique who stood up. I figured they were leaving.

"Do you mind," Wallace asked, "if we danced?"

I leaned back on the sofa. They were standing a foot apart like dance contestants, looking at me as if I had to tell them when to start.

"No, it's fine."

Wallace curled his arm around Dominique's neck. They moved slowly across the floor, dancing as lovers do, one step at a time in a tight square. Their hips snuggled closely together.

I sipped my wine, feeling the buzz in my head. I imagined I was back in high school, watching couples dance in the gym, beside my friend Jeff. We were two odd guys out, wishing we had girlfriends, and not daring to wish that we could dance, just the two of us, without anyone noticing.

They danced to one song after another on the album "Moonlight Sinatra." When it nearly ended, they stepped back from one another and held hands, satisfied. Wallace's lips were moist and swollen, his normally bleach-white skin rubescent. Dominique looked calm and controlled. They kissed. Wallace took several steps back and leaned on the mantel. Dominique sat across from me, dangling a leg dangerously close to one of mine.

The stylus clicked into place. Silence enveloped the room.

"Have you ever tried it with a man?" Dominique asked.

Chapter Twenty-Six

"Dancing?"

"No, the next step up from that."

"Why do you ask?"

He grinned. "It's better, man. Better than with a chick. There is so much more you can do." His palm traced a lazy pattern back and forth across my leg. A chill raced through me.

Wallace looked on with a smug expression. His right hand was deep in his pocket. As Dominique rubbed my leg, Wallace's expression changed to a sly grin. He stared at Dominique who looked at him. Wallace stepped to the door, whispering, "I'm going. Too tired to outlast both of you," and he slipped out the door.

I went over to the record player and put on a Johnny Mathis album, returning to the far end of the couch, getting as far away from Dominique as I could.

Dominique rephrased his question, "Do you want to try it with a guy?"

The wine had gotten to me. I took a quick slug which spilled down my chin. Dominique scooted over and, with his sleeve, wiped it off, his one leg drawn up at an angle so that it rested on his crotch.

He spoke in a soothing tone. "Come on, man, sit over here." He patted the place beside him—and I looked at his hand moving up and down on the couch, at the long, elegant fingers and the whiteness of his fingernails, at his muscular arm. His eyes were kind. He had high cheekbones. He wore a cherubic smile and furrowed his brow.

"You want to? I think, honey," he said and paused, "you do."

He seemed to know more about what I wanted than I did. I tried to think what to say but no words came out. He reached over and rested his hand on my shoulder. I tilted my head toward him. His arm came around my shoulder and rubbed it, prodding me to scoot over. I did. He slid next to me. *What the hell* is all I could think. *What the hell. Let me be wild.*

The bristle of his facial hair. His lips against mine. His tongue. My loneliness. His experience. My inexperience. His hands on my belly. My belt unbuckled. His shirt slipped off easily. The sound of my zipper. My jeans crumpling on the floor, looking sad and lonely. His face burrowing into my belly, pressing against it, nibbling on my flesh. It wasn't a woman's hand on my body, not the pliant, tentative hand of Tess. It was aggressive and assured, a hand that knew what another man wanted. His tongue licked my neck and ears, the inside of my thighs. He kissed me and I kissed him. He explored my body. I explored his. Our penises, hard and unashamed, speaking a language they knew of touch and counter touch. He lifted me up. I slung my arms around his neck. He carried me to my bed. I felt like a newlywed. He folded his body over me, pressed a finger against my anus, moistened it, probed it.

"Relax," he said. "I'll go easy."

Facing him on my back, my legs around his hips, I lifted my hips, letting him have me. When Dominique's penis pressed into me, there was a sharp pain. He pulled back, told me to breathe, to take it slowly. I thought to myself that it must be how a woman feels—the insistence of it, the way he gripped my back, thrusting back and forth with increased pace, his tongue in my mouth and his eyes, open, staring at me intensely. I must have swooned as he gripped my buttocks and lifted me up, pressing my body against his. Then his body let go, melted into mine. He drowned in the pleasure, the waves of which washed over us. As if swimming in

Chapter Twenty-Six

that mutual current of love, I mounted him and pushed into him. He pressed his hands against my face. "Easy. Easy now." He gradually let me rest, then, kissing me deeply, said, "Go on." He received perfectly to my thrusts. We lifted together off the bed. We drifted off in each other's arms, quietly content. Sleep overtook us.

In the morning, Dominique dressed and left, kissing me tenderly on the cheek and slipped out the door. By mid-morning three more cars pulled into the driveway. Dominique and Wallace greeted the new arrivals, a wiry black dancer, a stout broad-shouldered man with a cape, the opera singer, a red-haired man with a yellow bandana around his head. They hugged and kissed as if they were family. Shortly after that Doug pulled in, toting bags of groceries, cartons of beer, and a case of liquor.

I hid out in my apartment. The sun had come up and, in a matter of hours, not only baked off the chill, but became warm. Several of the men went out to the back lawn and basked in the sun, drinking, dancing, and belting out songs. The phonograph speakers, placed on the porch, blared at full volume. Men lying next to one another, kissing, drinking—a kind of frenetic madness to squeeze every delicious moment from the day. A homosexual entourage had spilled out of the Washington, D.C. area and splashed into the backyard, lounging on rocks. They were freed to be who they were. No masks.

At two in the afternoon, Doug knocked on my door, apologized for the racket, and invited me to join in. He wanted to introduce me to his friends, some of whom I already knew. I told him that I had already spent time with Dominique and Wallace. He seemed pleased.

"Aren't they a lovely couple!" he exclaimed. "I am so glad you got to know them. You're a dear to entertain them. That was above and beyond the call of duty."

I went out to chat with them and drank a glass of wine. Dominique was coy. As he brought drinks to some other guests, he offered to refresh mine. He sat by me and told me that he worked for a department store and did the window displays. He wore a white and yellow outfit. I couldn't get over how handsome he was. His eyes, liquid and inviting, told me that if he put his mind to it, he could seduce any man, or any woman if he was so inclined. I had trouble keeping my eyes off him.

Later that evening, after dinner, drinks, and conversation, when other couples, or singles who became couples, climbed the stairs to their rooms, Dominique followed me to the porch. It was warm and the air was still. He put his hand around my waist and asked if he could spend the night again. My body was screaming, yes, yes, yes. He knew it. Yet I told him, "No." I had crossed a boundary, strayed far from my comfort zone, given myself a chance to see what it was like to let go and be wild, and now, just hours afterward, I needed time to ascertain what it meant to have been in his arms, to have felt pleasure, unmitigated pleasure, holding onto him, feeling him inside me, and sensing that, however strange it was, however unusual, I went along and had enjoyed every minute. This was different than with Tom. I was so drunk when I was with him, I only remembered bits of the evening, little scraps of memory. With Dominique, I hadn't just gone along with it. I got immersed in making love. I thought of Eric. I had a whole batch of evidence and, like a lawyer with a new case, needed some time to make sense of it.

Chapter Twenty-Six

After I said no, Dominique kissed me, then touched his finger to my lips.

"It was lovely," he said. "I get it. Take your time, honey. Give it time."

I went to my room and wrote for hours. I recorded what had happened, what I felt, and what I didn't want to feel. I wrote until my open mind, luxuriating in the pleasures I'd just experienced, shut again, all the way back around to denial. I wrote until nothing was left to say except it was a mistake, a moment of weakness, and it wouldn't happen again. That is what I wrote. Mistake. Weakness. That is what I told myself.

In the film *Midnight Cowboy*, the hustler picked up two men, both pathetic, cloying, inept, and sad. I didn't want to end up like them.

From the exhilaration of being with Dominique, I soon slipped into despondency. It was as if my body wanted to go in one direction and my mind wanted to go in another. I felt split in half. I got drunk and felt wonderful, then became more tortured by each sober day that passed. Once more, the feeling of death—the sense of being closed off and trapped by my own feelings—came over me. I couldn't make up my mind. Something had to happen to free us from the labyrinthian doublethink.

When I came home at night from work, I would fantasize about putting an end to my struggle. But that wouldn't do. I'd tried that. Not for me.

It was the end of Head Start's year. For weeks, I met with Carol, helped close the Centers, did inventories, sent off reports, and wrote next year's grant applications. After nights working late, my head ached. On the drive home one night, I heard on the radio that the Viet Cong had invaded the central highlands. They were set to take over the southern areas that Americans had secured. This would split South Vietnam and make it harder to conclude the war. Nixon came on the air and said he would honor his commitment to withdraw the 400,000 American troops. He might do that, but he would probably increase his bombing of North Vietnam, I thought. He was a master of Orwell's double speak. I turned off the radio.

I needed a break from wanting to call Eric. At nights, my brain felt fried, and that was not a good time to call him. On top of my hesitancy about him being a guy, there was also the same hesitancy I had as an adolescent about asking a girl out on a date. I worried about rejection. "Do you want to go out?" would seem too forward. Putting off the call had become a neurotic habit. I would plan to do it, find an excuse not to do it, and then make a commitment to do it by Wednesday, then determine it would be better to wait until Friday, and the whole unbreakable cycle would repeat itself.

I spent nights playing with Toby, tossing a sock that he'd chase, boxing with him, letting him grab my hand with his two paws. If I had any energy, I'd write. It was late May. The air was lovely, warm, and light. The night sky, pocked with stars, invited exploration.

One night, on the back porch, gazing out at the river listlessly flowing under the willows, I remembered the two tabs that Larry gave me and what he said about a trip he'd taken.

I'd asked, "Where did you go?"

He'd laughed. "Not a car trip. An acid trip. LSD. You ever try acid? I have some really good stuff if you want."

Chapter Twenty-Six

That's when I'd accepted his offer and stuffed them in my pocket. I'd waited for the right time to try them—almost forgot about them—and fished them out of my sock drawer. The tabs looked innocent enough: like little, flat, orange-colored aspirin in a plastic baggy.

If you are going to use them," he had cautioned me, "give yourself plenty of time for the trip."

I fingered the pills for a moment, then threw them in my mouth. I went into the kitchen to fix some dinner while I waited.

The hamburger was good, juicy, medium rare—just the way I liked it. Initially impatient, waiting for the acid to do something. I assumed the tabs probably had lost their potency. I could read the new book I just had brought, *The Collected Poems of Wallace Stevens* or, perhaps, just do some writing. I'd always wondered how Stevens, a Vice President with Hartford Insurance, could manage to write poetry and still do his job. He claimed that imagination was the most potent faculty. Did he, when presenting to the board of directors, think how "the mimic motions made constantly a cry / although they were misunderstood?" I unwrapped the book with Stevens's executive face on its cover. Funny how executives looked the same, the same thick jowly faces with bland, indifferent expressions.

Not disappointed that the two tabs were flops—I had other things to do—I decided to clean up the kitchen and get to work. I went to wash off the dishes. As I turned on the water, I noticed the flow of water seemed to explode and splatter and spill out from the plate into the sink and from the sink into the kitchen, and from the kitchen into the other room. I waved my hand at the water—*it must be an illusion*, I thought—and my hand, as it swept through the air, created a rippling effect stirring the air, and it fluttered up in an arching rainbow, rippled downward as children do when they circle their arms with sparklers, creating the illusion of one continuous loop of color. I felt the water, distinctly warm, on my hand, but, as I looked at my hand, I could no longer distinguish what was my hand (its shape) and what was water (its flow).

This is not good, I thought. *I can't tell what is real and not real.*

I felt a panic in my throat. Every time I moved, I caused light waves to explode out from me, splashing against the walls and splattering into empty space. If I held still—and I tried to—the room, the walls, the windows, the floor, the sink, and the cabinets blended, shapeless splotches, amazing colors, blues, reds, yellows, greens, spurting to and fro as if I had unleashed them, totally independent of me. There was no solidity. Objects which had once stood by themselves—the desk, the couch, the chair, the dresser joined in and merged with the sweeping colors. I closed my eyes. No better. I could no longer distinguish what was outer and inner, me and not me, this or that.

I put my hand on the wall, feeling for the telephone, and the wall melted into reds and blues and greens, sparkling and spewing over my fingers like fingerpaint. I had to concentrate. It was hard to distinguish the wall from the phone. They flowed together in one stream, colors blending into colors, fused in a seamless kaleidoscopic mishmash.

I needed to dial Larry's number. I had to find out what to do.

Focusing on the white membrane of the phone for brief moments, I could make out numbers. 7. Got it. 7. Got it. 8. And patiently, found 4 and 3 and 6 and 2. The phone at the other end rang.

Chapter Twenty-Six

A voice.

"Hello."

"Lou, is Larry there?"

"You OK?" Her words rippled out of the mouthpiece.

"Larry?"

"Okay. Okay. I will get him."

When Larry came on the phone, I blurted out, "I took the two tabs!"

"Great!"

"Nothing is real. In the middle of the river, but underwater."

"Yeah, that's how it works."

"Works?" I screamed. "This doesn't work. I'm out of my fucking mind."

"Right."

"Right? How can you say *right*? Nothing is right."

"Listen to me. Can you listen?"

"The colors!"

"Take a deep breath, real slow. Yes, like that. Feeling better? Here's the deal. You have got to get real and not real out of your head. You understand? When you are on LSD, man, there is no reality. No binary systems. Things as they are—objects—are no longer distinct. Everything that is, is interconnected—every breath you take, every move you make, all you see and experience—it's all one. And, man, that's what's going on all the time. But people have lost the ability to see that. They live in compartments. With LSD, you need to let go of compartments. Forget normal. You need to find a way, any way you can, to find the flow. Isn't it amazing? Everything flows together. All the energy that's out there—now you can see it. Finally, you get to see it. It's also inside you. Just the flow.

It's a gift. You just have to accept what is. Go with it. Enjoy it."

"Accept what is?" I'd been unsuccessful at doing that for years. The wall melted before my eyes. If I traced my fingers over the panel's surface, they became like a brown river, the brown oozing out in a myriad of patterns that extended outward into space like a ripple in a pond.

"How can I enjoy it when nothing is real—it's all blur?"

He laughed. "That is, man, what is. Don't you get it? Remember what I said about letting the wildness in you be? We're just energy, all of us, and LSD just lets you see it as it is. Reality is not out there. It's in us and around us. It surrounds us. LSD lets you participate."

The gears in my mind started to shut down. Listening to words took too much work. He might be right. The visual fireworks shot off anywhere I turned. Panels melted into windows; the floor oozed out the door into the yard, and the yard, what there was of it, spun around in a kaleidoscope of shapes assembling and disintegrating into other shapes, all infused with brilliant colors like a Jackson Pollock painting except there was Pollock now live, splashing buckets of paint. I was dizzy. It was like the finale of a Fourth of July show, except it was in my kitchen by what had been my phone and what used to be my hand that had become a magic wand.

"So, what do I do? Tell me again. I do nothing? How long will it take?"

Tossed like Alice in Wonderland into a place that had no semblance to what I knew, I dropped down into a rabbit hole with no exit and no path to follow out of this new reality.

"Three, four hours, sometimes more. Just breathe. Let go and

Chapter Twenty-Six

enjoy the ride. Be wild. That's why they call it a trip. You are in the place you've never been in before."

I knew whatever he was saying, he was right. I could not change what was happening to me no more than I could change how I felt about sex. I had to give myself over to it. I had entered a movie theater of the absurd. The doors had locked behind me. No getting out. I had to let it play out. I took a deep breath.

I hung up.

I leaned my head against the wall. I felt like crying, but I took several long, slow breaths, as he said I should, and gazed up. The room and all the empty space within the room where normally there seemed to be nothing—just air—converged into a great, swirling galaxy. More energy, a pulsing force field I could not normally see but was here and now revealed itself to me. It was reality. It converged and dissipated and rushed at me, and over me, and around me.

I found the door handle—the metal cool on my hand—and opened the door on a world that vibrated with long sweeping stands of light darting up and out, down and across the field of my vision. I could see the air move. Careful to creep along the slate path by the house—the one sure reality I could count on was touch—I gathered confidence in my ability to swirl though the energy field like a dancer with colored scarves trailing ahead of and behind him. I made my way down the steps to the dock, sat, and listened to the river. Its blues, greens, yellows, reds, and violets are amassed. It took my breath away.

To think this was always here, this force of nature. The world felt incarnate, as alive as the flesh of my hand, which, when I slid it through the water, sent out a whirlpool of light. I thought that how I experienced the river at this moment was how fish must feel inside it.

This swirling current of energy lapped continually around their scales, playing musical notes on their heads and songs inside their mouths.

On the bank of the river, I began to enjoy the trip. I sat there like a tourist in a new country, taking in the view. I dismissed ideas of what to expect. Nothing kept its original shape. The dock, and river, and the air, and my body—all those names I gave different elements—blended. I was sitting within them, the force field of one intermeshing with the other.

When I first read Black Elk Speaks, Black Elk spoke of all of life being a circle, a large hoop, where everything, living and non-living, was part of a larger whole. I laughed at myself because, as much as I wanted to understand what was happening, I knew that I did not understand anything. The motion of my hand, the tip of my head, the blink of my eye—each was as momentary and ephemeral as light—yet enduring. It was always there and, as much as I tried to stop the movement, to create some stillness, it flowed, extended beyond me, rippled outward like sound waves, making the external and internal worlds indistinguishable.

I spent what may have been an hour, maybe more at the river. I walked back to my apartment, which no longer felt apart from everything else, and collapsed on the sofa, put my feet up and covered my face with my arms. I took out a journal, picked up a pen and, looking at the page, which still blurred with the coffee table, tried to write something, to put down what I was feeling in words. It took too much concentration to follow my hand, so I put the pen down. Exhausted, I gave up trying. I let go. I let the word phrases in my mind wave up and down and around just as the external reality was. Sleep released me from the phantasmagoric light show and the trip slipped into darkness.

Chapter Twenty-Six

◉

The next morning, when I looked at the shelves, each distinct spine of the books with its title and author, my desk with my journal, the floor with its blue and beige tile, I wanted to kiss them like old friends. I shook my head several times, shaking out any remnant hallucinatory images.

For a week, I had small flashbacks where a wall in my office would ooze colorful sprigs, then reestablish itself as a distinct entity. But on one evening, something had changed in the way I saw the world. Not binary. I had come to see reality as much more fluid than I had imagined it to be. Maybe the world wasn't made up of distinct objects, external and internal, but was made up by the interconnectedness of everything. Maybe Black Elk's large hoop did, indeed, connect us all. Infants, when they first open their eyes, must see as I had seen. If they are lucky, a kind voice calls out to them and points to the shapes of faces, of eyes and mouths, and of love for the things of the world that will sustain them. It's what Larry understood and why he was so comfortable with his body and with me. It seemed wrong that the world could be so fluid yet so fragile. If that were true, all the acceptable categories of what was right and what was wrong were up for grabs. I thought about my own life and how, those fast and true beliefs I had as a white suburban guy, had eroded in college.

Back in 1964, when I left home to attend college in Indiana, reality, as I knew it then, also shifted. I left the familiar life of my boyhood in the Chicago suburbs and lost my internal compass and came to question the truths told by my parents and other adults. Nothing was fixed and sure. I don't know why or how, in the years since, I'd forgotten that lesson. The objective world that, before I took acid, seemed so real had vanished in minutes, and was as ephemeral as my parents' world.

Much of what I had come to believe before college gave way under the weight of the civil rights and anti-war movements. Of course, I was not alone to find my footholds on reality shaken. By the fall of 1964, as President Johnson convincingly trounced the conservative Barry Goldwater, my parents drove me to Ashbury University. Cataclysmic societal upheavals were about to disrupt the world and change, for many of us, how we would come to see it. It happened so quickly back then and now, in my new life, as I floundered in my relationships, getting involved in one, giving up another, my whole world was still in upheaval. I knew I had to somehow grab hold of something I could trust, even if I wasn't sure of what it was and how long it would last.

Reflecting on what was real and what was not made my inclination to meet with Eric even stronger. Taking those tablets opened a door inside me. "The flow," Larry said. "Go with the flow. Forget the binary systems." I felt a terrible anxiety about what would become of me, as I felt when the pills first took effect. Confused as I was, I knew that I would only learn who I was by testing what I had never been willing to be, by letting go and claiming the wildness in me.

Chapter Twenty-Seven

I picked up the card, and dialed Eric's number. The phone rang. I blew out some air.

"Hello."

"Eric?"

"Yes, who is this?"

"Jason. Remember: I got locked out of my car at Suzie's party," I said, talking faster than I should.

"That wasn't Suzie's party," he said.

"You're right. It was what's his name?"

"Alex."

"Right."

"Nice to hear from you." His voice was soft.

"The same."

I fidgeted with a glass in the sink. I washed and rinsed it.

"So?" he asked.

This was my chance. I had to say something.

"I was wondering if you wanted to get together?"

"Get together? We could get together."

I took a breath, dried the glass, and put it in the cupboard. "Great. When did you want to—get together?"

"This weekend, I'm free," he told me. "Friday or Saturday, should be fine."

That was easy. I had done it. We settled on Saturday, and he gave me directions.

Chapter Twenty-Eight

When I arrived at Carole's early the next morning, she pulled me in and shut the door. She wasted no time in telling me what happened.

"There are some problems with Bertha," she said. Bertha, a black aide in the Petersborough Center, had a 21 year-old son, Barry, who had disappeared with his best friend and several white, teenage girls from Mooresville.

"Did they find Barry?" I asked.

"Yeah. But not good news. He was very sick when she found him. No, not sick. That's what Bertha called it. He was drunk. Totally intoxicated. He had gone with Reg, you know him, he works in the office sometimes, to help with typing. Barry and he had gone to Mooresville, looking for some action, as they say. They picked up the two girls. They went to a local motel. And you can figure out the rest. There may be morals charges."

"Are the police involved?"

"Yes."

"How old were the girls?"

"Fifteen."

"Oh, my God."

"It's bad. They were gone for two days. Police were searching for them. The girls' parents were on the local news."

When Bertha tracked him down—she recognized his car in the parking lot—he said that he felt so sorry it had to be her who found him. He was hiding out. He'd seen the news. The girls had already left. They'd said were they eighteen. How was he to know? He believed them."

"Is there anything we can do?"

"He is in custody. I don't know what the charges will be, if any. The parents weren't willing to press any. Something's up. Rumors are this isn't the first time for the girls. There isn't much we can do. Reg knows you. Maybe you can go down and talk with them, let them know we have a lawyer if need be. They're at his mom's house."

I nodded my head. "Sure. But am I—the right person?"

She knew what I meant. "They need someone. And they know you. They need to know that we're working to help them. I plan to call the local paper. I don't want this to be some front-page racial hullabaloo; we all know local Klansmen will eat up this shit. One of their kids goes to the Center."

"I imagine the girls thought it was an adventure, a way to defy their parents."

"You know how it will play in the community. A generation ago, there would have been a lynching."

We moved quickly. Conferred with an attorney. Called the paper editor who told us he couldn't pull the story, but he could push it to the back. The police chief was pleasant enough. I met with the boys who weren't boys; they were scared, young men who told me the girls solicited them, claimed to be eighteen, suggested the motel where they had gone before. I told them to tell that to the lawyer. I told them we'd do our best to make sure they were safe.

Chapter Twenty-Eight

Bertha agreed to meet with me. "This is gonna be trouble," was the first thing she said.

I said the truest thing I could think of. "Race never seems to go away. Every time we think, 'there, that will make the difference' the venom spills out as if it were just biding its time, waiting for the right moment. I'm so sorry."

Rather than drive home, I stayed overnight at Carole's house. In the morning, I tossed the ball with her son. In this last year, he had grown taller, skinnier, and quicker. But he never tired of playing catch.

In the paper, on page six, there was a small column about the missing girls. There was no mention of race.

"We'll have to wait. We must see if the parents will press charges."

We knew a time bomb was clicking. Something was bound to happen. We didn't know what it would be.

I had my directions. On Saturday, I drove up Route 28 to Cumberland, turned right at the main intersection, followed the road up a hill, turned left, went a half mile, and turned onto Apple Grove Road, to the third building on the right. Eric's house was set back from the road. The front yard, the size of two football fields, had several old maples and there was a parking lot big enough for eight cars. I pulled in.

I hopped out of the car and craned my neck to look at the house. It didn't look like apartments. It seemed like an old, refurbished Georgian mansion. Three stories, a white façade, Doric columns. A large veranda wrapping around it. A pavilion with an iron railing. Palladian windows gave it an air of quiet, *Gone with the Wind,* elegance.

To the right of the front door, there was a mailbox with names on it. Number 3, Eric Kendrick. I opened the front door and climbed the staircase like a teenager on his first date.

I knocked.

Eric opened the door, waving his hand. "So here you are. Come in." He was beautiful. His honey-colored complexion, strong jaw, and eyes that widened and took me in, made me feel I'd made the right choice.

"Can I take your coat?" he asked. He motioned to a living room with a large couch set in front of the Palladian windows.

He showed me around. A narrow kitchen hooked around behind the living room, and, on the other side, a bedroom ran the length of one whole side. Nestled at the end was a small bath. From his bed, he could look out at the back where a large pasture sprawled over rolling hills. Just off the bedroom was a small study with a desk and an easel.

"You like?" he asked.

I did.

There were two large walnut armchairs upholstered in a peach-colored fabric, but I sat on the couch. He brought in a tray of crackers and brie, and, for each of us, a glass of red wine.

We chatted for a while. He had taught school on Long Island, where he grew up. He dated a man, Larry, who had been discharged from the Army. They moved in together, thinking they could make a life together. But someone on the school board saw them getting on the ferry to Fire Island. Word got around. The principal told him he would not renew his contract. He left, enrolled in West Virginia University and got his master's in social work, then moved south to Cumberland where he worked as a counselor at a local health

Chapter Twenty-Eight

center. His partner drank heavily, and there was an ultimatum. The partner left. Eric had been single for twelve years.

I told him about my travels, Divinity school, how I'd come to West Virginia on the rebound from the failed folk school up in the Cumberland Mountains, taking the job as a Head Start Director. I told him about Jay, how he had been burned, how he disappeared. I described the lodge, its veranda where I could sit in quiet space and write. He asked what I wrote about. I talked about some of my poems.

"I sometimes think I may be straight," I said. "Other times, I don't. I wish I could decide what it is."

Eric laughed. "Our society is so fiercely heterosexual. Men are so obsessed with being straight, it's no wonder."

He asked if I still dated Suzie. I told him, no. It was over. "Free love was costly," I said.

He laughed.

"So why did you call me?"

"I'm not sure," I said. "Maybe I couldn't get you out of my mind."

He said, "I've thought of you, too."

He gazed at me, his lips pursed slight, his head tilted back, appraising. "Sex is complicated," he said. "Wish it wasn't. Just is. Don't you think?"

"Sure is."

"It isn't as if someone could draw a line and say, 'Everyone who is gay, stand over here, and everyone who is straight, go over there.'" He poured us another glass of wine. The sun had tipped into the trees.

He patted my leg. "So, you are here. That's good. Let's take it slow. That okay with you?"

"I would prefer that."

I looked at the paintings on the walls, the lushness of the colors, the vigor of the brush strokes. They were intense. The grass on the riverbank, the old boat against the falling sun—had a muscularity, as if they were warring against the setting sun.

"You like them?" he asked.

"Very much. That one, the one with a boat and one oar dangling, it's lovely." I stood to take a closer look.

"They're mine," he said.

"You painted them?"

"Yes."

He invited me to look at several more paintings in a back study. They depicted a man sitting in a blue lounge chair, his skin a luxurious fabric of russet, cobalt and green. It made him appear as if he, too, were a luxurious fabric. In one, his legs spread, his penis fell across his thigh. They were loving portraits. They were splendid. I noticed, as Eric looked at it, a sadness fell over his face. He sighed and offered a weak grin. I asked who the subject as. He told me he was a former partner.

"He was beautiful. But . . ." he said.

"Sorry."

"Don't be. It's better. I was miserable."

He took me to his bedroom where a small landscape was hung on the wall across from the bed. I sat back on the mattress to get a better view. He stood next to me. I had run out of things to say.

"Dinner," I said. I started to get up, but he pressed his hand against my shoulder.

"No," he said kindly. He put our wine glasses on the floor. He kneeled on the bed and put his lips to mine, gently. We kissed.

Chapter Twenty-Eight

"I know we said that we should—"

"Should do what we need to do," I said, kissing him gently.

We didn't hurry.

We seemed to be in an otherworldly dance. Our clothes loosened. His legs over mine. We held each other. We did not speak. We went slowly. We slipped off one article of clothing after another, taking turns. Shirt. Shirt. Undershirt. Undershirt. Shoes. Socks. We let the tips of our fingers explore our valleys and peaks, the concave of our collarbone and shoulders, the convex curve of our hips. I felt as if I'd been pulled out of a cave and exposed to light for the first time.

In the past when I made love with a woman—or a man—all I thought about was my cock, how it felt, how it wanted release. But with him, my whole body was singing and my cock, happy as it was, was just another member of the chorus. We made love. We never hurried. After we finished, our love juice warm between us, he leaned on his elbow and caressed my face. He said, "We forgot to eat."

He passed me a robe. We went to the kitchen and baked a salmon pie.

It might have been midnight when we ate, but it did not matter. He sat next to me, eating a sliced green pepper, and I sat next to him. His hand would sneak under the table and would caress my leg. Then, mischievously, he would touch my erection. I would laugh and he would laugh too, as I slid my hand onto him. We took our time eating and being aroused, the food of life and the joy of lust comingling in such a way I felt that, if I were ever to find happiness, this was as close as I had gotten.

We wandered into the living room, sprawled on the couch, our legs entwined, the soft caress of the moon snugged across the field. We slept and woke, made love again, and returned to his bed, pressed against one another.

"You feeling more assured?" he whispered in my ear.

"About . . . ?"

"Yourself," he said, letting his finger trace a question mark on my chest.

"I've never had anything like this before. Never," I said and kissed him.

"Then remember this when you're in doubt. Remember it and let it take you back to me," he said. He cupped his hand on either side of my head. He patted my chest.

I closed my eyes, but I couldn't close my body from him. His arms held me. His legs looped over mine. I could count his breaths. The night was on us now. We embraced it.

By the time I awoke in the morning, I knew that I had crossed over into another domain. I had never felt as happy nor enjoyed as much intimacy with another person. Eric's head was nestled in my arm. He yawned. We made love again.

At breakfast, he pulled his chair close to mine.

"I know you don't want to hear it," he said. "You're gay. I believe it with all my heart."

"You're right, I told him. "I don't want to hear it. Let's not go there. Let's not ruin things."

One morning the next week, late in May, I went for a swim before work. I'd been obsessing over Eric. I'd found myself, as he

Chapter Twenty-Eight

had suggested, going back to that night, his holding me. It was as if I was living in a wakeful fantasy.

As I sat by the river, a rotten leaf floated by, probably dredged up from the bank. Its edges were lace, held mostly together by the stem and veins. I looked at the dark copper green trees on the slope and the wisteria tangled among them, and one leg at a time, slid into the water. I spun in the current, paddling my arms, the blue misted hills on either side awakening me to the light spreading over the valley.

I swirled around to look back upstream at a fish, its tail swishing, pressed against the current.

I had received several letters from David, asking me to come visit in Italy. In return, I'd sent him a poem:

> A kind, northern face
> mingled such with an exiled guise
> of the everlasting eyes of Pierrot
> and, of Gargantua, the laughter,
>
> delivered me from the white coverlet
> and pillow—I see now, inheritances—
> delicate riders of the storm of lust
> and what had been hidden in us.

Eric had been calling. He wanted to talk, to ask when we could get together. Although I couldn't get him out of my mind, I also had begun to ask myself some serious questions. Part of me was convinced that I was finally putting aside one life so that I could find another, but I needed to be sure. If I were to swim against the current, I needed the inner strength to do it.

As I sat drying on the porch after the swim, looking out at the willows rustling in the wind, I noticed at the edge of the veranda, several black ants carrying a large termite. The first one parried with it, mouthing it, dragging it near a hole in the cement—probably where their colony was—and the others followed, tugging at the termite's legs, and wings, piercing it in the head. A few inches from the hole, a whole cadre of ants came out. One side tugged the termite one way, another tugged another. Clearly no one was in charge, but everyone knew their role, and they acted with expediency and efficiency.

To my surprise, still alive, the termite tried to break loose. The one busy ant who had led the initial effort to drag it in ran ahead of it, chafing his antennae madly. Others followed. They circled the hobbling creature. Trapped, surrounded, the termite flailed at its foes.

I felt sorry for the termite. I felt I knew it. The night before as it had tried to fly into my apartment, I had swatted it down, probably broke one of its wings. I had maimed it. His plight was my fault. With my finger, I squished an ant, picked him up and placed him—still wounded, not dead—by the hole, thinking his flailing might distract the ants and give the termite a chance to flee. But no one even looked at it. They kept at the creature and, with more reinforcements coming up every minute, dragged him into the hole. He would soon be breakfast for multitudes, be hacked and butchered limb from limb. I remembered Joseph Campbell, the mythologist, saying that life eats life. The secret was to find a way not to be the meal, not to be torn apart, which, at this moment, was what I was trying to prevent. And, as much as I wanted to avoid it, confront what was to become of me if I made a commitment to Eric.

Chapter Twenty-Eight

Carole threw a party for the end of the Head Start year. She invited her staff, my staff, Lou and Larry, and Ken as the representative of Community Action.

Ken premade his famous mint juleps and left them to chill in the refrigerator. Outside on Carole's porch, shaded by a large oak, the conversation drifted to the latest Washington Post story about the Watergate break-in.

"Nixon is complicit," Ken said. "This shows how the monies to pay for the break-in came from his campaign funds. Can you believe it? I admire that guy Sloan who said he couldn't work in good conscience for the campaign. He says there are people trying to cover it up."

"I know who that is," I said. "It's Nixon. I hate him. Look at what he's done in Vietnam. He says that he's going to pull back troops and he does, but then he expands the bombing."

Carole said, "It's on the news morning to night. I need a break." She refilled Ken's and my glasses, the ice clinking.

"Those are powerful," I said.

Ken said. "Boiled over two cups of sugar. Sweetness is the key. Add Wild Turkey Bourbon, more than called for, and mint, fresh from my garden. My, my, does it taste good. I'm not long for the world."

Later in the evening after the meal, Lou and I were sitting on a swing in the backyard.

I rubbed my head, drunk, lightheaded.

She patted my knee which meant, *Talk to me, friend.*

"I don't think I never told you," I said. "But there is this little guy inside me who, when faced with change, feels overwhelmed."

"What's worrying him now?"

If I were going to tell anyone, Lou was the one who I could trust to keep it to herself.

"Come on," she said. "Hey, it will be summer break soon. I don't want to see you carrying baggage when we'll not be seeing each other daily."

She pulled her fingers across her lips, miming, *I can keep a secret.*

"I have a new lover," I said.

"Oh, Jason, what good news," she said. "That's nothing to be down about. Who is she?"

I looked at her without saying a word.

"I'm missing something?" she asked.

"Yes."

She squinted her eyes and looked at me.

"I used the wrong pronoun," she said.

"Yes."

She turned in the swing, so she was facing me, put her hand on my shoulder, squeezing it.

"Confusing, right?"

"Very."

"Well," she said, "at your age, I don't think it's a phase."

I laughed. She had such way of lightening topics I dreaded.

"No, not a phase," I said and smiled.

"There's what I missed all evening. That beautiful smile of yours," she said.

"I wish I felt like smiling inside."

"Look, my brother who is a musician. I never told you about him. He had dated both girls and boys. Bisexual. I think that's what they call it."

"But, God, I don't want to be living with this back and forth. Why can't I just feel like other guys all the time?"

Chapter Twenty-Eight

"You have never been, even despite this, just like other guys, Jason. You have always been different. The artist in disguise. That's what I like about you. No, really, I mean it. Conventional guys are so boring. Sports. Girls. Sex. Not my idea of someone I want to spend time with. You are, my friend, always interested in talking about everything."

"But—"

"But what?"

"I want to feel one way. It's driving me crazy. I want to just feel one way."

"Give it time. Maybe you just need to trust with this new guy—what's his name?

"Eric."

"I like it. My best friend, back in Minneapolis, is Eric. I had a crush on him. Don't tell Larry. I was smitten. But in the end, I got the right one."

"I wish I could just let go of my fears." I put my hand to my eyes. Without knowing it, I had begun to cry.

She rubbed my shoulder. Her eyes were filled with compassion.

"Hey boss. It will work itself out. Eventually, your heart will tell you the truth."

From the porch, Larry called out," Hey, what's up with you two?"

Lou called back. "Just talking about old times."

Larry waved his hand. "Come on, Carole has a special dessert. A cake. Homemade. She wants us all here."

I reached over and grabbed Lou's hand. "You're a saint."

"Don't be too quick to canonize me."

"You know what I mean."

"Hey, if in the next months, you need to talk," Lou said, "remember, the phone. That's what it is for. Call me anytime. You hear me?"

In the living room, set in the middle of the table, was a three-layer German chocolate cake. Carole said, "In honor of his hard work and support for the program, I want Ken to do the honors." She handed him the knife.

We clinked our cups. The cake was delicious. Carole took me by the arm and whispered, "I was afraid I was losing you, the way you've kept to yourself lately."

The party lasted late into the night. No one wanted to leave. We knew that soon enough we would be going our separate ways for the summer, and that we would tell each other, as collateral against loss, that we would keep in touch until September, but we also knew that, as we got caught up in our own worlds, even just for a few months, things would change for all of us.

Chapter Twenty-Nine

Eric had planned a day trip to view the Moundbuilders' sites. He had studied about the ancient tribes who lived in the area hundreds of years before Christ. I arrived late. He was in a good mood and in a hurry.

"Let's get going," he said. "I'll drive."

Throughout the region, perfectly built mounds, some 35 feet high and 175 feet in diameter, contain remains of shamans or tribal leaders. The Adena and Hopewell tribes that built them existed 300 years before Christ and lasted 500 years afterward. Eric explained that they were sophisticated, wealthy, skilled craftsmen. They traded along the rivers as far as the Mississippi. He showed me their statuettes, copper jewelry, elaborate pottery, and delicate, mica cutouts.

We were standing atop a mound with a graceful, gentle slope. From the top, we could see for miles. "Just think," Eric said. "They lived and hunted right where we are standing. They flourished for hundreds of years. Then they vanished. Can you imagine? What was it that drove them away? So much buried history."

"Mysterious, isn't it?"

"It fascinates me. I wonder what will be left of our civilization. So many artifacts—hollowed out TV sets, hulking, rusted car frames, even toothbrushes—and what will other millennia make of them?"

I reached down and rubbed the crusted earth with my toe.

Beneath my feet, buried deep in the mound, a vault had been discovered with the remains of a large man, some seven feet tall. At that moment, I felt my little guy, the homunculus, buried in my chest. I was scared that Eric would find him and know what a fraud I was. I shuddered.

"You okay?"

"Just a little dizzy."

"Let's get out of the heat. And look here." Eric showed me an archaeological pamphlet with a man who looked like a middle lineman for the Chicago Bears. "Big, huh?"

"I thought primitive people were small as a rule. They must have eaten well."

We drove to several sites and visited a small museum. We went to a Chinese restaurant for lunch. He ordered for me since I'd only eaten Chinese food once before. He showed me how to use chopsticks. My fingers jerked and he held my hand and set a stick across the palm of my hand, letting it rest between two fingers, and demonstrated again.

"Once you get the hang of it," he said. "It will be as natural as using a fork."

"Natural. I want to feel like that. Everything is new to me these days."

He grinned. "Yes. That."

"But you don't act as if it is."

"Acting, that's my specialty."

"You're pretending when we—"

"No. Not at all. It's just that it's new," I said, grabbing a noodle from the chopsticks and swirling it so it clung to the chopsticks.

Chapter Twenty-Nine

"What's so new about it?"

I pointed beneath the table.

"Oh. I see. Yes, that would be new," he said.

When we made love later that evening, he scrunched next to me, his arms around me, his chest, belly, and legs snuggled against me. He reached his hand over and held my cock. "This is mine, now," he said. "Is that right?"

"Yes, it is."

"I want that as a promise," he said, pulling me closer.

"I have gone out with—"

He squeezed my cock that had gotten hard. "I know Suzie."

I pushed his hand away.

He leaned back and sat upright. I turned to face him.

His voice low, querulous, he asked, "Not just her? Another woman?"

"Do you want to know?"

"Let's be honest. I've been abstinent for years. Clearly, you have not," he said.

I scooted closer to him, placed my arm around his shoulder. He wore his monogamy with pride. I worried if I told him about my affairs, he might think less of me. "No. I haven't. I was so repressed for so long—for years I was afraid to do anything—once I started, sure, I played around. A married woman."

"Are you still?"

"No, not now. Not anymore." A bead of sweat on my forehead trickled down my face. I quickly wiped it off. I could feel the skin on my cheeks tighten against the bone.

He bit his lip, his eyes intently gazing at mine. "I think there is something you're not telling me. You might as well." He tapped my forehead. "Say it."

"You're not the first guy. A guy named Dominique. A one-nighter."

"A guy?"

"Several of them. They were flings. I was drunk. I was experimenting. I—"

"So?"

"I just thought I needed to tell you. I got drunk both times. Very drunk. One guy tried to sober me up and one thing led to another and I—"

"You fucked him."

"That's about it."

The wall clock ticked. Eric took my hand and brushed back my hair. "That was then. This"—he pointed to my chest—"is between you and me. Right?"

"Right."

"Unless you want to hook up with them again?" He cocked his head. "Do you?"

I started to protest, but he put his finger to my lips. "You think a lot. That's for sure."

He stood up and slipped on his pants. Standing by the bed, the afternoon light cast over his shoulder, his hairless chest, smooth, his abdomen taut, a godlike Adonis, he paused, reached down, and said, "Come on, get dressed. We haven't eaten."

Chapter Twenty-Nine

The next day, we sat outside under a white oak where two blue lawn chairs were kept. Long shadows stretched down the hillside. A few songbirds sang back and forth above us. He held my hand.

"Something is bothering you," he said.

"My brain keeps spinning. I feel as if I am losing and finding myself at the same time. Yet I feel so confused. Gay. Straight. Then there is a whole other battle that I'm fighting with my past. I want to break from it. I don't want to be like my dad. I don't want to be the guy in a grey flannel suit. Yet even that is appealing sometimes, the normality of it, the security of it. I would like to have a family, kids. I can't deny that. But what the hell I am, I don't know. I really don't. I don't want to be like Suzie. I don't want to flit from one person to the next. I'm not like her. I want permanence. I want to be myself if I can figure out what self I am."

He took my hand in his, looked away, said very slowly, "You're just experimenting. I'm not. As you said, this is all new to you. It's not for me. You're ambivalent. I'm not. You seem to want kids, a family, a white picket fence, and a dog. I gave up that fairy tale a long time ago. I do love you. I can't deny that. But I don't want to be living with uncertainty. I've done that before."

"I wish it weren't so confusing—"

He dropped my hand. "I'm *not* confused. Let's get that straight." His voice was sharp.

"No. I didn't say that. I'm the one who is living in the either/or."

"Exactly. I need you off the teeter totter. Either you want to make a go of it with me or—" he stopped. "I'm sorry. I don't want to be your therapist. I do enough of that already."

"You want me to go?"

He didn't say no.

I stood up and stepped toward my car.

"Not so fast. Wait a minute," he said. "You didn't let me finish." He reached his hand out to me. "I want you to go to bed with me first."

For much of the day and overnight, a heavy rain fell unrelentingly. After I went home, as I sat in my kitchen before going to bed, it intensified, trampled, splattered off the roof, overflowed the gutters, cut gulches in the driveway, charged by the front steps, funneled by the kitchen door and swept alongside the house toward the river.

For two days, I hadn't paid attention to the radio, hadn't even bothered to read the newspaper. I kept to myself, reading, staying up late, journaling, thinking about Eric and me.

Early one morning, I got a phone call from Doug. He was back at his home in Wheaton. Had I noticed that the rain had increased? He was worried about the rising river. Had I pulled the canoe up higher? Got it out of harm's way? No, I hadn't.

"It's supposed to flood," Doug said. "We're getting hit by Hurricane Agnes."

"I didn't know. I'll go now," I said. "I'll pull it up the bank."

From the veranda, I could see that the river had nearly crested its banks. I draped my raincoat over my head and sprinted toward the stairs. But, when I reached them, a spectacle stopped me short. The river had not only plunged over its banks and spread across the entire river valley, it had swallowed up the trailers across the river and the five willows beside them and had come two-thirds of the way up the embankment. Engorged with whole trees, fences, sides of barns,

Chapter Twenty-Nine

and swollen carcasses of cattle, sheep, goats, the river had become a bloated torrent of carnage. The canoe, whatever or wherever it was, had long been swept away. Gigantic whirlpools erupted, spinning around and sporadically spurting up five feet and higher like miniature volcanic geysers. Waves lashed back and forth, thrashing logs and debris into each other, growling, hissing, throbbing, deafening. It was a deep rumbling racket like the insides of the earth howling.

I sat down on one of the steps. For once the external world mirrored my inner world. My own floodgates had opened. I had unleashed the Freudian libido. I liked the excitement of feeling as deeply as I felt. But I feared where it might lead me. I needed to get some control. That I knew. I thought of how Eric told me to remember our moments together. And I had. I was happy then. I could hold onto that moment.

As I looked at the river, sitting there, my back being pounded with rain, drenched to the bone, I thought how life choices by their nature were a closing off, cutting one off from what was on the other side. That made the choices harder. They signaled an end of one set of possibilities, venturing into some other unexplored territory, and, trying as one did, not to be swept away in the current of confusion. Over a certain amount of time, one got used to the new territory and stepped into the drudgery of everydayness of another set of possibilities. Adulthood was not an expanding adventure as much as a delimiting of self.

How did entrapments seem for some not traps, but the road to freedom?

Five things I had learned that year: I could do a job as a competent director. I could earn a living without relying on my dad. I didn't need the confines of a you-have-to-do-it-this-way life. And, I had to mark my own course, to make my own destiny. And lastly, my sexuality was fluid like the river. If I wanted to keep my sexual drive contained, I would need to find my way to one side or the other. Right now, I was in the flow. And it was flooded.

I watched the river for an hour. From the debris coming down the water, the river appeared to have gobbled up whole farms, livestock, cabins, fences, and trees. There was no end of the debris. The rain kept pouring down. I was drenched. It cascaded down the steps, swirled off my back, around my legs, over my shoes as if the river was calling for me, too. I called Doug back and told him the canoes were long gone. And thought to myself, *as long gone as I am.*

Chapter Thirty

Since the rains weren't about to let up, since I needed to get away at least for a while, if nothing else, to clear my head, I called Eric and told him I planned to drive northwest to Glen Brook to visit my parents. He told me to keep in touch.

In touch, I thought. *Yes, that's what I want to do.*

Once I crossed the line into Illinois, the flat, uninterrupted rows of corn, acres of it, walled in the highway. As children, we played hide and seek down the narrow rows of corn, the tassels dappling pollen on our shirts like blessings. When it rained, when rolling blue-grey thunderclouds marched across the horizon, metallic sheets of rain pouring out of them, it was fun to wait until the crashing sound was nearly upon us, only a few yards away, and then to tear off toward some shelter, the torrents nipping at our heels. We'd duck under an awning, letting the rain pour over us, watch it parade by us, then step out into sunshine and resume our games. Life seemed simple then. Everything was black and white like the TV programs. Predominantly white. Matt Dillion was the sheriff of Dodge City. A man with a quick draw. David and Ricky Nelson were like my brother and me. It almost seemed that their lives were more real than our own. My father's company sponsored the show. He once met them and said they were just like they were on TV. Fiction had become reality.

Going back into that life, much as it had the tug of nostalgia, felt

River Crossed

like reentering a carefully arranged cage with all the appointments of luxury to make it seem hospitable. I had rattled the bars for years until my knuckles were raw. I wanted out, didn't care where out was, and now here I was returning, steeling myself for all the questions about why I'd taken a job so far away, why I wasn't making more money, and if I had met someone, a girlfriend, if I was finally settling down.

When I pulled up the driveway past the hawthorn tree and stand of oaks, my mother was on the front steps to greet me.

"How good to see you," she said. She eyed my hair. "You need a haircut."

"Good to see you, Mom," I said. I pushed my hair back from my forehead.

"Is Jack around?"

"Your brother is at work. But we all plan to have dinner at the club. We thought that would be nice, don't you think?"

"Where's Dad?"

"Your father is playing golf," she said. "We will meet him there." A worried expression crossed her face.

"Did you bring your clubs?"

I said, "In the trunk."

I lugged my suitcase up the winding staircase to what had been my room. The poster of Gayle Sayers was still on the wall, along with a paint-by-numbers Indian chief I had done when I was ten years old.

When we arrived at the club, Bob, the valet, opened the door for Mom. "Good evening, Mrs. Follett. Good to see you Mr. Follett."

I still knew how to play the part. I even enjoyed having someone

Chapter Thirty

wait on me, known by my surname, and act as if I was important.

I had gotten dressed as I always had, in my blue blazer, red tie, button-down shirt; appearances were everything. If you looked right, people at the club would greet you, welcome you, and know you were one of their kind. If you didn't, the host would give you a jacket and tie so that you fit in.

In the Green Room for cocktails, several other people—the bartender, and a waitress—greeted me, telling me how good it was to see me. I was still considered an insider.

My father arrived shortly afterward.

"How was your game?" I asked, shaking his hand.

"Not a good question to ask," he said.

"Bad?"

"Horrible. I never sank a putt and my drives—they never saw the fairway," he said. He squinted his eyes. "You need a haircut."

"Mom already told me that."

"She's right. It's longer than your mother's."

His ears had turned red and his jaw, clenched as it did before he snapped, was tightening.

Mom patted the seat next to her. "Have a seat, Howard. Order something. We were waiting for you."

My brother arrived with his wife and four-year-old son, Keith. Keith was dressed in a coat and tie, too. His hair was trimmed so that his big ears stood out.

I stood to greet them and pulled several chairs around the glass-topped cocktail table. My brother shook my hand. His wife leaned over and kissed my father on the cheek and said hello to my mom, ignoring me. Their son hid behind her skirt, his hand gripping her skirt. I bent down and greeted him.

"Hello, Keith. I'm your uncle and godfather. We met a while ago. I suppose you don't remember. You want to shake hands?" I held out my hand. Barbara took him by the shoulder and guided him toward a chair on the other side of my mom. "Barbara, good to see you, too."

Even after several drinks, the tension in the room never dissipated. Mom talked with Barbara; my brother talked with dad; I listened. I felt as if were a mannequin in a shop window staring at a crowd outside, able to hear them, but unable to talk. I got up to get another drink. My brother came with me. He hooked his arm in mine. "You made it back," he said.

"For whatever good it does."

"Your hair," he said. "I supposed they bugged you."

"You got it right."

He laughed. "You know at my age, just having hair is a bonus."

"If we end up like Grandpa," I said. "We'll be like billiard balls."

He rubbed his scalp, patting his thin hair over his forehead. "Hey, I wish you could give them some slack. I mean, look at this place, look at what they gave us. We have been pretty damn fortunate, don't you think?"

"What's your point?"

"My point is that they sense your disapproval."

"Lay off, Jack. I don't plan to kowtow to them. I know how it works. First, I cut my hair, then I take some corporate job, then I vote Republican, then I marry some sweet girl who fawns over dad, and I end up as some drunk in that bar across this room every other weekend night."

Chapter Thirty

Jack squeezed my arm. "Can you lower your voice?"

"All I ever hear from you is 'Be more appreciative. Respect their lifestyle. Make some compromises.' And do they care one damn bit about my life, about what I am doing? Do they ever ask how I am doing? Do you? Not a word."

"I said keep your voice down," he said. He steered me to the Oak Room, a men's only room with twenty oak tables and a bar. "Order a drink. Order several. You'll need them." He was smiling. "You know I get it. I know dad is always trying to divide us, me-against-you. I cave in sometimes. I admit it. Sorry. But I get what you are saying. I sometimes wish I'd kept up writing. I buried the artist. I was pretty good. But, hey, I'm doing well. I figure a few more years—"

"How can you stand it?"

"You want to know?"

The bartender came over, called me, "Mr. Follett."

I did what I had done my whole life. I acted as if I was someone, someone who was known, who had his father's name, a birthright who's who. I looked the bartender in the eyes. I wanted him to know I realized that he, too, was somebody. "Good to see you, Jerry. How is the family?"

"Fine. My boy's in high school now."

"That's swell."

My brother, who also knew how to act his role, saluted Jerry. "You're the best."

He took me by the arm again, said, "You mind if we just talk? It has been a year." He pushed open the outside door to the putting green.

Eighteen putting holes spread over twenty yards. We stepped on the green. Jack knelt and rubbed the smooth surface.

"Such an amazing color, don't you think?"

He looked out at the first tee. "How many times did we play that hole? How many balls did I slice out of bounds?"

"You had a mean slice," I said. "You hit a car once, didn't you?"

"Several times."

"And once you hit a house across the street."

"Broke a window."

The fairway spread straight ahead. On one side, a line of trees. On the other, more trees, a wire fence, and a few feet from the fence, a street. Out of bounds.

"What were we talking about?" I asked.

"You wanted to know why I do it all? Simple. I do it for this—I want to be able to be a member here, pay it on my own. I want to be my own man. I plan, and you may laugh at this to make more money than he ever has. I will show him. That's my plan." He pointed at my chest. "I worry about you, though. Dad, and Mom, too, they complain about you. You never write. They call, but you tell them nothing. They are hurt. I hate to see them that way. I guess I fall into resenting you, too."

"Resent, that's a big word," I said.

"You're the one who got away. I guess that's like an escapee."

I looked at the green of the first hole, some 400 yards away, remembering how difficult it was to reach it in two. I knew this world, whether I was proud of it or not.

"The course looks good, doesn't it?" Jack put his hand on my shoulder.

"You should at least come back more. We could hit the links, have a challenge match."

I looked at him. Below his eyes, there were puffy, lined bags. He

Chapter Thirty

looked tired.

"Promise me you'll come back more often," he said, nudging his head next to mine.

I laughed. "I don't want to be sucked back into this. Is that so bad?"

"Just cut them some slack. That's all I'm asking."

I said, "Can I ask you one more thing?"

"What's the cold shoulder bit with Barbara?"

He laughed. "She thinks you hate her. I think it's her way of protecting herself. She's Catholic, remember. And she likes things just so. You're not exactly 'just so.'"

He walked me across the putting green. "We must have spent half our lives out here," he said, kneeling over, looking at the break on the green's lower side.

"If I remember," I said, "it breaks severely, especially right around the cup."

I sat in my childhood room by the window that looked over the yard. Gnarled and thick, dense with leaves, dark oak limbs blocked the view of the fields that led to Cantigny Farms. I thought of McCormick, the old WWI Colonel standing in front of the Tribune employees like an overlord, passing out Christmas bonuses, and expecting the employees to act obsequious, to bow down to him, to appreciate how grand he was when, in fact, he was a paranoid, vengeful tyrant. Here I was not a mile from his house. I'd come home—or what used to be my home—to pay homage to my parents. I wasn't being very successful. At least I had my brother as an ally. There was something decent in him. I wrote in my journal.

River Crossed

What baffles me is how easily, like a fish in familiar stream, I can adapt to the conformities of my parents' world. I put on the right jacket and tie, polish my shoes with the automatic brush by the door, comb my hair back, and act as if I'm one of the Follett boys. The "as if" part is what drives me crazy, although there is a part of me that likes being known, enjoys someone opening the door, providing drinks, calling me by my last name, and waiting on me. It almost makes me think I am important.

The mothers in Head Start defer to me (even if they don't put on airs). The people here, in this life, at the club, serving me drinks, defer to me, too. But in both cases, everyone only knows by an image that they have of me. They don't know the real me. They don't have a clue how inadequate I feel.

I did call Eric. We had a good conversation. He wants to see me when I get back. Yet (and this troubles me) I can't imagine ever bringing him home to my parents. I will have to find a way to a home of my own—one that lasts.

I placed the journal on the nightstand, turned off the light, and gazed up into the oak. Nothing moved, not even the leaves. All was quiet. The night had come, but here in the midst of the suburbs with traffic coming and going, I had no interest in going outside. I hunkered down in my old bed and read from T.S. Eliot's collected poems.

Chapter Thirty-One

Eric invited me to dinner. He fixed a stir-fry and instructed me again about the use of chopsticks. We sat on his couch afterward. The window open, we could hear crickets grinding their night songs. A few fireflies blinked in the grass, like stars that had wandered off their constellations.

Having been away for some time, I wasn't sure what to say.

"I like this time of night," he said. "It seems everything stops. Even the air. The traffic, what little there is, seems far off. I can feel myself quiet."

"I sometimes sit out on the veranda at night, just sit and listen to the river. One night the moon, amazingly full, was reflected in the water. It seemed to be moving yet was still. The water seemed to be running through it. It was so close I felt I could reach out and grab it."

"Sounds wonderful."

I asked, "What do you want to do?"

"You mean with my life?"

I nodded.

"My life. I'm a therapist. I do some dancing in a local theater. Bit parts. Chorus. It's fun." He leaned over and kissed me on the cheek. "I'm glad you asked, since this part involves you. I could use that."

I took a deep breath. "I think I want that someone to be me."

"I think so, too. You share my same interests in ideas, in books, in the arts. You're active. You're sensitive." He brushed my hair back from my forehead. "Except I'm still not sure you're ready to settle down. I'm not sure you're ready for what this will be like for us, in these times."

I rubbed my head. He was asking a lot. I didn't want to lie to him. Yet I wanted whatever we had to work. "You have me nailed," I said. "I do love you. I just need time. Can we take this a week at a time?"

He didn't say no.

I slept over. His body next my body. My hand on his belly. His lips on mine

Chapter Thirty-Two

Later that week, Ken called me. He told it was work business. He knew it was summer vacation, but an emergency had come up. He needed to meet me at my office. It was the summer grant, he said, the one for the archaeological dig, the one I had worked on with the teenage boy, Terry, the one I had told Ken I didn't want to be involved with anymore.

Was there a problem with the grant? I asked. Something I hadn't done correctly? No, it wasn't the grant. Not the dig. No accidents. It was the professor, the expert, who led the expedition. Ken would tell me when I got there, he said. Soon as I could. He needed my support.

"I'm asking as a friend," he said. "Please come."

When I arrived at the office, Ken led me into the conference room where ten boys sat in a circle. Two I knew well—Terry and Mitchell, his friend—eight others I'd met. Ken wanted me to hear it from the boys, he said. He had persuaded them to talk but they would only do so if I was there.

"Sit down," Ken said. "We need to hear what they have to say."

Terry glanced at me, then dropped his eyes, his lip caught in the side of his mouth as if he were chewing gum. Mitchell sat on the opposite side of the room, his nostrils flared, his hands caught between his legs, his body rocking back and forth.

I asked, "What's happened?"

Terry had his hand to his mouth and had gnawed on his forefinger. He set his hands on his knees and looked up. "It was Professor Hammersmith, you know, the old guy."

"Yeah, I know," I said.

"He was good," Terry said. "I have to say that. The dig was incredible. We found muskets, some pots, some coins—"

Ken interrupted, "Tell him, Terry. He needs to know."

"First few weeks were fine." Terry hesitated. He licked his lips. "Can I have something to drink?"

Ken got him a Coke. Terry drank it, looking at me as he did, his eyes wary.

He continued, "I knew something was fishy." He looked at Mitchell and the two boys sitting on either side of him, one being Jeff, the basketball player. They stared at their hands, holding them tightly together like praying. "I knew something was up. He would take them into his office. He wanted to give us all, he said, individualized instruction on the findings. But Jeff, here"—the boy sitting next to him—"he came out of there upset and wouldn't say why. So, I looked one time though a keyhole and he was, you know . . ." He nodded his head, glancing at me to help him out.

I said, "I know." Ken nodded his head, too.

Terry completed the story. "I figured out that he paid them to keep quiet, paid them twenty bucks each time. That's a lot of money. He even offered me fifty dollars not to tell when he found out I knew. I wish there had been someone I could talk to." He looked at me. "You should have come visit us. Why didn't you come? You wrote the grant!"

Chapter Thirty-Two

Ken put his hand up. "No blame here, please. This is hard enough."

Terry continued. "I couldn't take it. No one was saying a thing. He was paying them off. I called Mr. Woodward. He'd been down to visit. He came and well—I guess here we are."

"Just stay put, boys," Ken said. "Let me talk with Jason. We'll be right back."

I closed the door to my office. "What do you want me to do?" I asked Ken. "This is really sick."

"I wanted another witness. We fired the archaeologist, of course. We informed the authorities, including his university. And the police. But have a meeting with the parents tonight. Can you make it?"

I nodded.

"They want the boys protected. I've just told the boys if they need to talk to someone, we have counselors who will keep it confidential. I'm worried, though. For their sakes, of course. You understand. About someone talking."

Terry was right. I should have been there. I hadn't followed up because of my own squeamishness about him, his coming on to me. I'd been a coward.

On the way out, Terry was standing beside the building, his hands in his pockets.

"I'm sorry," was all I could say.

He turned his head away.

"You okay?" It was a weak question, but it was all I had.

"Some of those boys got messed up," he said. "I should have acted sooner. It went on for a month—"

"But you—"

"I didn't do anything. I knew it was happening. I knew—"

"I understand. You felt compromised and—"

"I did. I did because Mitchell was there and we—"

"I know," I said, and I did. He wanted me there because he couldn't say that the old guy was gay like him, but unlike the professor, Terry was young and, even if he had sex with Michell and other boys, was not abusing them, since they were just boys having fun. Terry was struggling to differentiate himself from what the old man did and what we both knew had happened, consensually, at Orlando's.

Terry started to walk down the street. I followed. "It wasn't until Mitchell told me that it wasn't cool, you know, that he was thinking of leaving, that he was going to tell his cousin who would take care of the fag, I realized how messed up he and those other kids were. That's when I caught him. It was gross. I opened the door, and he was there on his knees."

"You did your best. You put a stop—"

"I fucked up. I should have done it sooner. I was the *lead* counselor. I was supposed to look out for them. I shouldn't have let it—" He began slapping his head. I grabbed his arm.

"Quit it. It's over."

"Oh, fuck, man. I messed up," he said, breaking into tears.

"Terry, you stopped it. Focus on that. You got him caught. He won't do it again," I said. "It took a lot of courage to act."

"You think?"

"Yes, I do."

We went to the Cozy Kitchen, sat in a booth, ordered fries and Pepsis. He told me Mitchell was disgusted by the whole thing, didn't ever want to have sex again.

Chapter Thirty-Two

"He wants nothing to do with me." He kept shaking his head, running his hand through his hair.

"It's alright, Terry." "It's alright," I said. "Let it go."

"But I don't want to end up like that, that professor," Terry said. "He's so . . ."

"Disgusting."

"Right. I get that. And he was wrong."

"I don't want to be like him," he said.

"You wouldn't be, man. You are better than that. It will be okay, trust yourself," I said, although I wasn't sure if it would be alright. I knew no matter what I said I had no guarantee, no assurance, that in our society, dead set against homosexuality as it was, he wouldn't end up like the professor in some ways, and for that matter, I wouldn't either. I did, however, want him to know that what the professor did was wrong, dead wrong. He should be punished. He had to face the consequences of abuse.

Terry asked if he could come visit. I told him that, given what just happened, that would be a bad idea. He shook my hand and left, his body, once proud and vibrant, slouched as he headed back home.

When Ken and I met with the parents, they wanted explanations. Why hadn't we known?

I showed them the professor's resume, his honors, his academic credentials, his years of teaching.

We told how he interviewed well, seemed to respect the boys. We informed them that we'd filed charges, that, if need be, the boys could testify using guardian ad litem, someone who could act as their support, make sure the court treated them fairly, but that, since it was being handled in Virginia, we had kept it out of the papers. The parents were worried, as were we, about the boys' reputations. Their disgust was plain. It so evidently went beyond the matter of consent.

One father screamed at us. "Trauma, that's bullshit. Where is the bastard? If I get my hands on him, he'll never touch another kid. I know a faggot when I see one. I'll take care of him."

Ken stood up and told him that he understood. He was also angry. But the justice system would take care of it behind closed doors.

"Take care of it, yeah," the man, beefy with a close-cropped beard, said, pointing at me. "That's what we get hiring a Yankee. I got a funny feeling he's—"

"Hey, none of that," Ken interceded. "Let's calm down and focus on what we can do."

I waited until everyone had left. I told Ken to check if anyone was on the street waiting for me before I went to my car.

Back at the lodge, I couldn't sit still. I went up to my perch over the river, leaned back, watched the clouds swirl across the moon, blotting it out, leaving a dark curtain across the river. For a moment the stark, horrid, terrifying reality of being gay washed over me. Here was a renowned archeologist who, for whatever reason, found himself with teenage boys and could not keep his hands off them and had, as such, brought shame upon himself and his career. I could hear the disgust and anger in the parents' voices. If they could have, they would have lynched him, cast him out of town on a rail, caked him with boiling

Chapter Thirty-Two

tar. Their fear, their dread of even saying the word, made my own feelings, even if they felt right, for Eric, seem even more dangerous than ever. How does one decide to commit to someone when such a commitment feels like a death sentence in the eyes of society? I caught my breath. My thoughts kept going back to being in Eric's arms that I hoped would never leave me. But I knew that we didn't live in Neverland. We were those who were, by our inclinations, damned by many in society. I could still feel that man's eyes staring at me, unmasking me. There was a vitriol in his eyes as if he had seen into me and hated what he saw, wanted to excoriate my very being, eviscerate me, leaving me a mere bag of bones.

I sat on the veranda and held my head in my hands and wept. I felt vanquished, defeated as if whatever barriers I'd managed to finally begin breaking down were now crashing down on me stronger than ever. I'd let myself be worn down. I'd met men at Doug's house who seemed content and happy, let that convince me the threat wasn't as bad as what it was, despite the new love I'd felt: that homosexuality was something reviled, scandalous, and sick. With the slightest provocation, I'd seen in the eyes of those parents a righteous rage. Who was I to tell them they were wrong? These were their children.

Eric and I were grownups. We had to face, if we were to live together, what still was considered a mental illness. For many, more than I even imagined before, we were perverts. I wasn't sure how I could cope with such rejection. To put it plainly, I felt as terrified as Terry had felt. I didn't want to find myself, late in life, like the professor.

Chapter Thirty-Three

I told Eric about the professor. There was a time in my life I would have just sat with the story and my concerns, kept it to myself, but I told him.

We were at my place, cuddling on the couch.

"That's the sorry case of someone in the closet," Eric said. "He's spent all those years in denial, and now, look what happens. Those poor kids, how will it mess them up, all because he couldn't be who he was. So here he is, a pedophile, something as disgusting as it can get, taking advantage of kids, living up to the worst stereotypes of gay men. But maybe that's not all his fault. Look at how people, those who think they haven't, although they certainly have, met a gay person. They rely on stereotypes. They think we're all perverts, when, in fact, most of those who abuse children are heterosexuals. They have laws that allow them to fire us if we are discovered. He had to live with such onerous constraints to preserve his job at the university. He was driven into his cave."

"I know," I said, pulling him close.

"Sure, you do."

The desk lamp, the only light in the room, spilled a puddle of light on the floor. Ambient light from the summer sky illuminated a tree outside the window. Sadness washed over me in a wave, as if the sorrow of all the years as a teen when I wanted to be loved, yet never dared to seek it out, to find someone who was like me to love. I had lived in a fantasy world. I'd let the slow drip of remorse about a life not lived spill over me. Eric held onto me. I didn't cry. I held onto him as if he were the only thing that kept me tethered, tenuously, to the real world.

Eric had bought Toby several toys that night, one a long rubbery pole with a wire and a play mouse at the end. Toby leapt at it and swatted. I was amazed how high he could jump, sometimes three feet off the ground. His antics made us laugh. We needed to laugh, even if it took a cat to do it.

Eric spent the better part of the next two weeks with me—on weekends, when he wasn't working, and weekdays, when he stayed the night. We explored each other's bodies as if they were a new continent.

I felt so alone until I saw his car coming down the drive. I'd raced out to greet him and we'd hug. The veil was lifted. As long as Eric was there, I felt free.

I took him to the river. We stood and listened to the water as it rushed over rocks.

"Is it very deep?" he asked

"Chest high in some places," I said. "Waist high in others."

He stripped off his shirt, pants, and shoes. "Let's go."

We swam upstream, held onto the boulders, let the faint moonglow gleam across our bodies. Then we let go, drifted downstream, holding hands. As we went past, I pointed out to him the cliff where I went some nights.

"You must take me there."

Chapter Thirty-Three

He swam back to the dock. He was carefree with his body, his sleek figure, his nearly hairless chest. His wiry hair dazzled, beaded with water. His cock, sleek, swayed with the current. He was self-contained as he sat on the dock, leaned back, shaking his hair, and licking the water off his lips.

We ate dinner late those nights, if at all. Every time I'd get up from bed to fix dinner, he'd pull me back as if he had to have my body. He never flagged. I kissed him from toe to earlobe. He wanted me as if starving for my touch. We never dressed. The moon never seemed to move. The stars kept still. When we did eat, we fed each other forks full of pink meat, baked potatoes. We drank Merlot like a sacrament, one I yearned for. We talked into the night about his loneliness, my doubts. We seemed to be two parts of a whole who had, by some force, come together. Every evening, whatever uncertainties I had vanished when he drove down the hill to spend time with me.

One night, I asked Eric if he wouldn't mind telling me about his family.

"My mother is Korean," he said. "My dad African American." He laughed. "When you date me, you get a triple header—gay, Black, and Asian, a full house of minorities." His mother had the worst time when he told her he was gay, because she wanted grandchildren. I asked about his work, too. For the sake of client relationship—Eric was a psychotherapist—he kept his sexual orientation to himself, not for public consumption.

"But, you know, there are other guys in town. We have potluck dinners. One thing I've learned is that when you're in a minority, you need to stick together, give each other support. For many of us, the minute we come out, tell our people what we are, we lose our families, and we lose friends. So, we need to create our own family, become a family of likeminded folks who can be open and support one another," he said.

Dating someone who had been out for a long time, I was learning quickly, that if we were to live together, I'd have to let go of many of my expectations—children, a normal life—and settle for the second family he talked about.

At the end of our summer together, swimming in our love, the startup of my second year of Head Start closed in on me. Keeping as close as we were would be difficult once I started back to work, once I reentered the Pearsall Flats community. If I was honest, I would need to tell Ken and Carole. But I felt even that would jeopardize the Head Start Program and compromise me. I talked to Eric about my worries.

"Hey," he said. "It's never easy casting off what others expect you to be. It's never easy to be free."

"Free?" I asked.

"Sure. Giving up what you've been trained to be is like unlocking a prison cell and stepping into the sunshine."

Free, I thought. *I've been trying to be free for years, having told how many girls I needed freedom to write, to be by myself. And yet never, not even when I was alone, not even when I came to this apartment, not even when I was writing, had I ever felt free.*

Eric pulled me close to him and brushed back my hair, one of his favorite ways to show affection.

"You don't want to know," I said.

"Oh, but I do," he said, kissing me on the forehead.

Chapter Thirty-Three

"I've been trying for years to be free. I keep thinking if I can get away from so many things, I will finally be free."

He scooted around, folding his legs in front of him, putting his hands on my thighs so we were facing one another. "I struggle, Jason. I do. I want to be more out than I am. I know it. I hate it. We're not that different, Jason. The biggest difference is that I've come to accept myself *for myself*. I've called a truce in my internal war, surrendered, put down my defenses, and come home to myself."

"I'm not there yet," I said.

"I know," he said. "But we have this." He looked around the room, our clothes on the floor, our naked bodies, the light coming in the window. "We have this."

The next morning, a car pulled in the driveway. I called out, "Get dressed. Someone is here." We pulled on T-shirts and shorts and looked out the window.

It was Carole. She waved. I opened the door and ran to greet her. "What brings you here?"

"You've been a stranger," she said. "I was worried."

"I'm fine. I have a friend over."

"Back with Suzie?" she asked.

"No. That's over."

"I'm relieved. But who is she?"

I took a deep breath. It was now or never. "Come with me," I said. Inside, Eric was sitting in one of the wicker chairs, petting Toby.

"Eric," I said. "This is Carole."

He stood and gave a deep-waisted bow. "I've have heard so

much about you," he said, smiling broadly.

Carole looked at me, nodded her head, and stretched out her hand.

"I'll get us some lemonade," I said. "It's a beautiful day to sit on the porch."

From the kitchen, I could hear Eric laugh and Carole laugh in return. I brought out the glasses and the three of us went outside together. Carole took a sip.

"Not too sweet. Just like I like it," she said. "My friend, I'm charmed with your friend. He has a wonderful sense of humor."

"Yes, he does," I said. "He's a dancer, too. He lives in Cumberland."

"A therapist!" Carole said. "I told him both of us practically need one on staff."

"You have been a lifesaver for Jason," Eric said. "He's told me how you sold the Presbyterian board to have a Center in their church."

"A woman's touch," Carole said. She turned to me and winked.

"You've been wonderful, you know it," I said, poking her lightly on the arm.

We chatted for an hour. Frivolous talk about her farm, the river and the weather.

After lunch, Carole and I walked down to the river. We sat on the dock, dangling our feet in the water. "He's a lovely man," she said. "How long have you known him?"

"Five months or so."

"And you didn't tell me," she said. "Not a word."

I couldn't look at her. "What was there to tell?"

Carole scooted next to me, her hand on my thigh. "Jason, I see the way you look at him. There's a sparkle in your eyes that I haven't seen in months."

Chapter Thirty-Three

I blushed and looked away.

She laughed. "I thought so."

"You're not upset?"

"Upset?" she said. "I've suspected something for quite a while. Oh, my poor boy, I've seen how, when certain men at the conference cross the room, how you look at them. There's something in that look that isn't just curiosity. It's a look of loneliness and I've been so afraid for you."

I felt like weeping.

"You might try to hide things from me, Jason. But for a country girl, I've been around," she said, slapping my leg. "What I'm most interested in is that you are happy. My sense is, he's a keeper. Quite stunning and I don't mean just looks. He's bright, sensitive, and clearly loves you. Oh, look at you. You're crying. Is there some—"

"No, nothing wrong. It's just what you've said. You've made it so easy for me to be me," I said and reached over to hug her.

We talked about how I met him, how I worried if the word got out, and how she also worried and thought that I better be careful. On the way to her car, she turned to hug me. "I'm so glad I got to meet him. I sense you wouldn't have told me. Am I right?"

"You are."

"Now, you'll be less a stranger?" she asked. She tilted her head down and gazed over the rim of her glasses.

I felt a weight lift off me. "We could all go out to dinner sometime up in Cumberland."

"It's a date."

She waved at Eric.

She drove off. Eric came up the driveway, took my hand, and

said, "What a remarkable woman. I don't think I've laughed as much in months." He squeezed my fingers. "She knows, doesn't she?"

I nodded. "I've just told her," I said. "She said she could already tell, by how I looked at you."

"You know, Jason, it's also the way you look at her. She touches your heart, doesn't she?"

"Yes. The best friend I've ever had."

"She's something else," he said. "Let's go for a swim."

As he'd asked, we went one full-moon night to my perch, walking up the road, holding hands, wending our way through the woods, brushing aside saplings and briars, until we came to the slate slope.

"Go on your hands and knees here," I said. "It's slippery."

"You sure you know what you're doing?" he asked.

"Careful, scoot down here," I said, leading him to the red cedar, "and hold on."

He shuddered.

"You're fine," I said. "Relax. You'll get used to it. Let your eyes adjust."

When we made it, I put my arm around him, remembering how he had done the same when we first made love. He leaned against me. The moonglow rippled on the water. A cool breeze coming up from the water wafted over us. We sat there, taking in the view, the lights of the houses far out in the valley, the dark sky with the stars like the lights of cities seen from a plane at night, the whole majesty of the heavens above us. I leaned back, careful not to stab myself on an errant slab of slate stone. He lay on me.

Chapter Thirty-Three

He eventually spoke. "I see why you come here. What did Thomas Hardy say, 'Far from the madding crowd.'"

"I suppose that's it."

"I feel so small here, so insignificant in face of the immensity." He nestled closer to me.

"Is that bad?" I asked.

He thought for a moment, patted my chest. "No, not bad. It's kind of comforting to know it's not us against the world. Not me against the natural world. It's me in the world, right here, just being part of it, being part of you. To think, we only live about an hour apart. Yet when I'm here in this place, I feel as if have come to another continent, a world quite separate from mine."

"A world quite separate?"

"Yes. It's magical and wonderful."

We stayed there and watched the moon lift higher in the sky. Then we went back, stripped, become quiet, and fell asleep in each other's arms as the immensity outside the window rose up in the night and brought in the new day.

The next morning, it was Sunday. The last day before work started again. I'd arranged a meeting with the staff, told providers when to deliver food and supplies to each of the Centers.

Eric stood in the doorway. I repeated to him our arrangement to come visit on weekends. When he left, when his car turned and drove up the hill, I felt as if my heart was being yanked out of me, dragged yard by yard up the road. I wanted to race after him and bring him back. Back to my bed. Back in time. But on he drove, and there I stood.

Chapter Thirty-Four

Three weeks after Head Start reopened, Dad hit a hole-in-one on the eleventh hole. Mother gave the updates, "the news" as she called it, about their Club friends: Mr. Hampton had died after battling cancer for two years; Dean, the Vietnam Vet, whom I had befriended, had been accepted into Harvard Graduate School to study James Joyce; the Lynche's and the Hirshe's got divorced and remarried within a month—Mr. Lynch married the former Mrs. Hirsh, and the former Mrs. Lynch married Mr. Hirsh. My mother loved the gossip.

I'd been driving six Head Start children to a picnic, one girl, Becky, asked what would happen if she pulled on the handle of the door. Before I could scream *Don't*, the door opened with the car going twenty miles an hour, and the air sucked her out. I pulled over and sprinted to her on the roadside ditch, ripped off my t-shirt and bandaged her head. Several other Head Start staff members who were in cars behind me stopped and transferred the other kids into their cars. I told them to call her parents and let them know.

I sped thirty miles to the Winchester Hospital with her lying in the back seat semi-conscious and bleeding. I ran into the Emergency Room with her in my arms. Nurses swooped her up and put her on a gurney. No one asked who I was. They assumed I was her father. They kept saying, "Don't worry. No permanent damage—hopefully."

After they patched her up, in a daze, quite overcome with the accident, I sat next to her. She was quite alert and showed no signs of a concussion. She was interested in what was going on, looking intently at the doctors in white jackets. "Why are they white?" she asked me.

I told her, "For cleanliness." She looked at the blue tile walls and asked why they were blue. I told her that it was to remind her of the sky.

"What is this?" she asked, tapping her head. I told her that her head was sewed up like her mom darned up a sock. The nurses pulled the skin together so it would be like new.

She asked me, "What color is my blood?"

I said, "It's red."

She smiled. "It's red and the tiles are blue, and the wall is blue, and the sky is blue. And that is white. Your pants are white, and the doctors and nurses are white, too."

When her parents arrived, they greeted me as if I were a family member.

I still had blood on my t-shirt when I was on the phone with my dad. He told me how he used a nine iron, how it took one bounce, and plopped into the cup. Now that he was retired, such moments took on great significance. After the round, my dad would have bought drinks for his friends. They would have shaken his hand, patted his back and made a big deal of it. He lived in a world far from mine. I hadn't played golf in a year. Families like Becky's probably didn't even know what it was, and, if they did, they couldn't afford it.

What came back to me, standing there talking on the phone,

Chapter Thirty-Four

was the haunting image of Becky's hand on the lever. The image, when the door swung open, of her body for a moment half-in, half-out. Like the abyss my old friend Erling Duus described as our fall from God's grace.

Falling? I wondered how it was that we all fell. That was how I fell for Eric. A door swung open, and I wasn't sure if I'd landed, or toppled, or slid into something—someone—beyond my control. This happened to many people living quiet lives who had fallen, were stitched up, and went on with their lives, their stories left untold.

Back in my office, I learned that a VISTA volunteer who had been assigned to our region was interested in working with Head Start. She showed up at my office and introduced herself. Her name was Debra. A red head, she was quietly intense. Her heavy-lidded eyes and trim athletic build attracted me. She spoke freely, smiled easily and displayed a keen intellect. She asked me to tell her what the town was like. Surprisingly, I hesitated. I realized the Pearsall Flats that I knew wasn't what it appeared to be. There was Orlando's clandestine world. There was the Black ghetto in the middle of town. There was the longstanding split between Yankee and Confederate loyalties. And there were the Federal programs like Head Start that were resented or appreciated, depending on who you talked to.

I asked about her background, whether she had any experience with young kids. She told me that she'd lived outside of Washington, D.C., in College Park, Maryland, and had worked in a children's Jewish Community Center. An English major, she was impressed with the poetry books on my office shelves. On the way out, she said that she enjoyed meeting me.

Debra joined the Pearsall Flats Center as a volunteer. Over the next weeks, when I visited the Center, I observed her on her hands and knees engaged with the kids and was impressed with how quickly she acclimated to the Center's routine. We chatted about the different children. Since Carole had also brought a VISTA volunteer in her program, Debra asked, if I wouldn't mind, driving her there.

On the drive, she talked about her family, how her father had died when she was teenager, how she'd attended John F. Kennedy's inaugural and met him.

Carole introduced Debra to Virginia, the other VISTA volunteer. They spent the day together.

Back at her office, Carole said, "Debra's impressive. She knows what she's doing. I'm glad you brought her over. Virginia is a nice gal but a little slow on the uptake."

On the drive back, Debra told me she wasn't sure if it right to ask me, given I was in a way, her boss, but she had tickets to a John Prine concert and wondered if I'd like to go. Never having heard him, I accepted. It wasn't as if I was dating her. I thought Eric would understand.

On the way to the concert, she invited me to College Park where I met her family. Her mother thought I was her new boyfriend, had me sit on the living room couch, and treated me like a son, listened to everything I had to say, lauded my commitment to those in need. She insisted that I send her my poems. She told me about her also being interested in the arts since she was trained as an opera singer.

Chapter Thirty-Four

At the Prine concert, Debra and I sat with two of her friends and afterwards, we went out to dinner. I drove back alone that night although Debra invited me to stay over at her house. I tried to justify my night and feelings. I told myself I was just experimenting, seeing what might happen.

◉

At the Center, Debra worked as an aide and did home visits. When I visited the Center, we chatted. The more time I spent with her, the more I discovered how many things we had in common—a love of literature, a strong commitment to civil rights, and a passion for music and politics. One afternoon, after visiting the Center as it was closing, I invited Debra to my place for coffee.

She browsed through my records and asked, "Who is Sir Dragon?"

Embarrassed, I explained that a friend had called me that since I lived in a cave by the river.

Toby had cuddled next to her on the couch.

"You have any cats?" I asked.

"I have two, Velvet and Fiddler," she said. "They get along with occasional spats."

"So, you don't mind?" I asked, looking at Toby.

"I love it. I miss having a pet. They are such comfort," she said.

I felt uncomfortable with my attraction to her. It was confusing. It didn't seem right for me to be with her, even interested in her after making a commitment with Eric. I also knew, despite our ages, I was not her peer. By all rights, I should need to keep my professional distance.

We should have met at the Cozy Kitchen.

◉

I told Eric about her.

"Are you dating her?" he asked.

"No. No. She just asked me to the concert."

"But you talk about her, how she likes literature, is interested in your poetry, and hates Nixon as much as you do," he said. "I think there is more going on here than you say."

"I don't think so."

"I do." He rustled my hair. "It's OK. I know you've wanted the normal life. Just be honest with me."

"I think you're jumping to conclusions," I said.

"We'll see," he said.

Lying in bed, his head resting on my chest, his body slack, warm, I thought about what he had said. Debra did make me feel normal, rediscovering my attraction to woman. I was grateful to her for that. I was even finding that I could envision myself with her. A politically active liberal Democrat, she resented Nixon, his handling of the war. She knew more than I did about English literature. She fit my ideal of what a woman should be.

I put my arm around Eric and pulled him closer, fearing that I was drifting away, becoming untethered, caught in my yearning to follow the script I'd been schooled to follow since I was a young boy.

◉

I continued to spend weekends with Eric, but I also went with Debra to films in Morganville and visited several local bars that had great dance music.

Chapter Thirty-Four

Although I still loved, or wanted to love, Eric, Debra who lived a mile away became a regular visitor to my cave. I felt my allegiances shifting. I'd almost given up the notion that I could ever live as a straight person, but a small, persistent voice still pestered me, told me I could never live as I wanted to live if I committed to being with Eric. That little voice began to speak louder as Debra sometimes stayed the night. I told her I was involved with someone else.

She became closer to me than any woman ever had, because we could talk about anything, from politics, to child development, to art, to history, to literature, to poetry. And she made me feel valued as a lover, an artist, a man, and thinker. I enjoyed the fact that I could tell others about her. No secrets. As it turned out, the door to the life I'd always hoped to live was still cracked ajar, and she held the key.

Since I didn't want to be dishonest with Eric, he and I talked about what was happening. We were walking in the fields by his house, something we had gotten used to doing. He seemed to like the outdoors more since I'd brought him hiking to my perch. We'd regularly begun to explore the fields for wildflowers.

"Hey, I'm not forcing you to be here," he said. "All l can say is I don't think it's right for you. As I told you, I tried that route. I gave it a shot. It worked for a while. I must say that my parents were delighted. Thrilled might be a better word. But in the end, having a normal life ended up being abnormal for me."

"Yet it might be normal for me," I said.

He sighed and shook his head. "I think your parents weigh on you more than you know. In your mind, you may think that you have rebelled. You may think you have separated from them. But they still cast a spell over you. They're under your skin. You're still their boy."

"That's not fair," I protested.

"Fair. Not fair," he said, shrugging. "Maybe so. But I think it's true."

I stomped off. My head felt as if it were being squeezed in a vise. I started to run. Where I was going, I wasn't sure. I had to get away. I ran up a hillside and stood. The valley below, washed in the late afternoon light, spread out toward the town. Eric hadn't followed me. He was walking back to his house, leaving me with my own thoughts.

Not being my own man, still being under the influence of my parents, wasn't what I wanted to hear. Eric was wrong. I'd spent my whole visit with them taking a stand, defying what they expected of me. What troubled me was not just them. It was my own self-image. It was also the eyes of that man at the meeting with kids from the dig. I could see the hate in them. That hate was the issue. I just could not push that aside.

I wanted to be a caring person. I wanted to be an artist. I wanted to find a community of people who valued the intellectual, who questioned our country's duplicity, who weren't just interested in keeping up appearances or making big bucks.

But Eric was right. I wasn't ready to say that I was gay. The word scared me. I wanted nothing to do with it. I stood on the hill for an hour, picking up stems of grass and chewing on them.

When I went back to Eric's place, he said, "You're back. Are you hungry?"

"Yeah, I guess I am."

Chapter Thirty-Four

"Guess?"

"I am," I said. "Thanks for cooking. What is it?"

"Polenta with spinach, some herbs. Concocted it myself," he said. "Sit. Let's eat."

We didn't discuss my ambivalence. I could feel the dread of something broken hanging over our conversations. I wanted to explain what I felt but I wasn't sure what I felt could be put into words. We made love. Our bodies were still talking with one another. My love of his body was stronger than ever—his sinewy frame, his touching me where the electricity charged through me wanting release. That was a relief, but it was also scary.

The next morning over breakfast, he said, "I can give you a longer leash for a time. But only for a time. My sense is if you don't find out what it is you need, you'll be resentful of me. I couldn't deal with that. So just keep me informed. Okay? Like with AA, a day-to-day thing."

I hesitated. I felt like crying.

"I know," he said. "It will take time. That is the one thing we have. We can take our time."

"I just hate the notion I'm a sexual deviant," I said.

"Who said that?"

"I read it in the Diagnostic and Statistical Manual of Mental Disorders (DSM)."

Eric laughed. "I thought I told you. Didn't I? Haven't you read about the movement, a strong one now, to expunge that diagnosis from the manual?"

"No."

"It's true. There have been protests. Gay and lesbian psychiatrists are putting pressure on the APA to change that classification. I think in a year or so that label will no longer hang over our heads. For now, say we forget about labels. What do you say?" He patted me on the leg.

I reached over to hug him. We spent the morning chatting about the recent news about Watergate, the break-in at the Democratic headquarters. Nixon was covering up something. The news was dribbling out, one trickle at a time, each pointing to some subterfuge among the higher ups. I hoped that Nixon would get his comeuppance.

My animosity toward Nixon, I realized, wasn't rational. Nixon's mannerisms were like my father's. He would say, as my father did, "Let me be perfectly clear," when he was about to denigrate some enemy or be uncannily obscure. My father would say it when he was reprimanding me for not acting properly. With the war continuing, even with Nixon's insistence that he would bring it to an honorable end, my fate as a guy with a draft number, even though it was a high number, hung over my head, made me feel as if, after avoiding the draft by attending Divinity School with a 4D status, I might still end up with a rifle in my hands. Eric was right: the ghost of my father, and his society, weighed on me.

I left Eric's house in a flustered state. Destiny seemed to be calling me, but it was calling from two opposite sides of a field. I needed time by myself to figure out what I needed to do. That night I woke at one o'clock sweating from a dream. I got up and wrote down what happened.

Dream of looking at a guy standing on his second-floor porch. He was handsome, charming, glib with the turn of a phrase. He acted out the Eroica Symphony as I once did before Dominique. Just

Chapter Thirty-Four

as I was enjoying watching his lithe body move, he leaned over the iron railing and tried to rip my dream apart. He toppled over the railing. He smashed on the ground, rolled over and knelt. He crept toward me. I became aroused. I awoke for a moment, wondered where the dream was headed, and then slipped back in. Everything shifted. The guy was gone. I was listening to Wallace Stevens reciting in his deep base, orotund voice, "The Large Red Man Reading." He had thick jowls, gray hair, deep-set eyes, and red pen marks on his cheeks. I was in the fourth row. After his reading, Debra went up to him to ask him a question about what he meant. I followed, asked him for an autograph. He was offended. He chided me in a severe manner, mocked me for liking his poems. Then the dream shifted. I am with Suzie. My penis in her as in a sheath, my seed wrapped like seeds in a pod ready to burst when, out of nowhere, the first dream guy who looks like Eric comes up to me and touches my arm and I become queer with pen marks on my face, deep oceanic blue marks that melt and I swim away in their wake.

All my feelings for Debra, for Eric and my wanting to be a poet—all there, all the different loves fighting for a place in my psyche and none of my selves seem to win. Each seems to confound the other. None of them can raise a flag and say, "Take me. Here I am. This is me. I surrender."

My instinct was to rip it out of the journal and toss it away. I closed the book. Stood on the veranda, watched the moon that had crested the ridge and was locked in the branches of a tree. I stayed there for a long time. It was quiet. Eric was right. I needed to make any decision, or else I had nothing.

Chapter Thirty-Five

The teacher in the Capart Center, the one nearest to the Virginia border, told me she was worried about a particular family. The children didn't have winter clothes and often came to the Center unkempt. One night, on a drive back from the Center, I stopped at their ramshackle house, twenty feet off Route 50, on a curve. The short clay driveway ended right at the front door.

The father was at home. His name was Charlie Burr. I'd been expecting the mother to be there. In his mid-thirties, thin, with deep set eyes, and a quick, staccato voice, Charlie wore baggy pants, the cuffs rolled up and a tobacco-stained white dress shirt. He opened and hid behind the door, blinking at me as if he'd just awakened from a deep sleep.

I told him who I was and that I'd come to see his wife.

"She's downtown someplace," he said.

I asked when she would be back, and he said he didn't know.

"That's too bad," I said, "I wanted to see how you're doing."

He pushed open the door, stepped out, squatted down on his heels. His greasy, matted black hair had a makeshift Beatles' cut as if someone had placed a bowl on his head, snipped the hair under it, and left the top ungroomed. His long Roman nose puffed out smoke. His eyes shifted between me his cigarette, and the floor.

"How have things been going?" I asked.

"Not very good. My wife and I are having trouble," he explained, not wasting time.

"Really?"

"She is so concerned with money," he said, taking a deep drag.

"I sympathize. Sometimes I'm glad I'm a bachelor, not married, having to face all that," I said, hoping to make him feel comfortable with me.

"You don't know the half of it. If it ain't money, it's sex. It's excuses, excuses, excuses. She said it was her father who told her, drilled it into her, that it was bad, and so she wouldn't do it. But she feels bad for me. She does. She knows I need it."

There was a hole in one of his shoes. He reminded me of a hurt little boy who'd been left out to play with no supervision. I said, "That must grind on you. With all these children, you have quite a load on your shoulders, a lot of responsibility." Seeing if I could shift the conversation to what their kids needed, I added, "Let me ask you, do you need some help? Your daughters look like they could use some winter clothes. It's getting cold. What say, can we help out?"

"Hey, buster, don't ask me. Ask my wife. She's the boss. She takes care of them if you know what I mean. And I don't think she'd take too kindly to handouts," he said. I stood up and shook his hand. "I will have our teacher speak with your wife. I wish you well. Hope things get better for you."

"San Francisco, that's where I'm headed. Count on that," he said. He threw another cigarette butt on the pile on the stoop.

As I drove off, I felt as if I'd spoken not to a person but to some tragic mythic figure who spoke so much of misery, he had become misery, a being who'd ceased to be present in his own life and to the daughters because he was caught up in his craving for lust.

Chapter Thirty-Five

I kept checking on him, dropping by. His story never changed. He didn't go out west. His wife became pregnant again. The teacher arranged for a local merchant to get them coats and winter wear. The program nurse set an appointment with a gynecologist and went with her, making sure she got what she needed. Whenever I drove by their house, I'd see several girls in the yard, playing in the dirt, no one there to watch them. I wondered how any of them would make it, given a dad who wasn't a dad and a mom who had to do it alone. I wondered what it was in our society that relegated so many families to live on the margins. I wondered how this man or other men got trapped and would breed another generation equally ill-equipped, how I had heard from a Head Start consultant a warning that even the best programs might never address the needs of certain people. I felt helpless. I wondered if anything we were doing in Head Start could reverse their fate.

When Eric came to visit—Debra had gone to visit her mom—I talked to him about what I was feeling. As a counselor, he could commiserate with my helpless feelings, but he admitted that he could offer no easy solutions.

"After some of my clients leave," he said, "I ask myself 'What good am I doing?' I've heard them out, even get them to make plans, but then it falls apart. That's when I go on long walks, you know, try to clear my head."

"On days like this I want to take a long walk out of here. I don't think I'm fit for this job. I hate to see what our society has done to people, me included. We just don't care. We don't care enough. We don't do enough. When I go visit my parents, I see the discrepancy. The haves and the have-nots. It drives me crazy. I feel so damn worthless," I said.

Eric took me by the hand. "Come on. Let's take my advice. Let's go for a walk."

With Toby beside us, we walked up the road and headed in the opposite direction of where I usually went. Beyond the lodge, the road rose steadily and wound up a hill, then leveled off parallel to the river, and came to an open field that looked over the valley below. We sat in the grass. Toby leapt in my lap and settled down. A faint breeze bent and swayed the grass like crosscurrents in the river.

Eric took my hand. "Some things don't make sense," he said. "The injustice irks me, too. I can't tell you how many times when I enter a store the way the clerks follow me with their eyes. Anytime I pass a cop car, I take my foot off the pedal. I slow down. If he finds any reason to pull me over, I know, before I even open my mouth, I'm guilty. Black. I live with that dread. I'm a marked man. It's not something white guys like you ever know. It's just how it is for me—"

"I'm sorr—"

"Don't feel sorry for me. I'm careful. It's all I can do. It doesn't change anything. I still feel enraged. I wish I could wave a wand and change it. But there it is. Those that try to make the change, you know, have too many bullets in their bodies. So, we make do." He tugged on my shoulder. "You have a good conscience. Makes me feel I'm not alone. You get it in some ways."

I leaned against his shoulder. He kissed me on the cheek. Toby purred and ducked his head under both our arms.

Eric said in a soft voice. "You remember I told you I dated a girl

Chapter Thirty-Five

in college?"

"I do."

"There was something I didn't tell you."

"Go ahead."

"We got married."

"What?" I lifted my head to stare back at him in shock.

"I knew it would surprise you. It's not something I'm proud of. As I said, she was also a dancer. I was clueless where I was going, what I wanted to do, and my parents really wanted grandkids. I wanted to be a good son. She and I worked in a local theater. At the time, I thought, 'wouldn't it be nice to settle down.'"

"How long did it last?"

"At least that I was honest about. A year or so. She was studying to be a dance teacher. I was working on my MSW. We were busy. I wanted it to work but, in my heart, I knew it wouldn't. We rarely slept together. I'd met a guy, an actor, and fell in love. Oh, I had a mean crush on him. Nothing happened, mind you. I kept trying to make the marriage work."

"How'd you know it wouldn't work?"

"My attraction to her faded. I was enchanted with her at first. I think, looking back, I was more in love with making it with a woman, than I was in love with her. The flame went out. She was okay with my being bi. She said it made me different. But later that year, I met another guy. We hung out, all three of us, and we became friends. But, on nights when she was working, he came over, and we became more. I had to accept the body has its own intelligence. I finally listened to it."

"Why didn't you tell me this before?"

"I figured we had something good. I needed to be the steady one, the one without doubts. I didn't want to let on that I once had the same ambivalence as you have. I don't know . . ."

He looked distraught. His face was flushed. I hugged him.

"I'm glad you told me," I said. "It makes me feel closer to you. And—" I laughed. "Not so much the fool."

We sat quietly for some time. Toby mewed. It was his dinner time. I picked him up, and we headed back to the lodge.

Hetzel, my Head Start driver, was arrested driving while intoxicated. I fired him, leaving one boy, Evin, without transportation to the Pearsall Flats Center. The lead teacher told me Evin didn't speak. He played well with other children; he wrote, read well, seemed smart, and sat by himself with a book, turning the pages, seeming to comprehend the words. But he was a non-talker. He lived far down River Road along a ridge that led deeper into the mountains. I ended up having to pick him up and drop him off, rising at 6:00 AM. His parents were tenant farmers.

The first day I drove, his mother stood at the doorway, afraid to let go of her son.

"So, you're the Director," she said.

"I am."

"How come you're picking up my boy?" she asked. She had her hand on Evin's head.

"I want to make sure he gets to the Center," I said. "And it's a nice drive up this way."

Evin, not sure who I was, grabbed ahold of his mother's dress.

Chapter Thirty-Five

He looked like a little elf with a compact body and spirited eyes. His hair combed over his forehead, he stared at me as if inspecting a new species. I knelt and introduced myself. I assured his mom I would pick him up and drop him off.

Evin came with me to the car. I had him sit in the front seat, belted in. When I asked him his name, he only shifted his eyes toward me, not saying a word. I kept up a steady stream of talk, trying to engage him.

For several weeks, as I drove along River Road, we drove in silence.

Some mornings as I turned onto River Road, a deer would appear out of the fog on the roadside, eating grass. It would take two or three ballet strides and then like Albrecht in Giselle, would leap, suspended for a moment in the mist ahead of me, as if bouncing off a trampoline into the brush.

Then, one afternoon as I was driving Evin home, I noticed a box turtle crossing the road. I pulled over and told Evin to wait. I trotted back to the turtle and scooped him up. About the size of a child's shoe, he scrunched inside his shell as I carried him back to the car. When I got in the car, I held it out to Evin, saying, "Here's a turtle for you."

He reached out, his hands, his mouth wide open. I showed him how to hold it by its sides so it could poke its head out.

He said, "It's a box turtle."

He knew exactly what it was. He told me where they lived, what they ate. He didn't stop talking all the way home. I found that I was having trouble driving because I started to tear up.

As he got out of the car, Evin called out to his mother, "Look, a turtle." She scampered down the steps to see it. I told her they could keep it. I'd get something for it to stay in if she wanted. The next morning, I brought a little aquarium with a rock and plants in it, along with some turtle food.

From that day on, Evin and I were buddies. He loved animals. I could see why. He had a dog and, across the street, a Billy goat. When I left him off at the barn across the street from his house, he showed me his Billy goat that he loved to chase and, in turn, would chase him. A few times, when he got out of the car, he ran after his goat, and, after three or four times racing around the barn, Evin screeching with delight as the Billy goat bleated, Evin would raise his arms straight to heaven, and the goat would chase after him.

Since some days I had to drive to Petersborough, I asked his mother if he could come with me, go to another Center, have dinner with Carole and me, if we had to work late. Some staff members wondered if he was my boy. The longer we spent time together, the more I wondered how Charlie Burr could detach from his nine girls. Just as with Jay, Evin energized my yearning to have a son. I imagined coming home with him there, greeting me, calling me Daddy, and racing into my arms. Something deep inside me, something deeper than a desire, was calling to me to be a father. It was as if I was being called to do something to make that possible.

Not out of any plan, nor out of any clear anticipation, nor even any sense I was violating my feelings for Eric, I had Debra stay over more often. I kept in mind how my romance with Suzie had fizzled, how I had gotten involved with Dominique, and how Eric had won me over to him. I kept saying to myself, "Don't rush, Jason. Just let it be. Trust it. Remember what Lou said. See what happens."

Chapter Thirty-Five

Debra and I had a routine. We'd have supper. She showed me how to use the oven. Like Tess, she knew how to cook, especially French cuisine from her grandmother. We talked about poets, about English novelists, her favorite being Jane Austen. Then, we slowly undressed in stages, first unbuttoning a shirt, a blouse, caressing our exposed flesh. She pressed her body on my pants, felt my cock. Light fell on her nose, the rest of her face black, flecked under the candle, which flickered on the table. I put on my robe, and she hers. We nestled close to each other on the couch, my mouth on her breasts, her mouth on my cock. I leaned back, her dark form over me like a wraith. We spent hours touching each other. She would ask why I always closed my eyes. "To let the pleasure seep in," I would say. But if closed my eyes, I could pretend it was anyone in my arms. It could be a god or goddess, Apollo or Aphrodite, Dionysus or Athena, a body, no gender, just flesh. I could give myself over to it.

When I was close to orgasm, I closed my eyes even tighter to give myself over to the ecstasy. We kept on swimming in the same current, mouth on body, mouth on mouth, like two merging dreamers in a river.

As the winter approached, as Debra and I spent more nights alone by the river, as I began to fall more in love with her and began to let Eric, however much I loved him, recede from my life, I felt as if my future had taken a turn. The river had also transformed into its winter garb. The ice, stacked high in the river, crashed through whole slabs along the river's bank, shoving them over the dock where, in the midday's sun, they'd melt and crack. The river sounded like a mammoth creature caught in a trap, moaning. If I were caught in a trap, it was of my own making. The more time I spent with Debra and the more time I spent with Evin, picking him up each morning, leaving him off at night, the more I craved a family life, the bliss of holding a child, the more I was feeling as if that life was calling to me in ways I could not resist.

Just as the river had begun to change, something began to shift in my mind. Instead of thinking of Debra as another, separate from me, I began to feel as if she and I had become a "we," two people united. I felt inspired to write a poem.

In Our Room by the River

Lumps of snow from the sycamore
Thumped on the porch. We opened our eyes.

Light fingered up white sheets.
Our different sexes bathed in light.

You slid over me. Winter ice had
masked the Potomac. Now it cracked.

White traffic jammed its banks.
Ice boulders shoved on shore.

Giant crystals glistened in light.
Our bodies pressed still and close.

The river rose with run-off and swept
the ice away. We shivered at the sight.

New lovers, we watched and wanted
to freeze how we came to be.

Chapter Thirty-Five

No longer do we live in that room. We're far
from the river. We're far from that shore.

Some mornings in these older years
when light slips in the window

faintly, yet surely, we hear
snow drip slowly off the sycamore.

She cried after she read it. "You are serious, aren't you?" she asked. "Of course."

"I am, too. We need to make plans. I think you should go back to Vanderbilt, see if that works for you. Head Start is wearing you down. And from there, we can decide what's next."

About this time, Eric came to visit twice. We had dinner, but we didn't make love. He suggested that we take a break.

"I need to ask you," he said. "Do you know if you *really* want to be with Debra?"

I studied his face, the soft, kind expression of someone who wanted to understand. "I wish I knew," I said. "I do have strong feelings for her. It's as close to love as anything I know. But I also have feelings for you, ones that I've never had for anyone else. I guess that I need to figure out which it is—which one will win out."

"Yes, you do. It's only fair. She needs to know that it's her. I need to know if, despite your fears, it's still me," he said.

When he drove off later that day, I felt as if someone had stabbed me in the heart. But I was also relieved. Whenever I was with him, the simple pleasure of his body in the same room, next to mine, I wondered if I would ever be able to commit to Debra. But I agreed with him. We needed a break. I didn't call him. I tried to put him out of my mind.

Chapter Thirty-Six

Debra's mother, Arlene, a sturdy woman with a strong, operatic voice, made me feel like I was a member of the family. Whenever I visited, she called me into her kitchen to show me how her family made certain recipes. "Jason, look at how I fix this. They're called latkes." Ever since she hugged me the first day we met, she kept repeating that she was glad Debra found me. She loved me. And she meant it. She had faith in people. Uninhibited, prone to say whatever was on her mind, she often embarrassed Debra.

One weekend, I had them over for dinner at my place. Arlene wandered around my living room, noticing the shelves of books, the poster of Beethoven, and the writing table with journals piled in one corner.

"You're a studious one," she said.

"I guess I am," I said.

"I admire that. Debra is too. She always has a book in her hand." She went to the back deck. "This view is breathtaking. To have the river right there, just steps away. "

"I think it's sacred," I said. "When I come back here from work, I can let go of everything."

Debra's sister, Nadine, three years younger than Debra, an aspiring actress, came to visit, too. She fought with Debra about everything—the length of Debra's hair ("Much too long"), the president ("Nixon should be trusted"), the future ("Everything will be fine"), and me ("You're too mean to him"), the last point being one I began to agree with more and more, since Debra took the liberty to correct me, often times legitimately, when I spaced out, drifting off into my own thoughts.

Debra was, in ways I didn't like to admit, like my father. They were both lambasters of points and people with whom they disagreed. As we spent more time together and as she became more propri- etary about our living space, she made me feel as if, up to now, I hadn't known how to keep house.

After a dinner and leisurely evening reading on the couch, as I prepared for bed, slipping off my clothes as I usually did, putting them wherever they happened to fall, I heard her cry out, "Would you please pick up your socks!" I had left them, as I often did, on the floor.

If I left the dishes in the sink, she asked, "Do you expect me to be a maid?"

When I was late to pick her up, she growled, "Are you ever on time?"

Altercations were as commonplace in her household as the sun rising in the morning and setting at night. I noticed how skirmishes between Debra, Nadine and Arlene would come at any moment. Once they ended, the air cleared, and everyone acted as if nothing had happened. I found it disconcerting. Sometimes, amusing. Other times, frustrating. In my household, growing up, arguments never happened. Never. My father would growl and snap at us, at which point I would make myself scarce. I somehow imagined that I would be immune from Debra's outbursts, as her lover. So, I was not prepared for them when they began being directed toward me.

One overnight in College Park, after dinner, I drove Nadine to

Chapter Thirty-Six

her ballet lessons. She had come to see me as a permanent part of the family and a good corrective to Debra's intensity. She confided with me about their family history. Their father, a lead chemist at a research lab, had been for years a wonderful dad, taking them swimming, teaching Debra to play golf, going to musicals, and involving them in State and National elections—including democratic presidential inaugurations. But something had gone wrong. He became temperamental, flying off the handle, screaming for no reason bigger than an overcooked brisket, one poor mark on a report card, a bicycle left in the driveway. He'd berate them, call them names, spank them, send them to their rooms. The next day, as if the clouds had lifted, he would be fine, happy the way he used to be, lifting them up, hugging them, acting as if whatever had happened the day before had been an aberration. As Nadine spoke, I thought of my own father, equally quixotic, prone to violent rages.

When Debra was a sophomore in high school, her father was in a car accident. Nothing serious. His car had veered off the road and hit an embankment. At the hospital, he was resting comfortably. He had bruised his abdomen. Nothing to worry about. He was in good spirits, said that the physicians wanted to do a few tests. It seems that before the crash he blacked out for a moment, which led to the crash. Debra was relieved.

The next day he was dead. He'd ruptured his liver which had been infected for some time, some vestige of a childhood case of scarlet fever, which explained his mood changes. His sudden death left Arlene in charge of finances and insurance, and she had a breakdown. That meant Debra had to step up, take over. And she did. She had never stopped.

I watched their dynamics closely—intimately. If the washing machine needed repair or replacement, Debra was the one who called the mechanic.

Nadine's volatile reactions to Debra were her attempts to have some say, to be her own person. It was between them. I wasn't about to be Henry Kissinger negotiating a treaty for what was an ongoing, internal conflict among two daughters and their mother.

As spring broke out in the hills, Debra stayed at my apartment most of the week. I wasn't sure if I was in love, at least not as passionately as it was with Eric, but I knew that I felt comfortable being with her, loving her as I would, passionate at times, guarded at other times.

With her I could have a child like Evin who I continued to drive to the Center, feeling the tug of fatherhood. I had to decide if I wanted normalcy in my life more than I wanted true love.

Debra liked to be with me, but not with some of my friends. She didn't enjoy loud parties with drinks, stories, and late nights. If I made plans to be with Ken, she would withdraw. Dark moods overtook her. At one moment, she'd be happy, spending the day reading, talking about poetry, drinking wine, and listening to music. Then, out of nowhere, she'd be sullen. She refused to talk, pushed me away when I tried to comfort her.

Those moments when she withdrew reminded me of lightning flashes that ripped across the sky and, once they were over, left the sky clear. It also remined me how open Eric was, how sunny he was by nature. But I still questioned what sort of life we could live: two

Chapter Thirty-Six

men, two sexual deviants to the minds of most people. Eric meant facing bigotry. Stigma. Social rejection. I yearned for certainty, to have a place in the world even if it was imperfect, I didn't need to worry about acceptance. Maybe Larry was right. I was afraid of the wildness. I wanted domesticity more than adventure.

One night, I went with Ken to a Rotary Dance with a woman he'd recently met. He thought I might be interested in joining the Rotary Club and invited Debra and me. Debra didn't want to go to anything sponsored by Rotary. Her mother had worked for them in College Park, and they had treated her poorly.

"No matter," Ken said. "There are a lot of guys who go stag. It would give you some status with local business owners. And should you want to look for another job, a great place to make contacts." I wasn't sure about wanting to be in any club any more than I was sure I wanted to stay with Head Start, but I owed him for all the times he stood by my side.

I danced most of the night. Women asked me to hit the floor. I had a great time doing the twist, funky chicken, and the fox trot.

Ken thought I'd made a big splash. "I heard several members want you to join," he said. "If I didn't know they were married, I might think they were fags. You should have seen how they looked at you."

I wasn't about to join. Besides the fact that the club reminded me of my parents' society. I didn't tell Ken that he may have been right. Some of the men who ogled me were probably men who frequented Orlando's place. I wanted to avoid them and, besides, I didn't want to alienate Debra by joining a group that felt alien to me.

When I got home, I closed my apartment door quietly, not wanting to awaken Debra. I took off my shoes and slid into bed on my hands and knees. I thought she'd turn, as she had other nights, to greet me with a hug and kiss. We could cuddle, and, if it felt right, to make love. She didn't move. Toby sidled near me and purred.

After a few minutes, I said, "Are you awake?"

I leaned over her and smelled her hair, the fresh smell of conditioner.

She didn't budge.

I stared at her body, her thin hip-high nightgown. Not an inch of movement, as still as the lamp that cast its light over us.

"Are you mad?" I asked, pressing my hand on her shoulder.

Not turning, her face against the pillow, she snapped, "What do you think?"

I said, "Have I awakened you?"

She said, "Yes."

"Well," I said, "it was quite a night. 1960's music. It was a good time. You would have liked it."

She remained silent. I felt a tightness in my belly as if someone had punched me. I expected that she would welcome me home. That wasn't too much to ask. After weeks of coping with her mood swings, I had reached a boiling point and, without thinking about it, not even knowing it was coming, I screamed, "Stop it. Quit acting like this."

Yet, the second the words flared out of me; I became frightened. Anger was not something I felt comfortable with. I'd seen my father lash out at my mother for no reason. I had to get away. If not from her, from my rage.

I laced my shoes and stormed out of the apartment, slammed

Chapter Thirty-Six

the door and marched up the road. I wanted to get as far away from her as I could, as far away from the anger seething inside me. The night sky felt as angry as I was, grayish black with a thin wedge of moonlight. It made it hard to see. I wanted to hit something, anything. I lashed at the brush along the road, shoved branches aside, stomped on fallen limbs.

Darkness hung low over the horizon. I tossed slate stones over the cliff and waited to hear them hit the water, a barely audible plunk.

I considered driving up to Eric's place to see if he'd let me stay the night.

Here I was, alone, thinking about him. I could imagine him right by my side, hear his voice, soft, gentle, inquisitive. He accepted me no matter what I did. Rotary. Knight of Columbus. Whatever group I was in. He wouldn't care. No matter who I danced with.

When had I seen him last? It was three weeks ago. He asked if I would marry Debra. We were at my place, and he walked to the window and looked out. Headlights grazed across his face, then left it in the dark. "Marriage. That's important to you?" he asked.

"I guess it is," I said.

"I get it in a way. I wanted the same. But isn't there something, some little voice in you that questions what's going on?" he said, turning to look at me. "Every bone in my body tells me that you're gay, and yet, here you are planning to give up those feelings for the great American myth of a wife and kids."

"It's no myth."

"It's your way out of this . . ." He motioned between me and to him. "I just think you're making a horrible mistake."

We talked well into the night.

"It hurts to see you do this to yourself, "he said. "From what you tell me about the way she treats you, even despite that, marriage is what's coming. I'm afraid, really afraid, I can't keep this up. I fear, and I guess I know, that I'll lose you."

I could still hear his words. "Lose you." They echoed in the night air.

It may have been an hour, maybe more, before I returned to the lodge. When I entered the bedroom, Debra reached out to me, unbuttoned my shirt, unzipped my pants, and pulled me toward her. Maybe she sensed I'd gone away, had drifted back to Eric. When we woke, her head on my chest, we made love again. We never discussed my shouting outright, but I felt as if I were a rubber band. I'd been stretched to the extreme, then released, and come back to a normal state all bent out of shape. Our love was mysterious, dual-faced, a give and take like nothing I'd experienced before, but it was something—maybe the uncertainty, maybe the excitement—that drew me in because the intensity of it demanded more than I had ever given to anyone else: the full emotional range of my being, both the dark and the light.

Chapter Thirty-Seven

I came back home one night after a meeting with Carole, driving along the river, a slight mist rising on its banks. Debra was there. She had fixed dinner. She kissed me and handed me a glass of wine—but was quiet. We sat on the couch with our plates. She shrank from me when I reached over to touch her.

"Don't touch," she muttered. "I'm not sure I'm right for you."

"What is it?" I asked.

Doug and his wife, Angel, had come down to check on the lodge, and found her here. I hadn't told them she'd be staying with me. They grilled her why she was at my place. She said they treated her "rudely."

"They don't like me," she said. "You—they think you're a god. But me—they almost spit at me." She thought it was because she was Jewish. "They could tell. I could see it in their eyes."

She asked why I hadn't told them? Was I serious, or wasn't I?

I said I was. It was my mistake. I would call and let them know.

"Angel yelled at me," she said, "because I used their damn washing machine. She told me never to use it. I had no *right*. No right? It's right there. All I used was water."

"Well," I said. I told her that I never used it. I did my laundry in town.

"What petty people," she said. "What the hell are we supposed to do? Are we together or not? Why don't you explain these things to me? I don't know what the rules are. How can I know? I'm sorry. I'm sorry." She cried. "You act as if I can read your mind." She gazed out at the rain. We sat on either end of the couch.

She moped, sighed, and read. I looked at her, offering a smile.

She said, "Don't try to flirt with me."

We slept with our backs to one another. The rain pattered on the roof. The room, cold and damp, felt like a prison cell.

In the morning, she asked, "Can we make this better?"

"I hope so," I said.

"What do couples do with their time?" she asked. "You know things we can do together to have fun. We should learn French together, have a project. We never do things together. You work. I work. Let's do something together."

She wanted me to teach her how to play golf. She had played it with her dad when she was young. I took her to a course in Winchester. She played well, a natural athlete. We had Chinese for dinner. She was surprised I knew how to use chopsticks.

Who taught you?" she asked.

"A friend," I said.

Later, we went to a movie. I didn't have to worry what people thought about us. We could hold hands in public. We could kiss. Everything was normal. We visited her mom, spent the night there, and drove back to my place the next day.

Chapter Thirty-Seven

Later the next week, in College Park, I got the flu. She took care of me, fixed soup, put cool compresses on my head, sat next to me, watched me, made me feel—I guess it was what I felt, although I wasn't sure—loved. Not erotic love as it had been with Suzie. Not passionate love as with Eric. It was familial.

While she nursed me, we discussed more intensely my interest in getting a PhD in theology and teaching, my desire to return to Vanderbilt, our getting out of West Virginia. The academic life appealed to me. It felt safe. It was something she, and her family, valued. I knew if I went back to Vanderbilt, no matter how many courses I took, no one, not for a minute, would ever mention the topic of sex. Not a word. I could read four hundred pages of text, incisive interpretations of the gospel, long theological tracts on religion, or radial discussions of liberation theology, and never see the word. I would be on my own to study theology and never have to think about my body. I would be with a woman. I could put some distance, something I had done with my parents, between myself and Eric and the gay underworld in Pearsall Flats.

Debra asked me, "Why would you want to go? You seem ambivalent about the church."

"Exactly. That's the reason. I want to challenge established religion. If I could teach theology, if I could get ministers to question the conventional way of interpreting the Bible, I feel that I could be of some service to them. I had a professor like that. He got me to ask questions. He got me to consider that what I had been told to believe was not what was in the Bible. Because of him, I took this job, broke in some small ways with my family, and am the person I am."

"It's a long road," she said.

"I need to make a change."

The next day, I called my old advisor and told him of my plans. He was delighted and told me to apply. I could start in September. Debra helped me complete the application. She applied for teaching jobs in Nashville. It was all happening so fast it made my head spin, but it felt right, I told myself. By moving to Nashville with her, I would have made an irreparable decision. Chosen a life. Crossed the river.

I would be able to calm her down, I told myself. My equanimity and our new, shared life together would make both of us new people.

Ruth, a friend of Debra's, a newspaper reporter, told me I was making the right choice. She spent the weekend with us and asked to speak privately with me, so we took a walk.

"You're the right one for her," she said. "Do you know why?"

I said, "Because I'm terrified of anger."

She laughed. "No," she said. "It's something more to do with your intellect and your disposition. Let me explain." She took my arm in hers. She felt physically strong. "In the Jewish culture, there is a great respect, even reverence, for the intellect. It's part of our tradition. Often families will designate someone as the scholar, the learned one, to study the Torah, to translate the rabbinical expositions. We are constantly looking to the texts and reinterpreting them to fit our present history. It's call midrash. We don't just follow them like Christians do, saying, 'It's the word of God. We must accept it on faith alone.' For that reason, even if a family has few resources, they will make sure that a designated person has the best education. The one to enlighten others. People will ask that person what they think

Chapter Thirty-Seven

because he or she becomes the vessel of the tradition—religiously, artistically, and intellectually. You are a person who values knowledge, who wants to learn, and as such, you will be honored in her family. You fit in perfectly. With my WASP friends, intellectuals are dangerous, not to be trusted, scoffed at, even resented. Am I right? But the Jewish culture values someone like you."

I told her that, indeed, my family had no interest in my education except as its utilitarian value to get me a good job. When I brought up topics about civil rights, the war, or my studies, I was told that they weren't appropriate conversation in polite society. "Don't say anything that might cause controversy," I said. "Keep up appearances. Talk about the weather or the dog. Perfect the art of small talk, which in my mind is no talk."

She said, laughing. "As you can tell from Debra's family if someone disagrees with someone else, they go at it, full bore, guns blazing. Have you noticed?"

"Oh, shit," I said. "Scares me to death when it happens. But I'm getting used to it."

"You'll be fine. You are calm and gentle. In time, I think that will have an effect. It will make her feel safe."

Our conversation made me feel more at home with Debra's traditions than I was with my own, if, indeed, I'd grown up with any worth preserving.

One evening, after Debra and I made love and were listening to the river, I surprised myself and asked her if, after we moved, maybe, if it worked out, we could get married. Lying on my arm, her head next to mine, she turned toward me. She lifted herself up so that she was looking down at me. "Are you serious?" she asked.

"I am," I said.

She rubbed her hand across my forehead. With one finger touched my lips. She sat up, crossed her legs and nodded her head, saying, "You've made me very happy. So, I guess, my answer is 'yes.'"

We told Arlene who was ecstatic, and we told Doug and Angel who were lukewarm. Carole was pleased.

When I told my parents, my father told me he'd have preferred meeting Debra in person first. He asked who she was. I told him that she was Jewish, majored in English, lived in Maryland. We would drive up in March, so they could meet her.

Instead of greeting me with a kiss, Eric said, "I think I know what you're going to say." We sat on the same couch where, on that first night, we had first kissed and made love.

"Yes," I said. "I suppose you do."

Eric bowed his head. His mouth opened as if he were about to say something, then closed. His lips drew thin, tightened. The space between his brows narrowed as he nodded his head. "I get it," he said.

"I'm sorry." I reached out and held his hand for a moment.

"No, you're not," he said. "You should be happy, Jason. It's what you want. Isn't it?"

"I think so."

"Think?"

I felt dizzy and rubbed my forehead. "I don't know. My feelings about you, no matter what I do, they're still there. I feel awful about us. Yet . . ."

Chapter Thirty-Seven

"Yet you've made a decision. A commitment. Right?" He spoke. "I don't like it. I think it's wrong. But I expected it." He stood. "I'll fix us some tea. You don't look well and it's a long drive back."

Before I left, he asked one more question. "Does she know about me? About you?"

I yearned to curl up in his arms, let him hold me. I think she suspects, I said. "She gets an expression on her face as if she knows something. We fight." I looked at his face, his eyes, his lips. They were tight. "I'll tell her. She needs to know."

He nodded. "She does."

After tea, he walked with me to the car. "Drive safely, dear one," he said. "And remember I'm here. If you need to call, do."

I didn't expect to cry, but I did. He held me and patted my back. "I know," he said. "I feel the same way."

My car headlights shone on him as he stood, waved, and smiled. His image, his kind face, that last moment, stuck with me. I believed if I could hold onto it, I could hold onto him, his image, for weeks, for months, maybe I could carry it with me into a new life without entirely forgetting the past. Even as I felt uncertain, I believed in him, and he'd told me to decide. And I had decided.

Chapter Thirty-Eight

It was cold, a Saturday in March, when Debra and I celebrated the end of the Vietnam War. Over the previous years, war had been like background music, something I'd paid little attention to, but was there, a whispering, insistent and unrelenting. My mind went backward in time to when I received my 1-A status, my Vietnam passport. When I sidestepped the war by enrolling in divinity school. When Dr. King declared the war racist. When our bombs fell on Cambodia. When I marched in the streets, and when the Kent State students were shot. When I learned that Bruce and Duffy, my high school classmates, were dead in some rice paddy. When Kissinger promised a de-escalation, then escalated. When Nixon declared 'Peace in our time.' When all those frightening moments flooded back to me, I realized the war years would in some ways always be imprinted on me like a scar, not impacting my everyday life yet still haunting me.

"This is like New Year's or Christmas for our generation, something we need to celebrate," Debra said. "The curse has lifted. The wicked witch is dead."

We held out our Rolling Rock bottles, clinked them together, and talked about a war that had begun when we were in high school.

I said, "I lived four years of my life praying I wouldn't have to go. It seems unreal. But did you hear him? He dismissed the war like someone sweeping crumbs off a table. As he did, he also managed to take a swipe at us. 'Despite an unprecedented barrage of criticism from a small but vocal minority' he stood firm for doing what was right. Yeah, right. I still hate the guy."

Debra said, "I was there at those marches. It was awful. Nixon came out one night, met with some of us. Then, days later called us thugs. He doesn't deserve to be president. Yet, I agree, here he's taking in all the glory."

I slammed my fist against the wall. "Why do we keep electing such men?"

Debra reached for a hug. "You can relax now. It's over."

She pulled out a copy of the Washington Post. "To lighten your mood, have you seen this?" She pointed to an article about Watergate burglar McCord. He had written a letter to Judge John Sirica. His previous testimony was a lie. A cover up. The burglary was not a CIA operation but had involved other government officials.

"You know what this means," she said. "Someone in the White House was involved. I bet it goes to the top. I've talked with my aunt, the one you've met, Jason, the one who works for the IRS. She's pretty sure it was Nixon. It's been a horror show for her, how he tries to use them to go after his enemies. If he could do that, he could do anything."

"I hope they nail him," I said. I looked at the poster of Beethoven. His Emperor Concerto composed when he once thought of Napoleon as a hero yet in the end, he despised him. How easily the great fall from grace. Was there any way to keep from falling? Maybe that was how it was for all of us.

Chapter Thirty-Eight

Debra grew up in the suburbs as I had. But she didn't grow up, as I had, in a Country Club that explicitly excluded Jews. (If you asked my father or his friends, they would have denied it). She was proud of being Jewish. Her parents socialized with brilliant academics, even some of the Nazi code breakers during WWII. With her father a chemist and many of her family members Kennedy appointees in the government, her social life revolved around serious discussions of national importance. In her early years, she didn't know anyone who was a Republican. Never went to cocktail parties. Never lived as I had in a world where being a Republican was almost a religious affiliation.

Debra presented herself, as she was: a woman who wore little makeup, dressed plainly, and spoke her mind. I enjoyed her intellectual repartee, her liberal political beliefs being tested. And I knew that wouldn't do in my parents' world. From their point of view, Nixon could do no wrong.

As we drove into my parents' new gated condo complex, we told the guard we were there to see the Folletts. He checked his notes, nodded, and opened the sliding gate. We parked in front of their condo, a two-story structure with a balcony on the second floor overlooking a recreational common area with a pool, tennis courts, a putting green, and a small garden with a gravel walkway.

My mother greeted us, giving me a kiss on the cheek. She smiled, as she always did, and graciously told Debra how pleased she was to have her visit. My father waited for us in the front hallway. I gave him a kiss. I introduced Debra. He studied her without saying a word. She took the initiative and said, "Nice to meet you, Howard."

My father's face tightened. The skin drew back, exposing a redness on his cheeks and forehead. For him, younger people calling him by his first name was disrespectful. I forgot to warn her.

With his best paternalistic manner, he said, "Dad will do."

She looked him straight in the eye and told him, "I prefer Howard. My father was the only person I called 'Dad'; and he died when I was younger."

She told my mother what a lovely place it was—how she loved how the kitchen looked over the gardens, and she and my mother went off to discuss the furniture and paintings in the living room.

My father glared at me. I offered him a weak smile as if to say, "Don't look at me."

From the onset of the visit, my father asserted his dominance. He told Debra not to tie up the phone. Her mother lived alone, she said, and if she remembered, she had talked to her each day—so that was how it was going to be. He told her that women wore skirts to the Club. She told him she had no skirts. He offered to buy her several and she politely declined. With amazement, I watched them parry. His ears reddened when he became angry, and it amused her. "Now, Howard," she'd say, "no reason to be upset. I just see things differently from you." For years, I learned to make myself scarce when he began to boil, but she hopped right into the kettle and stirred it.

It was as if she was giving me a short course in how to handle an overbearing parent. I loved it, yet I worried, too. When he boiled over, his rages scalded everyone in the room.

On our second morning there, I noticed that no one had brought in the newspaper. I opened the porch door, fetched it, and took it to the kitchen. My father was waiting for me, his hands on his hips, his

Chapter Thirty-Eight

face flushed, staring at me.

"What?" I asked.

"What? You ask me 'what'?" he shouted. "You went out on the porch in your bathrobe."

"So what? It's not the end of the world, Dad."

He pointed his finger at me. "Don't get sassy with me. Let me be perfectly clear. You are not living in the hills."

"What's the problem?"

"I'll tell you the problem. People can see you out there. It's a public place. Totally unacceptable. Out there you need to be dressed," he screeched. "Do you understand me?"

Debra had come in behind me. She stared at us. It was my moment of truth. I shook my head and said nothing. I threw the paper on the table. The salt and pepper shakers toppled onto the floor. I walked out of the kitchen.

She followed me.

"How dare you let him threaten you like that," she said, her voice raised.

"Forget it," I snapped.

"Hey, I'm not the one yelling at you," she said.

I showered. Debra and I ate on the porch. She had accomplished in two days what I had never done in twenty-seven years: confronted my dad and taken a stand. My parents joined us with their coffee. My dad had on a new face. He inquired how Debra's mother was doing. I was impressed. He was making an effort. That was the best I could hope for.

After breakfast, my father informed us they had set up a reception at the Sheraton in honor of our visit and our forthcoming marriage.

"Marriage?" I said, my mouth falling open.

"Yes, I thought you said that you were—"

"Planning, yes. Nothing definite," I said. "We'll go to Nashville together and—"

"So. You said, 'marriage.'"

I looked at Debra. She curled her lip and shrugged.

"Can you call it off?" I asked.

"Out of the question!" he said. "We have invited all our friends and, well, there must be a hundred guests—"

Debra interceded, "A hundred?" She sat forward. "We don't need that."

My father slammed his fist down on the table and sent the marmalade bouncing across the glass. He declared, "Young lady, you do not—you hear me—do not have the right to tell us what we can or cannot do for our son!" My mother put her hand out to calm him, but he stood and threw his napkin on the table, hovering threateningly over Debra.

I rose quickly, pulled him away from the table, and steered him back to the kitchen. As we walked together, I composed myself and asked him, "Dad, can you just give us some time? You sprang this on us without even letting us know ahead of time."

"I thought you'd appreciate it, give you a chance to see your childhood friends."

We stood in the kitchen. "It's the choice thing, Dad. We'd appreciate it if you give us a choice. Let me talk with Debra, alright?"

He turned toward me, his face close to mine, "I don't think she's the right girl—"

"Drop it, Dad. Drop it. It's my decision." I squeezed his arm gently.

Chapter Thirty-Eight

He backed away. "I don't get it. What has gotten into you?"

He went over to the refrigerator, poured himself some orange juice, looked out the window.

I went back to the porch where my mother and Debra were talking.

"Oh, honey," Mom said, "have a seat. I'm so sorry. We only thought you and Debra might like a special night, and your father, you know, he's hurt since he went to a lot of expense and, well, we've invited—"

I reached over and took her hand.

Debra, seeing how hurt my mom was, without my saying a word, said, "Yes, of course. We are delighted to go."

◉

Later that day, my mother went with Debra to buy a dress and have lunch. I sat on the porch. My father sat beside me. We didn't speak.

After Debra came back, we locked ourselves in my room. I explained what it would be like to prepare her: a reception line, meeting all the guests, probably gifts, lots of drinks, hors d'oeuvres and, afterward, Club dinner. I would wear a coat and tie.

She showed me her new dress—sleek, black with green and white trim. "I've never owned a dress like this," she said, rubbing her hand along the fabric.

"How much was it?"

"I don't know. Your mom insisted on buying it."

◉

My parents, Debra, and I stood in line for an hour. Father introduced Debra to each guest, acting full of pride, as his new daughter-in-law-to-be.

River Crossed

At dinner, he gave a toast to the bride-to-be and made the point that she was his second daughter—acknowledging my brother's wife Barbara. Debra clutched my arm, never let it go. "How can you stand it?" she whispered. One guest after another told us how lovely we looked, how pleased they were, and shared some anecdote about my childhood. Although I hated such affairs, I had been brought up going to them. This world was not a shock to me. I mingled with my parents' friends, made small talk, and found myself click into the host's role more easily than I expected.

Debra and I drank much more than we usually did. We danced to the band music and ate good food. I felt, more than ever, that she was the right one. She had stood up to my father, and she compromised.

The next day, we drove back to Pearsall Flats. Each mile along the interstate marked the distance we felt from the world we had temporarily entered.

Chapter Thirty-Nine

Carole and I worked out a plan for her to take over as director of my Centers, using my salary to hire more aides. I announced to the staff that I would be leaving in late August but would be with them to the end of this year's program. Going back to Vanderbilt felt like the right decision, but leaving the area, particularly my place by the river, felt like a horrible mistake. It was the first place I'd ever felt was home. The cave, my sanctuary where I could spend as much or as little time as I wanted writing, drawing, swimming, and being by myself, was sacred.

Late in May, the lead teacher of the Pearsall Flats Center called to tell me to come over. "Hurry," she said. "It's an emergency."

When I arrived, she pulled me to the side of the classroom and showed me a boy with a swollen foot, purplish, the color of an eggplant, clearly infected with a four-inch cut on the side. The boy, a pale, slight child, winced when we touched it. He was running a fever. I could smell the smoky coal odor in his clothing and the unwashed scent of his body. His name was Billy, and his parents lived off Black Strap Road. I'd driven many kids home along there. It was the same road where the Heavener's house burned down.

Unsuccessful in reaching his parents, I drove him out to their house, a one-story structure, a smoking stove pipe stuck out of the roof. I carried Billy to the door, and marched up the road.

His mother, a woman in her thirties with short, closely cropped hair, opened the door, and invited me in. At a pink, vinyl-covered table sat an elderly woman sewing a shirt, a shawl draped over her shoulder. She didn't look up. In the middle of the house, a pot-bellied stove pumped out the heat. Several windows were covered with plastic. Others had newspapers stuffed in them to keep out the morning chill, the sun barely shining through. There was one print of Jesus on the wall, his countenance aglow with a halo, and a picture of John Kennedy.

Billy's mother offered me a seat. I sat by the table and undid the makeshift bandage around the wound, tapping the distended skin, and told her that he had quite a serious infection. She came to sit by me, brushing back her boy's mop of brown hair. I asked why she hadn't taken him to the doctor.

The older woman said from her chair that she had taken care of it as she had done with all her boys, and it worked with them so it would work with him.

His mother whispered they couldn't afford a doctor. They had no insurance. Her husband had lost his job. I told her we could cover the costs, that there was doctor who would take care of him. She said that as soon as her husband came home, she'd talk with him.

The next day, Billy came to the Center with his foot covered with some mustard compound, a yellowish gel, and wrapped in a torn cloth.

I went over to the Center to see it in person. The swelling had increased, with a blue discoloration creeping up his leg.

"What are you waiting for?" the teacher asked.

"I'm not sure I can—"

"So, you're going to let this boy die because—"

Chapter Thirty-Nine

"Let me work it out," I said. "I'm as worried as you are."

Across the room, sitting on the floor, Debra played with several of the kids. She looked over at me, not wanting to intrude. We had to keep our distance. But I could see from her face that she was equally perturbed that I hadn't acted more decisively.

From the Center, I called the Billy's home again.

"Fine," the father said. "Fine. Fine. As long as there weren't no expense."

I drove Billy over to the office of the Dr. Owen's office who often saw indigent patients. Gruff and unfriendly, he had, nonetheless, a strong social conscience and had seen several of our students without charge. In the waiting room, he had a large tank of tropical fish, small orange ones called Platies with black tails and black stripes on their head. Billy was enchanted with them. I held him close to the tank. His body, clammy and warm, showed signs of serious infection. He felt as if the fever had gotten worse.

When the nurse came to get us, she took us to a room and unwrapped the infected foot. She asked what happened. I told her that he was barefoot and had stepped on a piece of metal, probably a car part, in the yard.

The nurse looked at me reproachfully and asked why I had not brought my son in earlier. I told her that his name was Billy, and I was the Head Start Director. Her demeanor changed.

She worked on his foot. She rinsed a cloth off in hot water, wrung it out, and pressed it to the wound again. With a soft voice, she explained to Billy what she was doing, how the heat would draw out the infection. She asked Billy if he would mind getting in a special gown since the doctor would need it to help him. He slipped off his socks, jeans, shirt and underpants, which were filthy. She whispered to me that she'd have them washed since the wound would have to be kept clean. We bathed him. Once he was in the dressing gown, he and I waited for the doctor. I held the warm, damp cloth on the wound the whole time.

When Dr. Owen came in, he told me to put the boy on the examination table.

"This boy should have been brought in days ago. What were they thinking?" he asked.

I told him, "No insurance."

He growled, "Damn the insurance, that's no excuse." He informed me that he had to lance the wound to drain the infection. His disposition changed as he knelt and put his arm around Billy, explaining he needed to get the bad stuff out of the wound, laying him down. He asked me to comfort him as the nurse came in with surgical instruments on a tray.

I could barely watch. I rubbed Billy's hair and explained that the bad stuff, the infection, was coming out of him. He held my hand and took long, slow breaths out of his mouth. Once Dr. Owen had drawn out as much as he could, he gave Billy a tetanus shot. He covered the wound, provided antibiotic lotion, more clean bandages, and explicit instructions. He told me to pick up more antibiotics at the pharmacy for the parents—or the teacher to give Billy each day.

I was startled, at the house, when Billy's father answered the door. He was a young, slight man with the same straight brown hair as Billy and the face of a child, round and guileless. I brought Billy inside and

Chapter Thirty-Nine

put him on his father's lap. I explained how to change the dressing on the wound. I told them that we *must* give him the pills twice a day, once in the morning, once in the evening. We could give him the morning pills at Head Start when he ate breakfast there.

I told him the foot had to be cleaned twice a day and he had to have clean socks and clean clothes.

"He can't be going barefoot," I said.

"He loves to do that, has done it his whole life," the father said.

My tone changed. I looked intently at the man. "If you want him to have the rest of his life, that can't happen. He must have the wound covered and shoes and clean socks on his feet."

The father glared at me and saluted me. "Yes, sir."

I smiled. "Sorry. But this is a matter of life or death." I added that no mustard plaster was needed. We needed to follow the doctor's instruction. The old woman grumbled in the corner, shaking her head back and forth to let me know that she didn't like being cut out of the care.

When I said goodbye, the father eyed me carefully and thanked me. "You done a good job there with my boy."

The goodbyes were difficult. But the worst goodbye was with Evin. I didn't know how I would keep myself under control when I left him for the last time. But I didn't want him to see me fall apart. I took him to lunch with me at the Cozy Kitchen, let him order what he wanted.

"Can I have a chocolate milk shake?" he asked.

"Sure."

We chatted about his turtle, his goat, and a new dog he'd named Zeus.

"Do you know who Zeus is?" I asked,

"He's my dog."

I laughed. "No, I mean, the word, where it comes from."

"Yeah, mom read about him. He was a god a long time ago," he said. "He got in a lot of trouble, and Zeus, he does, too."

He talked about salamanders he found under some rocks by the creek, the deer that slept in the corn field, the too-small fish he caught in the river and let go. He was a naturalist at heart. He made friends with creatures.

I figured the car was the best place. On the drive to his home, I told him that I had to say goodbye, that I was leaving, moving to another state. He pursed his lips. "Why?"

"I want to go back to school," I said. "Maybe look at a different career."

He was quiet for some time, then shook his head. "You'll miss this," he said pointing out the window.

"I know, I will."

At this house, his mom came out to greet us, standing on the porch. Evin grabbed my hand. We walked up the gravel walkway. I had already told her that I would be leaving.

"So, this is it," she said.

"I've worked it out with the school. He will get picked up when first grade starts."

She reached and took her son by his shoulders. "Much appreciate what you've done."

"No, I appreciate your letting me take him with me. He's become like a son to me."

Chapter Thirty-Nine

She smiled. "He calls you Turtle Man."

I looked at Evin, "Why you call me that?"

He blushed and shrugged his shoulders.

I crouched down. "I guess we started with that turtle in the road. Is that it?"

There was a mischievous sparkle in his eyes. He shook his head.

"Go ahead, Evin," his mother said. "You can tell him."

"It's that jacket and tie," he said. He stuck his hand under his shirt collar, hunched his shoulders, scrunched his face, and pulled his neck down as if inside a shell.

I laughed. He was right. On days I dressed up, when we met with federal officials putting on my businessman uniform, I did feel stuck in a shell.

"You're one observant guy," I said. "Come here." I held him in my arms. "I need to go now."

He said, "It hurts."

"What?" I said, afraid I was holding him too tightly.

"Right here." He pointed to his chest.

My resolve to keep in control collapsed. I couldn't help it. I was crying. "Yes," I said. "It does for me, too."

He wiped one of my tears away. For a moment, he was the elder taking care of me.

His mother reached out, and I passed him to her. She was crying, too.

"I'm sorry," I said.

"No. No. Don't be sorry. I know you love him. He loves you, too," she said. "You best be going. It's not gonna be easy. Just do what you said. Don't forget us."

River Crossed

◉

Almost as a distraction from the agonies of goodbyes, I became mesmerized by the unraveling Watergate story. I told myself that by focusing on the congressional hearings of each of the latest people in Nixon's administration indicted, I could put aside the ache that came from leaving a place that had become woven into my heart. But I watched the administration's little lies, one after another, become known, and it reminded me of my own cover-ups, the ways I'd acted as if I was just like other guys with nothing to hide. Still, I couldn't look away from Nixon. He became my fall guy.

Carole invited me to her house to watch the initial sessions of the Senate Watergate Committee. With the appointment of Archibald Cox as an independent prosecutor, I knew whatever cover-up had occurred was more serious than suspected.

She poured me coffee and we sat in her living room, watching the Committee tease out incriminating evidence from one official after another. Their inquisition reminded me of the whole set of secrets that, if I stayed, might have also brought me down. I had another life, one that I hid from nearly everyone, one that, if I wasn't careful, even after we moved to Nashville, might still expose me.

"I never have had much use for the man," Carole said. "I go way back with him. I remember his slandering that lovely man Alger Hiss. Ruined his career. Called him a Communist. This time it's him in muddy water."

The politicians were seated in a semicircle on a dais, asking questions. Some had prepared statements, some were probing for more information. Every time one of Nixon's underlings spoke, the veil of secrecy was pulled further away.

Chapter Thirty-Nine

"I don't know," I said. "Much as I dislike him, I do feel sorry for him."

"Why's that?" Carole seemed surprised.

"We all have things, don't we, that we'd just as soon keep under wraps?"

"Eric, I think you mean," she said. She looked at me and then back at the TV. "That's why the nation is captivated. Everyone's worst fear is being played out on TV."

Sick of politics, sick of his lies, I said, "Yeah, I haven't told Debra."

"You haven't?" she asked, reaching to turn off the TV.

Carole leaned forward, put her elbows on her knees, her hand on my arm, "Jason, her handling your father was one thing. Being your lover is another."

"What are you saying?"

"I saw you with Eric."

"I'm happy now," I protested.

"Not in the same way. She doesn't make you laugh as Eric did. I just worry, that's all," she said, patting my arm. She got up. "I made us lunch."

After we ate, we went for a walk. "Are you going to be alright?" she said pressing her hand on mine again.

"It's killing me, this leaving," I said. "I'm not sure I can—"

"Let it out," she said. "Just let it out."

I cried. She patted my hand. "Hey, you need to know we love you, too. We are going to miss you as much as you miss us."

"That's good to know."

"It's true."

An hour, maybe two, we chatted and remembered. When I got in my car, she said, "Call any time. You're family. You hear me? You are family."

Much of the work of closing the program was done. Debra had finished with her work at the Center, had gone home for the week since the weather had changed—the daytime temperature in the high 70s.

I spent a few days lounging around the lodge.

Doug had made flower beds, a tiny pond about the size of a bathtub and, next to the pond, a patio area large enough to hold a table and lounge chairs. Water lilies hugged the edges of the pond water. A small fountain kept the water clear. In the morning, in the languid sun, I'd sit in one of the chairs and take out my journal and enjoy the warmth of the sun, its gentle heat warming me.

One of these mornings, while I sat sketching, I noticed something move in the pond. A creature swimming across the surface. Without fanfare, the head of a snake peeked up and inspected his surroundings. Not sure what type of snake he was, I sat still. He swam to the edge of the pond and slithered out of the water, flicked out his tongue, and curled up on a sunny spot not six feet from me. I saw he was a cottonmouth.

I studied his body, the soft brownish white paisley skin and the taut musculature. He had no ill-intent. He was no Nixon. He wasn't threatening me. He was content to be where he was as long as I kept my distance. We shared our places under the soothing sun.

We were guarded friends. He would often be there when I went to the pond. He would gaze at me intently until I took up my perch in the chair and then he would go back to sleep. When I arrived, he would slip out of the water, coil up on the shelf of stones, and fall asleep. The longer we spent time together, the more I got to know him. His tail like

Chapter Thirty-Nine

that of a cat would wag back and forth and lurch if startled. He slept with his eyes closed. He'd stick out his tongue in my direction as if to say, "Lovely morning, isn't it?" and I'd nod at him in reply.

The first morning Debra was back, I was sunning, and she came out of the lodge fast, tripping down the stairs, excited to see me.

I held up my hand and called out in a muted voice, "Stop."

She thought I was joking and kept coming toward me. I put out both hands. "Stop, stop. For Christ's sake stop."

She halted not two feet from me.

She whispered, "What is it?"

I pointed to the cottonmouth who had felt her footfalls and coiled defensively.

Debra screamed, "There's a snake!"

The snake took one look at her, bowed its head, and slunk over the side of the wall, disappearing into the underbrush.

"Did you not see it?" she exclaimed.

"He's a friend," I said. I told her that he and I had been on good terms for nearly a week. "He suns here most mornings."

She could not believe it, even when I tried to explain. She would have nothing of my rationalization.

"It's time to stop pretending you're Tarzan, Jungle King, and come back to earth. I come out here to read, he must be gone. Hear me? It's too dangerous. It's asking for trouble."

When she was angry—or, in this case, worried and angry—she brokered no discussion. I knew her well enough to politely agree while planning to continue as I was.

Chapter Forty

In early July, Debra and I drove to Nashville to look for an apartment. We listened to the Watergate hearings on the way. They had become our soap opera. The Watergate Committee wanted copies of Nixon's tapes. Nixon refused to release them. The case went to the court. Who would win out? We barely talked with each other, captivated, as we focused on the radio. I kept thinking, if it were Eric in the passenger seat, we would still be talking. I needed to come clean with her. The more I heard of the cover-ups, the more I felt as if I was complicit on my own with a coverup.

Ironically, once we arrived in Nashville, we discovered that we also needed to cover up and lie.

A local friend told us, if owners knew we were unmarried, they wouldn't show us apartments. We had to put on fake wedding rings. When an agent asked, "Are you married?" we smiled, raised our hands, and testified, "We are."

Debra landed a job working as an aide in a high school. I found a job through the university as a waiter in the faculty dining room. We signed a lease, starting in August, on a three-room apartment ten minutes from campus. My misgivings about our relationship and our fights—the latest Debra's frustration with my needing time to write, with her needing more time with me, boiled over on our short visit to Nashville. The more she insisted I be with her, the more I wanted to be alone, the more I wanted to get back to the lodge and spend my last weeks there alone. I did introduce her to some faculty members who were excited to meet her and see that, at least to them, everything seemed fine. We were a young, newly committed couple.

Once we settled all the details about living in Nashville so that, when we did move there, we had an apartment, jobs, and familiarity with the city, we drove back to West Virginia. For more than a month, we could relax in the lodge, visit with friends, and prepare for the inevitable goodbyes before we headed to our new adventure.

On our return I found a letter from mother. She said grandmother was failing. I should visit her.

I decided to take a trip to Lake Worth, Florida, to see my grandmother—a perfect excuse to get away—and sort out any lingering misgivings about moving in with Debra. I could put some distance between us, making sure that Nashville was the right decision, although I knew I had, and really couldn't change, what we'd already committed to do.

As it turned out, my dad was going to be in Florida, too. I could visit my gram and see my father, perhaps, mend some of the hard feelings after our visit to their condo. He planned to meet me and to show me the new home he'd designed and was having built—he needed to confer with the contractor.

I drove all night and well into the next day. The Gulf Stream Hotel where, upon my grandfather's retirement, she had lived. It was a pink stucco three-story hotel that was once luxurious but had lost its luster. It reminded me of the hotel at Casablanca with Humprey Bogart. It stood across from the Intracoastal Waterway,

Chapter Forty

a body of water between the coast and the mainland providing safe passage for boats and protecting the mainland from storms.

My dad wasn't there yet. Wouldn't be for a few days. My grandmother—an upright lady with a stern yet engaging personality—greeted me and invited me inside. We sat on her porch. Dinner was brought up from the hotel's main kitchen.

I stayed for two weeks. On my fourth night, I received a letter from Debra. I read it and it made me sad. I had disappointed her. I had been distant when I was with her, I needed to respect her ability to see what was happening between us, and her ability to change.

She said:

The longer you are away, the more I imagine you must be questioning whether you want to return. I fantasize about your view of my shortcomings. Our differences can become quite vicious. But I long for you to come back.

I was touched by her honesty. It was clear she deserved more from me. She went on:

I am so sorry for the unhappiness I'm causing both of us. I seldom pray, because I seldom believe in God, but yesterday I needed something to believe in, and I prayed hard that I might find my way out of the hole I've dug myself into. Lord—if the hole gets deeper and I lose you, well, I just know I'll be in worse shape than I am now—which, as you know too well is none too good. I know that the degree to which I need you is something that you're not comfortable with, and probably makes you feel trapped. All I can say is please try to give me some time to straighten out my mind.

I want us, our relationship, to work, to have us live together more than I have wanted anything in my life. I will try to make it work. I'll try to be less possessive.

She signed it with a row of Xs and Os.

I sent off a quick note to her, letting her know I wanted to make it work, too.

During the day in Florida, I went to the beach, swam in the warm water, and walked back and forth on the bridges. I returned for lunch, and then swam in the pool, listening to men play gin rummy, talking of the old days, and complaining about Watergate and the Blacks who had moved into Fort Worth. At night, I took Gram out for dinner. If she was failing, she didn't act it. She got spruced up, even put on low heels. I talked to her about Head Start, my apartment, and Debra.

She listened.

When my dad arrived, he drove me north to see the construction of his new home, a permanent retirement home in the south where Mom and he could play golf all year long. Walking among the wood framing beams, he told me that Debra wasn't right for me. He went on about religious issues. Jews and Gentiles. I let him speak. He may not have sensed it, but I was making amends, letting him be in charge because I had come to see, no matter what he said, regardless of his biases, despite his disagreements, I was going to live my own life and what he said was just his opinion, and they couldn't change what I would do. His words fluttered from his mouth, lingered there like a bird in midflight, and then flapped away.

I borrowed clubs and we played golf. The golf course was the one place where we could get along. We discussed his swing. We

Chapter Forty

discussed my brother. Although we never talked about my going back to Vanderbilt, he never disparaged the idea either.

On the radio, the Watergate investigation ramped up. Every time I heard the word cover-up I cringed. I had to tell Debra. She was willing to face her possessiveness. I needed to face my coverup. I couldn't keep putting it off. A newly appointed special prosecutor was on the case and Nixon was feeling the heat. My father kept telling me to turn off the radio. "It's a bunch of claptrap," he said. "It's misguided, a waste of time. Congress should pay attention to the economy, not fuss with a silly break-in." I knew that he and I would never see eye to eye, and that was something I had to accept. In a way, even as we were so separate in our political views, we were still, no matter how I felt or believed, father and son. He was my dad. I could accept that. His flaws and his shortsightedness were his. I didn't need to make them my own.

Back in West Virginia, it rained and rained. I sat outside and watched it come down. Debra came out on the porch, sat sullenly in a chair, and asked, "When will this end?"

She wasn't just talking about the weather. Since I'd come back, I felt vacant, tired yet not fatigued, half here, half absent. For four days, I felt no urge to make love, and I couldn't explain it. It could be, I told her, the anxiety of leaving, but I doubted that. At night, even with her body next to mine, I'd drift off, and she'd ask where I'd gone. She sensed that I was somewhere else.

Finally, the rain stopped. We sat by the pond. July bugs clanked into the zapper and fell to the cement.

Debra glanced across the river valley. "It's so beautiful here," she said.

I looked out at the river and the land beyond it and knew it was time for a reckoning.

The moment was upon me. The snake was lurking somewhere nearby. I knew it. I took one huge breath, took her hand in mine, and told her.

I told her about Eric. What we were to each other. How intensely I felt about him, about how I'd covered up those experiences, tried to pretend that they hadn't happened. I said, "Odd as it may seem, I feel like Nixon. I should have told you long ago."

She scooted close to me, looked me in the eyes and said the opposite of what I suspected. "I know. I've known all along. I see it in the way you look at some men. It's okay. It makes you more interesting. I like that."

"You knew?" I asked.

"It's over. Right?" she said.

"In a way," I told her.

"Then it's fine."

"Really?"

"It doesn't mean anything," she said and in a strange and unexpected way, I took such offense to that, but I let it pass, as I had let what my father said pass. She added, and that's what I needed to hear, "You're a beautiful, sensitive man. That's all I care about."

When I came back from my office on the next to last night, cars were lining the road to the lodge, filling up the parking area. Debra

Chapter Forty

had prepared a surprise party for me with the help of my friends. She stood at the door and pointed to a parking slot left for me near the apartment. They all came—Ken, Lou and Larry, Edith, Bill, their gang of kids, Doug, Angel, Carole, even Arlene and Nadine. Everyone wanted Ken to make them his famous whiskey sours. They were his other speciality. He made batches of them. There were steaks on the grill, homemade potato salad, hotdogs for the kids, and marshmallows for roasting.

I didn't want the night to end. It was like a final passage at the end of a symphony when the music seems over but somehow there is another refrain, and still another, and each one more intense, seeming to take off in a new direction. The air was filled with the music of voices, laughter, and storytelling, going on and on.

Time seemed to stall. We sat on the porch, chairs pulled out of the main lodge to accommodate all of us. Toby checked out the guests, rubbing against their legs, allowing himself to be picked up by some and not by others. It was a mix of many different people I'd come to know in the new life I'd built for myself, all on my own. The small tensions that brewed up seemed fitting and were squelched as quickly as they emerged.

Edith said that she was afraid to travel west to Phoenix because they might get scalped by Indians. Debra told her, "That's racist. That doesn't happen anymore."

Edith said it was a joke, just a joke.

Nadine and Debra got into an argument about how to cook the hotdogs. One wanted them lightly charred, the other not charred at all. Larry picked up the tongs and said, "Ladies, let a gentleman take care of this." Lou joined him and they cooked them perfectly.

Debra mingled with Edith's and Bill's kids, taking them down to the river, letting them puddle on the shore, giving Edith a chance to mingle with Carole and me.

Larry and Lou smoked a joint and passed it to others, some who had never smoked before like Ken, who took offense, but had a hit and seemed mellow afterward. I smiled to myself. Arlene found the heat unbearable, went to stand by a fan in the cool living room of the main lodge. Carole kept by my side much of the time, nudging me, telling me to spend more time with Ken, who, she thought, was going to miss me more than I realized. Doug and Larry got engaged in an animated conversation about something. Doug's hands, all over Larry, checked his willingness, seeing if he might have a live one, someone he could invite on his special weekends for a tryst. Larry let him, and later came by me, for confirmation of what he suspected.

Larry laughed. "There's a homo behind every bush here."

Angel, busy as she was cleaning up, being the good hostess, didn't seem to notice, or, if she did, she never let on.

Later in the evening, Carole pulled me aside and said, "This isn't going to be easy for you. You sure about what you're doing?"

I took her by the arm and walked her to the lodge stairs. I admitted, "It's tearing me up inside. I have these aches in my chest as if my heart is restless, wanting to get out. I've come to realize this place"—I motioned to the lodge and river—"as a sanctuary. And the staff, those kids, particularly Evin, have gotten under my skin."

"Eric," she said.

I sighed. I nodded. "I wish not, but yes. Mostly him. Right here." I pointed to my chest.

"Give it time," she said. "Time mends." She glanced to the veranda.

Chapter Forty

"All these people love you. You can tell, can't you?" she said.

I had a hard time looking at them. I didn't want to say goodbye. "It's killing me, I know that. Gee, I don't know, not for certain. It's just—"

"It's just that you have to give it a shot, right?"

Finally, she had been able to put it into words for me, what I couldn't accept, but had to accept. Yes, I had to give it a shot. I nodded and got tearful.

"Listen, love." She never called me that before. "I know you've got to find yourself, your next self. I get that." She grinned and shook her head. "But leaving here is not something I understand. I've lived here for forty-eight years, never left except for college and that was local. Maybe you're another sort. A traveler. A vagabond. But let me say this again: if it doesn't work out, if you need a place to call home, you know where you can come. Our doors are open."

I said to her. "I may need that."

We watched the moon crest the hill and rise into the sky.

At the end of the night, Arlene needed help getting back to the motel. Debra left with her mom and sister, wanting to be sure they got settled into their room. Then, there were a series of goodbyes. As much as everyone said it wasn't goodbye, my heart knew otherwise.

Doug and Angel wished me good night and retired to the lodge.

Edith, one of her kids asleep on her arms, said they'd come by again before they left for Bill's new job in Phoenix. I didn't believe they would, though.

Lou and Larry left me a couple of joints. They said they'd give me their new address; they were moving on too, heading to the

Midwest, this time to farm, one they'd bought, one with as much promise as there was in their hearts.

I followed everyone to their cars. With each car that drove away, I felt more and more empty.

Ken took me aside. "Listen, buddy, I'm the one who got you here. But look at what you've done, the friends you've made."

"You've been more than a boss. A true friend."

"Cut the sentimental shit," he said, rubbing his hand against his eyes. "I get it. Let's just hug and stay in touch. Okay?"

He wrapped his arms around me, snuggled close, slapped my back. I could hear him sniffle.

He strode off, heading through my apartment. I held onto my tears.

Carole was the last to leave. "This is it," she said, standing by her driver's side door. "We've had amazing times, haven't we?"

I could not speak.

We hugged for a long time.

I went inside my apartment. The shelves I kept my books on. The couch where Terry passed out, where Suzie cuddled by the fire, where Toby boxed his paws at me, where Dominique was drawn to me, where Tess and the music became one, where Eric and I spent days together, and where Debra entered my life. The fireplace. The empty shell of it and the heat it had had.

I wondered, *who will live here next? What will it be like for them? What will be their name?* I remembered Eric when he came, those nights we spent together, how we swam naked in the morning, filled with the joy of our bodies and what they could do. I would leave that behind me and yet keep it inside me. I would leave all those who were here, whom I loved, and they would remain singular moments,

Chapter Forty

singular loves who would never be entirely lost, and never, as with Debra who would be with me, be strangers to me.

I took out my journal. Marked the date, sat on the porch, looked over the river, noticed some storm clouds circling above me, and knew I had to write everything I could of what I felt. I surprised myself—it was prayerful.

I have a little time to say a goodbye prayer to the lilies and the acorn; to the susurrant wind that surrounds me now; to the hush of morning; to the quiet nights; to the seasons and the rain; to the river, its quiet, its flood, the algae on its shore, its centuries-smoothed-over rocks, its jagged slate on the bottom, its power to cleave and to release, its deep secrets; to the day crickets and night crickets; to the cicada; to the hornets that built their dry nests and made thrumming sounds in the eaves; to my lapses at work, my growth despite them; to Carole who was my heart; how she had, more than others, come to know me as a man and an artist; to our walks by the falls; to Doug's Boys fondling in the sun, safe from society's prying eyes; to Doug himself and his gay life, and to his stern, Christian wife, Angel, both of whom were kind; to the night when day almost died and I cried because of a love so deep it hurt to breathe; to Suzie the sensual one who taught me to trust my desires, gave me love when I needed it, and let me go; to Ken who argued for a faith I never had in myself; to Evin who still holds my hand; to Dominique who invited me in, who danced with me even when the music stopped; to Tess and Sir Dragon, and the touch of an older woman, and her coffee done right; to David pirouetting across his room to Wagner; and the blood of his aunt on the carpet; to Lou who rowed me across the river; to Larry who challenged me to find my wildness; to the Old South; to those who speak fondly of Jefferson Davis and Stonewall Jackson who still feel the sting of defeat; to

River Crossed

old loyalties that seem to live on despite the centuries' sure passage unto another time; to the hours under the maple at Carole's house drinking her homemade ice tea; to the purple wisteria draped across her porch and hawthorn bush; to her unflagging hospitality; to the moonlight over the river; to the recrudescence of gay fears; to the spot where I first walked at night and the red cedar I held onto, and still hold onto; to the rain in the river, the ice on the shore, the strafing, the gnashing of ice on ice as the spring waters broke open its encasement; to the thaw that crept over the land, and the chill that lifted as the new season came; to words which I lack to do all that I wish they could, and are too weak to explain; to the surroundings; to the apple orchards on the verdant hillsides; to the corn fields by the river; to the birds of the ash and oak around me; to the cottonmouth that taught me how to be with him; to Toby who cried so I could find him and claimed me and stayed with me, lovingly, demanding no more from me than I could give and who gave me, when I had no one else, comfort; to Eric who taught me to love and not be afraid of love for another man and how to let go when needed, and who I carry in my heart, will always carry in my heart, and who I may never leave and who haunts me to this day; to Debra who gave me confidence I could live the life I want to live, need to live, and that will hopefully lead to happiness; to the layers of years and of time; to the last days here and the little quiet to write, as I do now; to the urban world I'm headed toward; to the green-to-orange transfigurations of leaves that turned inevitably brown and black and turned, yes, back to a minty green; to the blackened earth, to the loam, to the insects that regurgitate the decomposed leaves; to the waste that becomes new life; to a butterfly that patters at me now in the breathless quiet before the storm and the rain I feel coming in the air, coming and unloosing itself so that I may fully know I am of its element;

Chapter Forty

to those who still hunger for what they need; to the cover-ups and what they tell of who we are and who we don't want to be; to the walks on the dark roads where I found the self-outside-myself; to the sky and desire and the still strong current of the river which I saw fully that one night as I was seeing as I've never seen before the waves of energy surrounding us all; to this moment that may never be as it is now; to this present life; to my dumbfoundedness at the whole of it; to the slightest rain which now titters on the roof; to my need to defy death; to say something of all this and all my selves, both those hidden, and those revealed, I have known and have living inside myself. To all of this I offer a prayer of thankfulness to bless what is and has been and I hope, as best as I can, to hold all of you in my memory as dearly and pointedly as you held me.

I put the pen down and stood on the veranda, feeling reverberation in my chest that was at once joyful and filled with sorrow. I was weeping. I was not sure for what. Maybe for all of it. I knew I could not explain what I felt to anyone. It was as if this place had been like two cupped hands holding me as I experienced what I knew that I was not better for it, nor worse, but fuller. I was more than a self; I was a host of selves who could, if I gave them time, come to accept one another.

Debra came home. Later that night when I was reading and, out of nowhere, I began to cry again, she said, "Sometimes I think that place is more important to you than people," and she may have been right. But it wasn't just a place. It was the people, too.

"I envy Carole," I told her. "She has lived on the same acreage, worked, and tilled the same land that will be passed on to her son and daughter and to their children, and has been theirs before the Civil War and will be theirs for generations to come."

"I don't understand why that is important," Debra said. "But, yes, I know you've come to love this place."

I went out to the porch. The moonless dark shrouded everything.

I stepped on Toby's paw, and he darted away. I stood there as he scampered up the slate hillside.

Debra came up behind me and whispered, "He's gone. But he'll be here where he loves to be and Doug will take care of him, as promised."

I hugged her and nodded. I wanted to weep some more. I wanted to wring out all the sorrow, let it have its say, and leave it here where I felt most at home and most myself. It seemed fitting that Toby would go off into the woods to be by himself and feel as I felt, the loss of companionship.

Debra spoke softly. "I'm sorry about your leaving Carole. It must break your heart."

I said, "She was a great friend." I caught my breath. "Probably the best I've ever had."

Debra put her arm on my shoulder and turned me toward her, whispering, "She really loved you. I really believe this, for you, must be like severing an artery. Your best friend," she said. "I'm sorry."

"It's okay," I said, then hesitated and embraced her, adding, "It's just that I feel lost." I cried again. I let go of her and asked if I could walk down to the river by myself, just for a while.

"Sure," she said, squeezing my shoulder.

I walked, as I had walked hundreds of times, around the lodge to the veranda, down the steps on the terrace, then down the ones that led to the river. *God, I felt empty*. I would never know any

Chapter Forty

place as I had known this spot of land, this ledge, and this river. But mostly her. Carole. I was thinking of Carole, and I was thinking of Eric. The tears kept coming to my eyes, so it was hard to see the current below me. God, I felt empty—that's what I kept saying to myself. I felt as if I was going to crack open with grief. We had shared so much together. The little homunculus inside me. Our dreams. Our hopes. We laughed. God, how we laughed. We loved being together. Sure, I would try to come back. But it would not be the same. There was this closing off again, this loss, that I hated, and it felt so irremediable.

I knew that grief required you to let go, let it play like a violin straining to draw its bow over all the notes of sorrow, and then you had to move on.

The next day, we moved to Nashville.

Chapter Forty-One

One Year Later

I usually didn't watch television in the morning, or drink in the morning, but there I was, sitting on the couch, a glass of wine in my hand, with the TV on the floor at my feet, watching Nixon resign.

One month earlier, Debra had driven off with Valene, her new lover. They'd taken our bed, most of the kitchenware, the rocking chair, and a bookcase, leaving me to figure what to sleep on and what to do next with my life.

I'd tried hard to make our relationship work—I truly believe I tried—but no matter what I did to please her, I never could. My anxiety grew worse over the year we spent in Nashville, acting—I suppose that's what it was—like a happy couple. I dreaded making love to her. I spent all my time out, absorbed in my own inadequacy, working part-time at the University Club, studying for classes. I should have seen that she was attracted to Valene. I would have if I'd been there to look. As it turned out, Debra and I had far more in common than I ever realized. Too much, you could say.

The year we'd been together, we made the best of a failing relationship. We cared about the world. We watched the news every night, and sometimes during the day, almost as a diversion, Nixon's attempts to cover up the break-ins. I felt a vague sympathy for him in the end.

I sat on the couch watching Nixon's White House staff give him a round of applause. His family stood on a raised dais with him. I was still struck by how much he looked as he once had in my dream like my father—the receding hairline, the hair combed back, the heavy jowls, the thick eyebrows that looked as if they wanted to meet but could not quite pull it off. And even his dismal self-assurance that, as long as he had the platform, he was the authority, and others had to listen. He wiped the sweat off his lip. He nattered about his own father and mother. He dared to reference Teddy Roosevelt, call him a hero, read a quote from him about a loved one who died. Then he changed his tone. He said, "We think sometimes when things happen that don't go our way; we think that when you don't pass the bar exam the first time—I happened to, but I was just lucky . . . We think that when someone dies, we think that when we lose an election, we think that when we suffer a defeat, that all is ended."

He paused and I thought that he might cry. For once, for this instant, he seemed genuine. He was speaking from the heart. His face was the soft, agonized face of a man who had come to an end, and he knew it. Yet he said, "Not true. It is only a beginning, always." He repeated that line again as if trying to convince himself of its truth. He then went on to say something about greatness coming not when things go well, but when you are tested. He added, "Only if you have been in the deepest valley can you ever know how magnificent it is to be on the highest mountain." Then he reverted to his public persona and concluded with several lines that did not ring true.

A beginning.

That is what I struggled with for the last four weeks—and for too many years before that—how to face an ending and, once it

Chapter Forty-One

came, how to start over. Yet here was a scoundrel, a man I reviled for years, saying something from the heart to keep him going, and it made sense to me. I had to look at what I could do, where I could go, how I could find what mattered. I only had to admit where I was at fault and what had gotten in my way. I had to admit, as I suspect he did, that I had lied to myself for way too long. I had tried to cover up what was true. It wasn't a degree, or a job, or generosity of friends, or a place to live that I had to find.

It was Eric.

I drove east on the same Interstate that had taken me to Pearsall Flats years ago, roads I knew—the signs for Knoxville for Clarksburg, the curve on Route 50 that swung into a valley and crossed a bridge where the South Branch of the Potomac flowed eastward toward Winchester and Washington. I felt a strange exhilaration as if, as Larry once told me, the wildness inside of me was being given its due of free rein.

By early morning, I drove through Pearsall Flats and turned left, going by the South Branch, past Hanging Rocks cliffs, past the road where I had lived for two years. I was tempted to stop and see if the lodge had changed, but I kept going to Cumberland.

For so many years, I lived in fear, worried someone would find out about me. But now I realized that the person who I really didn't want to find out was me all along. I had to be a father to myself first. I had to let that small boy inside me know I would take care of him.

Outside of Cumberland, I stopped by a diner and ordered coffee. The waiter, a guy my age with an angelic face and a sweet disposition, asked me if I wanted anything else. When I said no, just coffee, he put his hand on the table, leaned over, and said, "Look, my friend, you look pretty grim. Your eyes are red. You look as if you've been up all night. Am I right?"

"You are."

"I've seen them come and seen them go, and I know what might do you a lot of good is a good clam chowder and a fresh roll along with that coffee. Put something in your stomach, sweetie. It will pick you up for whatever else you have to do. Shall I get that for you?" he said, tilting his head to the side, scrunching his lips to the side.

I liked how he called me sweetie, how he knew it was okay to do so, how he wanted to take care of me, and how, for some reason, I wanted him to. I nodded my head, "You got my number. Sure."

He brought the soup, two bowls of it with fresh rolls slathered with butter, and, as he predicted, it lifted my spirits. I noted that in the back of the diner, by the end of the counter, near the restrooms, there was a pay phone on the wall.

"Can I use that?" I asked.

"Please. Help yourself."

I took my coffee. I took an old card out of my wallet. I inserted a quarter and dialed the seven numbers, listened for how much more I owed, slipped in several more coins until the phone began to ring.

"Hello."

"Is this Eric?"

"Who's this?"

"Jason. It's Jason."

There was a pause. I could hear his breath on the other end.

"Nice of you to call," he said matter-of-factly. "Been a while."

"I wanted to call." I shifted from one foot to the other.

Chapter Forty-One

"Glad you did. How you been?"

"Fine," I said but quickly corrected myself. This call was one of honesty. "Well, not really. I've been messed up."

"Sorry to hear that."

"It's nice to hear your voice." I leaned against the wall, its coolness fine on my cheek.

"Good," he said, "Nice to hear yours. How long has it been?"

"A year."

"That long? My, my."

I traced my fingers along the numbers on the dial, 1, 2, 3, 4. I knew I had to say something.

"I want to see you," I said. "I just want to, that's all."

"Well, honey, you're a long way from here."

"I left Nashville," I said. My heart was racing. I felt dizzy.

"Well, where did you end up?"

"Here at the A-1 Diner in Cumberland."

There was a catch in his breath. And silence. Then he whispered, "What are you doing here?"

"I drove here last night."

"Are you kidding me?"

"No."

There was silence, but I could hear his footfalls on the floor.

"With Debra? She come along?"

"That's over."

"My, my. Aren't you full of surprises."

"It wasn't right, my being with her."

The dishes on the diner table clinked as the waiter picked them up. I pressed the receiver to my ear. I wondered if we had been cut off.

"I told you that."

"I know."

"You're one slow learner."

"I know."

I could hear him pacing back and forth. He always did that when he was upset. The waiter stood five feet from me, making the coffee. The machine that he filled was bigger but worked the same as Tess taught me. He pulled out the old filter. He replaced it with a new one, put in the grounds, poured the boiling water, waited until it settled in, then poured the rest. He glanced over. It was as if he, too, was waiting for something to be said.

I held up my cup.

"Eric?" I spoke.

Eric said nothing.

"Eric, can I see you?"

"You expect I'm going to say, 'Sure, come on over'?"

I winced. Nearly spilled my coffee. Why hadn't I called him? Why hadn't I written? What was wrong with me? He needed to know I had thought of him, yearned for him, the whole time I was in Nashville, but I couldn't tell him all that on the phone.

What should I expect? I'd given up wanting to be normal. All I needed was for him to forgive me.

He was silent. I sensed that I had lost him. What an idiot I was. Another dead end. Fuck. Fuck. Fuck. No beginning. Nixon was wrong, again. I wanted to hang up. I slammed my palm on the wall several times. The waiter turned to look at me. He stepped over toward me, the coffee pot extended like a peace offering. I smiled at it and waved him away. I had one chance here and I had to make the best of it.

Chapter Forty-One

"Listen, Eric. I messed up, I admit it."

"Glad to hear it. That's a good sign," he said, although coolness still ruled his voice.

I took a deep breath. My voice cracked. I said, "Eric, I love you. I always have."

The waiter stared at me. He smiled.

No sound came from the other end of the phone. I tapped my foot. I looked at the second hand of the clock over the counter, its black finger jerking from one line to another 5. . . 6. . .7. . . 8 . . .9 . . . to the next. I leaned on the wall, my hand pressed above my head. 10. . .11. . .12. . . Then a voice.

"It sure took you a long time to say that," he said. "But do you mean it?"

"I do, I really do." I was crying outright. The waiter handed me several napkins.

Eric asked, "You're sure?"

"Yes. Honestly. And I'm afraid—"

"Afraid of what?"

"Us."

"Us?"

"I love you; I want to be with you," I said.

"It's taken you a year to figure it out?" he asked, still cool in his voice.

"I'm slow."

"Yes, I grant you that." He laughed. "But, I suppose, slow is alright if you get it right. I just wish . . ."

"I know, I wish, too. But I had it all wrong . . ." I stopped to catch my breath and blow my nose. "I just couldn't see how wrong it was.

Don't you see? I was caught up . . ." I straightened myself. "I was trying to live someone else's life. I know that now."

"This has come so quickly," he said.

I could hear his hesitancy. "You need time."

"That would be right. Yes," he said. "And yet, you are here, aren't you?" His tone changed.

"I'm here."

"You are," he said, "Right up the road."

"I am."

"And you drove all night."

"I did." I took a breath. "Well, can I come over?"

The waiter stood beside me, arranging cups, and sorting out filters. Whatever happened, he wanted to know. If it went badly, I sensed that he would be there to help me out. His ear was cocked in my direction. I took a deep breath and waited for Eric to answer.

"The door is open," Eric said. "Let me see you!"

I was like a snake, poking its head out of the pond for the first time, feeling the sun on its scales.

I told Eric, "I'll be there." I put the phone in its cradle, my coffee cup on the counter, asked the waiter how much I owed him.

He shook his head, "Honey, it's on me. You take care of yourself." He winked, and I reached over the counter, right in front of the other customers, hugged him, and kissed him on the cheek, saying, "You're one sweet guy."

He put his hand to his cheek and said, "You be happy, hear?"

I walked out of the diner in the morning air and took a deep, cool breath of a new life.

About the Author

Bruce Spang, former Poet Laureate of Portland, Maine is the author of three novels: *The River Crossed* from Wisdom House Books, *The Deception of the Thrush*, and *Those Close Beside Me.* His new memoir *No Way Back: A Young Man's Search for Home*, comes out in 2026. He's also published five other books of poetry: *Twist* (2025), *All You'll Derive: A Caregiver's Journey, To the Promised Land Grocery*, and *Boy at the Screen Door* (from Moon Pie Press). Along with these, he has published several other books, anthologies, and two chapbooks. He is the poetry editor of the Smoky *Blue Literary and Arts Magazine* and the lead writer for *Asheville Poetry Review*. His poems have appeared in *Connecticut River Review, Puckerbrush Review, Red Rover Magazine, Asheville Literary Review, Great Smokies Review, Stoneboat Literary Journal, Muleskinner Journal, Kalopsia Literary Journal, Café Review,* and other journals across the United States. He teaches courses in both fiction and poetry

River Crossed

at the Great Smokies Writing Program at the University of North Carolina in Asheville. He lives in Candler, NC, with his husband Myles Rightmire, their three dogs, five fish, and twenty birds.

Other Books by the Author

Poetry

Twist. Warren Publisher, 2025

All You'll Derive: A Caregivers Journey, 2020

Not Just Anybody, BPS Books, 2015

Boy at the Screen Door, Moon Pie Press, 2014

To the Promised Land Grocery, Moon Pie Press, 2008

The Knot, Snow Drift Press, 2006

Poetry Chapbooks:

Tip End of Time, Smyle Publications, 2005

Once the First Berries Dissolve, 2003

Poetry Anthologies:

Passion and Pride: Poets in Support of Equality, Moon Pie Press, 2012

I Have Walked Through Many Lives, Young Voices-Scarborough, Moon Pie Press, 2009

Libretto:

Reckoning, the Musical, 2010.

Novels:

The River Crossed. Wisdom House Books, 2024

Those Close Beside Me, Piscataqua Press, 2018

The Deception of the Thrush, Piscataqua Press, 2014

Memoir:

No Way Back: A Young Man in Search for Home, Piscataqua Press, 2026

Dear Teen, Dear Poet: Coming of Age in Letters
Warren Publisher, 2026 with Peter Orne